John Ferguson Nisbet

The Insanity of Genius

and the general inequality of human faculty - physiologically considered

John Ferguson Nisbet

The Insanity of Genius
and the general inequality of human faculty - physiologically considered

ISBN/EAN: 9783337367855

Printed in Europe, USA, Canada, Australia, Japan

Cover: Foto ©Andreas Hilbeck / pixelio.de

More available books at **www.hansebooks.com**

THE INSANITY OF GENIUS

AND THE

GENERAL INEQUALITY OF HUMAN FACULTY

PHYSIOLOGICALLY CONSIDERED

BY

J. F. NISBET

AUTHOR OF 'MARRIAGE AND HEREDITY' ETC.

NEW EDITION

London

WARD & DOWNEY

12 YORK STREET, COVENT GARDEN

1891

PREFACE

MEN of genius have exercised a powerful influence in the world since history began. Yet they are still more or less of an enigma even to themselves. As chiefs and warriors among savage tribes, as men of letters, art, or science, statesmen or military commanders in civilised communities, they win the admiration of their fellows without furnishing in their own lives any conclusive indication of the means by which their success is achieved. They strike out a path for themselves, and seem to owe little or nothing to help or example. Genius has never been the monopoly of any class or system. It is as likely to manifest itself in the peasant as in the peer, and, indeed, in any list that might be drawn up of the great men of the world, examples would be found of intellectual capacity asserting itself in all conditions of life, and quite independently of the much-vaunted advantages of education. By what fatality a small number of individuals thus find themselves born to pre-eminence in every successive generation—carrying, so to speak, the marshal's baton in their knapsack—is one of the most interesting questions that can engage the human mind, and many, accordingly, have been the speculations indulged in with regard to the nature and origin of the gifts which lift the favoured few above the general level of their species.

For over two thousand years some subtle relationship has been thought to exist between _genius_ and _insanity_. Aristotle noted how often eminent men displayed morbid symptoms of mind. Plato distinguished two kinds of delirium—one being ordinary insanity, the other the spiritual exaltation which produced poets, inventors, or prophets, and which was not an evil but a gift of the gods. The *furor poeticus* and the *amabilis insania* of the Romans had reference to the same phenomenon. Dryden borrowed from Seneca the suggestion of his well-known line as to great wit and madness being near allied. Lamartine spoke of the *maladie mentale qu'on appelle génie*, and Pascal pointed out that *l'extrême esprit est voisin de l'extrême folie*, furnishing in his own person a sad exemplification of his view. In modern times the connection of genius with insanity has been scientifically insisted upon by Lélut, Moreau (de Tours), Lombroso, and one or two more recent writers. Lélut, in 1837, scandalised the world of letters by declaring upon the physiological evidence furnished by the life of Socrates that the 'father of philosophy' was not figuratively, but literally the victim of sensory hallucinations, and, ten years later, the same authority passed a similar judgment upon Pascal.[1]

Following up this line of inquiry Moreau, in 1859, laid down the principle, based upon a number of rather doubtful examples, that genius was essentially a *névrose*, or nerve affection, his contention being that originality of thought and quickness or preponderance of the intellectual faculties were organically much the same thing as madness and idiocy.[2] A few years later Lombroso, in Italy, supported this *névrosité* theory, quoting some further examples of insanity in distinguished men or their near relatives, but admitting that many others had shown no trace of mental aberration.[3] Various German writers, notably Hagen[4] and Radestock,[5]

---

[1] Lélut : *Du Démon de Socrate*, and *L'Amulette de Pascal.*
[2] Moreau : *La Psychologie morbide.*   [3] Lombroso : *Genio e Follia.*
[4] Hagen : 'Ueber die Verwandtschaft des Genies mit dem Irresein,' *Allgemeine Zeitschrift für Psychiatrie*, 1877.
[5] Radestock : *Genie und Wahnsinn*, 1884.

have since given a similarly qualified adherence to Moreau, while Ribot,[1] in France, touching incidentally upon the question, has remarked that the objections taken to Moreau's theory have mainly been sentimental and not very distinguishable from prejudices, and that genius, whatever it may be, is but rarely transmitted.

On the other hand, there has always been a strong body of opinion, philosophical and scientific, against the supposed connection of genius with insanity. Locke, Helvetius, and other early authorities, ascribed all intellectual superiority to education; and, in the last century, in England, it was generally believed that men were not naturally adapted by mental constitution to one pursuit more than another, but that, when a particular aptitude was evinced, it was due to the direction given to the mind by casual events or circumstances. In accordance with this view Dr. Johnson maintained that genius resulted from a mind of large general powers being turned in a particular direction. Charles Lamb, forgetting the fact that he himself had been confined in a lunatic asylum, expressed a similar opinion. ' So far from the position holding true,' observes Lamb, ' that great wit (or genius in our modern way of speaking) has a necessary alliance with insanity, the greatest wits, on the contrary, will ever be found to be the sanest writers. It is impossible for the mind to conceive of a mad Shakespeare. The greatness of wit by which the poetic talent is here chiefly to be understood manifests itself in the admirable balance of all the faculties. Madness is the disproportionate straining or excess of any one of them.' Goethe, also, was opposed to the mad view, holding that the man of genius summed up in his own person the best qualities of the family or the race to which he belonged.

Unsupported as it was by any evidence except the

---

[1] Ribot: *L'Hérédité psychologique* 1887.

recorded insanity or eccentricity of a few great men, and
leaving unexplained the cases of the many who had lived in
the full enjoyment of their faculties, Moreau's theory naturally aroused the keenest opposition. The great physiologist, Flourens published, in 1861, a treatise contemptuously
refuting it as absolutely fatal to the dignity of man. 'I
could as soon believe in the assimilation of virtue and vice,'
said Flourens, 'as in that of genius and insanity. Although
vice has so long flourished in the world, virtue, as Fénelon
has remarked, is still called virtue, and cannot be dispossessed
of its name. So,' added Flourens, 'will it be with genius;
and what vice has been unable to do with regard to virtue,
that will science be unable to do with regard to genius.
Genius, in short, will always be genius. . . . We are eter-
nally reminded of the hallucinations of Socrates and Pascal.
Socrates believed he was accompanied by a demon or familiar;
Pascal thought he saw a precipice open at his feet. But
what does all this prove? Does it prove that hallucination
is genius, or that it produces genius? Without their hallucinations would not Socrates still have had his good sense
and Pascal his *grand esprit*? Is it not the fact that the
relations of genius and insanity are merely external, occasional, and fortuitous? . . . Genius is the faculty carried to
an extreme of seeing and thinking justly. Many roads lead to
the truth. The man of genius is he who opens these roads.'[1]

Among English scientific men Moreau's views have
found little favour. Galton, in 1869, put forward a theory
of hereditary genius,[2] maintaining that intellectual gifts of
whatever kind—literary, poetic, artistic, philosophical, or
administrative—were the attributes of a superior type of
humanity, and that, like the physical perfections of the race-
horse or the prize-bullock, they were transmissible from one
generation to another in the favoured families where they

---

[1] Flourens: *De la Raison, du Génie, et de la Folie.*
[2] Francis Galton: *Hereditary Genius.*

occurred. Maudsley has also thrown the weight of his authority into the scale against Moreau. 'It is undoubtedly true,' says this writer, 'that where hereditary taint exists in a family, one member may sometimes exhibit considerable genius while another is insane or epileptic; but the fact plainly proves no more than that in both there has been a great natural sensibility of nervous constitution, which, under different outward circumstances or internal conditions, has issued differently in the two cases. Such a condition, moreover,' Maudsley goes on to say, 'is not characteristic of the highest genius, since anyone possessing it lacks, by reason of his great sensibility, the power of calm, steady, and complete mental assimilation, and must fall short of the highest intellectual development—of the truly creative imagination of the greatest poet, and the powerful, almost intuitive ratiocination of the greatest philosopher. His insight may be marvellously subtle in certain cases, but he is not sound and comprehensive. Although it might be said then, by one not caring to be exact, that the genius of an acutely sensitive and subjective poet denoted a morbid condition of nerve-element, yet no one, after a moment's calm reflection, would venture to speak of the genius of such as Shakespeare and Goethe as arising out of morbid conditions.' Again, ' the acts of the genius may be novel, but they contain, consciously or unconsciously, well-formed design,' whereas ' the acts of the person who has the evil heritage of an insane temperament are purposeless, irregular, and aim at the satisfaction of no beneficial desire. . . . In both cases there may be an uncommon deviation from the usual course of things ; but in the one case there is the full recognition of the existing organisation as the basis of a higher development, in the other there is a capricious rebellion as the initiation of a hopeless discord.'[1] And George Henry

---

[1] Maudsley: *The Pathology of Mind.*

Lewes's studies led him to the conviction that nothing was less like genius than insanity, although unquestionably some men of genius had had occasional attacks of this malady.[1]

Latterly, heredity and environment have been recognised as factors in the moulding of genius. Herbert Spencer regards the great man as the product of many co-ordinated social influences over which he personally has no control.[2] 'Along with the whole generation of which he forms a minute part,' says the eminent evolutionist, 'along with its institutions, language, manners, and its multitudinous arts and appliances, he is a resultant. The genesis of the great man depends upon the long series of complex influences which has produced the race in which he appears and the social state into which that race has slowly grown. . . . Before he can remake his society, his society must make him. All those changes of which he is the proximate initiator have their chief causes in the generation he is descended from.' This view is controverted, however, by a recent writer of some distinction in America. 'The causes of production of great men,' says William James, 'lie in a sphere wholly inaccessible to the social philosopher. He must accept geniuses as data, just as Darwin accepts his spontaneous variations. For him, as for Darwin, the only problem is, How does the environment affect them, and how do they affect the environment? Now, I affirm that the relation of the visible environment to the great man is in the main exactly what it is to the " variation " in the Darwinian philosophy. It chiefly adopts or rejects, preserves or destroys—in short selects him.' The determining causes of the great man, in Mr. James's opinion, are, 'molecular and invisible, and inaccessible, therefore, to direct observation of any kind. . . . The same parents, living in the same environing conditions, may at one birth produce

---

[1] *Fortnightly Review*, February 1872.
[2] Herbert Spencer: *Principles of Sociology*.

a genius, at the next an idiot or a monster . . . and the more we consider the matter, the more we are forced to believe that two children of the same parents are made to differ from one another by a cause which bears the same remote and infinitesimal proportion to its ultimate effects as the famous pebble on the Rocky Mountain crest, whose angle separates the course of two rain drops, itself bears to the Gulf of St. Lawrence and to the Pacific Ocean.'[1]

And more recently still, Henri Joly, rejecting Moreau's views, which he holds to be untenable, concurs to a large extent in the environment theory of William James and in the physiological view expressed by Goethe. 'The great man,' says Joly, 'is evidently the culminating point of his race, and all experience shows the unlikelihood of two geniuses following each other in the same family. If, however, by the side of an extraordinary individual immediately preceding or succeeding him, there should be found a nature resembling his, it appears almost always under a feminine form. Here may be found maintaining for a time, or reviving, their lustre, those gifts which the head of the family has brought to perfection, and whose fertility at the same time he has exhausted.'[2]

The merely literary theories of genius are numerous, but too vague to call for serious consideration. For example, Oliver Wendell Holmes conceives genius to be a 'creating and informing spirit which is with us and not of us. This,' he goes on to say, 'is the Zeus that kindled the rage of Achilles; it is the muse of Homer; it is the demon of Socrates; it is the inspiration of the seer; . . . it shaped the forms and filled the soul of Michel Angelo, when he saw the figure of the great law-giver in the yet unhewn marble, and the dome of the world's yet unbuilt Basilica against the black horizon; . . . it comes to the least of us as a voice that

---

[1] *Atlantic Monthly*, October 1880.
[2] Henri Joly: *Psychologie des Grands Hommes*, 1883.

will be heard ; . . . it lends a sudden gleam of sense and eloquence to the dullest of us all ; we wonder at ourselves, or, rather, not at ourselves but at this divine visitor who chooses our brain as his dwelling-place and invests our naked thoughts with the purple of the kings of speech or song.'[1] Very pretty, but very unsubstantial ! Mrs. Oliphant, again, wonders whether not only an infusion of Irish blood, but the breathing of Irish air, for a generation or two, has not quickened the imagination of the Irish descendants of English settlers in Ireland ;[2] while ' Ouida,' greatly daring, urges that the social atmosphere of England is fatal to poetic genius and that of Italy peculiarly favourable to it.[3]

From this review of authorities, great and small, it is clear that no convincing explanation of genius has yet been put forward. The various theories above set forth are one and all open to the fatal objection that they do not cover all the admitted facts of the case. While insanity treads upon the heels of genius in quite a remarkable number of instances, the fact remains that many men of the highest attainments retain full possession of their senses to the last, and otherwise display no outward affinity with the insane and the idiotic. Equally insufficient is Galton's theory of hereditary genius. For if there is one thing more clearly established than another in this connection, it is that the families of men of genius, so far from exhibiting any of the qualities of prize stock, fall considerably below the average both in point of numbers and fitness. If education be pointed to as an all-important element in the making of character, we may ask what it did for Faraday, Dickens, or Burns, who received but a very insignificant amount of schooling. Year by year thousands of young men are turned out by the universities and the higher schools of the country, but very few rise to the level

---

[1] Oliver Wendell Holmes : *Mechanism of Thought and Morals.*
[2] Mrs. Oliphant : *Life of Sheridan.*
[3] *North American Review,* February 1890.

of genius. Such education as is received in his youth by a great man has seldom much to do with the shaping of his career. It was not education that made Shakespeare a poet, Reynolds a painter, or Darwin a naturalist. As to the Johnsonian theory of genius, one can hardly believe that it was ever based upon practical observation. Diversity of tastes and aptitudes is shown by boys in the schoolroom long before circumstances influence their lives materially, and if an eminent poet or painter could be found willing to take the command of an army in the field, it is inconceivable that a successful general should, by taking thought, excel in writing poetry or painting pictures in times of peace. Much is said, again, of the importance of taking pains. But nothing is more certain than that industry alone is not enough to enable the aspirant in any walk of life to become distinguished. Some men toil hard to learn what others acquire by the slightest application. Nay, more, the art of taking pains is, itself, a natural endowment, like a good or a bad memory, and is probably responsible for much of the difference existing between the reckless, scatterbrained ne'er-do-well, who never accomplishes anything, and the steady, persistent worker who, with similar faculties, carves his name indelibly upon his epoch.

Turning now to the philosophical view that the great man is the resultant of many co-ordinated social factors, it is not easy to realise how such influences should have so impinged at the little town of Stratford-on-Avon, on April 26, 1564, as to ensure the birth of one William Shakespeare. Admitting that the sixteenth century in England was favourable to the advent of a great dramatic poet, we are entitled to ask why William Shakespeare, the third child of his father, was the chosen man rather than his brother Gilbert, who became a respectable hosier, or his brother Edmund, who was an actor of no repute. The man of genius necessarily contains within the four corners of his system all the elements of his greatness. Environment may be favourable or unfavourable to him ; he may be unnoticed by his contemporaries, and obtain merely the tardy recognition of posterity, or conceivably he may be snuffed out altogether by adverse circumstances before being able to make his power felt. With the genius that perishes in embryo, or that never comes to perfection, we are not here concerned; for, although it might be curious to speculate as to the number of able generals unhappily shot as subalterns in their first engagement, or as to the village Hampdens who have lost their opportunity through the passing of the Reform Bill, the inquiry could hardly be of a practical character. To the genius that contrives to assert itself environment is more or less an accident. It is true that we do not look for the rise of a great dramatic poet like Victor Hugo among the Zulus, or of a Mozart among a tribe of tom-toming savages. But this admits of easy explanation. The great man assimilates and recasts the material supplied him by his epoch. It is the faculty of utilising existing material that constitutes his genius, and this he cannot be said to owe to his environment. It is something personal to himself; something due to his physical organisation. For, clearly, the social influences which act upon a Victor Hugo and a Mozart, act equally upon masses of their totally undistinguished countrymen. The ' heir of all the ages ' is never alone in the enjoyment of his privileges; he shares them with multitudes of his fellow-men. Merely to be born in an epoch favourable to the advent of a great poet, a great commander, or a great statesman, implies little or nothing, therefore, as to the individual's chances of distinction. Looked at from any point of view, in short, the inadequacy of the existing theories of genius is manifest.

This is obviously one reason why another attempt should be made to solve the problem of what constitutes genius. It is not, however, an entirely sufficient reason. If so many distinguished philosophers and physiologists have been unable to come to any agreement upon this subject, what justification, it may be asked, have I for taking it up? The answer to this is simple. Within the past few years science has opened up new methods of inquiry, thrown new light upon many cognate subjects, and placed new instruments in the hands of the investigator for getting at the truth. The results of modern research affecting most intimately the question of genius are, first, the localisation of the functions of the brain, and, secondly, the established kinship of an extensive group of brain and nerve disorders, of which insanity or paralysis is the more obvious expression, and gout, consumption, malformations, etc., the more obscure. Both these branches of knowledge are of greatest utility in solving the problem before us; and their due application to the facts of biography will be found to rob genius of much, if not all, of the mystery which has hitherto enshrouded it.

The result is to place upon a solid basis of fact the long-suspected relationship of genius and insanity. Apparently at the opposite poles of the human intellect, genius and insanity are, in reality, but different phases of a morbid susceptibility of, or a want of balance in, the cerebro-spinal system. This conclusion is arrived at from a close examination of the lives of all the greatest men whose personal and family history is authentically known. For obvious reasons I have refrained from dealing with living personages; but the abundance and sufficiency of the material to hand happily renders this restriction of no moment. In the selection of names I have been guided solely by the desire to obtain a representative list. I have, indeed, been under no temptation to trim or square the facts, for whenever a man's life is at once sufficiently illustrious and recorded with sufficient fulness to be a subject of profitable study, he inevitably falls into the morbid category—a remarkable proof, surely, of the soundness of a theory which after all need not, like a chain, be tested by its weakest link.

My method of inquiry is not unlike that of the family doctor who is called in to examine a patient. With the help of the biographer I ask the great man, figuratively speaking, to stand up; I look at his tongue, feel his pulse, and inquire into his family history. By this means a wholly different view of genius is obtained from that generally current. The biographer, unfortunately, is too often as troublesome a person to deal with as the family nurse. It is difficult to learn the essential facts of a great man's life if they conflict, as they not infrequently do, with the biographer's notion of greatness. Commonly, the writer falls in with the popular view of genius, which is that a certain quasi-divine influence, or *afflatus* of an inscrutable nature, descends upon certain individuals after the manner of the Holy Ghost. If, however, he happens to be of a scientific turn of mind, he affects to believe that the great man has inherited his genius from his mother, or that, as Goethe held and as Joly has further insisted, he is the culminating point of his race, the crowning triumph of a sound and vigorous ancestry on both sides. In any case, the smallest suggestion that the object of his veneration has not been entirely sane, affects the ordinary biographer as a red rag affects a bull. He loses temper and treats it as a shameless affront to the great man's memory; for insanity, in his view, seems to be a sort of reprehensible thing which no well-conducted person would be guilty of. Sometimes he condescends to argue the point with the subtlety of a special pleader, and when the facts happen to be too strong for him, he is ready with an explanation as to 'over-work,' 'anxiety,' 'excessive strain,' 'excesses,' and the like.

Still, patient research in biography brings to light a vast number of facts of an instructive character, all helping to solve the problem of that diversity of faculty which is seen to exist among men born under similar circumstances. The heredity of genius is abundantly established, but it is not heredity of the simple and direct kind imagined by Galton when he wrote his treatise on the subject twenty years ago. Variation steps in at every point, and an instability of the nervous system of one or both parents manifests itself in the off-spring in a manifold shape, the sensory or intellectual faculties being quickened at the expense of the nutritive, and *vice versâ*, upon a scale of almost infinite complexity. The word genius is susceptible of many interpretations. For the purposes of this inquiry I give it the widest, applying it not merely to the creative gift in literature and art, but to that inherent ability which enables its possessor to excel in any given sphere of human activity, literary, artistic, scientific, administrative, military, commercial, religious, philanthropic, or even criminal. Genius is essentially a manifestation of nerve energy, and the scope of a man's faculties is necessarily determined by a physical organisation over which he has no control. In thus asserting the principle of a fatalism in the lives of great men, like that which Orientals conceive to exist in all human affairs, I am well aware that I am flying in the face of many excellent treatises written for the edification of the young; but no fiction, however well-intended, can, after all, be as beneficent as truth, and if any prejudices suffer from contact with the facts set forth in the following pages so much the worse for them.

Incidentally, I endeavour to lift the veil from one or two obscure but interesting subjects, which, in an inquiry of this kind, force themselves upon the attention. The cause and the manner of Shakespeare's death are, for the first time, investigated in the light of his family history, or such of it as is known to us, and the result is to convey a different impression of the man from that hitherto prevailing. From the neuropathic point of view there are incidents in Shakespeare's life, which, though small, are extremely significant, and by a new chain of circumstantial evidence, of which the signatures attached to his will are an important link, the death-bed scene of the poet is reconstituted in a manner which only the latest advances of physiological and medical science have rendered possible. For the first time, also, the difficult subject of Inspiration is made to yield up, as it seems to me, some portion at least of its secret. ' The great desideratum in the theory of intellectual character,' says Bain, ' is to give an intelligible resolution of the innate power of recasting and moulding the raw material of thought, of the determination to self-activity, so to speak, in place of remaining content with the received forms and order of the communicated impressions. In short, it is the problem of original genius that is the reproach of the schools of mental philosophy.' To some extent, I venture to think, this reproach is now wiped away, and here, again, I avail myself of the latest discoveries with regard to the mechanism of the brain and nervous system. Phrenology necessarily receives some share of attention, and is, in a limited degree, rehabilitated, or, at least, shown to have more foundation in fact than seemed at first compatible with the mapping out of the sensory and motor areas of the brain upon Ferrier's system.

Lastly, this investigation of the neuropathic side of genius will be found to throw fresh difficulties in the way of an application of the principle of Natural Selection to the human race. In his latter years, Darwin's confidence in his theory as applied to man was somewhat shaken, and his distinguished co-worker, Alfred Russel Wallace, has since admitted that the ' noblest and most characteristic of human faculties ' do not appear to come under the Darwinian law. Whatever may be man's relations with the lower animals, and whatever may be the causes of Darwin's spontaneous variations, the fact, now clearly established, that the progressive achievements of the intellect are wholly unconnected with a survival of the fittest, may be allowed to have an important bearing upon the evolution theory.

LONDON : *March*, 1891.

PREFACE

THE SECOND EDITION

FROM the rapid sale this book has met with, a second edition being called for within the space of a few months, and the keen controversy it has excited in many quarters, it would appear that I did not over-estimate the desirability of endeavouring anew to solve the perplexing question of genius, and to ascertain, in the light of the latest discoveries in physiology, its bearing upon the progress of the human race. 'The Times,' in a leading article, characterised the subject of my inquiry, namely, the genesis of the better members of the community, as 'one of vital importance to every civilised country.' Acknowledging the force of the evidence brought forward in support of my view, the leading journal went on to say : 'History seems to teach that the continuance of great gifts, either mental or physical, for several successive generations, although not unknown, is at any rate highly exceptional ; and that the rise of individuals above the current level of humanity is most frequently compensated for, so to speak, by a swing of the pendulum in the opposite direction. . . . At present, we fear, in so far as the facts offer themselves to experience, the inheritance of great qualities is the exception rather than the rule.' Mr. Galton himself, whose opinions as expressed in his work on 'Hereditary Genius' I had set myself to refute, felt constrained to admit, in an address delivered before the recent Congress of Hygiene and Demography, that the best, like the worst, members of the community, did not seem to be able to hold their own in point of fecundity.

Professor Huxley also has been good enough to express his general agreement with me on this question in the following terms: 'Genius to my mind means innate capacity of any kind above the average mental level. From a biological point of view, I should say that a "genius" among men stands in the same position as a "sport" among animals and plants, and is a product of that variability which is the postulate of selection both natural and artificial. In my apprehension, Darwin's theory proper assumed variation as a fact, and does not attempt to account for it, nor can be called upon to do so. And ever since the subject was first discussed, I have tried to insist upon this. On the general ground that a strong and therefore markedly abnormal variety is, *ipso facto*, not likely to be so well in harmony with existing conditions as the normal standard, which has been brought to be what it is largely by the operation of those conditions, I should think it probable that a large proportion of "genius sports" are likely to come to grief, physically and socially, and that the intensity of feeling which is one of the conditions of what is commonly called genius, is especially liable to run into the fixed ideas which are at the bottom of so much insanity.'

That such weighty support as the foregoing should be lent to my view, in however qualified a degree, more than compensates me for the obloquy I have incurred from anonymous reviewers who have roundly asserted my theory to be that all men of genius are lunatics. No intelligent reader of the book need be told that such an assertion is nonsense. Genius is not lunacy; it is insight, power, and energy in excess of the normal allowance, and my contention is that such great gifts, however desirable in themselves, are not obtained, as a rule, without some disturbance of the healthy equilibrium of the brain and nervous system. Emerson had some inkling of this truth, though he knew nothing of the mechanism of mind upon which I am able to base it. 'In the chief examples of religious illumination,' he observes, 'somewhat morbid has mingled, in spite of the unquestionable increase of mental power. . . . Shall we say that the economical mother disburses so much earth and so much fire to make a man, and will not add a pennyweight though a nation is perishing for a leader? . . . If you will have pure carbon, carbuncle, or diamond to make the brain transparent, the trunk and organs shall be so much the grosser; instead of porcelain they are potter's earth, clay, or mud.'

It has been objected to my theory that neuropathy exists among the 'dolts and dunderheads' of the world in perhaps as great a degree as among the men of genius. I dare say it does. Indeed, I should expect this to be the case wherever the dolts and dunderheads fall as much below the average level of mental capacity as men of genius rise above it. I expressly say that the soundest man is he who most nearly approaches the average. It is upon the medium type that Nature evidently relies for the continuance of the species, not upon extremes or accidental variations. All Darwinians will admit in the abstract that divergencies or variations from the main type are bad and bound to come to naught. Nevertheless, there is one variation for which some among them deem it their duty to stand up at all hazards, namely genius. I can attribute this only to prejudice—to the rooted conviction which has obtained for so many years that exceptional ability of any kind denotes the superior animal. It will surely be evident on a moment's reflection, that if the musician with his exceptional ear, or the painter with his exceptional eye, were as sound and as prolific as his neighbours, and if his gift were freely transmissible, the human race would soon be splitting up into a number of distinct species, each with a special endowment. On Professor Huxley's showing it is inevitable that all departures from the mean, in the human species, including those which constitute genius, should be unsound.

In the face of the existing evidence, it cannot be asserted that among the general population of the country there is to be found anything like as much nerve disorder as among men of genius of the first rank. For the purposes of comparison in this respect I fortified myself, while writing the book, with the health-record of a number of average men of my acquaintance, but I thought it safer on the whole to take the wider basis afforded by the Registrar General's returns, in which, be it observed, the dolts and dunderheads are thrown into the scale against me, since they tend to make the total amount of neuropathy greater than that existing among average individuals. Some of my critics have sapiently inquired why nothing was heard of neuropathy in Homer's time, or in Shakespeare's, forgetting that the very anatomy of the body, to say nothing of the causes of the nervous ailments, was not then discovered; others, with as little justice, have commented adversely upon the very slight evidence offered at the close of the different chapters as to the ailments or the causes of death of the eminent men who flourished from two or three centuries ago. With regard to the latter I would observe that my reason for mentioning them in the lump is to show that although only the slightest evidence is procurable respecting them, that evidence, as far as it goes, tends to support my view. The whole strength of the case for the insanity (i.e. the unsoundness) of genius lies in the lives of the great men of the past few generations, about whom nearly everything is known. And it is worthy of remark that, as a rule, in their case the greater the genius the greater the unsoundness.

September 1891.

CONTENTS

CHAPTER I

CHAPTER II

CHAPTER III

CHAPTER IV

CHAPTER V

CHAPTER VI

CHAPTER VII

CHAPTER XI

CHAPTER XII

THE
INSANITY OF GENIUS

CHAPTER I

MUCH of the uncertainty prevailing with respect to the nature of genius and the conditions of its appearance, is due to a habit of looking upon the human mind as an intangible something, a spiritual essence, associated in some way with the body, but not governed by the laws of matter. Upon reason, judgment, imagination, and other abstract terms of a like degree of vagueness, there have been endless disquisitions by eminent men of past ages, who have never succeeded in establishing among themselves a definite or incontrovertible basis of agreement. While there has been but one truth requiring exposition, there have been many different and opposed schools of philosophy professing to expound it. The cause of so much divergence of opinion is plain. Until the anatomy of the brain and nervous system was as closely studied as it has been within the past twenty years, all reasoning as to the processes of sensation and thought was necessarily as unsound as the methods of treating disease which obtained before the discovery of the circulation of the blood. The Lockes, the Dugald Stewarts, the Benthams, the

Humes, and other distinguished writers of a bygone day, who discussed the operations of the mind, were somewhat in the position of a man who should presume to lecture upon the steam-engine without knowing anything of its internal arrangement of valves and pistons. Happily the inquirer into the mysteries of thought is no longer constrained to wade, as in the past, through a bottomless quagmire of speculation; he has now something like a solid footing to go upon, and the relations of mind and matter have become like other branches of science, the subject of exact investigation.

It is to physiology more particularly that the world owes its deliverance from the long reign of error or misconception as to the operations of the mind. The development of the brain and nervous system is traced from the most rudimentary beginnings. In the lowest living forms nerve does not exist. We see merely a sensitive pulp moving without any apparent organs of sense, though possibly in its seemingly homogeneous substance there may be differentiated tracks—the rudiments of nerves—along which sensation travels. The earliest appearances of a nervous system as we ascend the scale of life are a few filaments connected by a nerve cell or a group of nerve cells. These, by-and-by, show a tendency to cluster at one point, to lay the foundation of a brain, but we get as high as the fishes before discovering any more complicated structure than sensory ganglia and nerves. The rudimentary brain consists of the cerebellum and the medulla oblongata, those portions of the brain substance which are in immediate connection with the spinal column, and where the various organic and automatic functions of the body appear to be carried on. Many grades of the animal creation get on very well with no other mental equipment. In the higher animals, including man, there is found, superposed upon the cerebellum, the cerebrum, which fills the upper portion of the skull in the shape of the right and the left hemispheres, and where, in a manner presently to be indicated, sensory impressions are received from the outer world, ideas formed, and orders given for transmission to all parts of the muscular system.

All mental processes are now shown to be an unbroken

material chain of causes and effects. As in the analogy of the steam-engine, there are no doubt certain ultimate facts in materialism—facts beyond which it is impossible to go. The force of the steam-engine and the force of the nerve cells of the brain are alike mysterious in their origin; both are manifestations of the unknown and unknowable Power underlying the universe. Nevertheless, if we do not know what force primarily is, we can at least tell the conditions under which it is exercised, whether in the case of the steam-engine or in that of the brain, and an investigation of genius and other forms of mental faculty consequently resolves itself into an investigation of our cerebral mechanism.

The hemispheres of the brain consist mainly of a mass of white substance overlaid with a thin coating of gray matter. This outer layer varies in thickness, averaging, however, about one-tenth of an inch, and extends to upwards of 300 square inches, its surface being enormously increased by being thrown into numerous folds or convolutions. On microscopic examination the gray matter proves to be thickly charged with nerve-cells of various shapes—round, oval, pear-shaped, tailed, and star-like, or radiated—each having two or more slender threads or nerves connected with it, while the internal white substance is made up entirely of nerves. Both cells and nerves are excessively minute, and form an extremely complicated network. The cells are evidently the sources of some power which the fibres conduct, and may be roughly compared to galvanic batteries generating electricity, which is carried by wires wherever it may be wanted. Indeed, this analogy holds good to a remarkable extent, inasmuch as the conducting nerves, like the electric wires, appear to be insulated by sheaths or coverings. In the interior of the brain are two large ganglia containing a certain amount of gray matter, and known as the optic thalamus and the corpus striatum; these are both connected by fibres with the outer gray coating, and are evidently important centres for the generation, collection, and distribution of nerve force. The radiating fibres from the central ganglia bear but a small proportion, however, to the fibres passing from one portion of the surface to another. The different convolutions and areas of the brain are very extensively connected, and it is obvious that a disturbance in one region is liable to be communicated to all adjacent regions, and even to distant ones. The hemispheres being the counterparts of each other, the brain is double, but uniformity of action seems to be ensured between its two sections by a broad connecting band of fibres called the corpus callosum. The cerebellum differs in appearance from the hemispheres, but nerve-cells and fibres are its main constituents; its connection with the hemispheres appears to be chiefly through the motor paths.

So much for the general structure of the brain. How does it act? The phrenologists conceived that each portion subserved a special faculty, and that the mental aptitudes of an individual could be read from the greater or less development of the bumps on his skull. Their system was based upon the comparison of a man's known character with the size and shape of his head; it was necessarily a very loose and untrustworthy system, and modern physiologists do not speak of it with respect, though, as we shall see in a subsequent chapter, it contains a basis of truth which is considerable and in some degree unsuspected. Whatever may be said of the overweening confidence of Gall and Spurzheim in their method, they are entitled, at all events, to the credit of perceiving or divining a fact which has only been conclusively proved in our own day, namely, that the brain is a sort of mosaic, and that its various parts are charged with special functions. The discovery of the true state of the case was very gradual. Long after Gall formulated the phrenological doctrine, Flourens found that removing slices of the cerebral substance caused loss of function in the animal operated upon; Schiff afterwards discovered that different portions of the cerebral substance were raised in temperature by different sensations; and it was observed that disease of certain regions of the brain had more or less definite results. In 1870 a flood of light was thrown upon the subject. It would have been a sad shock to the eighteenth century philosophers to be told that the true science of thought was to be initiated by experiments upon the brain of a dog. Nevertheless, when Fritsch and Hitzig bared a dog's brain upon their dissecting-table and found that an electric stimulus applied to certain convolutions caused spasmodic movements of the opposite side of the animal's body, they laid the foundation of the modern system of metaphysics. Since then Ferrier, Horsley, Schäfer, Goltz, and a host of investigators have been in the field and have reaped a rich harvest of observations.[1]

Broadly speaking, the hemispheres of the brain have been mapped out into centres of sight, hearing, touch, smell, taste, and muscular movement. Upon the main lines of these all physiologists are agreed, though observers differ as to the precise limitations of each area. Considering the methods employed in the localisation experiments a slight diversity of opinion is not surprising. The operator first applies the electric stimulus to a given convolution of the brain and notes the muscular or other results produced. With a knife or the electric cautery he then destroys the same convolution and notes the animal's corresponding loss of muscular power or sensation. It is clear, however, that the electric stimulus cannot be rigidly confined to a small region, and that the shock of the knife or the cautery may likewise have a disturbing effect for some distance around. Hence, no doubt, the tendency of the various spheres in the reports of different observers to overlap or encroach upon each other. Besides, as already remarked, there exists between all the areas a most intimate system of intercommunication, a sensation in any one region reacting at once upon various other regions so as to produce a highly complex and co-ordinated series of effects in the feelings, ideas, or action of the individual. It is found that each hemisphere of the brain controls the movements and sensations of the opposite side of the body, the nerves crossing over before entering the spinal column. Thus an injury to the motor area for the leg or foot in the right hemisphere causes paralysis in the left limb and *vice versâ*.

At first sight it would appear that the phrenologists have

---

[1] Ferrier: *The Functions of the Brain*, 1886; and *Cerebral Localisation*, 1890; *Philosophical Transactions of the Royal Society*, 1887–8. Bastian: *The Brain as an Organ of Mind*. Luys: *Le Cerveau et ses Fonctions*, etc.

been ludicrously wide of the mark in their reading of the
bumps. Injury to, or stimulation of the gray matter along
the upper portion and sides of the hemispheres where they
locate self-esteem, firmness, benevolence, imitation, wonder,
hope and ideality, paralyses or excites muscularly the entire
opposite side of the body, the area in question being sub-
divided into centres for controlling the movements of the feet,
legs, arms, hands, head, face, mouth, and eyes. This motor
region is now very well defined, partly by observation of the
results of disease in the human subject, partly by experiment
upon the brains of monkeys, which are constructed on the
same plan as the brains of human beings. On the left temple
is a centre roughly corresponding to the 'constructiveness'
of the phrenologists, whence the movements for speech are
controlled. Destruction of this centre produces the condition
known as aphasia, in which a person understands perfectly
what is said to him, and thinks an answer without being able
to utter it. Habit, which seems to be the cause of our right-
handedness, is probably responsible for the location of the
speech centre on the left side, for in left-handed individuals
it is found on the right side of the brain. Hard by is the
centre for agraphia, or the condition in which one is unable
to express oneself intelligibly in writing. When it is destroyed the patient loses control over the movements of his
hand.

Impressions of sight are received in the occiput—in plain
English, the back of the head—the region appropriated by
the phrenologists to self-esteem, approbativeness, inhabitive-
ness, adhesiveness, and even, in part, philo-progenitiveness.
The hearing area is over the ear, where phrenology places
acquisitiveness and secretiveness, while smell, taste, and touch
are centred in the lower convolutions. If these different
centres are injured or destroyed the faculty concerned suffers
accordingly. The frontal lobes of the brain are supposed to
play some part in arranging or co-ordinating the material of
thought. Electrical excitation of this region yields no results,
but as the stimulus is directed towards the motor region at
the temples, movements of what Ferrier calls 'attention' are
observed.

The frontal lobes reach their highest development in man, and an ample forehead is, no doubt, the general indication of a clever mind. Intellect, however, is not the product of the frontal lobes alone, or indeed of any one region of the brain; it is rather the outcome of all the cerebral centres, sensory and motor, in combination. If nothing more could be said of the different cerebral centres than has been done in the foregoing pages we should still be far from understanding the mechanism of thought. But we are not solely dependent for our knowledge of the brain upon the results of the electrical stimulus or the cautery as applied by the physiologist. Where experiment or direct proof ends, induction begins. The line of active research known as the localisation of the functions of the brain suggests where the truth lies if it does not bring us to the truth itself.

What happens when we receive a sensory impression, say, through the eye ? There is a disturbance of the nerves of the eye in the first instance. The impression is then conveyed to the visual centre of the brain by what, for want of a better term, is called a nerve-current. When a nerve is excited there is a change in its substance, probably chemical. This change, once begun, propagates itself along the nerve at the rate of ninety feet a second. Nothing is really known of its nature, but exercise is seen to exhaust the carrying power of the nerve, while repose and the circulation of healthy blood restore it. We are temporarily deafened by a loud noise and blinded by an intense light, because, for the moment, the energy of the nerve cells is exhausted by the strain put upon them. From the eye the nerve-current duly arrives in the visual area of the brain, and, according to its character, throws the nerve-cells of that area together with their extensive network of fibres into activity. The impression conveyed from the eye to the brain is most likely of a twofold character, optical and muscular. While one set of nerves conveys the shades of light and colour, another takes note of the muscular adjustments of the eye which are concerned with form, so that every object seen calls into play certain groups of nerve-cells and fibres in the visual and motor areas: and it is probable that every group thus formed is capable of being revived under an appropriate stimulus.

Herbert Spencer reduces all mental action to a sense of likeness and unlikeness in the things perceived—change or no change in consciousness.[1]   A red light, for example, affects our nerves in a certain way. We then pass to the contemplation of some other object. By-and-by the red light comes again; the result in our minds is a flash of recognition, a renewal of the first experience, together with a feeling of identification; and the repetition of this enables us to class redness as a definite sensation. We next see a green light, which affects our nerves differently from the red. It brings about, let us say, a different grouping of nerve-cells. There is now a shock of difference or change, and we discriminate between the past impression and the present one.

So with all impressions conveyed to us from the outer world through the various channels of sight, hearing, touch, taste, and smell. The grades of discrimination are many. The eye distinguishes an immense variety of shades; a fine ear is sensible to a small fraction of tone. In sight and hearing there are probably thousands of grades of discrimination; in touch, taste, and smell they are fewer though still numerous. To the perception of likeness and unlikeness, Bain adds as one of the fundamentals of thought the faculty by which a past impression, that is to say. a past combination of nerve-cells, is revived under an appropriate stimulus.[2] This is the principle of memory. ‘Working together,’ observes Bain, ‘ our sense of agreement and our sense of difference exhaust the meaning of what we call knowledge. To know anything as a tree is to discriminate it from all differing objects, and identify it with all agreeing objects. We are perpetually reminded of objects by the presence of something of a resembling kind.’ On this point the conclusions of Bain and Herbert Spencer are identical. ‘Our reason,’ says Bain, ‘essentially consists in using an old fact in new circumstances through the power of discerning its agreement or disagree-

---

[1] Herbert Spencer: *Principles of Psychology.*
[2] Bain : *Body and Mind.*

ment with them.' 'Our various states of consciousness,' says Herbert Spencer, 'are elaborated out of our perceptions of change, kind of change, degree of change, facility of change, arrangement of change, etc., all running together in larger and larger groups and series until they embody to us what is called the outer world.'

It is the power of associating one impression with another that makes the difference between the richly endowed and the poorly endowed mind. How does one impression just received arouse another impression previously received? Evidently by the passing of a nerve current from one group of cells and fibres to another group. If the passage is easily effected, and if the nerve-cells of the second group are lively, the revived impression will be strong; if the connection is uncertain, if the bridge, so to speak, is in a bad state of repair or the nerve-cells sluggish, the revived impression, in other words our memory of the past fact or sensation, will be weak and partial. There is no doubt that a constant repetition of this process of association tends to make the connection easier. In the nerve-cells, where the currents meet and join, there is, in consequence of the meeting, says Bain, 'a strengthened connection or diminished obstruction, a preference track for that line over other lines where no continuity has been established.' Whether in these established connections or groupings the nerve-cells increase in activity, or whether the conducting power of the fibres improves, it is impossible to say. Probably both causes operate. Some authorities suppose that as the cell-junctions of the fibres are the places where a great many independent nerve-circuits come into close neighbourhood, these affect one another by a process in the nature of electrical induction.

Both our sense of likeness and our sense of unlikeness in the objects perceived have their bases in memory, which is the power of continuing or recalling impressions no longer stimulated by the original agent. 'If we suppose the sound of a bell striking the ear, and then ceasing,' observes Bain, 'there is a certain continuing impression of a feebler kind, the idea or memory of the note of the bell, and it would take some very good reason to deter us from the obvious inference

that the continuing impression is the persisting (although
reduced) nerve currents aroused by the original shock.   And
if that be so with ideas surviving their originals, the same is
likely to be the case with ideas resuscitated from the past—
the remembrance of a former sound of the bell.   All observation confirms this doctrine.   The mental recollection of language is a suppressed articulation ready to burst into speech.
When the thought of an action excites us very much, we can
hardly avoid the actual repetition of it, so completely are all
the nervous circuits repossessed with the original currents of
force.   The lively remembrance of a pleasant relish will produce the same expression of countenance, the very smack of
the reality.   In strongly imagining a kick, we can scarcely
refrain from giving one.   As we rehearse in thought the
movement of a dance, we almost join in it.   It has even been
shown by experiment that the persistent imagination of a
bright colour fatigues the nerves of sight.'

A curious experience related by Wigan, who, fifty years
ago, wrote about the functions of the brain, illustrates the
revival under morbid excitation of a special nerve-grouping
in the auditory centre.   'I remember hearing a bell,' says
Wigan, 'at Mola di Gaeta, with a very peculiar sound; it
probably was a musical note of an exact pitch which had
never struck my ear before from any instrument, or it might
have been something in the quality of the tone independent
of its position in the musical scale.   I happened at the
moment to be in the midst of a long train of painful emotions,
and the two things became associated in my mind.   I never
heard the same bell again, but in passing Mont Cenis I en-
countered one of those whirlwinds called a *tourmente*, and felt
that I had taken cold in my ears, which began to be slightly
painful, when I suddenly heard the peculiar sound of the bell
of Mola di Gaeta.   I was entirely convinced that I heard a
bell; I looked round for a campanella in vain, and tried, with
a little success, to persuade my companions of the truth of my
convictions.   All the way thence to Beauvoisin the same
sound continued in my ears, renewing all the painful impressions connected with my first hearing it, and it was not till I
had sat for some time in a very hot room at Martigny that

it ceased to annoy me. On resuming my journey the sound was renewed, and it was not till after a hot bath and free injection of the ears with warm water at Lyons that I finally got rid of the distressing delusion.' 'The comparative feebleness of remembered states or ideas,' says Bain, 'is, we may presume, an exact counterpart of the diminished force of the revived currents of the brain. It is but seldom that the re-induced currents are equal in energy to those of direct stimulation at first hand.' Formerly it was believed that the brain was a sort of storehouse for ideas which were docketed and put away in pigeon-holes for future use. With our present knowledge of its structure this is no longer a tenable hypothesis. 'It must be considered as almost beyond a doubt,' says Bain, who, in this matter, is fully supported by Ferrier, 'that the renewed feeling occupies the very same parts of the brain and in the same manner as the original feeling.'

What is implied by this modern anatomical theory of the intellect? This, that for every act of memory, every exercise of bodily aptitude, every habit, recollection, train of ideas, there is a specific co-ordination of nerve-cells and fibres in the brain resulting in a specific set of sensations or movements. That is to say, every stimulus from the outer world conveyed through sight, hearing, touch, taste or smell, actuates in the brain some group of fibres and cells between which connections have been established, partly by inherited structure and partly by custom. The instincts of the lower animals are the outcome of an inherited structure, a permanent grouping of nerve-cells which always respond in a given way to a given stimulus. Many of our own bodily functions are similarly regulated. In the case of acquired knowledge, lines of preference for the nerve-currents seem to be determined by circumstances. It is in this manner that the social instincts—the general habits, the likes and dislikes, the morals of a community find a physical embodiment. They are the outcome of established methods of brain action which, as I have shown in a previous work,[1] vary as between one community and another, and even in the same com-

[1] *Marriage and Heredity.*

munity as between one period and another. In proportion as acts become habitual, they cease to be conscious and tend to become instinctive. Tricks of habit are a result of the tendency of certain nerve-groupings to be revived, for it seems to be a law of nerve tissue that what it has done once it is prone to do again.

On the principle here laid down it will be seen that every sensory area of the brain has its own memories or cohesive nerve-groupings, each liable to be revived directly through its own centre, or indirectly by nerve-currents from other centres. Our ideas of the commonest and simplest objects are made up of the impressions derived from many centres, sensory or motor; and the due co-ordination of such impressions is only effected by practice. As we have been sorting our impressions from childhood we have ceased to become aware of the complexity of the process which is gone through. With regard to the acquirement of voluntary movements Ferrier observes: 'Some particular object held before a child recalls by sight a pleasurable sensation and excites desire (which is the ideal persistence of a sensation and its tendency towards repetition); but, instead of inducing as yet a definite action for its gratification, it excites only vague and undefined movements of arms, legs, and facial muscles—the expression of general excitation of the motor centres. In process of time the centre of the special differentiated movement necessary to the gratification of the desire can be thrown individually into action, and thus a definite act of volition is for the first time fairly accomplished. . . . And it is curious and interesting to observe in a child how, in the growth of volition, the first action fairly differentiated in response to any particular sensation or desire is repeated in response to desire in general, however ludicrously insufficient to accomplish the desired end. The individual activity of the various motor centres having once been fairly established, at first in response to particular sensations and desires, voluntary acquisition proceeds apace, the centres being free to form new associations. The associating fibres between the one motor centre and the various sensory centres may thus become innumerable. Complex and intricate movements are longer in being acquired than those which are simple or reflex, and already hereditarily organised. Hence, the movements of articulation in combination with those of vocalisation are longer in being acquired than those of the arms and legs.'

To persons who have been born blind and who have afterwards gained their sight, an object seen for the first time appears to touch the ball of the eye and is not recognised as what it is, say a stick or a stone. The optical effect of the stick or the stone comes gradually to be associated with the muscular adjustment of the eye to particular distances, to form, etc., and with its weight, hardness, coldness, and other qualities ascertained through the sense of touch, and when all these sensations and associations are completed by practice, then, and not till then, do we arrive at a perfect conception of the object before us. To vary the illustration, we see a carving-knife. Its optical effect is produced in the visual area. Instantly by the multitudinous lines of communication which exist, other nerve-groupings in other areas are aroused by association and offer suggestions as to the weight, hardness, smoothness, cutting, and pain-producing qualities of the knife, all based upon experience tactile and motor; the memories of taste and smell stimulate the glands of the mouth and the action of the jaws, they even react upon the visual area, calling up the picture of a dinner-table set with articles of food and drink. Perhaps the auditory centre is aroused to furnish impressions of something that has been told about a carving-knife, or, if the story has been read in a book, the visual and motor centres are once more called into play to reproduce the impressions originally derived from a succession of printed pages. In short, the sight of the carving-knife causes a nerve-thrill to spread over the greater portion of the cerebral hemispheres, arousing trains of impressions, or, in other words, reviving cohesive nerve-groupings in the various centres as it passes. A powerful stimulus throws all our centres into activity. When a man is angry, his features, limbs, and body are all agitated.

If one centre is incapacitated, the other centres form cohesions of their own. A person born blind has ideas from which every visual impression is excluded. He knows, let us say, a pair of scissors by touch, and instantly names them. When he gains his sight and the scissors are held up to him he does not at first know what they are. The optical effect has, as yet, formed no associations in his brain. A lady shown a tea-cup under such circumstances could not tell what it was until she had felt it; only after repeated experiments with sight and touch combined could another patient distinguish, at a distance, a cat from a dog. The form, size, and weight of objects are slowly discovered by similar means. Colour is necessarily learnt by the association of a particular impression with a name. Five and twenty days after gaining the use of her eyes, a lady, operated upon by Waldrop, had constantly to be informed of the meaning of objects around her, whether in or out of doors. 'What is that?' she would ask, 'A soldier.' 'And that thing which has just passed us?' 'A man on horseback.' 'And that bright thing on the pavement there?' 'A lady in a red shawl.' The same training has to be undergone by the other centres of hearing, taste, smell, and touch. A rat's tail was cut off and engrafted in its back, where it took root. After the nerve-connection had been formed the animal could feel a pinch in its new tail, but was unable at first to locate the sensation. In about three months it learnt to turn and try to bite the offending object.[1]

Our knowledge of men and things is made up of an incalculable number of cohesive nerve-groupings in the different centres. Persons are associated with places, occupations, amusements, property, age, rank, and position, and with the many attributes that make up character and reputation. The links of association are almost infinite, and, if one set fails us, another will be found to hold good. In trying to remember a thing it is usually sufficient to be able to alight upon some limb or fragment of the necessary cohesion; the entire group of associated impressions is then revived. Persons who tie a knot on their handkerchiefs in order the better to recall some fact at a given time unconsciously avail themselves of this cerebral mechanism; they associate the tactile and motor centres with the thing to be remembered, and

---

[1] Taine: *De l'Intelligence.*

when accidentally pulling out their handkerchiefs they come upon the knot the whole set of impressions hanging upon it is liable to flash upon them. Acquisitions of knowledge are the formation of nerve-groupings in endless variety, the most richly endowed mind being that in which such groupings are most numerous, most extensive, and most easily revived.

In man, the visual, auditory, motor, and tactile centres appear to be the chief spheres of cerebral action; he has very little cohesive faculty in the centres for smell and taste. Perhaps the visual and the motor centres are the chief, and it is an anatomical fact that, between these, in the human brain, the nerve communication is very extensive. Great bands of fibres also extend from these areas into the frontal convolutions, which, being larger in man than in the monkey or the lower animals, are believed to be a sort of intellectual centre, or centre for the sorting of impressions. Many animals have acuter senses than man, but they are not so well able to found abstract ideas upon them. The dog's sense of smell is much keener than ours, and the corresponding portion of its brain is larger, showing that some relation exists between the development of an organ and its efficiency. In cats and rabbits, as well as dogs, the olfactory bulbs and tracts are very large; in amphibious animals they are small; in fishes they are rudimentary or nil. In the monkey and man, where smell is good but subordinate to other faculties, the olfactory apparatus is small though distinct. Some animals use their noses to investigate the nature of substances which man would examine by means of sight or touch; and, as every sense has its memory, we need not be surprised at a dog, for example, finding his way back over long distances by smell alone. He is guided by a train of smells as effectually as we are guided by a train of sights, or, in other words, a succession of objects impressed upon our visual centre.[1] Yet, acute as he is, a dog cannot reason abstractedly upon impressions derived through his nose as a man does, for example,

[1] In man the memory of smells does exist in a certain degree. Maudsley says of himself: 'There are certain smells which never fail to bring back to me instantly and visibly scenes of my boyhood, though I was not in the least thinking of them at the time.'—*Physiology of Mind*.

with reference to the smell of sewer gas, and the chances of
its being followed by typhoid fever. The animal's reflective
mechanism is defective, and does not enable him to do more
than put together a few general ideas. Savages, whose
frontal lobes are smaller than those of civilised man, show a
similar incapacity for abstractions, their speech containing
only such phrases as are required to describe the most striking
objects of nature and the experiences of their daily life.

Contrary to the belief of Gall and his disciples, the cerebellum is most assuredly not the seat of 'amativeness.'
Experiment shows it to be the centre of those automatic
movements whereby our equilibrium is maintained. A bitch,
mentioned by Ferrier, in which only a small fragment of the
right lobe of the cerebellum existed, showed 'heat,' became
impregnated and bore young, but could not stand erect or
move from place to place except by 'butting forward, and
proceeding by force of her falls.' Men who sustain injuries
to the cerebellum reel as if intoxicated, though if the affection
be of slow and partial growth, they are able to accommodate
themselves to it, probably by an adaptation of the faculties
of sight and touch. Hitzig placed the poles of an electric
battery behind a man's ears. The patient experienced a
feeling of giddiness, and the direction in which his equilibrium was disturbed depended upon the direction of the
current. With his eyes closed he felt as if he were being
whirled from left to right, or from right to left, or as if the
basis of support on one side were withdrawn. With his eyes
open, he saw objects whirling round him in one direction or
the other. In experiments upon monkeys, it has been found
that injury to the after part of the middle lobe of the cerebellum causes a tendency in the animal to fall backwards.
If one of the lobes on either side is affected, there is a disturbance of equilibrium on that side amounting to constant
rotation of the body. Electric stimulus of the cerebellum
causes spasmodic movements of the eyes and limbs, showing
the relation of ocular movements to those required for the
adjustment of the equilibrium. The mechanism of the cerebellum is, perhaps, largely independent of the hemispheres.
Nevertheless, these interest themselves in all, or nearly all,

automatic movements. The main seat of the sexual feeling is probably the centre of touch, with extensive connections in all the other centres except that of taste. No feeling is more widely diffused or more powerful. It is capable of throwing the whole of the hemispheres into activity, not excepting the purely intellectual regions, and the shock produces extensive exhaustion of the nerve-cells, which then require sleep or rest.

If not only every thought and feeling, but every fragment of a thought and feeling, is the outcome of a certain grouping of nerve-cells and fibres, the number of such nerve-cells and fibres available in even the poorest brains must be enormous. Yet, in point of variety and complexity, the nerve elements of the brain would appear to be by no means disproportionate to the intricacies of mental function. The following calculation is given by Bain: 'Allowing for intervals, we may suppose that a line or row of 500 cells occupies an inch of the gray matter of the brain, thus giving a quarter of a million to the square inch for 300 inches. If one half of the thickness of the layer is made up of fibres, the cells, taken by themselves, would be a mass one-twentieth of an inch thick; say sixteen cells in the depth. Multiplying these numbers together we should reach a total of 1,200 millions of cells in the gray covering of the hemispheres. As every cell is united with at least two fibres, often many more, we may multiply this number by four for the number of connecting fibres attached to the mass, which gives 4,800 millions of fibres. Assume the respective numbers to be (nerve-cells) 1,000 millions and (fibres) 5,000 millions, and make the comparison with our acquisitions as follows: With a total of 50,000 acquisitions evenly spread over the whole of the hemispheres, there would be for each nervous grouping at the rate of 20,000 cells and 100,000 fibres.

'With a total of 200,000 acquisitions of the assumed types, which would certainly include the most retentive and most richly endowed minds, there would be for each nervous grouping 5,000 cells and 25,000 fibres. This leaves out of account a very considerable mass of nervous matter in the spinal cord, medulla oblongata, cerebellum, and the lesser gray centres of the brain, in all of which there are very large deposits of gray matter with communicating white fibres to match.   Such an estimate, confined to the hemispheres of the brain, is enough to show that, numerous as are the embodiments to be provided for, the nervous elements are on a corresponding scale, and that there is no improbability in supposing an independent nervous tract for each separate acquisition.'[1]

In the process of waste and repair that goes on, the molecules of the system are constantly renewed, but each new set takes the stamp of its predecessors, and thus the continuity of our personality is assured.   That all kinds of sensorial and motor activity depend upon the soundness of the nerve-connections existing between the different areas of the brain, is shown by some curious results of brain disease. Spoken language is carried on between the auditory centre and the motor centre for articulation.   It is in the auditory centre that the nerve-groupings which constitute the memory of words are formed, and upon the efficiency of this centre depends our faculty for remembering things we have heard, for learning languages by ear, for appreciating music.   A word, whether spoken or written, is only a symbol.   It is custom that associates the word bread in English with something to eat.   The French adopt *pain*, the Germans *Brod*, to signify the same thing.[2]   Before a word is learnt a nerve-connection has to be formed between the nerve-group embodying it in the auditory centre, and the nerve-group required in the motor centre for giving it articulation.   Now, suppose this nerve-connection were to break, either through the decay or the imperfect nutrition of some set of nerves, what might be expected to happen?   Surely this, that the patient would know perfectly well a word when he heard it, but that he would not be able to say it.   He would be suffering from the well-known malady called aphasia.   Some-

---

[1] Bain : *Body and Mind.*

[2] Dr. Samuel Wilkes says his parrot associated things with words.   It never caught, however, the word nuts ; but, when nuts were on the table, it uttered a peculiar squeak, which the members of the family fully understood to mean nuts.—*Journal of Mental Science*, 1879

times the nerve-connection between the auditory and the speech centre is not broken but only deranged. In that case the patient speaks freely, but his words are wrong—he calls pills 'potatoes,' a stick a 'cord,' and so on. The nerve-group of the auditory centre throws into action the wrong nerve-group of the motor centre. If the derangement is great the patient's attempts to speak will result in an unintelligible jargon, as in the case of the French lady (mentioned by Trousseau), who, wishing to bid a visitor take a chair, said, 'Cochon, animal, fichu, bête.' Sometimes the patient knows, sometimes he does not know, that he has wrongly used a word. In the worst cases, short of absolute dumbness, only one set of nerves between the auditory and the articulatory centres are open; the patient then uses one word for everything, sometimes not even a word, but a sound.

Similar defects are found in connection with the visual and other centres. The patient sees properly, but loses the power of naming objects. With a horse before him, he cannot remember what to call it. He will ask for a glass of ——, without being able to recall the name of the drink required. A friend will offer him beer. 'No,' he will answer. 'Water?' 'No.' 'Milk?' 'No.' 'Whisky?' 'Yes.' He knows the thing when he sees it, but cannot mention it by name. There is a derangement of the nerve-connection between the centre for sight and that for speech. Abernethy tells an amusing story of a friend who could not recollect a person's name, and who dragged him into a neighbouring street to show it him on a door-plate. The printed word is as much a symbol as the spoken one, only it appeals to the eye instead of the ear. Consequently, a defect in the visual centre, or in the ocular adjustments that convey the form of the letters, causes inability to read, while the faculties of hearing and speaking remain. It will thus be seen that learning to read a foreign language is a wholly different process from learning to speak it; in the one case the visual centre, with its muscular adjustments of the eye, in the other the auditory centre is employed. In both cases extensive nerve-groupings have to be established and linked with each other. For the reading of ordinary literature in Chinese, some 10,000 separate characters have to be learnt and re-membered. The nerve-groupings in connection with language generally will be much greater than this, though their intimate association with each other will cause them to be easily revived. In language, as in our acquisitions generally, the various centres act and re-act upon each other. The student will frequently remember a word by sight, that is to say, by its place in some printed page, when his auditory centre is powerless to recall it. It is also a common experience that a fact read in a book is forgotten, but remembered if we make a note of it. The reason is that, in the latter case, two centres instead of one are brought into play; a double memory is established, that of sight and that of muscular movement. It is like the tying of the knot on the handkerchief. Letters, especially initial letters, cohere in the memory independently of words. Hence, a person may recognise individual letters when whole words are Greek to him. W. W. Ireland knew an aphasic patient who could not read written-out numbers, such as 'thirty-seven' or the corresponding Roman numerals 'XXXVII,' but who could read the ordinary figures '37,' while perfectly understanding all that was said to him. His age was 32; when this was written 42, he corrected it.

Applying the same principle to the malady called agraphia, many things that perplexed the wisest of our forefathers become as clear as day. A woman, who has somehow lost the faculty of writing, consults a specialist. He asks her to write her name. She takes a pen, and in all good faith scribbles:—

Sunnil Siclaa Satreni,

adding by way of an address,

Sunesr nut ts mer tinn lain.

The defect here is similar to the misuse of words in speech. There is something wrong with the nerve-groupings and their connections employed in the movements for writing. As in the case of speech, the defect may be great or small. Sometimes a patient can begin writing a word correctly, but inevitably lapses into meaningless combinations of letters like 'ffg' or 'ndend.' Asked to spell cat, a patient so affected will say, properly enough, c, a, t, and then write 'caudd.' In extreme cases, one meaningless group of letters is written for all words. Persons unable to write their own thoughts, or perhaps to think coherently, may still be able to write correctly to dictation, though unable to read afterwards what they have written. In this case the connection between the auditory centre and the writing muscles is good, while that between the writing muscles and the visual centre is impaired. It may happen that a person to whose visual centre a written word makes no appeal, will learn what the word is by tracing with his hand the outlines of the letters, thus bringing a motor centre with its memories into play. It is on the same principle that comparatively illiterate people help themselves to understand a printed page by audibly or silently articulating the words.

Thought, like our impressions of the outer world, is necessarily the product, not of one centre but of many centres combined. A blind man learns to read with his fingers, a nerve-connection being formed in his brain between the centre for touch and that for articulation. The often-quoted deaf-mute, Laura Bridgman, was observed during thought, or when dreaming, to execute unconsciously the same movements as she was accustomed to make in the actual exercise of her manual speech. The paralysis of the first Lord Denman was accompanied by total inability to form letters into words, or words into sentences. He could only sign his name by seeing it written out and copying it. But his intelligence seemed to be unaffected; law reports and parliamentary debates interesting him then as much as ever. Men could play chess without knowing the names of the pieces, or even the name of the game. And it is surely a common experience to elaborate ideas before, and sometimes without being able to express them in words. John Hunter, although a great thinker, had a poor command of words, and Turner was wholly unable to express his ideas of art in intelligible language. Still, there can be no doubt that speech powerfully supports thought. Lordat, the distinguished professor of

medicino, lost his power of speech after a fever, understanding what was said to him, but being unable to express himself except in writing. During his malady he professed to
combine abstract ideas as freely as before, but his friends
noticed a deterioration of his intellectual faculties. Ferrier,
Bastian, and other specialists, note that aphasic patients lose
their powers of abstract thought, or think with difficulty.

Music, like speech, resides in the auditory centre, with an
executive faculty in the motor centres. An impairment of
the nerve-connection between the auditory and the motor
centres gives rise to the same sort of disabilities as we have
seen existing in the case of speech. Kussmaul mentions a
patient who could compose music, write musical notes, and
recognise an air which he had heard, but who could not play
from notes. Another had lost the value of musical notes, but
could play an air after hearing it. Frederick Clay, the composer, who died, in 1889, of paralysis, from which he had suffered for some years, presented curious symptoms. He lost
the art of reading music, but when a piece of his own composition was played in his presence, and played inaccurately, he
stopped the performance at the faulty passage. His speech was
mainly confined to monosyllables. When asked to name his
favourite opera, he replied ' Don,' meaning ' Don Giovanni.'
Along with the faculty of reading music, he had also lost that
of ordinary reading and writing, but he could recall the names
of Derby winners for many years back.

All partial disorders of memory and impairment of intelligence or modes of feeling will be understood from the foregoing pages. Linné forgot his own works and read them
with pleasure as the writing of a stranger. Walter Scott
forgot a novel which he had dictated. The poet Rogers had
to ask his servant whether he knew the people he met.
Wycherley's memory played him tricks in his old age; if
anything was read to him over night he would rise next
morning full of the ideas and expressions he had heard, and
write them down in the full belief that they were his own.
After an attack of apoplexy a patient of Brown-Sequard's
lost all memory of events that had occurred during a period
of five years, this period, which comprised his marriage, finish-

ing about six months before the attack. As the result of a knock on the head a man is said to have forgotten his Greek but nothing else. Abercromby relates that a surgeon whose head was injured by a fall from his horse, could give instructions for treating the wound, but completely forgot the existence of his wife and family for three days. Sharpey tells of a young woman who, after an irresistible tendency to sleep, forgot everything she knew, recognising nobody, not even her parents, and had to begin to learn reading and writing like a child. Amid the wreck of her acquisitions only some knowledge of music remained, but she was not conscious of how or when she had studied music. Double personality is not unknown. There is a recorded case of an hysterical woman who, in her normal state, was 'grave, reserved, and laborious,' but who, after recovering from a fit of unconsciousness, was 'gay, turbulent, imaginative, and coquettish,' this continuing until she was seized with torpor, when she became as before. Forbes Winslow tells of a young married woman who, after a period of debility, lost all sense of the time that had elapsed since the day of her marriage. She remembered with remarkable vividness every previous event of her life ; but when her husband approached her she repudiated all knowledge of or relation to him. She acted in the same way with regard to her child. Her parents and friends by their authority succeeded in persuading her that she was in reality married, and had given birth to a son, but she beheld her husband and child without being able to imagine how she had come by them. Men have been known to forget their own names, and to beg their friends to tell them from time to time who they were. As the result of shock to their nervous system, people in danger of death by drowning or otherwise find memories revived which previously would have seemed to be entirely obliterated from their minds. The long-forgotten languages and prayers of youth return to them, together with pictures of the scenes of their childhood.

Luys lays claim to have solved the uses both of the optic thalamus and the corpus striatum. From an anatomical examination of the radiating nerves in connection with these organs, he holds that the optic thalamus collects the sensory impressions arriving from the outer world as well as from all parts of the body and nutritive system, and launches them into the appropriate areas of the gray matter; and that the corpus striatum is, inversely, an intermediate station for sensory impressions passing into muscular action. If these conjectures are well founded, a disturbance of faculty, sensory or motor, will be produced by disease in the optic thalamus or the corpus striatum as well as in the various outer centres. Records of cases seem to bear out Luys's view. Thus, a young woman, mentioned by John Hunter, successively lost smell, sight, hearing, and touch. After death it was found that her optic thalamus in both hemispheres had been progressively destroyed by disease. Stimulation of the corpus striatum in one hemisphere, again, causes a general contraction of the muscles on the opposite side of the body, as if the whole motor area were being excited at once. Hæmorrhage into the brain commonly proceeds from the rupture of small arteries passing through these internal ganglia; hence, a very small derangement here produces extensive paralysis and loss of sensation, precisely as the traffic in all parts of the city of London is deranged by a block at the Mansion House.

In hypnotism certain areas of the brain seem to be stimulated in an extraordinary degree at the expense of others. When the body is torpid the senses are excessively acute. The ticking of a watch, the smell of a flower, can be detected by the patient at incredible distances. Through a layer of cotton wool placed upon his eyes he can read a newspaper, and colours influence him through a wooden screen one-fifth of an inch thick. The emotional areas, also, become extraordinarily susceptible. The picture of a merry face makes the patient laugh, a gloomy one makes him cry. The memory is enormously quickened. 'I once heard a young married lady,' says Luys, 'who had listened to one of my lectures, repeat the lecture several months afterwards in a state of somnambulism, with the utmost accuracy, reproducing, like a phonograph, the very tones of my voice, using every gesture that I used, and adapting, too, in a remarkable way, her words to her subject. A year afterwards this lady had still the same capacity, and displayed it every time she was put into a state of somnambulism. And, extraordinary as it may seem, when once awakened she was utterly unable to repeat to me a single word of the lecture. She said she did not listen to it, she understood not a word of it and could not say a single line.'

An unequal distribution of blood in the brain would seem to be the more immediate cause of the hypnotic condition. The operator's first step is to fatigue one of the senses, usually the sight, by causing the patient to gaze fixedly at a bright object; sometimes the hearing, by a regular beating of the notes of the scale; more rarely the sense of touch, by gently rubbing a particular part of the body. By this means seemingly a disturbance of the circulation is set up. There is probably an excessive flow of blood to the fatigued region, which then becomes unduly sensitive. When there is a full supply of blood in the brain all the senses are active; when the circulation is feeble the functions are depressed or suspended. Sleep is caused by a withdrawal of the blood-supply of the hemispheres; dreaming arises from a partial circulation through the various centres; in sleep-walking the motor centres are thrown into activity. Brain disease is sometimes indicated by an unusual delicacy of the centres of sight and hearing—the result of an excessive blood supply; and defects in the speech centre have been found to be due to the plugging of an important artery in that region. A sudden excitement in one centre seems to draw away the blood from other centres, whose efficiency is thereby reduced. The physical process of digestion hinders intellectual activity. An idea occurring to us makes us cease any bodily exercise in which we may be engaged until the new excitement subsides. The fear of shipwreck, or any violent emotion, checks sea-sickness. The poet Moore, in crossing the Irish Channel, was sea-sick when news was brought to him of his father's death, whereupon his disorder left him.

Drugs and poisons taken into the blood produce various intellectual disturbances, as does also the vitiated circulation caused by malignant fevers. Of alcohol most people have some experience. Its first effect is to loosen the connecting links of the different centres, producing a want of harmony between sensations and motor acts and impairing the various kinds of memory. It is for this reason that a drunken man is reckless and irresponsible. Finally, alcohol paralyses all sensation and movement. The staggering gait of a drunken man is probably due to a disturbance of the cerebellum, for which alcohol would seem to have a special affinity, like that of strychnine for the spinal centres. In drunkenness the weak points of the character are thrown into relief, one man becoming morbidly irritable and quarrelsome, another ludicrously affectionate, a third stupid, a fourth obscene, a fifth sordidly avaricious, a sixth profusely generous, a seventh vain, an eighth silly, a ninth superstitious. In hypnotism it has been observed that the patient's faculty for falsehood is largely if not wholly suppressed; in drunkenness there is the same deficiency in the organic cohesions of the different centres where a lie might be concocted. Whence the proverb, *In vino veritas.* Opium, according to De Quincey, does not affect the equilibrium, its action being apparently confined to the hemispheres, where it stimulates past and forgotten 'memories' into great activity. Chloroform, in addition to paralysing the hemispheres, like alcohol, acts upon the medulla oblongata, affecting chiefly the breathing power—an important fact established by the Hyderabad Commission of 1889. Hashisch, with which interesting experiments were made upon himself by Moreau (de Tours), produces errors of sense and false convictions. 'The mind has a tendency to exaggerate everything, and the slightest impulse carries it along. By a word or gesture our thoughts may be successively diverted to a multitude of different objects with a rapidity and a lucidity which are truly marvellous.'

In the modern theory of brain-function above set forth there is no place for that bugbear of the older metaphysicians, the will. If it be admitted that what men call mind is only the working of a sensitive mechanism called the brain, which is acted upon by stimuli from the outer world, through the senses, pretty much as a weather-cock is acted upon by the wind, it follows that in speaking of the will as an agent in our mental processes we mistake a word for a thing. A railway engine is not thought to exercise will, when, in obedience to the force of the steam generated in its boiler, it moves backwards or forwards, slowly or quickly, according to the setting of its gear for the time being. It is not responsible for the steam or the mode of its action. A ship, again, is not credited with volition when it sails before the wind or obeys its rudder. Equally with the locomotive and the sailing vessel, man is moved hither and thither by external influences acting upon an organisation with which he has been endowed at birth or, rather, at conception. At every step in life he is driven one way and another by different impulses, all having relation to the general question of pleasure or pain, profit or loss, to the individual. He is required, as he thinks, to make up his mind as to which way he will go. The forces acting upon him are numerous and subtle, some obvious and material, others purely ideal, many hereditary and unconscious. There is a multiplicity of motives counteracting and reacting upon each other in the various centres of his brain. To all, he is more or less responsive, just as the memories, or experiences, or hereditary predispositions concerned in the conflict, are strong or weak. In the end, one impulse or set of impulses proves itself the strongest, and he is carried along by it. Meanwhile he flatters himself that he has made an effort of will in this direction; in reality, he has been as passive as a musical instrument that is played upon. He thinks he commands whereas he only obeys. ' Will,' says Herbert Spencer, ' is spoken of as something apart from the feeling or feelings which for the moment prevail over others; whereas it is nothing but the general name given to the special feeling that gains supremacy and determines action. Will,' he adds in a forcible metaphor, ' is no more an existence separate from the dominant feeling than a king is an existence separate from the man occupying the throne.'

Some men are as rash as others are cautious. The rash man has imperfect links of association between one centre and another, or one set of impressions and another; when, therefore, a pleasurable object is presented to him in the form of a sensory impression, past impressions of an opposite character in the same or in other centres are not aroused. He is in the position of a judge arriving at a decision upon incomplete evidence. The cautious man, on the other hand, is one in whom a long series of impressions, recorded in different centres, link themselves together and become successively revived, the strongest finally asserting itself and passing into the motor area. Both men believe that the course they take is volitional ; in reality they are unconsciously governed by the mechanism of their brain-centres, which may be good or bad, efficient or inefficient. Honesty, therefore, is no guarantee that we shall hold sound views or do wise deeds. To go one step further, no man can be said to be responsible for his opinions. Everyone expresses himself according to the manner in which he has been impressed, and this depends altogether upon the state of the cerebral organisation with which he happens to be endowed. Obstinacy arises from conditions similar to those of impulsiveness, one set of impressions being more readily and vividly aroused than others ; and selfishness, benevolence, vanity, in fact all the varied characteristics of human nature, are to be explained on the same principle.

All extreme or fanatical views are attributable to defective comparison, that is to say, to a defective revival of counteracting memories in the brain. The delusions of insanity would also seem to have defective comparison as their chief basis. The morbid excitability of a sensory centre produces an effect appropriate to that centre—an hallucination of sight, hearing, smell, touch, or taste. If the cohesive memories aroused in the other centres by this action, memories of time, place, touch, movement, etc., are sufficiently extensive and vivid, they correct the false impression ; the patient knows that what he sees or hears is an hallucination. If, on the other hand, through the destruction or the inactivity of certain areas, the cohesive memories are poor, so that the individual has but a slender basis of comparison whereon his judgments may be formed, the hallucination begins to wear the aspect of reality ; the sight or the sound is accepted as a fact, and the patient is mad. Fixed ideas, rooted and unreasonable prejudices, general narrowness of view, are minor manifestations of the same infirmity. Each half of the brain appears to be capable of elaborating thought, as instances are recorded of men exercising their intellectual faculties after one of their hemispheres has been destroyed by disease. In ordinary health, the hemispheres no doubt act in unison, owing to the extensive system of fibres binding them together. Some of the forms of insanity may be due to an impairment of these connecting fibres, especially when the patient has insane impulses which his reason seems to hold in check. Not infrequently patients feel a desire to murder somebody, but have sense enough to control it, and even to place themselves voluntarily under restraint lest the impulse should overpower them. In such cases we may suppose one hemisphere to be morbidly active while the other is sound, or nearly so.

The dependence of will upon physical conditions of a purely hereditary kind is curiously exemplified by the experience of twins. A close physical resemblance between twins is often accompanied by a similarity in their ideas. No less than eleven out of thirty-five cases examined by Galton [1] testify to this. The twins make the same remarks on the same occasion, begin singing the same song at the same moment, and so on. 'An observer and friend,' adds Galton, 'graphically described to me the effect produced on her by two such twins whom she met casually. She said, " Their teeth grew alike, they spoke alike and together, and said the same things, and seemed just like one person. . ." One twin, A, who happened to be at a town in Scotland, bought a set of champagne glasses which caught his attention, as a surprise for his brother, B ; while, at the same time, B, being in England, bought a set of precisely the same pattern as a surprise for A.' Upon this theory of the will, which, by the way, abolishes that freedom of judgment upon which men are accustomed to plume themselves, and which forms the basis of so many religious systems, it is possible with the exercise of a little patience to explain even the most trivial volitional acts, so called, of one's daily life. An ingenious writer, [2] in a passage too long to quote, shows how absolutely conditioned is such an apparently free act as the determination to touch, *by accident*, some one of the squares of a chess-board.

[1] Galton : *Inquiries into Human Faculty.*
[2] Jonathan Edwards.

Hypnotism throws an instructive light upon the so-called operations of the will. The operator obtains control over the sensory and motor faculties of his subject, who then has no sensations or desires that are properly his own, but performs extremely complicated and apparently rational acts in obedience to suggestion. If told that he is hot, he takes off his coat and fans himself; he accepts a candle as a cigar and smokes it; if a knife is put into his hand, a train of muscular associations is aroused, and he cuts with it; an umbrella being given him, he opens it and believes he is in a shower of rain; dance music makes him dance, and if the tune is suddenly changed to a religious one, he falls on his knees in the attitude of prayer. A suggestion conveyed to the patient while he is in a hypnotic state may remain latent in his mind after he is restored to himself, and in due time be translated into action. He is told, for instance, that in ten minutes he is to get up and open the door. He is thereupon restored to consciousness and remembers nothing of what has been said to him, but when the ten minutes have elapsed he gets up and opens the door. On being asked why he does so he says he does not know; he obeys an unconscious impulse, communicated to his muscles by the automatic mechanism of the brain. At Nancy, where extensive experiments in hypnotism are carried on, a suggestion is said to have been latent in a patient's mind for 172 days. To a hypnotized subject, Mdlle. A. E., the operator, Beaunis, said: 'At ten o'clock on the morning of New Year's Day you will see me appear in your room. I shall wish you a happy New Year and disappear again.' This was in July. On waking, the lady remembered nothing and no more was said. At the given date Beaunis happened to be in Paris, but at ten o'clock the lady, being then busy in her room, heard a knock at the door, and said, 'Come in.' To her astonishment Beaunis entered, dressed in his *summer clothes*, wished her a happy New Year and retired. She looked out of the window, but did not see him leave the house. Soon afterwards she went downstairs and told a friend Beaunis had paid her a visit. Nor could she be persuaded that he had not actually been there in person.

Whence, then, comes the common delusion that will is an integral part of our mental equipment? The belief seems to have its root in consciousness. Of consciousness we can only say that it is a fact in connection with our nervous system. It appears to come into existence only when a variety of nerves are stimulated. The power of discriminating between successive sensations has already been described as one of the fundamental conditions of knowledge. Now, discrimination is but another word for consciousness, a necessary element in this being a change from one nerve-state to another. If we could conceive the weathercock as being endowed with a discriminating faculty, we should perceive that whatever might be its belief as to the voluntary nature of the movements it was executing, these movements would in every case have been entered upon before it began to discriminate them. This is precisely what happens in the case of our own so-called volitions. They are begun before they come within the sphere of consciousness at all. When actions are so often repeated that the requisite nerve-groupings become closely organised in the brain-centres, such actions cease to be conscious. Memory, reason, feeling, and will simultaneously disappear in proportion as mental changes become automatic. We act then from force of habit. Much of our mental action takes place thus unconsciously, as when a man goes to bed with his head in a state of muddle and gets up in the morning with a clear perception of the course he ought to take; or when, after he has been vainly trying to remember a thing and has apparently ceased to think of it, it flashes upon his consciousness. As Taine remarks, there are many stages or platforms where our mental action is carried on, though only one may be lighted up at a time. It was force of habit, with perhaps some hereditary tendency, which constituted the Greek Nomos, or custom having the force of law, as described by Grote—the established fact and condition of things which each new member of the community is born to and finds subsisting, the aggregate of beliefs and predispositions to believe, ethical, religious, æsthetical, and social, respecting what is true or false, holy or unholy, honourable or base in all the relations of life.

The identical modes of feeling and judgment that prevail among masses of human beings are the result of brains of similar organisation being acted upon by similar stimuli ; and it is in accordance with this principle that an author, an orator, a painter, or a musician, counts upon producing his effect. Common-sense is the established groove of thought in a community. It varies with time and place. The social virtues of to-day are not those of 500 years ago. Our English common-sense is not the common-sense of the Zulus. It is not even that of our near neighbours the French, in some particulars. Much of this effect is educational, but the special grouping of nerve-cells, the persistent nerve-thrill which is involved in the operations of common-sense, must be such as falls within the capacity of the average brain of the community. Special susceptibilities, or want of susceptibilities, in the individual will always lead to deviations from common-sense, that is to say to originality. Most minds have little bents of their own. A person will be found at a given moment repeating a given thought. Examiners put the same questions year after year. In conversation we unconsciously drift into our favourite subjects. The efficiency of a musical instrument does not more depend upon its construction than does the scope of the mind upon the cerebral organisation.

While there is a pretty general level of intellect in communities, individuals differ widely from each other in mental development. 'I was present,' says Forbes Winslow, 'at the post-mortem examination of the body of a gentleman who died of visceral disease at the advanced age of eighty-four. Up to this period he had been remarkable for great vigour of intellect and for extraordinary elasticity and retentiveness of memory. He appeared to have forgotten no impression that had ever been made upon his mind, in early as well as in advanced life. During the examination of the brain I was repeatedly struck with its anatomical appearance. The gray matter was by no means diminished in quantity or consistence. The fissures were well marked, and both as to volume, character, and depth of its convolutions, the brain presented an aspect similar to what a pathologist would expect to detect in a person dying in full intellectual power at the age of thirty or forty. In another case I examined the brain of a gentleman whose mind had become prematurely enfeebled for six years previously to his death. He died at the age of fifty-six. The convolutions of the brain had greatly diminished in depth as well as in complexity, and the encephalic mass also presented a general shrunken or atrophied appearance.'[1]

Insanity in all its degrees is to be ascribed to a lowered or heightened susceptibility of brain tissue. If a morbid change is not always visible after death, it does not follow that it has not existed, for in the groupings of nerve-cells and fibres in the brain, we have to deal with phenomena transcending the highest powers of the microscope. Violent mania and imbecility are probably due, the former to an excessive susceptibility of the nerve-cells, the latter to their decay. In the one case, hallucinations of the senses occur, according to the area affected, with imperfect reasoning powers, arising from insufficient comparison; in the other, the perceptive faculties as well as memory in its various forms cease to act, the brain gradually becoming an inert mass, incapable of responding to any external impressions whatever. In acute delirium the exciting cause is usually found to be inflammation of the brain or its membranes. 'Cases of chronic insanity, in which all anatomical lesions are wanting observes Maudsley, 'are rare. Many of the more advanced cases exhibit some degree of atrophy of the brain, especially of the convolutions, effusion into the subarachnoid space, discolouration of the gray matter, and general hardening of the white substance.' Insanity attended by symptoms of depression is often due to a deficiency of blood in the system, in which case the patient is pale and emaciated, with little or no sensibility.

Among individuals of the same race, a greater or less capacity of mind may be attributed with perfect confidence to a greater or less development or susceptibility of the different areas of their brain. There are persons with poorly constituted brains in which a sight or sound—an impression from the outer world—arouses few cognate or secondary

---

[1] Forbes Winslow: *Obscure Diseases of the Brain.*

impressions—few memories, that is to say. Dolt and block-head are the words commonly applied to these unfortunates who are governed almost wholly by the sensory impressions of the moment. The possessor of a well-endowed visual centre in conjunction with a poor auditory one, will remember things he has seen better than things he has heard. He will have a good memory for faces, and a bad one for related facts. He will have a clear perception of surrounding objects, with their colours and their relations to each other, but he will be a poor hand at remembering a tune. He may be a painter, he will never be a musician. In the musician the auditory centre is necessarily the most susceptible, since it is here that his memories are the most cohesive and the most easily revived.

In intellectual or artistic pursuits of every kind, the power of concentrating one's thoughts is of great importance. Upon what does this power depend? As sensory impressions tend to call up appropriate movements, so induced movements call up the sensory impressions commonly associated with them. So much is clear. By throwing himself into the physical attitudes of joy or sorrow, the actor contrives to bring his sentiments into a corresponding state. In view of this, Ferrier offers the ingenious suggestion that a person whose motor centres are highly developed may, by the agency of these, be enabled to control his ideas, just as one may call up a state of grief, more or less pronounced, by assuming the physical expression appropriate to it. He concludes that, as the motor centres are not merely the basis of sensori-motor cohesions and acquisitions, but also the basis of the powers of concentration and control of ideation, a relatively high development of the motor centres, as compared with the sensory centres, will be found in those animals and individuals capable of the highest intellectual achievements. There is no necessary contradiction here to the theory, above adopted, of the will. The highly developed motor centres spoken of by Ferrier are but the means whereby a communicated impulse from the outer world is carried into effect. Will still remains essentially a matter of cerebral organisation, which the individual is powerless to alter.

That persons are born with richly or poorly organised brains is beyond all question. The fact is as indisputable as that they are born potentially tall or short, stout or lean, dark or fair, and although education helps to increase their mental acquisitions, it cannot add to, nor can anything but disease or accident take away from, their native capacity. Rudolph Wagner, an authority on the physiology of the brain, observes: 'Between the convolutions of different individuals there are remarkable differences, so that one may distinguish richly convoluted and poorly convoluted brains. These relate only to more numerous divisions and to bendings, etc., of the primary convolutions, which retain the same number and essential position in all normal brains of whatever race. The most notable differences occur in the convolutions of the frontal lobes. There are to be found brains of adults which in this respect resemble the brain of a seven months' fœtus, and of which it may truly be said that, in their outward configuration at least, they have remained in a fœtal condition. The slighter development of the frontal convolutions occurs more especially in female brains, so that it may be said that they resemble in this respect the fœtal brain in its later stages of development, before the final evolution of the frontal lobes. There are to be found also male brains of the same character, which may, therefore, be said to belong to the female type, and female brains which in their richness of convolution approach the male type. As a rule, however, the convolutions and fissures are better developed in all the lobes when the frontal convolutions are especially complex.' As Ferrier and others have shown, there are many grounds for believing that the frontal lobes form the substrata of these physical operations which lie at the foundation of the higher intellectual processes, and their varying degrees of development in individuals is a matter of common observation.

Diversity of brain mechanism necessarily produces diversity of function. It is not alone the poet who is born, not made. As much may be said of the painter, the musician, the commander, the administrator, the philosopher, the man of science or the inveterate criminal. Macaulay, before he

was eight years old, wrote a Compendium of Universal
History. Reynolds began to paint and Handel to compose
without instruction; Napoleon studied war in the playground;
Samuel Taylor Coleridge, before his fifteenth year, was im-
mersed in metaphysics and theological controversy. Environment may do much for the species, but it does little for
the individual. All special aptitudes and predispositions
depend upon the preponderance of certain areas of the brain
possessing more enduring records, more vivid recollections,
a greater supply of nerve force, active or latent, than other
areas, and thus providing a richer store of material together
with a more efficient means of utilising that material for
intellectual or artistic operations. Here we have the key to
genius in all its forms, creative and destructive, nay, to all
the diversities of human faculty, whether in the direction of
plus or *minus*. We have now to discover how the inequalities of brain structure, underlying these diversities of faculty,
arise.

CHAPTER II

ORGANIC FUNCTIONS REGULATED BY THE BRAIN AND SPINAL CORD—
ALLIED NERVE DISEASES—INSANITY, IDIOCY, PARALYSIS, EPILEPSY,
CONSUMPTION, GOUT, ASTHMA, DEFORMITIES, BLINDNESS, DEAFNESS,
ETC.—ILLUSTRATIVE TABLES—DRINKING HABITS, CRIMINAL INSTINCTS,
NE'ER-DO-WELLISM, PIETY, AVARICE, PHILANTHROPY, AND OTHER
MORAL CHARACTERISTICS IN RELATION TO THE CEREBRO-SPINAL
SYSTEM—THE VARIATIONS OF HEREDITY—THEIR PROBABLE CAUSE

THE operations of the brain are not purely sensory, motor, or intellectual; they are also, and to a very large extent, administrative as regards the living body. For all practical purposes the brain and spinal cord are one. Not only does the spinal cord convey the impulses of the cerebral hemispheres to the trunk and limbs; it is in itself an organ of nervous activity, as is shown by the persistence of reflex action in the lower portions of the body after their connection with the brain has been cut off. Many important functions are regulated by the medulla oblongata, the bulbous head of the spinal marrow, situated just inside the skull. If an animal is deprived of its brain above the medulla oblongata it loses the faculties of sensation and of voluntary motion, but it still lives and breathes. Under due stimulation the eyelids will close, the muscles of the face and tongue contract, and the ear twitch; if food is put into the mouth the act of swallowing is performed; the placing of the nipple to the lips excites sucking. What is still more remarkable, the animal so mutilated utters a cry as of pain when pinched; yet it cannot feel anything, the cry being only a result of the reflex action of the larynx and the lungs. When the medulla oblongata is destroyed the animal can emit no sound, though pinching may still produce reflex action in its limbs; and respiration also ceases. The movements of the heart are caused by the intrinsic ganglia of the heart itself, for it will beat even after its removal from the body, but over the heart's action and the state of the blood pressure the medulla oblongata exercises a controlling influence. By the gray matter of the spinal cord, the tone of the muscles, the secretions of the skin, and the nutrition of the tissues are regulated. All the functions necessary to life, indeed, are organised in the cerebro-spinal system independently of consciousness; this is shown by the simple fact that they are carried on during sleep. The hemispheres, when active, take note of much that is done by other portions of the cerebro-spinal system; it is in them, as we have seen, that memories of various kinds are stored up to serve as the fabric of thought. Without hemispheres, no animal, we may suppose, can have any conscious thought, and in proportion as the cerebrum is organised will the mental powers, apart from the instincts, which are purely reflex, be developed. But although the hemispheres may look on, so to speak, at the organic functions, they have comparatively little to do with them. We cannot hold our breath for any length of time; we cannot voluntarily stop the heart's action. If we had this power, suicide would be a much easier matter than it is. To a limited extent respiration is under our control, and it is not improbable that the Indian fakirs who feign death so successfully are able to weaken the action of the heart. Practice enables an actor to turn pale at will. The influence of the hemispheres in the organic functions is also shown by the fact that in hysterical or epileptic subjects like Louise Latour hallucinations may so affect the nutritive system as to produce in the body and limbs a semblance of the wounds of Christ. The result of hypnotic suggestion in the cure of disease and in the production of morbid symptoms in a healthy body point to the operation of similar causes.[1]

What is more particularly to be noted in connection with the present inquiry, however, is the broad and indisputable fact that the growth, nutrition, and maintenance of the body depend upon the efficiency of the cerebro-spinal system, and that defects in this may be productive not only of deformities

[1] Tuckey: *Psycho-therapeutics.*

but of a whole group of constitutional diseases, comprising scrofula, rickets, gout, rheumatism, consumption, asthma, diabetes, and even dipsomania, as well as intellectual and motor disorders. This subject has been zealously studied of late years by Charcot, Bouchard, Möbius, Féré, Dejerine, Revington, and others, and from their investigations [1] the whole neuropathic family of diseases would appear to be but different manifestations of a single evil, namely, an instability of some sort in the nervous system, betraying itself in one form or another according to its seat in the body. If the brain is deranged, the various forms of hallucination or insanity ensue ; if, on the other hand, the seat of the evil is the spinal centres, an impairment of the nutrition and vital forces of the body takes place.

In these varying complications, heredity plays an important part; for the origin of all the nerve diseases from insanity downwards probably lies in that common physical condition known as ‘ lowness,’ or ‘ being out of sorts.’ This is induced in a man by fatigue, exposure, or unsuitable diet ; he marries a woman suffering from the like weakness, and the evil becomes aggravated in their children. That it should have been reserved for the science of the present day to discover the family relationship of a number of maladies as old as mankind, is not surprising when we consider how diverse in their symptoms these allied diseases are. Until the functions of the brain and the nervous system came to be as fully understood as they have been of late years, it was naturally impossible for any observer, however shrewd, to discover the relation say of insanity to ‘ club-foot.’ For the problem is complicated by the indirect operation of heredity. The nerve-diseases seldom descend in a simple and direct form from parent to child ; they become metamorphosed in passing from one generation to another, and even assume different forms among members of the same family. Ignorance of the subject, be it remarked, is still very wide-spread. People are not unwilling to confess to having gout in their

---

[1] Dejerine: *L'Hérédité dans les Maladies du Système Nerveux*, 1886. See also ‘The Neuropathic Diathesis,’ by G. T. Revington, *Journal of Mental Science* 1887-88.

family, but they scrupulously hide the existence of insanity.
Yet, at bottom, the one disease is no more respectable than
the other, and may indeed claim it as a near relative. The
connection of diabetes with the neuropathic group was
discovered by the merest accident. It was found that
puncture of the fourth ventricle of the brain produced the
diabetic condition, sugar appearing in large quantities in the
urine; and further investigation showed the formation and
excretion of the sugar to be the result of vaso-motor paralysis
of the liver, the immediate consequence of the injury in
question.

Morbid heredity follows the same lines as normal heredity;
it is direct or indirect, it may throw back, appear collaterally,
or occur in parent and child at corresponding periods of life.
There is no ascertained law governing the alternations in the
form of the disease; the insanity of a parent may be metamorphosed in the child into general ill-health, dyspepsia,
liability to neuralgia or headache, or even excessive physical
activity; it may, on the other hand, descend directly, so that
the son becomes as mad as the father. The importance of a
proper selection of partners in wedlock can hardly be over-
rated. If the members of a family in whom nerve-disorder
prevails marry into families similarly affected, the chances
of a healthy offspring being born to them are exceedingly
remote. Nerve-disorder in one parent is, however, counter-
acted by the soundness of the other, and the children in such
a case are likely to show a mixture of healthy and unhealthy
tendencies. Many unsound families are saved from extinction by the accident of one of their members selecting a
healthy partner. In families suffering from nerve-disorder,
some members die young, while others attain a great age.
If the evil happens to affect any important seat of organic
life, the patient succumbs early; if, on the other hand, the
intellectual regions alone are impaired, he may complete, and
in consequence of excessive stimulation of his vital functions,
even exceed the ordinary span of human life. Both short
life and long life in excess are, therefore, symptoms of the
neuropathic condition, as, indeed, is every marked departure
from the mean of existence. It has been remarked that while

certain unions are sterile, the same parties, differently united, are prolific enough. The explanation of the fact must be sought in the neuropathic condition of the couples. Suffering from the same nerve-disorders they make an unwholesome blend; if they are not childless, their children, unfit to live die young. There is another important fact to be noted. Like long and short life, irregularities of growth, such as excessive stoutness or leanness, great height or dwarfishness, may also be looked for in families where nerve-disorder prevails.

Practical illustrations of heredity in mankind bear out to the full the variation theory. Möbius gives the following family table: A drunkard dies of delirium tremens at fifty, leaving a daughter who is a 'little excitable' in temperament. This woman marries an apparently sound man, and has a mixed offspring, namely:

1. Daughter. Melancholic, with suicidal tendencies. Marries a man suffering from tuberculous disease. Of this union are born a daughter who dies of a puerperal disorder, a son who is tuberculous, a daughter who dies in infancy of convulsions, and a son who dies at twenty-six of spinal disease.

2. Son. Melancholic and suicidal. Marries a healthy woman and has several children, apparently sound.

3. Son. Melancholic, and actually committed suicide. Married a woman of unknown character, and leaves eight children, of whom two die of convulsions, two suffer from neuralgia, and one is epileptic. Others apparently well.

4. Son. Suffers from neuralgia. Marries a woman of 'nervous temperament.' Leaves a son with a deformed ear, a daughter who dies of convulsions, a second daughter who is six-fingered and slightly hydrocephalic, and a third who is apparently sound.

In 1884, a Calabrian soldier named Salvator Misdea shot several of his comrades in cold blood, and was sentenced to death by court-martial. His pedigree was investigated by Lombroso, Blanchi, and Basilei, who tabulate the result as follows:

Grandfather unintelligent, but of very active habits. Of his sons, the eldest was extremely hot tempered, and died of asthma; the second was eccentric, the third lame, irascible and homicidal, the fourth semi-imbecile, the fifth (Salvator's father) eccentric, drunken, and extravagant, married to an hysterical woman, who had one brother a brigand, and another a thief. Salvator, the offspring of this ill-starred union, was himself epileptic, hypochondriacal, feeble in memory and intelligence, and drunken. He had brothers and sisters, of whom one was epileptic, another sound, a third impetuous and hot tempered, a fourth obstinate and unteachable. One of his uncles (the second) had a family of idiots and imbeciles.

Among the children of epileptic parents the mortality is enormous. About half the number born die in childhood, principally of convulsions. They have so great an instability of nerve-element that convulsions result from the slightest irritation. Indeed, any sort of disease of the nervous system in the parents seems to dispose to this ill condition of the child, the acquired deterioration of the parent becoming the inborn organic feebleness of the offspring. Convulsions, as Maudsley remarks, are the sure sign of a weakness or lowered vitality of nerve-element—a defect which implies an unstable equilibrium of its organic constitution. Of the children of epileptic parentage who survive the perils of infancy only one in seven, apparently, inherits directly the complaint of its parents ; the others are hysterical, paralytic, idiotic, insane, cross-eyed, or subject to St. Vitus's dance, pretty much in the order named. Among the morbid conditions which, in parents, lead to epilepsy in the children, Dejerine enumerates alcoholism, persistent headache, suicidal tendencies, neuralgia, deafness, blindness, club-foot, paralysis, and ataxy. Other observers have noted in addition melancholia, somnambulism, apoplexy, nervous excitability, meningitis, softening of the brain, and lock-jaw.

The mixed conditions resulting from healthy blood on one side, and a morbid taint on the other, are well illustrated by the following family history : An 'eccentric' man marries a healthy woman, and has three sons and a daughter. The eldest son is sound, the daughter is weak-minded, the second son is also weak-minded, and the third is eccentric and ailing. This third son, who, in spite of his ill-health, lives to be seventy-one, marries an intelligent and apparently sound woman, and has a large family with the following characteristics:

1. Alexander: imbecile; dies at sixty-nine of peritonitis due to congenital hernia.

2. Ellen: sound and long-lived.

3. Mary: imbecile; dies at twelve.

4. William: idiot; alive at sixty-eight.

5. John: idiot; dies at fifty-six.

6. Robert: imbecile; dies at sixty-one of debility, due to disease of bones of the foot.

7. Joan: consumptive; dies at forty-four, leaving a daughter who also dies of consumption.

8. Thomas: a sufferer from chronic bronchitis with nervous exhaustion; marries a sound woman and has an imbecile son.

9. Anne: imbecile; dies at forty-four of consumption.

10. James: well and long-lived; marries and has eight healthy children.

11. Charles: imbecile; dies at four.

In this singularly corrupt and numerous family, two children, and two only, escape the hereditary taint on the father's side. Morbid heredity in both parents seems to leave almost no loophole of escape for the offspring, judging from the following table by Möbius:

A man who has suffered from St. Vitus's dance in his youth, and is intelligent but rather singular in his habits, and deformed, and who has a sister subject to nervous attacks, marries a woman belonging to a neuropathic family. Their children are one and all morbidly affected as follows:

1. Daughter: deformed and hysterical; marries a sound man, and has hysterical, nervous, or tuberculous children.

2. Son: suffers from St. Vitus's dance; is cross-eyed and melancholic, marries a sound woman, and has a child subject to convulsions.

3. Daughter: deformed and hysterical: marries a sound man, and has four daughters—the first, scrofulous and nervous; the second, deaf; the third, scrofulous and deformed; the fourth, nervous.

4. Son: intelligent, but of extremely variable temper;

marries a woman who is sound mentally, but tuberculous, and has a scrofulous, nervous, hysterical, ailing, and melancholic family.

5. Daughter : subject to St. Vitus's dance and hysterics.

None of the family tables yet given shows an access of any particular faculty along with general morbid conditions, but the case is not rare. I quote again from Möbius. A medical man of position, gay and active, marries a woman of unknown characteristics and has a family :

1. Son : small, deformed, of mediocre intelligence ; marries a sound woman and has, *a*. son : deformed and weak-minded ; unmarried. *b*. daughter : of quick intelligence, a little deformed ; married but childless. *c*. daughter : bright and witty, exhibits some mental derangement at the age of puberty ; marries a sound man and has four children, three of whom die in infancy, and one is idiotic. *d*. daughter : indolent, suffers from pains in the head, eccentric.

2. Daughter : of unknown characteristics ; has a son *superior morally and intellectually*, who marries his cousin (*b*) and is childless.

3. Daughter : also of unknown characteristics ; has a son of *vigorous intellect*, but melancholic, who is married to his cousin (*d*), and has a nervous, epileptic, and melancholic family.

4. Daughter : intelligent, but gluttonous ; childless.

5. Daughter : quick and imaginative, a little eccentric end capricious ; marries a sound man and has, *a*. son : *intellectually vigorous*, but hypochondriacal and capricious ; marries a sound woman, and has six children, three of whom die young, while one is an invalid, and two well. *b*. daughter : nervous ; marries a nervous man, and has an extremely nervous daughter, a son of feeble intellect, and another son who dies young of brain disease. *c*. son : *intellectually vigorous, gay, imaginative*, but capricious and hot-tempered ; marries a sound woman, and has four daughters, three of whom die young, while the fourth is nervous, and a son who is an invalid.

In a family table given by Vizioli, there appears to have been born to a neuropathic couple (the husband gouty and apoplectic, dying at seventy-five, and the wife dying of gangrene at seventy-two), no fewer than sixteen children, the majority suffering from paralysis, impediments of speech, apoplexy, ataxy, hypochondria, dipsomania, or deformities. In two cases there occurs *remarkable intelligence* combined with apoplexy, ataxy, heart disease, hypochondria, and early death. There are also two cases in the same family of *extraordinary sexual power*. Concerning the latter characteristic it may be noted that whereas, formerly, medical authorities were wont to attribute paralysis and kindred affections to the sexual excesses that so often precede them, they are now disposed to reverse the order of matters, and to recognise such excesses as a mere symptom, an effect and not a cause of the morbid state of the nervous system. As much may be said of the extraordinary weakness or total absence of the faculty observed in certain cases, and also of the perversion of the sexual instinct.

The frequent occurrence of alcoholism in the group of allied nerve diseases is remarkable. It would appear that the drunkard's vice is not solely acquired by the unhappy individual himself, but is due to hereditary predisposition. No authority who has lately studied this question entertains any doubt as to the persistence of the alcoholic taint in families, or as to its metamorphosis into other forms of nerve disease in passing from parent to child. It is found in close family connexion with insanity, epilepsy, violent temper, paralysis, imbecility, suicidal tendencies, deaf - mutism, and kleptomania. '*N'est pas alcoolique qui veut*,' observes a well-known medical authority; and, indeed, it is a matter of common observation that there are not only people who have acquired no excessive liking for drink, whatever their opportunities or temptations may have been, but to whom alcoholic liquors are positively distasteful. Dejerine gives details of a case in which a man of alcoholic tendencies, marrying a sound woman, engendered an hysterical daughter and a son who was dipsomaniac and epileptic. On the authority of Charcot, the same writer publishes the pedigree of a family whose members suffered variously from St. Vitus's dance, paralysis, hysteria, impaired sight and speech, and other affections. The father was epileptic, the mother subject to headaches and attacks of nerves. The grandfather was eccentric, and had a sister who suffered from asthma, and who had a son alcoholic and irresponsible ; the grandmother was of violent temper, and had a nephew who committed suicide. Magnan has observed epilepsy and alcoholism existing side by side in the same individual. It sometimes happens that a man becomes a settled drunkard at forty, and that his son, born twenty years before, develops in due time the same habit. What the father transmits to his son in such a case is not the vice of drunkenness itself, but the physical condition which conduces to it. Some authorities endeavour to establish a distinction between alcoholism and dipsomania—between acquired and inherited habits of drinking. The line of demarcation is one very difficult to draw. Both evils are the result of a craving of the stomach, due to some perversion of the gastric sensibility, and both in extreme cases are accompanied by affections of the brain and organic disturbances, particularly of the liver.

Similarly it may be said that consumption or tuberculosis is not transmitted directly, but is the result of a transmitted physical condition. There is no doubt but that tubercular disease propagates itself in numerous families from generation to generation, and that such families show a special susceptibility or tendency to it in one or other of its forms. At the same time there is reason to believe that the structural disease itself is not hereditarily transmitted, but that it is directly excited in each individual in whom it appears by a process of external infection due to the action of the tubercle bacillus. In other words, if the disease itself is not inherited, a particular temperament which renders the constitution liable to be attacked by it is capable of hereditary transmission, and is found alternating with diseases of the nervous order.

Ne'er-do-wellism, profligacy, or general good-for-nothingness, is as much the product of a defective brain organisation as insanity itself, of which, indeed, it is a variety. Only to be found in families where there is a neuropathic taint, it is a frequent concomitant of genius, if not in the individual, at all events in his near relatives ; and its physical basis is to be sought, partly in an excess of sensual appetites, partly in the same order of nerve-groupings as caution, caution and ne'er-do-wellism being due, respectively, to an excess and a deficiency in the revivability of those past impressions which serve as a guide to present conduct.

'Crime, vice, and insanity,' says Féré, ' are only separated by social prejudices, they are united by their character of fatality.' The hereditary nature of crime has been maintained by Maudsley, Jacoby, Lombroso and other writers ; and the case of the infamous Jukes family in America, whose criminal pedigree has been made out for seven generations, and who now number over 600 individuals, lends much support to the theory already well established by the frightful ravages of epilepsy and other nerve diseases among the criminal classes. Gluttony figures among Dejerine's tables as a vice of the epileptic order ; so do avarice and excessive piety. Here is the family history in which the latter characteristics occur :

A man of eccentric habits, very intelligent, but opposed to the education of his children and extremely avaricious, has a family of seven. Of these the eldest is violent in temper and has a child insane ; the second is obtuse, avaricious, and devout, having one child obtuse, and another deaf-mute and imbecile ; the third, a daughter, is avaricious and devout, is attacked by puerperal mania, has a tuberculous daughter, two other children who have died of meningitis and convulsions respectively, and two sons of defective intelligence, one being a somnambulist ; the fourth is maniacal and devout ; the fifth devout ; the sixth insane, and the seventh imbecile.

As piety is a frequent symptom of the epileptic condition, and as vanity and many faculties of a simple or complex character are occasionally found in an inordinate state of development when the cerebro-spinal system is unsound, it is not surprising that avarice should be a member of what Féré calls the ' neuropathic family.' Philanthropy itself may be placed upon the same footing. Howard, the prison reformer, was a tyrant in his own house and had a son who was insane. So also with selfishness. The explanation of these facts, so subversive of the current notions of morality, will be found in what has been said concerning the operation of the will. Owing to the non-receptive or the irresponsive action of one or more centres of the brain—a question of cell or nerve-nutrition—certain sets of ideas maintain themselves in the field of consciousness to the exclusion of others, or certain impulses independently of consciousness obtain the upper hand. There are people who, as the saying goes, do not listen to reason, who are insensible to all save their own interests; others, again, may be so self-sacrificing as to denude themselves unreasonably of their comforts and possessions for the benefit of their neighbours or possibly of the heathen. Both classes may be as truly neuropathic as the dyspeptic or the sufferer from tic-douloureux. Intense convictions of all kinds, including the most bigoted professions of religion, will generally be found associated with an ailing, sickly, or nervously unsound constitution. On the other hand, the man of robust health is of necessity tolerant and many-sided in his views.

There are various physical or mental defects of a minor character arising from anomalies of the nervous system which it is hardly necessary to enumerate. They will occur to the intelligent reader on a moment's reflection. Stuttering, due to a defect in the motor centres of articulation, bad teeth, excessive hairiness or baldness, albinoism, all arising from defects in the nutritive process, together with writer's cramp, which is known to occur in people who do not write, are as truly nervous in their origin as congenital blindness and deafness, or physical malformations.[1]

Gout, popularly believed to be the result of good living notwithstanding its frequent occurrence in poorly-nourished people, is an important member of the group of nerve diseases now under consideration. With its kindred affection of rheumatism it is perhaps more liable to transmission in a direct form than some others. Dyce Duckworth, the latest English authority on gout, states that in those families whose histories are the most complete and trustworthy, the influence is strongly shown, and occurs in

[1] Féré: 'La Famille Névropathique,' Archives de Neurologie, 1884.

from fifty to seventy-five per cent. of the cases; further, that the children of gouty parents show signs of articular gout at an age when they have not assumed those habits of life and peculiarities of diet which are commonly regarded as the exciting cause of the disease. But gout also alternates with neuropathic troubles. Bouchard, a French authority, is clear upon this point; he finds it intimately associated with insanity, epilepsy, hypochondria, asthma, St. Vitus's dance, etc. Various examples of this kind are given by Dejerine. A man suffering from rheumatic gout, gravel, neuralgia, and headaches engenders three children, of whom the first dies at thirteen from meningitis, the second suffers from headaches and fainting fits, and the third is subject to convulsions and hysterical crises. In another case, the father, suffering from eczema, dies suddenly (presumably from brain or heart disease, the common cause of sudden death), the mother is hysterical, and their children suffer from diabetes, consumption, sciatica, hypochondria, and other evils. *Per contra*, any one of the nerve diseases enumerated, from insanity downwards, may be accompanied or followed in members of the same family by gout or rheumatism. Suppressed gout may cause paralysis, hallucinations, or attacks of mania. These troubles cease when the gout returns to the joints. Gairdner, Lynch, and other writers note affections of speech alternating with gout. Féré has had under treatment a gouty subject in whom fits of hypochondria preceded attacks in the joints and ended as these began; a son of the same patient escaped gout, but was subject to hallucinations. Another individual known to Féré suffered from violent explosions of temper, headaches, and sciatica; at thirty-three he was attacked by gout which was followed by shaking palsy. In other cases gout is attended by intellectual torpor, imbecility, or malformations. Asthma is also of frequent occurrence in gouty families.

The interesting question remains: By what process is the transformation of one nerve disease into another effected? Of late years the labours of Van Beneden, Hertwig, Weismann, and others, have thrown some light upon this mystery and have furnished a plausible explanation of the variations of heredity. It is now well established that a young animal arises from the fusion within the female ovum or egg of an extremely minute particle derived from its male parent. The ovum is much larger than the male germ or spermatozoon, but it contains a nucleus which is believed to be the bearer of the hereditary characteristics. Technically, these particles are termed the male pro-nucleus and the female pro-nucleus, the body formed by their fusion being known as the segmentation nucleus, which is, properly speaking, the starting-point of every individual organism.

If the male and female particles were always combined in equal proportions, and in precisely the same way, the young animal would, no doubt, be an exact reproduction of its parents in equal parts. But this is not so. There is a certain amount of variability to be observed in the transmission of characteristics, the young animal taking more after one parent than another, and even throwing back in a greater or less degree to more distant ancestors. The highest power of the microscope does not reveal the exact composition of the pro-nucleus supplied by each parent, though it has been established that the double nucleus of the fertilised ovum is accurately composed, half of female and half of male elements. At this early stage the segmentation nucleus is not a homogeneous, structureless body, but is built up of different parts. It contains extremely delicate threads, which are either coiled up or intersect each other to form a network, the meshes of which are filled up by a viscous substance; and these various parts evidently consist of molecules having, like those of other matter, the property of self-adjustment. By a process of division, cells, similar to those already existing, arise, and these in turn also multiply by division. In course of time the various cells arrange themselves into layers, and from these are derived all the tissues and organs of the body. Whether in the embryonic or the adult stage of life, therefore, every cell in the body is derived by descent from the segmentation nucleus through repeated divisions.

It is clear that the segmentation nucleus embodies the characters of both parents, and, in a lesser degree, of their immediate ancestors, and observation of the offspring points to the conclusion that in each successive act of generation the admixture of parental and ancestral characters takes place in different proportions. How this is effected the microscope partly shows. Prior to the conjunction of the male and female pro-nuclei in the segmentation nucleus, portions of the germ-plasm are extruded from the egg, forming what are called the polar bodies. This curious phenomenon Weismann aptly explains on the hypothesis, that a reduction of the number of ancestral germ-plasms in the egg is a necessary step towards fertilisation and the development of the young animal. He supposes that by the expulsion of the polar bodies one-half the number of ancestral germ-plasms is removed, and that the original bulk is restored by the addition of the male pro-nucleus to that which remains. He further supposes, though this is not proved, that a similar reduction takes place in the ancestral elements of the male pro-nucleus. As precisely corresponding molecules of this germ-plasm are probably not expelled from each ovum or each male pro-nucleus, similar germ-plasms need not be retained in each case; and thus diversities may be expected to arise between the offspring of the same parents.[1]

[1] Weismann: *Biological Memoirs,* 'On the Number of Polar Bodies and their Significance in Heredity.' This theory covers the facts better than any other hitherto put forward. The nuclear substance does not appear to be sexually differentiated; that is to say, it appears to be pretty much the same in the male and female pro-nucleus—seeing that the female germ-cell transmits the male characters of the ancestors of the female quite as readily as the female characters, and that the male germ-cell transmits the female quite as readily as the male characters of the ancestors of the male. In all sexual eggs two polar bodies are observed. The first is presumably a part of the nucleus which was required to complete the growth of the egg, and which, once the growth is complete, becomes superfluous. The second is believed to consist of germ-plasms, bearing hereditary characteristics, by the removal of which from the egg, the excessive accumulation of different kinds of hereditary tendencies is prevented, and room made for the introduction of the male or sperm-nucleus. It is an essential part of Weismann's theory that there should be complete or approximate equality between the quantities of hereditary substance derived from either parent. As to the germ-plasm of the offspring, it follows that the latter can only contain half as much paternal germ-plasm as was contained in the germ-cells of the father, and half as much maternal germ-plasm as was contained in the germ-cells of the mother. There is no room for more. With each succeeding generation the original quantity of germ-plasm becomes reduced until it reaches the vanishing point, its place being taken by due proportions of germ-plasm derived

By a sudden change after the entrance of one male cell, the ovum usually ceases to be receptive. Occasionally, however, two spermatozoa are believed to enter. Twins thus born of two germinal spots in the same ovum appear to be invariably of the same sex, and amazingly like each other in body and mind, whereas the resemblance between those derived from separate ova is much less close. On the subject of twins Galton has collected some interesting facts. The father of two twins writes :—

'Their general health is closely alike; whenever one of them has an illness the other invariably has the same within a day or two, and they usually recover in the same order. Such has been the case with whooping cough, chicken pox, and measles; also with slight bilious attacks, which they have successively. Latterly they have had a feverish attack at the same time.'

Another parent of twins says :—

'If anything ails only one of them, identical symptoms nearly always appear in the other; this has been singularly

from more recent sources. Although the microscope has not yet revealed a similar reduction of the germ-plasms of the male, the reduction, according to Weismann, must, somewhere or somehow, occur, as otherwise the number of male ancestral germ-plasms would be increased by one-half at every fertilisation. 'If then,' continues Weismann, 'we consider how numerous are the ancestral germs which must be contained in each nucleus, and further, how improbable it is that they are arranged in precisely the same manner in all germ-cells, and finally, how incredible it is that the nuclear thread should always be divided in exactly the same place to form corresponding loops or rods, we are driven to the conclusion that it is quite impossible for the reduction of the nucleus to take place in an identical manner in all the germ-cells of a single ovary so that the same ancestral germ-plasms should always be removed in the polar bodies. But if one group of ancestral germ-plasms is expelled from one egg and a different group from another egg, it follows that no two eggs can be exactly alike as regards their contained hereditary tendencies; they must all differ. In many cases the difference will only be slight, that is when the egg contains very similar combinations of ancestral germ-plasms. Under other circumstances the differences will be very great: namely, when the combinations of ancestral germ-plasms contained in the egg are very different. . . . According to my theory the differences between the children of the same parents becomes intelligible in a simple manner from the fact that each maternal, and presumably each paternal, germ-cell contains a peculiar combination of ancestral germ-plasms, and thus, also, a peculiar combination of hereditary tendencies.'

visible in two instances during the last two months. Thus, when in London one fell ill with a violent attack of dysentery and within twenty-four hours the other had precisely the same symptoms.'

A medical man writes of twins :—

' Whilst I knew them for a period of two years there was not the slightest tendency towards a difference in body or mind ; external influences seemed powerless to produce any dissimilarity.'

The mother of the two other twins, after describing how they were ill simultaneously up to the age of fifteen, adds that they shed their first milk teeth within a few hours of each other. Trousseau tells of twins having a remarkable pathological resemblance. When one had an attack of ophthalmia, the other in a distant town was simultaneously attacked by the same disease. Moreau knew twins who were not only so nearly alike as to be easily mistaken the one for the other, but whose dominant ideas (they suffered from monomania) were absolutely the same. They both considered themselves subject to persecutions; the same enemies had sworn their destruction and employed the same means to effect it. Both had hallucinations of hearing ; both were melancholy and morose. Being confined in different wards of the same hospital (at Bicêtre) they had no communication with each other. Yet, from time to time, at irregular intervals, without appreciable cause, and by the purely spontaneous effect of their illness, a very marked change took place in the condition of the two brothers. Both about the same time roused themselves from their habitual stupor and prostration and made the same complaints to the superintendent. The same thing occurred when they were confined in different asylums, one being at Bicêtre, the other at St. Anne. Baume (' Annales Medico-Psychologiques,' 1863) speaks of two brothers, twins, who had nearly simultaneous attacks of insanity, and who, being miles apart, dreamt a remarkable dream on the same night and about the same hour (they believed they were catching a thief who, a few days before, had robbed a box containing their joint savings); during a subsequent attack of insanity, one attempted to drown himself, and the other, knowing nothing of the incident, actually did so. In other cases it has been found that twins have both been born ruptured, that they have suffered from toothache at the same age and have had the same tooth extracted, that their hair falls off at the same period, that identical diseases attack both, and that they die at very nearly the same age and from the same cause. It has already been shown that in life and in a state of health the same ideas occur to both.

The observed facts of nerve disease carry us a little further than the microscopic investigations of the physiologist. In families where there arises some instability of nerve element, we have seen how diverse are the forms it assumes from simple neuralgia to insanity. The obvious conclusion is that the symptoms of the evil vary according to the function of the particular portion of the cerebro-spinal system which happens to be morbidly affected. The change is, probably, for the most part of a molecular character, undiscoverable by the microscope. In pronounced cases of insanity and paralysis, however, some actual deterioration of the brain-substance is visible, and various organic disorders have been found associated with an impaired condition of the spinal marrow. How the metamorphoses of nerve disease are regulated it is impossible, in the present state of our knowledge, to say. They appear to be capricious, but as the facts of heredity continue to be observed and recorded in all their aspects it is possible that some law will ultimately be evolved from the existing confusion.

As already remarked, the earliest irregularity, the first disturbance of the healthy equilibrium of the nervous system, is probably the very common condition known as 'being out of sorts.' There is a loss of nervous force, betraying itself in headache, languor, want of appetite, impaired digestion, weakness, excitability, and kindred symptoms, the result of mental worry, business cares, want of exercise, insufficient sleep, improper food, and excesses of all kinds. 'Being out of sorts' is sometimes said to be a disease of civilisation and to be most commonly met with in great towns. This, however, is a mistake; it appears in all conditions of society. Where it does arise it is apt, unless promptly checked, to become permanent, in which case it leads to an innate weakness or nervous instability in the second generation. The operation of congenital causes of this kind is fully admitted by Weismann in his theory of 'the Continuity of the Germ-plasm.' Whether such a temporary condition as drunkenness in one of the parents at the moment of conception could exercise an injurious effect upon the child is not proved, although many observations to that effect have been recorded. Chronic alcoholism, however, does almost certainly affect the nurture of the germ-cells, and thus react disastrously upon the offspring.

Although most of the organic functions are withdrawn from the control of the hemispheres we are made generally conscious of anything being wrong in our systems. The feeling of health is not the feeling of disease. 'That the sensations of organic life,' says Ferrier, 'are represented in the cerebral hemispheres directly or indirectly is plain from the extraordinary influence which states of the viscera exercise on the emotional tone of the individual. Organic sensations generally, with one or two exceptions, are, unless rising to the pitch of painful intensity, obscure and non-localisable, and the healthy or morbid psychological activity is expressed subjectively as the vague and ill-defined feeling of well- or ill-being. Whether the centres of organic sensation are fused with those of tactile or common sensibility, or whether they are specially represented in and through the optic thalami or elsewhere, are all questions as yet unsolved. But, wherever situated, they seem to be the foundation or universal background of pleasurable or painful emotions in general. As healthy states of the viscera produce pleasurable feelings, and morbid states of the viscera produce painful or depressing feelings, so conversely, on the principle that the revived feeling occupies the same parts as the original, pleasurable emotions exalt and painful emotions depress the vital functions. Visceral derangements are frequently the cause and always the accompaniment of melancholic depression.'

CHAPTER III

IT is chiefly through insanity that a view can be obtained of
the workings of genius, and, from the facts I propose to bring
forward, it will be seen that the two conditions of mind have
much in common.   The man of genius overflows with ideas;
countless memories are stirred in his brain, and he discovers
combinations and affinities in facts, tones, and colours, that
lie beyond the scope of the ordinary mind.   In all these accomplishments the madman is his equal.   Both the man of
genius and the madman owe their characteristics of thought
and action to the excessive stimulation, the depression, or
the excitability of certain regions of their brain.   The difference between them is hardly a question of degree of susceptibility; it is rather a question of area.   As an exciting cause
in both cases, there may be an excessive or vitiated blood
supply to the affected portion of the brain, or the nerve-cells
and fibres of this portion may be naturally super-sensitive—
it is impossible to determine which. Genius frequently
merges into insanity, and insanity into genius, and both
are attended by a common train of functional disorders.   For
it appears to be a law of Nature that excessive activity or
depression of one region of the brain or spinal system entails
a depression or an excessive activity of some other region,
with a consequent loss of healthy function, affecting either
the sensory or motor apparatus or the numerous channels

through which the growth and nutrition of the body are regulated. All this will be seen from the investigation to be made in subsequent chapters of the lives of great men in all spheres of human activity. Genius, insanity, idiocy, scrofula, rickets, gout, consumption, and the other members of the neuropathic family of disorders, are so many different expressions of a common evil—an instability or want of equilibrium in the nervous system.

There may be hallucinations of most of the senses without any appreciable impairment of the reasoning faculties. This is the explanation of the phenomena known as spectral illusions—figures of persons or animals or inanimate objects persistently occupying the patient's field of vision, although he knows them to have no actual existence. It is commonly thought that spectral illusions have no connection with insanity, but there is no doubt that the local disorder of the brain from which they arise would, if more widely extended, produce insanity. As accompaniments of insanity, hallucinations of the senses are very frequent, particularly of the sense of hearing, whereby the patient believes that he is addressed by spirit voices. The most striking case on record of hallucinations without insanity is probably that of Nicolai, the Berlin bookseller. One day, while walking with his wife and friend, Nicolai suddenly saw at a distance of ten paces the figure of a deceased person. This, after causing him great alarm, soon vanished, but afterwards he was assailed by swarms of figures day and night. 'I saw,' he declared, in a report made by himself to the Royal Society in Berlin, 'for almost two months constantly, and involuntarily, a number of human, and other apparitions, and this while I was in the full enjoyment of my senses, and even, after I had overcome the terror which at first seized me, perfectly composed in mind.' The apparitions consisted of human figures of both sexes; they commonly passed to and fro as if they had no connection with each other like people at a fair, but sometimes they appeared to converse. Once or twice he saw among them persons on horseback, also dogs and birds. They all appeared their natural size, and absolutely life-like. Nicolai could not summon up the figures by an effort of will

or imagination; they came and went as they pleased. He
was attended night and day by two female spirits about
three feet in stature, and of brown complexion. 'They
called each other by their names, and several spirits,' he
adds, 'would call at my chamber door and ask whether such
spirits lived there, and these would answer they did.' The
application of leeches to the patient's neck banished this
affliction, the figures becoming paler and paler until they
disappeared, and Nicolai was troubled with them no more.
Here there were hallucinations of hearing as well as of sight,
obviously the result of an excessive supply of blood to certain
areas of the brain.

In true insanity there is frequently a very general disturbance of faculty, as is shown by the case of Kadinsky, a
physician of Moscow, who, having been insane for two years,
has left an interesting record of his symptoms. His illness,
he relates, began with an irregular mental activity, a headlong race of thoughts, delusions, and dominant ideas, after
which came hallucinations of all the senses, except taste.
He felt abnormal pressure on the neck and other parts of
the body; simple and co-ordinated sounds assailed his ears,
sparks floated before his eyes, and there was sometimes a
universal lighting up of the field of vision. Once he saw a
statue of white marble—a Venus in a stooping position.
After some seconds, the head of this figure seemed to fall off,
exposing the muscles of the neck; the head, moreover, when
it fell, broke, exposing the brain; and the contrast between
the white marble and the red blood, adds the patient, was
especially striking. The equilibrium of the body was also
disturbed. The patient had a sense of rolling down a slope,
of being whirled round or thrown into the air, and of flying
through space. At other times it happened that to the
right eye the wall of the room seemed to be moving upwards,
while to the left eye the opposite wall seemed to be moving
downwards, the painful feeling of a sundering of the brain
being thus produced. And all this while he was fully conscious of himself and able to take note of his abnormal impressions. In epilepsy or falling sickness there is a violent
agitation of the motor centres, affecting successively different

groups of muscles; temporary delusions of the senses are also produced, and the disease has a tendency to spread to other regions of the brain, insanity being a frequent although not an invariable result. It is observed that while hallucinations of sight are not infrequent in sane people, hallucinations of hearing are nearly always followed or accompanied by insanity. Probably this arises from the relative situation of the different centres of the brain. The visual centre lying at the back of the head is far removed from the supposed seat of what may be called the more intellectual faculties, namely, the frontal lobes, while the auditory centre is more forward and in greater proximity to that region. It need hardly be said, however, that in insanity all the senses are liable to derangement. Some lunatics eat the most disgusting substances without the smallest inconvenience. Others are utterly insensible to pain, and have been known to wilfully hold their hand or foot in the fire till it was burnt to a cinder. Others, again, constantly suffer the sensation of smelling putrid matter.

Among ordinary persons there seems to be as much diversity of faculty as there is of feature. Galton has collected statistics showing that, among one hundred sane people taken at haphazard, the power of mentally calling up some past scene varies greatly.[1] Some see vividly in their mind's eye the breakfast table of the morning with each object upon it distinct and properly coloured; others find the general image faint or misty and wanting in detail, while others, again, appear to have almost no power of visualisation whatever, but reconstitute the scene by an exhaustive process of association. Here we have really examples of the different kinds of memory to which reference has been made—memories of sight, smell, taste, or movement, each depending upon the efficiency of its particular centre in the brain. Some persons possess an accurate appreciation of form without being able to fill in a mental picture, in which case there is probably a deficiency in the colour sense. Colour blindness is understood to have its seat, not in the visual centre, but in the eye itself, or in the nerves of the eye, whereby imperfect sensations

[1] Galton: *Inquiries into Human Faculty.*

are transmitted to the brain. When the visual centre is highly developed, it is extremely responsive to impressions made upon the other centres. Thus, a person so endowed, on hearing a number pronounced, say the number ten, at once sees it in outline before him ; numerals in certain minds have even a habit of arranging themselves in geometrical patterns. So with the sense of hearing. Sounds are associated with particular colours. There is an old, and no doubt a true story, of a man who always pictured to himself the sound of a trumpet as red.

As to the law of excess and deficiency in brain-function, it is observed in idiocy, which is due to the imperfect structure of the brain, that one faculty, either sight, hearing, smell, taste, or touch, is occasionally extraordinarily acute. 'The senses of many idiots and imbeciles,' says Ribot,[1] 'are unequally affected. The arrested development is not uniform at all points. The sight may be remarkably good while the other senses are obtuse, and a weakness of the memory in general may coincide with an excessive development of some portion of it. Certain idiots, insensible to every other impression, have a pronounced taste for music, and can retain an air which they may have heard but once. Others (the case is rarer), have a recollection of form and colour, and display an aptitude for drawing. More frequently one may meet with idiots having a special memory for figures, dates, proper names, and words generally. Dr. Herzen informs me of a Russian of Archangel who became imbecile at twenty-seven, and who, of the brilliant faculties of his youth, retained only an extraordinary memory, which enabled him to solve the most difficult problems in arithmetic and algebra, and repeat word for word long poems after once hearing or reading them.' Drobisch relates the following, of which he was an eye-witness :—' A boy of fourteen, who was almost an idiot, had great difficulty in learning to read. He had, nevertheless, a marvellous faculty for remembering the order in which words or letters were placed. If he had two or three minutes to run over a page printed in a foreign language, or treating of questions of which he was ignorant, he was able to

<hr>

[1] Ribot : *Les Maladies de la Mémoire.*

repeat the words from memory as correctly as if the book had been lying before him.' 'There was,' says the Rev. Henry Fearon, 'a man in my father's parish who could remember the day when every person had been buried in the parish for thirty-five years, and could repeat with unvarying accuracy the name and age of the deceased and the mourners at the funeral. But he was a complete fool; outside the line of burials he had not one idea, and could not give an intelligible reply to a single question, or even be trusted to feed himself.'

The reports of the Massachusetts Asylum for the Blind make mention of a female deaf and blind mute, Julia Brace by name, in whom the sense of smell was extraordinarily keen. Anybody whom she had met before, she recognised by smell. She knew all her acquaintances by the smell of their hands, being able, in fact, to perceive and distinguish odours unfelt by other persons. In sorting clothes that had come for the wash, she could distinguish those of each friend. If half a dozen strangers threw each his glove into a hat, and the gloves were mixed, Julia would take them up, and by means of smell alone assign them to their owners. She could also tell brothers and sisters by smell. In the same institution there was a blind boy in whom hearing was carried to a wonderful pitch, and who was lent to a locksmith on one occasion for an extremely delicate experiment. There was an iron safe to be opened by means of a key, but to avoid deranging the mechanism it was necessary to know which one of ten bolts should be shot back. The bolt sought for was longer than the others, and the locksmith argued that if lifted by the key and allowed to fall without being shot back, it would have a different sound from the others. His ear, however, could detect no difference between the different bolts. The blind boy being called in, listened as the bolts were tried one after the other, and declared that the sixth one struck a little the loudest. Upon this, the locksmith lifted and turned back the sixth bolt, and the lock was opened without the combination being deranged. Maudsley says : ' I have seen an imbecile in the Earlswood Asylum for Idiots, who can repeat accurately a page or more of any book

which he has read years before, even though it was a book
which he did not understand in the least; and I once saw
an epileptic youth, morally imbecile, who would, shutting his
eyes, repeat a leading article in a newspaper word for word
after reading it once.   I have also been informed of a similar
case in which the person could repeat backwards what he had
just read.'   The late Mrs. Somerville, in her autobiography,
mentions two idiots, whom she had known, possessed of extraordinary memories.   The first never failed to go to kirk, and,
on returning home, could repeat the sermon word for word,
saying, ' Here the minister coughed . . . . here he stopped to
blow his nose.'   The second idiot knew the Bible so perfectly
that, if you asked him where such and such a verse was to
be found, he could tell without hesitation, and repeat the
chapter.   A female child, three and a half years of age, the
offspring of a paralytic father, that came under the treatment
of Brierre du Boismont, was subject to violent fits of rage
and caprice, but at the same time was intelligent far beyond
her years.   Dr. Robert Jones, resident physician of Earlswood
Asylum, informs me that he has recently had two imbeciles
under his care, of whom one could play any difficult piece of
music after once hearing it, and the other was able to repeat
word for word whole pages of Gibbon's ' Decline and Fall of
the Roman Empire.'   A third idiot now in Earlswood possesses
an extraordinary arithmetical faculty, and another, great constructive ingenuity in making models of ships.

In insanity, where there is a wide disturbance of faculty,
the patient's general character undergoes a change.   Wigan
tells of a gentleman who, by dint of long and exemplary
services, rose to a position of great importance, in which he
exercised a paternal control over his subordinates and was
much respected by all who knew him. Gradually, towards
the age of sixty, this gentleman became garrulous and light
in his conversation, and the others in his office suspected him
of drinking.   He had many rebuffs from the persons under
his command, but this in no degree changed the indecorous
levity of his conversation, which had formerly been remarkably
dignified and as reserved as was compatible with his excessive
benevolence of disposition.   Months passed on, his language

became gradually worse, and despite repeated warnings from his employers he sank at last into the most depraved obscenity, which led to his dismissal. Not long afterwards he died of brain disease. Without being positively insane, a person may have what is called the 'insane temperament'— a condition characterised by singularities of thought, feeling, and action. He is eccentric in his habits; he does apparently purposeless acts, and he is often either extremely obstinate or given to violent fits of temper. With his children he is usually severe; it is the man of insane temperament who cuts off his son with a shilling for some trifling peccadillo. If not engaged in family quarrels he carries on a bitter feud with a neighbour. The insane temperament rarely lands its possessor in an asylum, but his children are apt to go there or to suffer from some of the diseases which alternate with insanity or follow in its train. 'Moral insanity'—another name given to the insane temperament—'is,' says Forbes Winslow, 'responsible for a vast amount of domestic discord, disunion, and misery. It often co-exists with great talents and high attainments, and is compatible with the exercise of active philanthropy and benevolence.' It cannot, indeed, be too emphatically urged that what is variously called moral principle, the law-abiding instinct, or conscience, is largely the result of constitutional causes over which we have no control—a physical condition, which may be inherited in a more or less perfect degree.

To the category of morbid inheritance belongs the case of a 'rather sharp-looking lad,' described by Maudsley. 'He could not hold his attention to anything, though very quick in instant perception. He was, however, most ingenious in mischief, and delighted to talk of playing some viciously malicious trick, in the imaginative description of which he exulted in a braggart and grotesquely dramatic fashion, chattering incessantly, and running from subject to subject without any other connection than the unity of character given them by the leading bent of his distinctive disposition. Though he could tell stories of the events, and even minute experiences of years back with surprising exactness of detail, he had no perception of truth, but evinced an inexhaustible and

uncontrollable craving for what might have been called lies
had his nature been in the least sensible to truth, but what
were really the constructions of a vivid and busy imagination
revelling in its vicious activity. His continual talk was
of killing persons or animals that had in any way offended
him or ruffled his prodigious self-conceit; and he was ludicrously ferocious and boastful in his dramatic conceptions
and circumstantial descriptions of the grand way in which
he would do it. His father had died of what was called
softening of the brain soon after he was forty years old,
having been insane for some time before his death; his
paternal grandmother had died demented in an asylum at a
great age, having lived there for upwards of twenty years.
On his mother's side, also, there was insanity, and she herself, though not actually insane, was extremely excitable, and
a singularly insincere and shifty-minded person.'

Morally insane, also, was the man mentioned by Forbes
Winslow, who was discarded by his family for his gross and
inexplicable acts of impropriety, and who abandoned himself
without restriction to all kinds of debauchery, vice, and
profligacy, squandering, meanwhile, in the most reckless
manner, a fortune which he had obtained with his wife. At
the age of fifty he became clearly insane, and was placed in
confinement. The conduct of a clergyman, also known to
Forbes Winslow, had, for years, been marked by great eccentricity and caprice before his insanity became sufficiently
acute to justify the interference of his friends. Yet, during
the whole time he wrote and preached capital sermons and
attended faithfully and zealously to all his parish duties.
Similar causes were responsible for the behaviour of a young
gentleman mentioned by the same writer, who, for a long
time, had been a cause of much unhappiness to his family.
' He drank to a frightful excess, indulged in the society of
the most degraded, depraved, vicious men and women, and
squandered in a few years a splendid patrimony. He married
a respectable girl much below him in social rank and station,
whom he in a short time brutally ill-treated; he then deserted
her and an infant child, leaving them both to the charity of
friends. Towards his own immediate family he manifested

no kind of interest or affection. His father, who was a man very advanced in years, was subjected to a murderous assault on one occasion because he refused to attach his signature to one of his son's reckless acceptances. The young man was eventually accused of various acts of gross brutality as well as of theft. There never was known such an instance of accomplished vice and cold-blooded depravity.' His friends did not think him insane, but a post-mortem examination showed the enveloping membranes of the brain to have been affected for years. A young man of good family, known to Wigan, had an irresistible impulse whenever he passed a church door during divine service to run into the organ loft and play some well-known jocular tune attached, perhaps, to profane or indecent words. This he would do so suddenly that it was impossible to prevent it before he had thrown the congregation into confusion. He was always sorry for it, and declared that he tried with all his might to prevent it. In all other respects he was perfectly sane, but he was subject to periodical epileptic fits, and the propensity was at last observed to have some connection with the malady. For several years this mild and equivocal form of mental disturbance continued; the patient then entered into great sexual excesses and sensual indulgence, and died of what his friends called brain fever. A young lady patient of Maudsley's, who became wilfully passionate, impulsive, eccentric, developed, at the same time, an extraordinary vanity and was able to write letters containing vigorous and clever remarks.

So much for the results of disease upon the general character. Those of accident may be illustrated by a patient of Forbes Winslow's, a tradesman, who fell from the top of an omnibus in Oxford Street and suffered concussion of the brain. 'For some hours after the accident he continued in a state of semi-unconsciousness. At length he opened his eyes, gazed listlessly around him and asked, " Where am I ? What has happened ? " In the course of a fortnight he was able to resume his business. About twelve months afterwards, a marked difference was observed in his character. He became peevish and quarrelsome, discharging his principal clerk for some trifling inaccuracies. A short time subsequently to this change being observed, he had, whilst in his country house, an attack of epilepsy. His mind appeared clearer and more composed than it was previously. He exhibited great self-command and acuteness in matters of business and appeared to be less irritated by family affairs. In about six weeks he showed symptoms of mental depression, which were soon followed by uncontrollable paroxysms of violent and furious passion. He had a second epileptic seizure, and on recovering from this fit a kindliness of disposition and affection again showed themselves. The change in the state of his intellect, and the altered condition of his emotions after each attack of epilepsy, were remarkable.' Other recorded cases of epilepsy show an alternation of extreme wickedness and extreme piety in the same individual, both states being most probably due to defective cohesions in the various centres.

Occasionally there is great intellectual activity produced by the epileptic condition, which seems to be caused by a wave of morbid excitement passing over the different cerebral centres. There is then a wonderful aptitude to conceive things quickly and to examine them under their most brilliant and poetical aspect. Previous to attacks of paralysis or apoplexy, the sight or the hearing may become abnormally acute, so that the patient sees objects at an unusual distance, or is oppressed by such a slight sound as the humming of a fly. Forbes Winslow had a patient who was able, while occupying a room at the top of the house, to hear, with remarkable clearness, the conversation taking place in the kitchen. 'In another case,' says the same writer, 'a few hours prior to an apoplectic seizure, a man remarked to his son that, when in a distant part of the house, he could hear distinctly a conversation that was taking place in the dining-room at a time when no one else could distinguish the sound of human voices.' The quickening of the senses in hypnotism produces intellectual effects of a surprising kind. Patients drawn from the inferior classes throw themselves into suggested characters and present them with a power and a truthfulness beyond, not only their own waking capacity, but that of the most intelligent and cultivated persons. Insane patients of little or no education astonished Lombroso by the depth of their remarks upon philosophical and scientific subjects. One, a tailor, named Farino, placed in confinement for killing the mother of a girl with whom he believed himself to be in love, wrote a long, detailed, and extremely graphic account of the crime. Several members of his family were insane, and he himself was undoubtedly so. He was without the smallest literary culture. Nevertheless, his memoir, quoted in full by Lombroso, is a curious example of hallucinations existing side by side with perfect reasoning powers and a consciousness of right and wrong, and is marked, not only by clearness and propriety, but even by eloquence of style, and shows in particular an extraordinary tenacity and correctness of memory for the smallest events of bygone years. His reminiscences, in fact, exhibit much greater variety and accuracy than would those of an ordinary person of sound mind.[1]

Forbes Winslow knew a gentleman who, whilst insane, wrote an able, philosophical, and critical essay on 'Original Sin.' It was found among his papers after death. He was, when he penned the dissertation, under the delusion that there was a family conspiracy to poison him. The same writer declares that men, naturally most dull of apprehension, in fact, nearly half-witted, exhibit both in the early and in the advanced stages of insanity 'considerable intellectual acuteness and capacity. . . . Mechanical ingenuity, acute sense of hearing, seeing, and smelling, as well as wonderful powers of adaptation to all possible physical conditions are often observed among a certain class of the insane, utterly incapable of appreciating a rational idea.' Forbes Winslow once attended a young man whose attack of insanity was supposed to have been caused by ill-usage whilst at school. ' I was informed,' he says, ' that this youth had never exhibited any particular talent for arithmetic or mathematical inquiries; in fact, it was alleged that he was incapable of doing even a simple sum of addition or multiplication. After his recovery from the acute symptoms of his maniacal attack, and when he was able to employ his mind in reading and conversation, it was found that an extraordinary arithmetical power had been evolved during his illness. He was able with wonderful facility to solve several rather complex problems. This talent

[1] Lombroso: *Genio e Follia.*

continued for several months, but after his complete restoration to health, he relapsed into his former natural state of arithmetical dulness, ignorance, and general mental incapacity.' The wife of a clergyman, also attended by Forbes Winslow, exhibited during her paroxysms of maniacal excitement a wonderful talent for rapid and clever versification. The disposition to improvise was manifested mostly at night. After her recovery all capacity for rhyming appeared to subside. Previous to her mental illness she had not exhibited the slightest poetical inclination or ability. Van Swieten speaks of a woman who, during her paroxysms of mania, showed a rare facility for versification, though she had before been occupied with manual labour and her understanding had never been enriched by culture. He also quotes the case of a young workman, who, never having dreamt of making verses, during an attack of fever became a poet and was inspired.

In their lucid intervals, insane people speak of the clearness of intellect they experience during their attacks. 'I always awaited with impatience,' said a patient to Willis,[1] 'the accession of the paroxysms of insanity, since I enjoyed during their presence a high degree of pleasure. They lasted ten or twelve hours. Everything appeared easy to me. No obstacles presented themselves in theory or in practice. My memory all of a sudden acquired a singular degree of perfection. Long passages of Latin authors occurred to my mind. In general I have great difficulty in finding rhythmical terminations, but then I could write in verse with as much facility as in prose. I was cunning, malicious, and fertile in all kinds of expedients.' 'The records of the wit and cunning of madmen,' says Rush,[2] ' are numerous in every country. Talents for eloquence, poetry, painting, music, and uncommon ingenuity in several of the mechanical arts are often evolved in a state of madness. A gentleman whom I attended in a hospital often delighted, as well as astonished, the patients and officers by his displays of oratory in preaching from a table in the hospital-yard every Sunday. A female patient of mine, who became insane after parturition, sang

---

[1] Francis Willis : *A Treatise on Mental Derangement.*
[2] Benjamin Rush : *On the Diseases of the Mind.*

hymns and songs of her own composition during the latter state of her illness with a tone and voice so soft that I hung upon it with delight every time I visited her. She had never discovered a talent for poetry or music in any previous part of her life. Two instances of a talent for drawing evolved from madness have occurred within my knowledge. And where is the hospital for mad people in which elegant and completely rigged ships and curious pieces of machinery have not been exhibited by persons who never discovered the least turn for a mechanical art previously to their derangements?' W. W. Ireland knew a patient in an asylum who could not talk reasonably on any subject, his speech being an incoherent torrent of words, but who was able to make an ingenious snare for catching birds.

As a prelude to positive insanity, patients often feel alarmed at the excessive rapidity of their thoughts. A gouty patient told Wigan that, at times, there seemed to be another person thinking with his brain, and telling him things which he knew to be false, but which he had the greatest difficulty to prevent himself from uttering as his own. This gentleman's delusions became so pronounced that he was in imminent danger of being removed to an asylum. At this juncture the gout came out in his toe, whereupon his brain was suddenly cleared of its delusions and his reasoning powers became extraordinarily acute. 'In some preliminary stages of insanity,' observes Conolly, 'the patient displays an unwonted vivacity of attention and an incredible activity of memory. Nothing escapes him, every subject receives illustration from his lips, his observations on common things display unusual acuteness, his art is irresistible, and his sentiments are exalted. He marvels within himself that he is a master of such varied stores as are now revealed to him.' Abercrombie treated a boy who suffered from nervous attacks resulting in blindness, loss of speech, and paralysis of the right side. Meanwhile the patient's intellect was not affected, but was 'extremely acute.' The same authority notes generally in the insane a 'fertility of imagination which changes the character of the mind without remarkably distorting it. The memory,' he adds, 'is even more ready than in health, and old associations are called up with a rapidity quite unknown to the individual in his sound state of mind.' In a case of insanity that came under Pritchard's care, the earlier symptoms displayed by the patient, a commercial man, were 'greater energy in business and more acuteness in buying and selling.' Penel says : ' I have often stopped at the door of a literary gentleman, who, during his paroxysms of insanity, appeared to soar above his usual mediocrity of intellect, solely to admire his newly-acquired powers of eloquence. He declaimed on the subject of the Revolution with all the force, the dignity, and the purity of language that this very interesting subject would admit of. At other times he was a man of very ordinary abilities.' Lombroso had under his care a poor woman who, in her insanity, developed a remarkable faculty for drawing and embroidery, tracing butterflies, which were so natural that they looked as if they had alighted upon the fabric. Luys observes that patients under an attack of mania will improvise, make quotations, associate ideas with extreme rapidity, say witty things, make puns, and generally perform mental feats of which they would have been incapable in their ordinary state. A young butcher confined in Bicêtre asylum astonished his keepers by reciting whole speeches from the 'Phèdre' of Racine. In a lucid interval he stated that he had but once heard the tragedy in question and that, despite his efforts to recall it, he could not recite a single verse. One of De Quincey's friends, Charles Lloyd, who had attacks of insanity, in one of which he died, was a most interesting talker. And 'the splendour of his talk,' says De Quincey, ' was quite hidden from himself, he was as free from vanity or even complacency in reviewing what he had done as it is possible for a human creature to be.' On the other hand, the vanity of the insane may be excessive. An insane volume of poems was published in Brussels in 1839; its author, an undoubted lunatic, observed in his preface, ' A man who writes on subjects as vast as these here treated ought to be possessed of all human knowledge. Such a man am I ; my works prove it, and by my works I desire to be judged.' This gentleman at the same time, like many sane people of the same type, disclaimed all idea of vanity.

The journals composed and printed by the inmates of lunatic asylums in different European countries abound in poems, articles, and scientific speculations of a high order of merit, proving the truth of the remark of Nathaniel Lee, the ' mad poet,' himself long an inmate of Bedlam, that ' it is difficult to write like a madman though it may be easy enough to write like a fool.'   Of the literature of the insane in Italy, Lombroso gives numerous examples, and Octave Delepierre has collected many curious facts bearing on this subject from France, Germany, and America, as well as England.[1]   There are not a few literary madmen—unquestionable lunatics—known to history.   Nathaniel Lee, whose compositions were praised by Addison, wrote poems and tragedies while confined in Bedlam.   Christopher Smart, a contemporary of Dr. Johnson's, confined as a dangerous lunatic, and deprived even of pens and ink, wrote a long poem on the walls of his cell with the aid of a key.   It was in honour of King David, and the following verses will give an idea of its nobility and elevation of style :—

> He sang of God—the mighty source
> Of all things—the stupendous force
>   On which all strength depends ;
> From whose right arm, beneath whose eyes
> All period, power, and enterprise
>   Commences, reigns, and ends.
>
> .   .   .   .
>
> Glorious the sun in mid career,
> Glorious the assembled fires appear,
>   Glorious the comet's train ;
> Glorious the trumpet and alarm,
> Glorious the Almighty's outstretched arm,
>   Glorious the enraptured main.
>
> .   .   .   .
>
> Glorious, more glorious is the crown
> Of him that brought salvation down
>   By weakness called the Son ;
> He that stupendous truth believed,
> And now the matchless deed 's achieved,
>   Determined, dared, and done.

[1] Octave Delepierre : *Histoire de la Littérature des Fous.*

Thomas Lloyd, one of the notabilities of Bedlam in the early part of the present century, was an extraordinary compound of vanity, malice, and poetic talent. He believed himself to be the sublimest poet that the world had seen, and that he had a universal acquaintance with ancient and modern languages, science, history, and music. More than once his extraordinary gifts secured his liberation, but he had always to be shut up again, and, like Christopher Smart, died in confinement. Here is a sample of his verse :—

> When disappointment gnaws the bleeding heart
> And mad resentment hails her venom'd darts ;
> When angry noise, disgust, and uproar rude,
> Damnation urge, and every hope exclude ;
> These, dreadful though they are, can't quite repel
> The aspiring mind that bids the man excel.

In 1811 London was surprised by the publication of a drama by one Thomas Bishop, entitled ‘ Karanzzo's Feast ; or, The Unfair Marriage : a tragedy founded on facts 2366 years ago, and 555 years before the birth of Christ. In five acts, embellished with sixteen descriptive plates by the first artists, ancient and modern. Printed by George Smalton, and sold by Hookham, and at the author's, 22 Clarges Street.’ The author divided his work into ‘ Prologue, epilogue, dirge, and design,’ and among his characters were the King of Babylon, the King of Persia, Lord Strawberry, Dr. Pill, four queens, Mrs. Hector, three savages, and five ghosts. In his preface he took credit to himself for being the first writer to convey to the public an exact idea of the characters, scenery, weapons, etc., existing at the date of the action. Grotesque as it was, the treatment of the subject was not without ingenuity. The closing scene contained the following stage directions. ‘ On one side a forest, part of which is dark. Two sofas and the appearance of a clock. Three savages in the distance.’

The case of a lawyer named Milman excited much attention in Pennsylvania at the beginning of the present century. He went out of his mind on hearing that his bride had been struck dead by lightning, and, whereas, before his insanity, he had no literary aptitudes, after it he developed a very pleasant talent for satire, humour, and description, and wrote copiously. A similar change of capacity under similar circumstances is recorded of Luke Clennel, a painter and *protégé* of the Earl of Bridgewater. In 1817, while engaged upon an important picture for his patron, he suddenly lost his reason. Being a violent lunatic he was shut up in a madhouse, and here, curiously enough, he took to writing verses, of which the following, addressed to the Evening Star, are a specimen :—

> Look ! What is it with twinkling light
> That brings such joys serenely bright,
> That turns the dusk again to light ?
>   'Tis the Evening Star !
>
> What is it with the purest ray,
> That brings such peace at close of day,
> That lights the traveller on his way ?
>   'Tis the Evening Star !

About the same period a farm labourer of Northamptonshire attracted attention by his verses. A volume of his was published in London in 1825. Soon afterwards he became insane, but in the asylum he retained all his talent for versification and rhythm. His memory was astonishing. He seemed to assimilate everything that he read or heard, picturing events so vividly in his mind that he related them afterwards as if he had seen and taken part in them. Of the execution of Charles I. he believed himself to have been an eye-witness, and he was accustomed to tell most graphically his pretended experiences of the battle of the Nile and of the death of Nelson.

As there have been poets, so there have been philosophers undoubtedly mad. The scientific world was much perplexed in 1529 by the publication at Florence of a treatise on the anatomy of language. This proved to be the work of a doctor, one Joseph Bernardi, an inmate of a lunatic asylum. The author's contention was that the whole race of monkeys possessed the faculty of speech, but were too well advised to employ it; and he sustained his views with such ability

as to call forth from a Jesuit Father a refutation of them,
based upon Scripture.   In 1622 an insane professor of Sala-
manca, Miguel de Flores, published an ingenious theory of
the universe, according to which the Supreme Being occupied the centre of creation with all matter moving round him
in concentric circles.   And some accompanying engravings
showed the Deity working the universe by the mechanical
action of his arms and legs.   In this country, at different
periods, nonsensical books on scientific subjects, showing
much misdirected ingenuity, have been put forth with every
appearance of good faith on the part of their authors.   The
more curious among these, perhaps, are Thomas Wirgman's
' Devarication [*sic*] of the New Testament,' and ' Grammar of
the Five Senses,' published in the time of George III. ; and
William Martin's ' New System of Natural Philosophy on the
Principle of Perpetual Motion,' dating from 1821.   There
was a scintilla of genius in Martin's family, his brother
being the painter John Martin.

Many men who might be described as half-geniuses
are known to history—men extraordinarily gifted, but too
insane to turn their gifts to proper account.   Such was
George Burges, the college friend of Bulwer Lytton, who
astonished people by his cleverness and oddity, and of whom
some account is given by Lord Lytton in his biography of
the author of ' Pelham.'   ' While still an undergraduate at
Trinity he published an edition of Euripides, with a preface
and critical notes in Latin, which astonished by its excellence
the best Greek scholars of the time, and raised the highest
expectations of his future achievements as a Hellenist. . . .
After leaving the University he was known chiefly by the
eccentricities of his conduct and the absurdity of his speculations.   He used to drive about London in a two-horsed
vehicle of peculiar shape, the panels of which were painted
with hieroglyphics, emblematical of his views as to the origin
of language.   He started two coaches, which plied up and
down the New Road, and he inscribed upon his visiting cards,
" Mr. George Burges, $\alpha\rho\mu\alpha\tau\sigma\pi\sigma\iota\acute{o}s$ " (coachbuilder).   He in-
vested a large sum of money in the construction of a huge, whale-
shaped machine for the aërial conveyance of passengers from

Dover to Calais. He invented a coat fastened only by a single button in the centre of the back, and wore it in the streets of London, where it attracted general notice, but none of those who chanced to see him in his model dress were induced to adopt it. He then set up as the maker of a new kind of stays, which he called *corsets à la Venus*, and he frightened and offended some of the leading ladies of fashion by the earnestness with which he requested their permission to try this invention upon them. About this time he married, perhaps in order that the *corset à la Venus* might have at least one fair trial under his personal superintendence. Matrimony, or the ill-success of his other occupations, disposed him again to authorship, and he wrote an unreadable play called "The Sin of Erin; or, The Cause of the Greeks," which he published with a dedication from "George Burges to George Byron," greatly to the annoyance of the poet. His next experiment was a series of public lectures upon ancient and modern literature. In the course of these lectures he asserted that the pyramids have a foundation exactly corresponding in shape, as well as in size, with the above-ground portion of them (a foundation consisting, in short, of an inverted underground pyramid), and he sang to the tune of " Malbrook," the θέλω λέγειν 'Ατρείδας of the pseudo-Anacreon. His Greek, indeed, overflowed on every occasion. His knowledge of it was extraordinary, and he especially loved to exercise his fertile ingenuity in amending the text of the Greek dramatists—emendations marked by the same kind of wild invention which distinguished his innovations in dress and carriages. His lectures on literature shared the fate of all his projects. They were neither popular nor remunerative, notwithstanding the apparent attractiveness of the following advertisement:

    ' " Good and Cheap Food,
   ' " *Without Ruin to the Farmers.*

  ' " The nobility and gentry in and out of Parliament, and now nearly ruined by the awful depression of the landed interest, are respectfully informed that Mr. George Burges, M.A. of Trinity College, Cambridge, will, in his seventh lecture, detail an easy plan by which his Majesty's ministers may, if they will, increase the revenue a million sterling annually, and so improve the soil of England as to enable it to feed sixty millions of mouths on cheaper and better bread than can be grown upon, or imported from, any other part of the globe."

'In the meanwhile his fortune had vanished into the coaches, the flying machines, the *corsets à la Venus*, and other creations of his genius, and for some years he earned a scanty subsistence by teaching and by drudgery work for the book-sellers. In this long period of toil and penury, with a wife and family to maintain, his buoyant hilarity and self-complacency triumphed over his fits of depression at every monetary gleam which broke in upon his burdened existence. In 1856 a legacy from a friend and the assistance of Bishop Blomfield saved him from absolute destitution, and he then settled with his wife at Ramsgate, where they kept a lodging-house, and where he died soon afterwards from the effects of a paralytic stroke.' Theology has also had its share of visionary geniuses, some of whom, like Mahomet, Luther, and John Bunyan, have exercised an influence in the world, entitling them to be placed in somewhat better company than the foregoing.

Quite on the borderland of genius and insanity stands William Blake, the contemporary of Charles Lamb. Blake, who was the son of a hosier and of stunted growth, developed in his youth a genius for art and poetry. As a boy in his father's shop he drew pictures on the counter, and wrote poetry on the backs of the bills. He was moody and mystical, living a life of dreamy abstraction. He had hallucinations of hearing; celestial voices seemed to call him. He took to engraving as a means of livelihood, but he wrote poetry copiously, turning out between his twelfth and fifteenth year no fewer than seventy pages of verse. By-and-by, hallucina-tions of sight beset him. Historical figures of poets, heroes, and princes swarmed around him. These he mistook for reality, and he gave out that his designs were not the work of fancy, but revelations made to him in visions which he was commanded by celestial voices to publish. He held consultations with the spirit of his deceased brother, and from him obtained, as he said, a valuable art secret—the truly beautiful and original method he employed in the engraving and tinting of his plates. The spirit also counselled him as to the treatment of one of his best known and most successful works, 'Days of Innocence.' 'Write,' said the spirit, 'the poetry and draw the designs upon copper, with a certain liquid (which he named and which Blake ever kept a secret), then cut the plain parts of the plate down with aquafortis, and this will give the whole, both poetry and figures in the manner of the stereoscope.' 'The Gates of Paradise,' another of Blake's works, although ambitious in scope, is quite incomprehensible. It consists of twenty-seven designs, extracted, possibly, from many visions, and seems to embody the fall of Lucifer and the creation of man; but, in truth, all that can be truly said of it is that it swarms with fantastic figures, human, demoniac, and divine. In a letter written by the artist to Flaxman in 1800 he says :—

'I am more famed in Heaven for my works than I could well conceive. In my brain are studies and chambers filled with books and pictures of old, which I wrote and printed in ages of eternity—before my mortal life, and these works are the delight and study of archangels. Why, then, should I be anxious about the riches or fame of mortality ?'

Moses, Homer, Virgil, Dante, and Milton, were Blake's constant companions in visions. When asked how these great men looked, he answered: 'They are all majestic shadows, gray, but luminous, and superior to the common height of men.' 'Did you ever see a fairy funeral, Madam ?' he once asked a lady in company. 'Never, sir,' was the answer. 'I have,' said Blake, 'but not before last night. I was walking alone in my garden. There was great stillness among the branches and flowers, and more than common sweetness in the air. I heard a low and pleasant sound, and knew not whence it came. At last I saw the broad leaf of a flower move, and underneath I saw a procession of creatures of the size and colour of green and gray grasshoppers, bearing a body laid out on a rose leaf, which they buried with songs and then disappeared. It was a fairy's funeral.'

Subsequently to this period, he designed an extravagant and incomprehensible work called 'Jerusalem,' embodying aspects of earth and heaven. Plate after plate is meaningless as a whole, yet many of the figures looked at from the point of view of form and effect belong to the highest art, being marked by wonderful freedom of attitude and position. Others of his works, if less ludicrous, are quite as natural and poetic, so that it is impossible to deny to Blake the possession of true artistic genius. Curiously enough, he believed the spirit of Titian to be the evil genius of art, and professed to suffer from his persecutors. Blake drew visions for his friends. Sometimes a shape was long in appearing, and he sat with his pencil and paper ready, and his eyes idly roaming in vacancy. All at once the desired vision would come upon him, and he would work like one possessed (as indeed he was). A friend asked him to sketch the figure of William Wallace. He consented, and there was a pause. At length 'There, there!' he exclaimed, 'I see him now. How noble he looks! Reach me my things.' Having drawn for some time with a careful hand and steady eye, as if a living sitter were before him, the artist stopped suddenly, saying ruefully, 'I cannot finish it. Edward I. has just stepped in between him and me.' 'That's lucky,' said his friend, 'for I want the portrait of Edward too.' Blake took another sheet of paper and sketched the features of the Plantagenet king, whereupon his Majesty vanished, and the head of Wallace was then duly finished. The informant of Allan Cunningham, from whose life of Blake I have been quoting,[1] saw these pictures. They represented two warlike heads of the size of common life. That of Wallace was noble and heroic, that of Edward stern and bloody.

On one occasion Blake sketched the ghost of a flea which appeared to him. 'I felt convinced,' relates Varley, who saw the artist make the drawing, 'by his mode of proceeding, that he had a real image before him; for he left off, and began on another part of the paper to make a separate drawing of the mouth of the flea, the opening of which

---

[1] Allan Cunningham: *Lives of British Painters, Sculptors, and Architects.*

prevented him from proceeding with the first sketch for the time being.' Sometimes Blake desired to see a spirit in vain. 'For many years,' he said, 'I longed to see Satan. I could never believe he was the vulgar fiend our legends represent him to be. I imagined him a classic spirit, with some of his original splendour about him. At last I had my wish. I was going down stairs in the dark, when suddenly a light came streaming amongst my feet. I turned round, and there he was, looking fiercely at me through the iron grating of my staircase window. I called for my things. My wife (for Blake was married to a woman who loved him and believed in him) thought a fit of song was on me, and brought me pen and ink. I said, "Hush! Never mind, this will do." As he appeared so I drew him.' 'Upon this,' says the biographer's informant, 'Blake took out a piece of paper with a grated window sketched on it, while, through the bars, glared the most frightful phantom that ever man imagined. Its eyes were large and like live coals; its teeth were as long as those of a harrow, and the claws were such as might appear in the disturbed dream of a clerk in the "Herald's" office.' 'It is the Gothic fiend of our legends,' said Blake, 'all others are apocryphal.' Another friend of Cunningham's once called on Blake, and found him sitting, pencil in hand, and drawing a portrait with all the seeming anxiety of a man who is conscious of having a fastidious sitter. He looked and drew, and drew and looked, yet no living soul was visible. 'Disturb me not,' said Blake in a whisper. 'I have someone sitting to me.' 'Sitting to you,' exclaimed the astonished visitor, 'where is he? I see no one.' 'But I see him,' answered Blake, haughtily. 'There he is, his name is Lot; you may read of him in the Scriptures. He is sitting for his portrait.'

As Cunningham rightly observes, 'Had Blake always dealt with such visionary matters, he would have no claim to be a man of genius, some of whose works are worthy of any age or nation.' Even while indulging in these hallucinations, he drew and engraved one of the noblest of all his productions, the 'Inventions of the Book of Job.' His poems, too, are, some of them, admirable. His 'Songs of Innocence' are introduced with the following pretty verses :—

Piping down the valleys wild,
Piping songs of pleasant glee,
On a cloud I saw a child,
And he, laughing, said to me—

'Pipe a song about a lamb ;'
So I piped with merry cheer.
'Piper, sing that song again ;'
So I piped—he wept to hear.

'Drop thy pipe, thy happy pipe,
Sing the songs of happy cheer ;
So I sang the same again
While he wept with joy to hear.

'Piper, sit thee down and write
In a book that all may read.'
So he vanished from my sight
And I plucked a hollow reed.

And I made a rural pen,
And I stained the water clear,
And I wrote my happy songs
Every child may joy to hear.

Blake died at seventy-one, childless. He was too flighty and eccentric to attain a commanding position as an artist, but his imagination undoubtedly glowed with what is called the ' divine fire.'

CHAPTER IV

EXAMPLES OF MEN OF LETTERS LAPSING INTO OR APPROACHING INSANITY—SWIFT, JOHNSON, COWPER, SOUTHEY, SHELLEY, BYRON, CAMPBELL, GOLDSMITH, CHARLES LAMB, WALTER SAVAGE LANDOR, ROUSSEAU, CHATTERTON, PASCAL, CHATEAUBRIAND, GEORGE SAND, TASSO, ALFIERI, EDGAR ALLAN POE, ETC.

AMONG English men of letters and poets who have become actually insane, or who have had hallucinations and idiosyncrasies characteristic of insanity, may be mentioned Swift, Johnson, Cowper, Southey, Shelley, Byron, Campbell, Goldsmith, Charles Lamb, Walter Savage Landor, and Edgar Allan Poe, with whom may be coupled, among foreign writers, Rousseau, Pascal, Chateaubriand, Tasso, Silvio Pellico, and Alfieri. Swift has been harshly judged by those who regard genius and wisdom as interchangeable terms. There was certainly much eccentricity, and even cruelty, in his conduct, especially in his treatment of the two hapless women known as Stella and Vanessa, to whom he held out delusive hopes of marriage, but he was never quite responsible for his actions. His insanity was congenital. A paternal uncle, Gordon Swift, was ' seized with lethargy, lost both speech and memory, and died insane,' and Swift, from. his boyhood, was full of crazy impulse. At Dublin University he led a wild, vicious life, for which he was severely censured by the academical authorities. The same irresponsibility marked his conduct as a man, and from his correspondence and other sources we learn that he suffered at various times from giddiness, deafness, impaired sight, muscular twitchings, and paralysis of the muscles of the right side of the mouth—all symptoms of brain disease. He had violent explosions of temper, and sometimes addressed strangers in an abrupt and enigmatical fashion. Before he became a

G

celebrity, he astonished the frequenters of Button's coffee-house by the singularity of his actions, and was known for a time as the 'mad parson.' He was always haunted by the dread of going out of his mind. On one occasion, observing by the wayside an elm that had been blasted by lightning, he said to a friend, 'I shall be like that tree, I shall die at the top.' As old age approached, his condition worsened. He developed violent mania, and had to be placed under a keeper. Some time before his death, however, he lapsed into a state of imbecility, in which he is said to have kept silence for months together. A post-mortem examination revealed extensive serous effusion upon the brain and also softening of the cerebral substance.

Ninety years after Swift's death, that is to say in 1835, his bones were exhumed in the course of some alterations made in St. Patrick's Cathedral, Dublin, and the skull was then found to present abnormal characteristics. 'The condition of the cerebral surface of the whole of the frontal region,' said a medical man who examined the skull, 'is of a character indicating the presence during life of diseased action in the subjacent membranes of the brain. The skull in this region is thickened, flattened, and unusually smooth and hard in some places, whilst it is thinned and roughened in others. The marks of the vessels on the bone exhibit, moreover, a very unusual appearance; they look more like the imprints of vessels which had been generated *de novo* in connection with some diseased action, than as the original arborescent trunks. The impressions of the middle arteries of the dura mater (an enveloping membrane of the brain) are unusually large and deep, and the branches of those vessels, which pass in the direction forwards, are short and thick, and terminate abruptly by dividing into an unusual number of minute twigs, whilst those of the same trunks that take their course backwards are long and regular, and of graduated size from the beginning to the end of their course. . . . The internal parts corresponding to the frontal protuberances were unequal in concavity.'[1] From the peculiar formation of the

---

[1] Wilde: *Closing Years of Dean Swift's Life.*

skull, the cerebellum, it was thought, must have been 'exceedingly small.'[1]

As the cerebellum has since been shown to be the centre for movements connected with the equilibrium, we have in this circumstance, no doubt, an explanation of those fits of giddiness of which Swift constantly complained in his correspondence. 'A sudden turn at any time,' he wrote, 'makes me feel giddy for a moment'—showing a deficiency in the balancing mechanism. His giddiness began, according to his own account, at the age of twenty-three; his deafness a few years later. As he died at seventy-eight, he suffered from active brain disease for over fifty years—an unusually long period. Wilde concludes from Swift's treatment of Stella and Vanessa, that he was constitutionally incapable of any passion stronger than friendship.

From his father Dr. Johnson inherited 'a vile melancholy,' which, to borrow his own words, made him 'mad all his life, or, at least, not sober.' This parent was a Lichfield bookseller of obscure extraction; Johnson's mother, according to Boswell, was a woman of 'distinguished understanding.' There was a second son of the marriage, Nathaniel, who died in his twenty-fifth year. At twenty, Johnson was in a state of 'perpetual irritation, fretfulness, impatience, dejection, gloom, and despair.' From hypochondria he was never afterwards free. He suffered, likewise, from convulsive cramps and scrofula—a well-known concomitant of nerve disorder—and he had the use of only one eye, though the other was very little different in appearance. On one occasion he had a paralytic seizure, which deprived him for the time being of speech, and in this state he wrote a prayer entreating the Almighty to allow him, as long as he should live, the enjoyment of his understanding. The dread of insanity haunted Johnson as it did Swift, and he must sometimes have been on the very brink of mental derangement. Upon his other disorders hallucinations of hearing supervened. 'One day at Oxford,' says Boswell, 'as he was turning the key of his chambers, he heard his mother distinctly call "Sam," although she was then at

[1] Wilde.

Lichfield.' So morbid was Johnson's constitution, that he 'never knew the natural joy of a free and vigorous use of his limbs.' Concerning his hypochondria, Boswell naïvely remarks: 'How wonderful, how inscrutable are the ways of God! Johnson, who was blest with all the powers of genius and understanding, in a degree far above the ordinary state of human nature, was, at the same time, visited with a disorder so afflictive, that they who know it by dire experience will not envy him his exalted endowments. . . . Insanity was the object of his most dismal apprehension, and he fancied himself seized by it, or approaching to it, at the very time when he was giving proofs of more than ordinary soundness and vigour of judgment.' The complaint that carried Johnson off was asthma, attended with dropsy.

The ancestry of Cowper was distinguished on both sides. It must, however, have been corrupt in an equal degree, COWPER inasmuch as symptoms of mental derangement declared themselves in the poet in his boyhood. His father, a clergyman, was a son of Justice Cowper, and nephew of the first Earl Cowper, Lord Chancellor; his mother, Anne, boasted a connection with several noble houses, and could trace her descent from Henry III. Which parent was the more responsible for the transmission to Cowper of his insanity, and with this of his genius, it is now impossible to say. Nor is the point material, seeing that the neurotic condition of the poet speaks for itself and does not require to be established by collateral evidence. Southey states that Cowper's father and uncle could both write verses—an ominous gift! while his mother died at the early age of thirty-four, so that there was probably a condition of nervous unsoundness in both parents.

At eight or nine years of age, Cowper was threatened with loss of sight; the progress of the disease was stopped, but his eyes remained liable to inflammation all his life. At twenty-one, when Cowper was studying for the bar, he fell into melancholia. 'Day and night,' he says in his autobiographical notes, 'I was upon the rack, lying down in horror and rising up in despair. . . . . . This state of mind continued near a twelvemonth, when, having experienced the inefficiency of all human means, I, at length, betook myself to God in prayer.' Throughout his life Cowper's hallucinations had a strong religious colouring. The long fit of depression above referred to ended as suddenly as it began. He was walking one day on the cliffs at Southampton.

'On a sudden,' he says, 'as if another sun had been kindled at the instant in the heavens on purpose to dispel sorrow and vexation of spirit, I felt the weight of all my misery taken off me. My heart became light and joyful in a moment.'

Such lightning-like changes of mood are frequent in insanity, and, however subtle they may seem, are known to be dependent upon strictly physical conditions. In another year Cowper's melancholia returned with redoubled force, inspiring him, to use his own words, with the 'dark and hellish purpose of self-murder.' His attempts at suicide are detailed with curious minuteness in his autobiographical sketches.[1] First he bought laudanum. This was when he was twenty-two and already writing poetry. 'The apothecary of whom I bought the drug,' he says, 'seemed to observe me narrowly, but if he did I managed my voice and countenance so as to deceive him.' Here we have a good example of the madman's cunning; and another marked characteristic of insanity is disclosed in a subsequent hallucination. He kept the poison in his pocket for some time, but one day, happening to read a letter in a paper which he took up in a coffee-house, a strange sensation came over him. 'The author seemed to be acquainted with my purpose of self-destruction, and to have written that letter in order to secure and hasten the execution of it.' Flinging down the paper he rushed out to seek a convenient spot for suicide, but before he had gone far the idea occurred to him that he would go to France and enter a monastery. He accordingly went home to the Temple and prepared for his departure. Again his mind changed, and the suicidal impulse once more possessed him. He called a cab and drove to the Tower Wharf, intending to throw himself into the river from the Custom House Quay, but on arriving there he

[1] Southey: *Life of Cowper.*

'found the water low, and a porter seated upon some goods as if on purpose to prevent him.' Returning to his chambers in the Temple, he tried to take the laudanum, but could not bring himself to do so, and the same irresolution defeated his efforts to cut his throat. Hanging was his next thought. He fastened a thong to his bedroom door, looped it round his neck as he stood upon a chair and then threw himself into space. As he did so he distinctly heard a voice say three times, ' 'Tis over.' The voice, however, was mistaken. The frenzied poet hung by the neck until he lost consciousness, and his next impression was finding himself lying face downwards upon the floor ; the thong had broken.

After this providential escape Cowper abandoned the idea of suicide, though ' a frequent flashing like that of fire before his eyes and an excessive pressure upon the brain made him apprehensive of apoplexy.' He gave himself up to religious despair ; he thought he had committed the unpardonable sin and was oppressed by uninterrupted misery by day and terrifying visions by night. To reassure himself in this condition he tried to repeat a prayer, but could not remember the words of it. In the effort to recall them, he says, ' I perceived a sensation in the brain like a tremulous vibration of all the fibres of it. Afterwards a numbness seized upon the extremities of my body, and life seemed to retreat before it. My hands and feet became cold and stiff, a cold sweat stood upon my forehead, my heart seemed at every pulse to beat its last, and my soul to cling to my body as if on the brink of departure. While traversing the apartment in the most horrible dismay of soul, expecting every moment that the earth would open her mouth and swallow me up . . . a strange and horrible darkness fell upon me. If it were possible that a heavy blow could light on the brain without touching the skull, this was the sensation I felt. I clapped my hand to my forehead and called aloud through the pain it gave me. At every stroke my thoughts and expressions became more wild and indistinct ; all that remained clear was the sense of sin and the expectation of punishment.' This crisis ended in Cowper's removal to a lunatic asylum, where he was confined for eighteen months. On his release he composed the well-known hymn :—

> The soul, a dreary province once
> Of Satan's dark domain,
> Feels a new empire formed within
> And owns a heavenly reign.

The improvement in his condition, however, was not permanent. Attacks of insanity occurred at intervals, and once he nearly succeeded in hanging himself, being discovered and cut down while on the point of strangulation. Throughout his life he was a victim to religious melancholia, and in this state—one, as he described it, of 'unutterable despair,' he died in his sixty-ninth year. More clearly marked symptoms of insanity could not be found than in this man of genius, rightly described by Southey as 'the most popular poet of his generation.' Cowper's brother John, a clergyman, died of asthma.

Southey himself retained the use of his faculties till within a few years of his death, but he came of an unsound stock on his mother's side. He had a maternal uncle who was an idiot, and a peculiarity of this relative was that, though he learnt to know the letters of the alphabet separately, he could never be taught to combine them into words, but yet possessed 'an excellent memory,' and a sort of shrewdness which, says Southey, 'would have qualified him had he been born two centuries earlier to have worn motley and figured with cap and bells and a bauble in some baron's hall.' Apoplexy carried off this weakling of the family. Southey's mother, 'while a mere child, had a paralytic affection which deadened one side from the hip downwards, and crippled her for almost twelve months.' 'In quickness of capacity,' says her son, 'I never knew her equal.' Southey's father kept a shop, but was 'passionately fond of field sports.' Extraordinary physical energy is often found in connection with nerve-disorder, the result of an excessive stimulation of the motor centres of the brain. Whether on the side of Southey's father some neuropathic tendency existed, there is nothing very positive to show.

An uncle, Thomas Southey, appears to have been rather eccentric. At his death this relative left a considerable amount of property to his footboy, Tom, and another stranger, ignoring the claims of an aged sister who kept house for him and who was unprovided for. This poor old lady, indeed, he turned out of doors for no other reason than that ' she discovered some regret at seeing the footboy, Tom, preferred to her nephews.' As to Southey's father, a passion for field sports is a somewhat suspicious attribute of a shift-less young tradesman, who tries his luck first as a grocer and then as a linendraper. It is to be noted that the physical energy which is so indispensable an element in productive genius was possessed by Southey in a remarkable degree. His literary output was enormous, consisting of some forty or fifty volumes of poems, history, biography, and essays on general subjects. Literary exertion, he himself remarked, was as necessary to him as meat and drink. As a child he was precocious, and wrote verse before he was eight years of age.

Whether as the legacy of one or both parents, Southey's sensibility was extreme. In a letter written in his forty-fifth year, he says : ' It is a matter of surprise to me that this bodily machine of mine should have continued its operations with so few derangements, knowing as I well do its excessive susceptibility to deranging causes. If I did not vary my pursuits, I should soon be incapable of proceeding with any, so surely does it disturb my sleep and affect my dreams if I dwell upon one with any continuous attention. If it were not for great self-management, and what may be called a strict intellectual regimen, I should soon be in a deplorable state of nervous disease.'

Carlyle, who saw Southey in his latter days, thought him the ' excitablest man' he had ever met. ' The shallowest chin, small, care-lined brow, the most vehement pair of hazel eyes! A well read, honest, limited, kindly-hearted, most irritable man ! I said to myself, " How has this man contrived, with such a nervous system, to keep alive for near sixty years ? How has he not been torn to pieces long since under such furious pulling this way and that ? " [1]

[1] Thomas Carlyle ; *Reminiscences*.

Not long after these words were penned, Southey's mind did give way. He sank into a condition of imbecility, in which he died. 'The approaches of his malady,' says his son, 'had been so gradual as almost to escape notice. A loss of memory on certain points, a lessening acuteness of the perceptive faculties, an occasional irritability wholly unknown in him before, a confusion of time, place, and person, the losing of his way in well-known places—all were remembered to have taken place when the melancholy fact had become too evident that the powers of his mind were irreparably weakened. . . For a year before his death, he passed his time as if in a dream, with little, if any, knowledge of what went on around him.' In addition to his mental instability, Southey exhibited some irregularities of physical growth. Carlyle noted the fact at their first meeting. ' He ' (Southey) ' had only half risen, and nodded on my coming in, and all along I had counted him as a lean, little man ; but now (as Carlyle was taking his leave), he shot suddenly aloft into a lean tall one, all legs, in shape and stature like a pair of tongs.' At eight-and-twenty, Southey suffered from ' an ominous dimness of sight at times,' but this weakness appears to have worn off.

Most of Southey's brothers and sisters died young, and in one instance, hydrocephalus is mentioned as the cause of death. The same form of brain disease carried off some of Southey's own children, though, as his wife also became insane, this result need not be ascribed to Southey's organisation exclusively. Of a daughter, who died at twelve months from hydrocephalus, he remarked that previously she had given no sign of disease save a ' somewhat unnatural quickness and liveliness.' Side by side with the genius of a family occurs with strange frequency and regularity the ne'er-do-well, a brother or other near relative possessing the sensibility and the waywardness of genius without its faculty of self-control. Southey's youngest brother Edward was of this stamp. ' The subject,' says Southey's biographer, ' is a painful one, and I may be excused from entering into it further than to say that every effort was made both by my uncle, Mr. Hill, and his brothers, to place him and keep him in a respectable line of life. He possessed excellent abilities, and had received a good education, and, if he had chosen a profession, they would have prepared him for it. He was placed first in the navy, then in the army, but in vain ; for he finally took to the wretched life of an actor in provincial theatres.'[1] Miss Tyler, a relation of Southey's on the maternal side, rendered herself notorious for her immorality.

The immediate progenitors of Shelley were eccentric. His grandfather, Bysshe Shelley, had a melancholy temperament, which is ascribed to his having been crossed in love in his youth. He invited no friendships, SHELLEY and lived apart from persons of his own station. Although wealthy, he hoarded money, and was indifferent to his personal appearance. Similar characteristics appeared in Timothy Shelley, the poet's father, whom Dowden describes as a 'kindly, pompous, capricious, well-meaning, ill-doing, wrong-headed man.' Timothy married a Miss Elizabeth Pilfold, who had a 'violent and domineering temper,' and the poet was the offspring of this union. From boyhood, Shelley was of a peculiar disposition. He was fond of musing alone, and was thought to be a strange and unsociable being. At Eton, he was known as 'mad Shelley.' He combined the diverse qualities of shyness, singularity, carelessness of attire, and unusual excitability of temper. Often he lost himself in waking visions, which were followed by much nervous excitement, his eyes flashing, his lips quivering, his voice being tremulous with emotion, and a sort of ecstasy coming over him. His sleep was disturbed by frightful dreams, and he was a somnambulist. As he grew to manhood, the excitability and impulsiveness of his temperament increased rather than diminished. He had a small, piercing, discordant voice, but his features breathed animation, fire, enthusiasm, and a vivid and preternatural intelligence. In conversation, he was impetuous and argumentative. About his twentieth year, the general state of his nerves was such that he had constantly to take laudanum to calm them. Hogg says he always looked 'wild, intellectual, unearthly, like a spirit that had just descended from the sky, or a demon, risen at that moment out of the ground. In telling a story

---

[1] Cuthbert Southey : *Life and Letters of Robert Southey.*

he would shriek with paroxysms of the wildest laughter.'
Hogg adds that Shelley had 'singular caprices, unfounded
frights and dislikes, vain apprehensions, and panic terrors. . .
He was unconscious and oblivious of time, places, persons, and
seasons; falling into some poetic vision or day dream, he
quickly forgot all that he had repeatedly and solemnly
promised. Or he would run away after some object of
imaginary urgency and importance which suddenly came
into his head, setting off in vain pursuit of it, he knew not
whither.'

There is no doubt that Shelley had actual hallucinations.
While staying at Keswick, he was alarmed early one morning by a noise outside the cottage he occupied. He went to
the door, opened it, and instantly received a blow which
struck him to the ground, where he lay for a while unconscious. This was Shelley's account of the affair, but the
neighbours were sceptical as to his supposed adventure, and
believed him to be the victim of a delusion. Trelawney
thought that Shelley's imagination played him false as to
occurrences. Certainly Shelley indulged for a time in the
foolish belief that he had elephantiasis, and if the Keswick
hallucination is a doubtful one, there is proof of his having
had visions in Italy. 'After tea,' wrote Williams, shortly before
he and Shelley were drowned in the Bay of Spezzia, ' Shelley
complained of being unusually nervous, and, stopping short,
he grasped me violently by the arm and stared steadfastly at
the white surf that broke upon the beach under his feet.
Observing him sensibly affected, I demanded of him if he
were in pain, but he only answered by saying, " There it is
again—there! " He recovered after some time, and declared
that he saw as plainly as he then saw me, a naked child rise
from the sea and clap its hands as in joy, smiling at him.
This was a trance that it required much reasoning and
philosophy to awaken him from, so forcibly had the vision
operated on his mind.' [1] Again, it is related by Medwin on
Byron's authority, that Shelley thought he met one day on
the terrace near his Italian residence a figure wrapped in a
mantle, which lifted up the hood of its cloak and revealed the

[1] Dowden: *Life of Percy Bysshe Shelley.*

phantasm of himself, saying, 'Siete soddisfatto?' (Are you satisfied?). Mary Shelley also mentions this vision, adding that Shelley often saw such figures when ill. Seeing a spectral image of oneself is a form of hallucination that occurs among the apoplectic and the insane; and it is also observed during the delirium of fever. Goethe experienced it in open day as well as Shelley. To the last, Shelley's terrifying dreams, a sure sign of morbid cerebral action, continued to afflict him, and he seems occasionally to have been in doubt as to whether they were dreams or waking visions.

In forming an estimate of Shelley's conduct as a man and as a husband, it is obviously unfair to judge him by the ordinary standard of sanity. Like Swift, he was the slave of morbid impulse, and who can say what developments of moral unsoundness his accidental death at the age of thirty may not have nipped in the bud? Both he and his brother John left issue, but it is strange to note how many of their descendants have been childless. Among the half dozen adults forming the first generation, three, if not four, cases of childlessness occur, an enormous proportion, testifying to the existence of neuropathic conditions.

'Some curse,' wrote Byron to a friend, 'hangs over me and mine.' He was right. It was the curse of heredity. On both his father and his mother's side Byron came of a vitiated stock, although with the fatuity of the common run of men who look at the extent of a genealogical tree, and not at its vigour or freshness, he was proud to an extraordinary extent of his descent, prouder, it has been said, than of his works. It is unnecessary to go deeply into the poet's pedigree in order to ascertain its neurotic character. In his immediate progenitors the 'insane temperament' stares us in the face. The ancestor whom he succeeded in the title, his grand-uncle, was a licentious, quarrelsome, vindictive man, feared or hated by everybody, and popularly known as the 'mad,' or 'wicked Lord Byron.' There was no enormity of crime of which this representative of a noble house was thought to be incapable by those who knew him. Under circumstances that forcibly suggested murder, he killed his friend and neighbour Chatworth, in a room where, by the feeble light of a single candle and without seconds or witnesses, a so-called duel was fought about a trifle. Shunned by his equals and deserted by his wife, he led a morose and lonely existence. From hatred to his son and heir he let the family seat go to ruin, cut down the timber on the estate, and sold illegally a portion of his property. His son and his son's son, however, died before him, whereupon the miserable old man transferred his aversion from them to the 'little boy at Aberdeen,' as the poet was then called. The brother of this ' mad Lord Byron,' was Admiral John Byron, the poet's grandfather, in whom the devil-may-care nature of the family happened to be turned to good account. Admiral Byron was a man of remarkable courage and endurance, and distinguished himself both in peace and war; but in his son John, father of the poet, the worst characteristics of the Byron blood re-appeared.

' Mad Jack Byron ' led such a dissolute life, that, before he was out of his teens, he was held in general disrepute. At twenty-two he ran away with the Marchioness of Carmarthen, married her after her divorce—she was an heiress—and, after squandering her fortune, killed her, it was said, by his ill-usage. When penniless, he looked about for another heiress, and found one in Miss Gordon, whose money also, after marriage, he spent like water, leaving her almost penniless with her only child. To such straits was the fine gentleman subsequently reduced by his own extravagance that, after separating from his wife, he had the meanness to write her a begging letter, imploring her to give him a guinea. He went to France and died there in his thirty-sixth year. To Harness, the poet more than once stated that his father ' was insane and killed himself.' The suicide has not been clearly established, but circumstances point to it. Jeafferson observes that the man who was known throughout life as ' mad Jack Byron,' may be presumed to have been a person whose ' eccentricity bordered upon insanity,' and that having gone abroad with a few guineas in his purse, just enough to keep him for a few weeks, suicide was with him a very likely resource.[1] In any case, ' mad Jack's ' character and his early

---

[1] J. Cordy Jeafferson : *The True Lord Byron.*

death, leave no room for doubt as to the morbid condition of his faculties.

The poet was no less unfortunate in his mother. His maternal grandfather, who was subject to melancholia, drowned himself at forty, and another near relative attempted suicide by poison.[1] His mother, inheriting thus a strain of insanity, was a woman of very unbalanced temperament. At the theatre in Edinburgh she went into convulsions on seeing Mrs. Siddons act. Her husband had good reason to fear her temper; to be sure, it was sorely tried, but towards other people she fell into 'frequent fits of uncontrollable fury.' Jeafferson says she rarely allowed a week to pass without 'a wild outbreak of hysterical rage.' She even mocked at her son for being 'a lame brat,' and Disraeli hints that she was addicted to drink. As a child Byron feared this unnatural mother, as a man he ridiculed and despised her; but the biographical theory which attributes the poet's unhappy characteristics to maternal ill-treatment in his boyhood, obviously does not take sufficient account of the evil heredity to which he was subject. While still a youngish woman, Mrs. Byron died suddenly, owing, it was said, to a fit of anger into which she had been thrown by an upholsterer's account, but more probably as the result of some affection of the brain or nervous system, and Byron, instead of following the body to the grave, engaged with his servant in a bout with boxing-gloves!

Combining thus, in himself, two converging lines of morbid heredity, Byron was necessarily a being of strange and wayward habits. It is such parentage as his that fills our mad-houses with patients. For, be it remarked, there can be no pretence of any inheritance on his part of intellectual gifts in the common acceptation of the word. 'Mad Jack Byron' may have had captivating manners, but he never gave proof of possessing even average mental ability, while Mrs. Byron, despite a distinguished lineage, was deplorably lacking both in intelligence and refinement. The poet's deformed foot is supposed by the biographer to have been due to an accident at birth; but malformations, as we have seen,

[1] Elze: *Life of Byron.*

are a common accompaniment of nervous disorder, and the
deformity, which resisted all attempts to cure it, may be
regarded as congenital. Owing to Byron's sensitiveness on
the point, none of his friends, even the most intimate, appear
to have known precisely what he suffered from; nor is the
question ever likely to be settled. Trelawney's account is the
most positive and authentic. He saw Byron lying in his
coffin; impelled by curiosity, he sent the servant out of the
room and uncovered the feet of the dead man. 'Then,' he
says, 'the mystery was solved; both feet were clubbed, and
his legs withered to the knees, but the right foot was the most
distorted, while the right leg was also shorter than the other.'
Byron's life, from first to last, was that of a man governed by
morbid impulse and scarcely responsible for his actions. In
friendship, politics, religion, and love he was uniformly unstable and insincere, and his strongest motive in everything
was probably vanity.

Although his whole life might be cited as a proof of the
neuropathic character of his genius, the evidence directly bearing on the subject, apart from heredity, admits of being given
within small compass. His diary, written in the very heyday
of his youth and fame, reflects a distempered mind. 'When
I am tired,' he says, 'as I generally am, out comes this and
down goes everything. But I can't read it over, and God
knows what contradictions it may contain. If I am sincere
with myself (but I fear one lies more to oneself than to anybody else) every page should confute, refute, and utterly abjure
its predecessor.' The entries abound in expressions of indifference and callousness, of vacuity and satiety, of loathing and
contempt for his fellow-mortals. 'What have I seen!' he
exclaims. 'The same men all over the world. Aye, and
women too. . . Hang up philosophy! To be sure I have
long despised myself and man, but I have never spat in the
face of my species before. Oh, fool! I shall go mad.' A fear
of going mad haunted Byron through life, as it often does
those who are destined to that fate—Swift, for example.
Lady Caroline Lamb's first impression of him was that he
was 'mad, bad, and dangerous to know.' Lady Byron left him
after one miserable year of married life, and explained that she

did so because it had been strongly impressed upon her mind
that 'Lord Byron was under the influence of insanity.' Sixteen
points in support of her contention were submitted to the
judgment of the medical men in the investigation which she
promoted, but they were never disclosed. This is understood
to have been one—that Byron was thrown into convulsions
by Kean's performance of the part of Sir Giles Overreach,
just as his mother had once been by the acting of Mrs.
Siddons. On another occasion he was said to have thrown
his watch, which he had worn from his earliest boyhood, into
the fire, and dashed it to pieces with the poker. That he once
discharged a pistol in his wife's bedroom is admitted even by
the Countess Guiccioli.

The grossest excesses and the keenest nervous suffering
marked Byron's life in Venice. 'His harem on the Grand
Canal, to which he gathered frail women from the homes of
artisans and the cabins of suburban peasants, was fruitful of
scandals. . . Little or nothing, however, was heard in England of the degree to which the poet now succumbed to the
appetites of the glutton and the sot. . . In the increasing
violence of his temper, ever too fervid, in the alteration of his
voice, once so clear and musical that children turned from
their play for the delight of listening to it, and in his penman-
ship, always indicative of irritability, and now growing so
illegible that it troubled the best compositors to decipher it,
there were signs of the nervous distress caused by drinking.
. . . At night he would roll in agony through long assaults
of acute dyspepsia, more often lie in melancholy moodiness,
or endure the torture of afflicting hallucinations. . . To
Byron, with a nervous idiosyncrasy that rendered him peculiarly sensitive and impatient of physical discomfort, the pain
of these spasmodic seizures was almost maddening torment.
The mental anguish that came to him from dreams was no
less acute.' [1]

The epileptic attacks preceding Byron's death sufficiently
explain his restless, extravagant, and impetuous life. He
was the victim of his organisation as truly as the violent
lunatic who has to spend his miserable days in a padded

---

[1] Jeaffreson.

room. It was at Missolonghi, in his thirty-sixth year, that the first epileptic seizure occurred. It appears to have been sharp and severe, lasting about a quarter of an hour. 'Every reader of the Byronic biographies has heard of this attack. A fact less generally known,' says Jeafferson, 'is that this seizure was the first of a series. . . In fact the poet had five epileptic fits within thirteen days.' Two months later he passed away, the immediate cause of death being said to be 'fever' arising from a chill. Probably the end was hastened a little by the excessive bleeding to which the patient was subjected, the doctors fearing that the epileptic attacks would be followed, as they so often are, by mental derangement. How near to insanity Byron's condition was, the following glimpse of it, given by his companion Leicester Stanhope, will show :

'The mind of Byron was like a volcano, full of fire and wealth, sometimes calm, often dazzling and playful, but even threatening. It ran swift as the lightning from one subject to another, and occasionally burst forth in passionate throes of intellect nearly allied to madness. A striking instance of this sort of eruption I shall mention. Lord Byron's apartments were immediately over mine at Missolonghi. In the dead of night I was frequently startled from my sleep by the thunders of his lordship's voice, either raging with anger or roaring with laughter, and arousing friends, servants, and, indeed, all the inmates of the dwelling from their repose.'

In Byron's offspring neurotic characteristics are to be detected. His daughter Ada suffered from determination of blood to the head and died at thirty-seven, leaving by her husband, Earl Lovelace, a son, who appears to have inherited all the eccentricities of the Byrons, saving only his grandfather's genius. This young man, Byron Noel, Viscount Oakham, mixed little with people of his own rank, but served as a common seaman, and then worked for some time as a ship carpenter at Millwall. The abnormal character of his organisation is suggested by his death occurring at the early age of twenty-six.

A tendency to insanity was strongly marked in Thomas Campbell, and reflected in his family. The evil appears to have been mainly on his mother's side, for insanity existed among his maternal cousins, while his mother herself is described by an indulgent biographer [1] as excessively 'irritable,' and 'unnecessarily severe or even harsh in the exercise of her authority,' a phrase of much significance to the student of mental disease. In old age she became paralysed. The poet's father was a merchant of good repute. Both parents were long-lived, and transmitted their longevity to some of their numerous children, who, in their several ways as the brothers and sisters of a poet of undoubted genius, present an instructive study in pathology. The family record is as follows :—

Mary Campbell	died at	86	Paralysed, childless.
Isabella	„ „	79	Paralysed, 'poetical,' childless.
Archibald	„ „.	70	Childless.
Alexander	„ „	65	Went abroad, prospered, and had a large family.
John	„ „	43	Childless.
Elizabeth	„ „	64	Suffered from protracted ill-health, childless.
Daniel	„	—	Died in infancy.
Robert	„ „	35	Childless.
James	„ „	13	Drowned while bathing.
Daniel	„	—	Nothing known of his death, a ne'er-do-well.

The poet was the eleventh child. Besides his genius, the characteristics of the family, it will be seen, were paralysis, infertility, and ill-health. The presence of the ne'er-do-well, as in Southey's case, is also noteworthy. This member of the family was put into business, but, as the biographer remarks, he had 'either too much genius or too little perseverance to keep there.' A 'boon companion,' and a 'man of infinite humour,' he became unfitted for his calling, which probably means that he gave himself up to drinking ; he then went abroad and was no more heard of. He had one son, who died early. As a child Campbell was precocious ; he wrote verses at ten, was imaginative, sensitive, and passionately fond of music. At eighteen he was attacked by melancholia,

[1] Charles Rogers : *Life of Thomas Campbell.*

and Professor Pillans of Edinburgh, who knew him a year or
two later, wrote as follows to a friend: ' He accompanied me
to my father's in the lowest state of depression, so much so
that my father taunted me with bringing to his house a man
who seemed to be bordering on insanity.' The Campbell
blood being so unquestionably corrupt, it was unfortunate
that its evil effects should have been intensified in the poet's
case by a consanguineous marriage. Such, however, was
the case. Campbell married his maternal cousin, who had a
sister insane, and who herself was very ' vivacious,' ' energetic,'
and ' irritable,' and the one son of his who survived the perils
of childhood was a lunatic. At the height of his reputation
Campbell showed signs of insanity, believing that he was
ruined, for example, while he was really in the most prosperous circumstances. He was eccentric in many ways, and
also, which is important in a pathological sense, suffered
from gout or rheumatism. His habits were most unsettled,
and his nerves so troublesome that he resorted to stimulants. In his latter years he sank into a condition of mental
debility, in which he died at sixty-seven.

Little is known of Oliver Goldsmith's personal and family
history, but such facts of his career as have been recorded,
tend to qualify him for a place in the group of dis- Goldsmith
tinguished men now under discussion. There was .
a strong tincture of ne'er-do-wellism in his character, and
much foolish moralising on his account has been indulged in
by biographers, who see in him only the man of genius
condemned to live from hand to mouth, and to write immortal
works in a garret. In truth, few young men had better
chances in life of comfort and respectability—if such be the
biographer's ideal of happiness—than Goldsmith, and none
assuredly threw such chances more perversely away. He
was maintained at college till he took his degree (in spite of
his being a ' dunce ' at learning), and neither then nor for
some years afterwards did he do a stroke of work of any kind,
but preferred to live on the bounty of his relatives. The
intermittent literary occupation that he finally settled down
to suited his temperament as an idler and a vagabond ; but
with money pouring in upon him whenever he chose to do

anything for it—Macaulay calculates that during the last
seven years of his life Goldsmith made 800*l.* a year in English
currency—and with not a soul in the world to keep but
himself, he still lived in squalor, had to be dunned for his
milk bill, and died 2,000*l.* in debt, this sum representing loans
that he had cadged from his friends, probably without the
smallest intention of repaying them. Of Oliver's brothers,
one was a humble village preacher, who appears to have died
early, another ' departed a miserable life ' as a cabinet maker,
and a third, after a career of adventure abroad, died in
wretched lodgings in London. Considering that their father
was a Protestant clergyman of some position in Ireland, this
must have been a very thriftless family altogether. Oliver
was a most unpromising boy. Though he scribbled verses
early, he was 'impenetrably stupid' at school, and, according
to his sister, was 'subject to the most particular humours,'
with the 'most unaccountable alternations of gaiety and gloom.'
This mental condition explains his boyish freak of running
away from home for six weeks, and also his prolonged
vagabondage on the Continent. Boswell says, Goldsmith
' disputed his way through Europe.' It is more likely, as
William Black remarks, that he ' begged his way through
Europe.' The portrait by Reynolds does not convey a
favourable impression of Goldsmith's character, exhibiting a
heavy, receding jaw, thick lips, a bulging brow, and a listless,
idiotic expression. Goldsmith died of some nervous affection,
the most clearly defined symptom of which was 'a violent
pain extending all over the fore part of his head.'

Charles Lamb appears to have owed his poetical and
literary faculties to a converging heredity of brain and nerve-
CHARLES disease. His father, who occupied the humble
LAMB position of a servant in Lincoln's Inn, wrote verses,
and about his fiftieth year lapsed into a state of imbecility;
his mother became paralysed. This couple had three children, John, Mary, and Charles Lamb. John is described in
one of the ' Essays of Elia' as a man ' of fiery and tempestuous temper,' unable to reason logically, but jumping at
' most admirable conclusions;' he held some position in the
South Sea House, and died respectably at sixty or thereabouts.

Mary became subject to fits of insanity, in one of which she stabbed her invalid mother to the heart and killed her. Charles Lamb was himself confined for six weeks in a madhouse about his twentieth year—the period at which he wrote most of his sonnets. He was of puny physique, constitutionally nervous and timid, subject to stammering, and to violent headaches. In his later years he gave way to what he called his 'cursed drinking.' The immediate cause of his death at sixty was erysipelas, but Talfourd says his constitution was by that time thoroughly broken down.

In her lucid intervals Mary Lamb had a fine poetical taste, very like Elia's own. Describing her insanity, Charles Lamb says :—'Her ramblings often sparkled with brilliant descriptions and shattered beauty. . . . She would fancy herself in the days of Queen Anne or George I. and describe the brocaded dames and courtly manners as though she had been bred among them, in the best style of the Old Comedy. It was all broken and disjointed, so that the hearer could remember little of her discourse, but the fragments were like the jewelled speeches of Congreve, only shaken from their setting. There was sometimes even a vein of crazy logic running through them, associating things essentially most dissimilar but connecting them by a verbal association in strange order. As a mere physical example of deranged intellect, her condition was, I believe, extraordinary ; it was as if the finest elements of mind had been shaken into fantastic combinations like those of a kaleidoscope.' Throughout life Mary and Charles Lamb were devoted to each other, having a perfect community of literary and poetic tastes.

In his defiance of all authority, his reckless impulse, his fierce outbursts of temper, his swift changes of mood, his general singularities which the most indulgent of biographers do not attempt to conceal, Walter Savage Landor would most certainly have been entitled to be classed as a victim of the 'insane temperament,' even had his closing years been unmarked by any of the more unmistakable characteristics of insanity.[1] He belonged to a

LANDOR

---

[1] John Forster : *Walter Savage Landor, a Biography.*

gouty family. As early as the age of twelve he had a violent attack of gout, and his father and brothers were sufferers from that malady. In a previous chapter gout has been shown to alternate sometimes with mental disorder. Landor's first attack was his last; the gout never returned, but, on the other hand, his mental condition was ever afterwards peculiar. His laugh is historical; it must have surpassed in volume even that of Shelley or Byron. 'Higher and higher,' says Forster in describing it, 'went peal after peal, until regions of sound were reached very far beyond ordinary human lungs.' Landor was consumed by an irrepressible energy, for which his poetic and literary occupations afforded some outlet. Poetry and literature he turned to instinctively, for, being possessed of private means, he was never under the necessity of writing for a livelihood. 'He had the power, sudden as thought itself, of giving visual shape to objects of thought, and with all this, an intense energy of feeling and a restless activity of imagination eager to reproduce themselves in similar forms of vivid and picturesque expression. He had an exceptional faculty for Latin verse, his excellence in which was a tradition at Rugby for half a century after he left. In every other study or pursuit he was the creature of caprice. At Oxford his character was ungovernable; he held fierce and uncompromising opinions, and once fired a fowling-piece into the window of a political opponent—an offence for which, refusing to apologise, he was rusticated for a year and very nearly expelled. Nor did time soften his asperities. He was always uncontrollably impetuous, and so prone to act from undisciplined impulse . . . that during hardly any part of his life could he live with other people in peace for any length of time; good-humoured for a while, he was apt gradually to become tyrannical where he had power, and rebellious where he had not.'

On one occasion, Forster had the greatest difficulty in restraining him from sending a challenge to Lord John Russell for some fancied slight to the memory of a supposed ancestor, Sir Arnold Savage, Speaker of Henry the Seventh's first House of Commons. After succeeding to the family estates, he so embroiled himself with tenants and neighbours, that the control of the property was taken out of his hands, and during a great part of his long life he lived abroad, owing, as he said, to the many acts of injustice and unkindness he met with in England. He was himself, however, his greatest enemy. In public and private affairs his plan of proceeding was on the eccentric principle of differing as widely as he could from everybody else. He was ever swayed by the mood that possessed him for the moment, and 'though it was easy by humouring this to continue friendly with him, it was yet easier to quarrel with him by opposing it in however slight a degree.' Changing his clime, Landor did not change his nature, for in Tuscany he contrived to get himself expelled by order of the Government. The mental breakdown in his latter years was complete. Referring to an action for libel in which Landor had enmeshed himself in one of his storms of frantic passion, Forster remarks that the old man had ceased to be a 'responsible human being.' He had not now even memory enough to recollect what he was writing from day to day, and 'while the power of giving keen and clear expression to every passing mood of bitterness remained to him, his reason had too far deserted him to leave it other than a fatal gift. He could apply no gauge or measure to what he was bent upon either doing or saying; he seemed to have no longer the ability to see anything not palpably before him; and of the effect of any given thing on his own or another's reputation, he was become wholly powerless to judge.'

Shortly afterwards, Landor persisted in printing, in spite of the remonstrances of his friends, the worthless scraps of his writings, which he called ' Dry Sticks;' the proofs had to be altered without his consent; and he had tried, though unsuccessfully, to make it a condition with the publisher that his name should appear on the title-page as 'the late W. S. Landor.' He talked of a 'swimming in his head,' of inability to remember places and faces, though verses of the ' Odyssey' and ' Iliad ' were perpetually floating before his mind. In this condition he lived six or eight years longer, incurring another action for libel, in which damages of a thousand pounds were awarded against him. The close of his life was spent in

Italy, where, according to a letter of Browning's, he required to have some one always at hand to explain away his irritations and hallucinations as they arose.   He suffered severely from sciatica, and upon his loss of memory deafness supervened.   His death at eighty-nine was brought about by his abstaining for three days from food, whether as the result of weakne-s or of some hallucination is unknown.

Thomas Chatterton, the most precocious literary genius that the world has ever seen, was the offspring of a 'drunken, wild-eyed' choir singer, who died before his mar-

CHATTERTON

vellous son was born, and of a woman who was long afflicted with a 'nervous disease,' probably palsy.   His sister, a Mrs. Newton, had an attack of insanity.   The boy's temper had 'something in it quite unusual in one so young. Generally very sullen and silent, he was liable to sudden and unaccountable fits of weeping, as well as to violent fits of rage.'   In his eighteenth year he committed suicide.   It is generally thought that this was due to his finding himself in a state of destitution in a humble lodging in London. Before his suicide, however, his landlady 'did not think he was quite right in his mind.'   He showed a 'growing restlessness,' and 'sudden fits of vacancy or silence that came upon him sometimes while he was talking rapidly.'   He would often 'look steadfastly in a person's face without speaking or seeming to see the person for a quarter of an hour or more, till it was quite frightful.'[1]   Young as he was, the boy had acquired a name for immorality in his native town of Bristol. He appears also to have been enormously vain.   Mrs. Newton had an only daughter who died young.   This was the last of the Chattertons.

Jean Jacques Rousseau was of melancholy temperament, and more than once had hallucinations of persecution.[2]

ROUSSEAU

There seems to have been insanity on his father's side, a cousin of the name of Rousseau having been afflicted with that disorder.   He was a weakly and ailing child, and a ne'er-do-well brother was a precocious libertine. Corancez, a friend of Jean Jacques', has left on record some

---

[1] Masson : *Essays Biographical and Critical.*
[2] Moreau : *La Psychologie Morbide.*

curious details as to the philosopher's mental condition.
Rousseau lived under the constant belief that his life was
being conspired against; and in the most trifling circumstances he saw a confirmation of his suspicions. 'My
enemies,' he remarked on one occasion, 'employ more ingenuity in persecuting me than would be required for
governing Europe.' Corancez discovered Rousseau on several
occasions in a convulsed state, in which his features wore a
strange and terrifying expression. At such times the philosopher's discourse was incoherent and wild, one of his remarks
being that his misfortunes had been specially predicted by
Tasso. Rousseau's condition at the time of his acquaintance
with Hume was clearly a dangerous one. What could
better reflect the hallucinations of a disordered mind than
his own account of his experiences? 'One evening,' he says,
'a remarkable circumstance struck me. As we were sitting
by the fire, I caught sight of Hume's eyes intently fixed on
mine, and that in a manner of which it is difficult to give an
idea. He gave me a steadfast, piercing look mixed with a
sneer, which greatly disturbed me. To get rid of my embarrassment, I endeavoured to look full at him in my turn,
but, in fixing my eyes on his, I felt a most inexpressible
terror, and was obliged soon to turn them away. . . . My
trouble increased even to the degree of fainting, and if I had
not been relieved by a suffusion of tears, I should have been
suffocated. Presently after this I was seized with the most
violent remorse, and in a transport of joy I sprang upon his
neck and kissed him. I felt my heart yearn towards him.
. . . The first night after my departure with Hume for Paris
we slept in the same chamber, when, during the night, I
heard him cry out with great vehemence in the French
language, "Je tiens Jean Jacques Rousseau." I knew not
whether he was awake or asleep. The expression was remarkable. I took the words, however, in a favourable sense,
notwithstanding that the tone of voice in which they were
spoken was still less favourable than the expression. It is
indeed impossible for me to give any idea of it, but it corre-
sponds exactly with those terrible looks I have before mentioned. At every repetition of them I was seized with a

shuddering, a kind of horror. I could not resist, though a moment's recollection restored me, and made me smile at my weakness. The next day all this was perfectly obliterated.'[1] Rousseau died of apoplexy.

According to Lélut, who made a complete study of his case from the pathological point of view,[2] Pascal suffered

PASCAL from hallucinations, one of which was, that there was a yawning abyss by his side. He was all his life a victim to extreme nervous suffering. As a child he had a sort of hydrophobia, being unable to look upon water without falling into convulsions. Another idiosyncrasy was that he could not bear to see his father and mother together, they had to approach him separately. His headaches were of extraordinary intensity, and afterwards he had epileptic convulsions, which were the cause of his death. A post-mortem examination revealed a strange condensation and solidification of portions of the brain, and an infusion of blood into certain cavities, together with some irregularities in the form of the skull. A sister of Pascal's, Jacqueline, wrote verses, was very precocious and sensitive, and became excessively pious, passing the latter part of her life in a state of religious exaltation.

Chateaubriand belonged to a mad family, and was himself of a melancholic temperament. His father died of

CHATEAU apoplexy; a brother and sister were eccentric and
BRIAND   vicious. The illustrious author of the ' Mémoires d'Outre-Tombe ' was haunted by ideas of suicide. As he himself relates, he one day loaded a fowling-piece, sought a retired spot, and tried to fire the weapon into his mouth; it failed to go off, and he was disturbed before he could carry out his intention. This occurred in his youth, but his suicidal ideas never quitted him. ' My great defect,' he writes in the work above mentioned, ' is *ennui*, a distaste for everything, and a perpetual doubt.'

Not a few other writers of eminence have shown symptoms of insanity. George Sand was, in her youth, profoundly melancholic and felt tempted to commit suicide.

---

[1] David Hume: *Philosophical Essays*
[2] Lélut: *L'Amulette de Pascal.*

'This temptation,' she writes, 'was sometimes so strong, so sudden, so strange, that it can only be described as a species of insanity. It partook of the character of a monomania.' The sight of water, of a precipice, of a loaded pistol, or of bottles containing poison was sufficient to arouse suicidal ideas in her mind, and her father, it appears, was subject to a similar weakness.—Tasso's homicidal mania and other eccentricities caused him to be confined for a time as a lunatic. He saw apparitions, sometimes glorious, as when the Virgin appeared to him in a crimson vapour, sometimes hellish and impish; he heard aërial laughter, hissing, and the ringing of bells. He believed himself to be accompanied by a familiar spirit with which he held sublime conversations. In the presence of his friend Manso (who was also Milton's friend), he summoned up this spirit and was surprised that Manso did not see· and hear it also.—Silvio Pellico had hallucinations of sight, hearing, and touch. The stillness of his prison cell was broken by groans and laughter, while spirit hands seemed to pluck him by the garments or to try to extinguish the light. 'These apparitions,' he says, 'became at times terrible realities.' In the dark he often saw phantoms.—Both Tannahill and Lenau committed suicide. The latter, who ranks high as a poet in German estimation, was, from his boyhood, of a restless and extravagant disposition, and notorious for his excesses in wine and love. Like Byron, he often felt he would go mad. His deep melancholia was followed by a stroke of paralysis. In a sudden frenzy he threw himself out of a window, and from the injuries so received he died. The brain proved on a post-mortem examination to be profoundly diseased.—Hölderlin's insanity lasted nearly forty years.—Although never placed under restraint, Edgar Allan Poe was undoubtedly an insane subject. More than once he attempted or threatened suicide under delusions of persecution.[1] He was, moreover, very erratic, hypochondriacal, and from his early years a confirmed drunkard, and he died of brain disease at forty. The family stock was radically unsound. The poet's father, David Poe, was a drunkard, and given to extravagances

---

[1] W. J. Gill: *Life of Edgar Allan Poe.*

which 'excited great solicitude among his family and friends.'
At eighteen David Poe eloped with and married an actress,
and both he and she died early of consumption, leaving, besides
the author of 'The Raven,' a daughter and another son
named William. The daughter died young. William Poe
was a poet of some promise, but, like his brother, of very
'irregular habits,' and short-lived.—Diderot had a sister
insane, and a brother inordinately pious; Kerner's aunt
was of a poetic disposition but melancholic, and had a
daughter insane, another daughter, who was a somnambulist,
becoming the mother of the poet Hauff.—Alfieri had fits of
extreme exaltation and melancholy, was eccentric, and more
than once attempted suicide.—The Roman poet Lucretius
suffered from intermittent mania, in the lucid intervals of
which he composed his great work 'De rerum naturâ.' At
forty-four he is said to have committed suicide.

CHAPTER V

METAMORPHOSIS OF NERVE-DISORDER IN CONNECTION WITH GENIUS—
GOUT, BLINDNESS, DEFORMITY AND NE'ER-DO-WELLISM IN MILTON'S
FAMILY—THE NE'ER-DO-WELLISM OF THE SHERIDANS—THE COLE-
RIDGE FAMILY PRESENTING EXAMPLES OF GOUT, INSANITY, DIPSO-
MANIA, PARALYSIS, AND CONSUMPTION—WORDSWORTH'S SISTER IN-
SANE—BURNS'S HYPOCHONDRIA AND DRUNKENNESS—UNSOUNDNESS
OF WALTER SCOTT'S FAMILY—BULWER LYTTON'S CHARACTERIS-
TICS—MACAULAY AS A PRODIGY—THE BRONTË FAMILY—PATRICK
BRONTË INSANE, HIS DAUGHTERS CONSUMPTIVE, HIS SON A NE'ER-
DO-WELL—DICKENS'S GOUT AND PARALYSIS—THACKERAY, GEORGE
ELIOT, WILKIE COLLINS, AND BROWNING AS NEUROPATHIC SUBJECTS
—THE ECCENTRICITIES OF BALZAC, DUMAS, AND ALFRED DE
MUSSET—GUSTAVE FLAUBERT AN EPILEPTIC—INSANITY IN VICTOR
HUGO'S FAMILY

As insanity is only one of the family of nerve-diseases, genius
will be found combined, in most cases, with some other of
the many ailments, mental and physical, which MILTON
spring from the neurotic condition. Evidence of
the morbid character of Milton's genius is furnished by the
threefold fact that he lost his sight from congenital causes,
that he was a gouty subject, and that a well-marked strain
of ne'er-do-wellism ran through his near collaterals. Milton's
father was a scrivener and a musician of considerable attainments, who lived to a great age. Of the poet's mother the
suggestive fact is recorded by Aubrey that she 'had very
weak eyes and used spectacles presently after she was thirty
years old.' She died rather early, though of what disease is
not stated. To this couple six children were born, three of
whom died in infancy, leaving John, who was the third child,
an elder sister, Anne, and a younger brother, Christopher.
Anne married a man named Philips, and had two sons,
Edmund and John Philips, the black sheep of the family.
Both these nephews of the poet possessed literary ability,

but they led shiftless lives and died miserably poor. The former, who was a clever hack writer, married a widow with children, but whether he left descendants is unknown. John Philips wrote both prose and verse, and is described as a 'man of very loose principles, who forsook his wife and children without making any provision for them.' He had gout both in his hands and feet. In the memoirs of one John Dunton, published in 1705, it is said of him, 'He'll write you off a design in a very little time, if the gout or claret don't stop him.' From this it would appear that to his other vices he added drinking. Of his children we know nothing. The poet's sister, after the death of her first husband, married one Thomas Agar, who appears to have brought a corrective influence to bear upon the Milton blood. At all events, Agar's offspring by Anne Milton proved to be vigorous enough to leave respectable and prolific descendants, whence it may be concluded that the Philips blood was not a desirable blend. Milton's only brother Christopher became a disreputable judge, whose descendants do not appear to have outlived the third generation.

As a child, Milton was a prodigy ; at ten years of age he was a poet, or at least a writer of verses. Unlike most poets, however, he was from his earliest years austere and serious, albeit not free from a certain 'haughty self-esteem.' A stickler for moral integrity, he was, as Masson expresses it, 'dead against the wild-oats theory,' holding that sensual indulgence at any period of life was the cause of spiritual incapacity. He had a judicial though somewhat contentious mind, and a total lack of humour. As a boy he suffered with his eyes, and had torturing headaches. Soon after his thirtieth year—the period from which his mother's infirmity dated—his eyesight began seriously to fail, and at the age of forty-four he found himself totally blind. As his eyes never showed any structural blemish, or his visual memory any falling off, the seat of the evil was probably the optic nerves. The morbid condition he transmitted to his descendants. His daughter Deborah had in turn a daughter who became a Mrs. Foster, and this lady, Milton's granddaughter, being visited by one Thomas Newton in 1749, when she was sixty-one years of age, was found to be 'extremely short-sighted,' as well as 'weak and infirm.' She told Newton that her mother Deborah had inherited Milton's weakness of eyes, having been obliged to use spectacles from about the time of her marriage, and that she herself had been 'unable to read a chapter of the Bible these twenty years.'

Milton's nerve-disorder revealed itself most unmistakably through his daughter Anne, who was lame and otherwise deformed, and who suffered from an impediment in her speech.[1] Deborah, with her weak eyes, was 'likest her father.' A third daughter, Mary, appears to have been of an ailing disposition, for she remained unmarried and died about forty. These were the children of Milton's first wife, of whose character nothing is known except that she found in the poet an uncongenial husband. There was a son born, but he died in infancy, according to a biographer, 'through ill-usage or the bad constitution of an ill-chosen nurse.' More probably he fell a victim to the same inherent weakness that crippled Anne, that blinded Deborah, and that brought Mary to an early grave. By a second and a third wife Milton had no family. The daughters lived most unhappily with their father. They found him tyrannical, while he thought them undutiful, and he accused them of cheating him in money matters and stealing his books in order to sell them. Genius may be a golden idol, but, if so, it too often has feet of clay. The dissensions of the Milton household tell their own tale of what the world is accustomed to venerate as greatness. Milton died at sixty-five of gout 'struck in,' and some further indications of a neurotic condition is furnished by the fact that he was physically undergrown.

In a Darwinian sense the poet's descendants are to be numbered among the unfit. The only one of his daughters who had offspring was Deborah. She married a weaver named Clark, and had ten children, of whom only three attained to adult age. The first of these survivors, Urban Clark, died unmarried; another, the Mrs. Foster above referred to, had seven children, none of whom left issue; the third, Caleb Clark, went to Madras, and with the record of

[1] Masson: *Life of Milton.*

the death of a single grandchild of his all trace of Milton's posterity ceases.

Of the parentage of Richard Steele there is nothing known, in a medical sense, except that he lost his father at five years of age, that his mother died soon afterwards, and that, in his thirty-sixth year, he speaks of himself as being 'divested of all relations' that might enjoy anything after him. A medical man named Woodward had Steele under his care, and in a posthumous volume, published in 1757, makes the following reference to the case of his eminent patient: 'He had the gout by fits for years, it constantly growing upon him, and in the winter of 1715 (when Steele was forty-three) and the following spring the fit was more severe than ever before, and continued for several months.' Woodward represents that he cured Steele's gout, although the patient 'frequently drank hard.' 'Only sometimes, after a great excess, his limbs became heavy, clumsy, and stiff, but never to such a degree as not in a little time to come to themselves.' In a diary kept by Steele in 1721 the writer deplores 'the miserable habit of mind' which he has contracted through a guilty indulgence of his appetites and passions. Here Steele probably refers not only to his drinking, but to his notorious thriftlessness and extravagance. In 1727 Steele had 'a stroke of paralysis, accompanied by a partial loss of speech, and he never completely recovered his mental powers.'[1] Two years later, at the age of fifty-seven, he died. By a second wife, who was not long-lived, Steele had two sons and two daughters. The boys passed away at six and eleven years of age respectively; Mary, the second daughter, died soon after her father of a 'lingering consumption.' The elder, Elizabeth, lived to become Lady Trevor. Aitken says she 'inherited something of her mother's beauty and her father's thriftlessness ;' she had two children : one was still-born ; the other, Diana, Steele's only grandchild, lived to the age of thirty-four, but was an idiot. 'It was thought,' says Aitken, 'that her idiocy was due to a fright which her mother had from a stag previous to her birth,' but her grandfather's gout and paralysis, her

STEELE

---

[1] Aitken : *Life of Richard Steele.*

aunt's consumption, and the fact that Lady Trevor her-self
died of paralysis, give a different complexion to the
matter.

Joseph Addison, Steele's more eminent colleague, died at
forty-seven of asthma. There is evidence that he ADDISON
was addicted to drinking, and that, despite his
brilliant social position, he suffered from depression of spirits.
He left a daughter, who was weak-minded.

For several generations the Sheridan family were no-torious
for their ne'er-do-well qualities.[1] Thomas Sheridan,
grandfather of the author of 'The School for Scan- SHERIDAN
dal,' was a strange, mercurial person, possessed of
an 'extraordinary gift for occasional poetry,' but careless,
eccentric, and ever the butt of fortune,'—always struggling
with debt—the victim of perpetual failure. He died of
asthma. The only one of his children of whom anything is
known, 'Tom,' the actor, was a man of ability, but like his
father, thriftless, and, according to Boswell, had ' a Quixotic
mind.' This erratic personage, who was ruined by his own
extravagance, did little for himself, but, by his marriage
with Miss Chamberlane, he presented to the world Richard
Brinsley Sheridan, the dramatist. Tom's wife was, like him-self,
a neuropathic subject. Her father, the Rev. Mr.
Chamberlane, sank into imbecility and left behind him a
weakly, ailing family, who died in their prime. A son, the
Rev. Walter Chamberlane, was a poet, and was given to
'absent-mindedness,' with reference to which peculiarity
various anecdotes are told. The mother of Richard Brinsley
Sheridan was the eldest of this family. As a child she
had a paralytic affection which induced permanent lameness.
Gifted, or cursed, with a ' strangely sensitive temperament,'
she wrote verses, and a novel that had much success in its
own day. From a memoir by her granddaughter, Miss
Alicia Lefanu, it appears that Mrs. Sheridan was, all her life,
subject to ' fainting fits ' and ' absent-mindedness,' and that
she was 'often a sufferer from her health.' She died at
forty-two. The day before her death she became speechless,
probably from paralysis, but a post-mortem examination, it is

[1] Percy Fitzgerald : *Lives of the Sheridans.*

I

stated, revealed the presence of 'four internal maladies, each of which must have proved fatal.'

From the pathological point of view, the union of this nervous and suffering lady with the thriftless and eccentric Tom Sheridan could not but be disastrous. Richard Brinsley Sheridan was a dunce at school, and a weakly boy; but he had hardly attained to manhood before he launched out in the true Sheridan style. His thriftlessness and extravagance are well known. He abandoned himself to riotous living without a moral check of any kind. 'There was hardly a single person,' says Fitzgerald, 'with whom he had ever been intimate that he did not alienate or injure.' That he ran away with Miss Linley was the smallest of his moral offences. She became a most unhappy wife. Sheridan wore her out with his 'unreasonableness and unintelligible folly.' Within a few weeks of her death he married again, the victim on this occasion being a Miss Ogle, whom he won by love-letters copied from those previously addressed by him to Miss Linley. The second wife was as much to be pitied as the first. As he advanced in years Sheridan's vices became more and more intolerable. He drank to excess; his friends cut him dead; he became a *déclassé*, miserably poor, if not in absolute want; his debts were 'la mer à boire.' At the age of sixty-six he was seized with epileptic fits, in which he died. His genius was of the most unpainstaking kind. 'The Rivals' he dashed off in six weeks at the age of twenty-three; the 'School for Scandal,' his masterpiece, dates from his twenty-fifth year. With ordinary restraints his career would have been a brilliant and honoured one, but this was not a condition of his genius. If he ever had any moral compunctions as to anything, they were merely impulses of the moment, too ephemeral to pass into acts.

The Linley family, with whom Sheridan allied himself by marriage, appears to have been as unsound as his own. Mrs. Sheridan's father was a musician and composer, who became imbecile. His sons were 'a compound of musical gifts and eccentricity!' One of them, Thomas Linley, who was accidentally drowned at twenty-two, was a prodigy as a composer and violinist, and was declared by Mozart to be a true genius. The daughters, beautiful and fascinating, sang like nightingales. All the family died young, Mrs. Sheridan falling a victim to consumption. By his marriage with Miss Elizabeth Linley, Sheridan had several children, only one of whom, Tom, left descendants. Short-lived himself, for he died at forty-seven, the son appears to have had the good fortune to marry healthy blood in the person of Miss Callender, who saved the direct Sheridan line from extinction. The family born to this couple comprised the Hon. Mrs. Norton, and one of their grandchildren is the present Lord Dufferin. Throughout both the Sheridan and Linley stock nerve disorder and genius are found side by side.

The father of Samuel Taylor Coleridge, the Rev. John Coleridge, was eccentric and absent-minded, and died suddenly at sixty-one. Anecdotes illustrative of his peculiarities will be found in all the poet's biographies, and need not be repeated here. Coleridge's mother was an uneducated woman, simple in her habits, and long-lived. To the medical expert, eccentricity in life and sudden death —the latter being due almost invariably to apoplexy or failure of the heart's action—are eloquent indications of nerve disorder, and in the family of an individual so afflicted, morbid symptoms are naturally to be looked for. In the Coleridge family such symptoms are not wanting. The Rev. John Coleridge had three daughters by a first wife, and nine sons and one daughter by a second. Of the lives and deaths of the first family there is no record; the second, of which 'S. T. C.' was the youngest member, was certainly not robust. Five of the poet's elder brothers, and his only sister, were in their graves before he was twenty-one, and the history of the surviving members of the family, though meagre, is significant. Luke Coleridge, dying at twenty-four, left a son, William Hart Coleridge, afterwards Bishop of Barbadoes, who had to resign his see 'through ill-health' at forty-two, and who 'died suddenly' at fifty; while of the family of the poet's brother James, Hartley Nelson Coleridge died at forty-five of spinal paralysis, and a daughter, Mrs. Patteson, of a 'wasting illness.' The issue of James Coleridge possessed the necessary vigour to survive and even to become prolific; but another brother, the Rev. Edward, had no children by a first wife, and by a second had a son and daughter, who died childless; while a third brother, George, left a son, who died unmarried.

Upon Samuel Taylor Coleridge himself the family heritage of nervous instability appears to have descended in a specially aggravated form. As a child he was weakly, self-absorbed, and morbidly imaginative. In his fifth or sixth year, in consequence of some quarrel with a brother, he ran away from home and passed the whole night, a night of rain and storm, on a bleak hill side, where he was found at daybreak, numbed in every limb. The same kind of morbid impulse caused him afterwards to run away from college and enlist as a private soldier, and later still to betake himself to Malta for no intelligible reason, leaving his friends in ignorance of his fate, and his wife and children dependent upon charity. From his earliest years he was also extremely precocious. 'I never thought as a child,' he says, 'never had the language of a child.' By his eleventh year, according to his son and biographer, the Rev. Derwent Coleridge, he was 'already a poet, and yet more characteristically a metaphysician.' Coleridge's own account of the matter is that ' at a very premature age, even before my fifteenth year, I had bewildered myself in metaphysics and in theological controversy,' particularly with reference to ' fixed fate, free-will, and fore-knowledge absolute.' The poet's youth and early manhood were the only period of his life during which he enjoyed a truce from bodily and nervous ailments. This blessed interval, as he calls it, appears to have lasted some ten or twelve years. At the age of thirty his health was completely broken by gout, and bodily suffering drove him to the use of opium. He lived to be sixty-two, but the latter half of his life was a wreck. In personal appearance Coleridge was far from prepossessing. 'His whole figure and air,' says Carlyle, was ' flabby and irresolute, expressive of weakness under the possibility of strength.' He hung loosely upon his limbs, with knees bent, and in a stooping attitude. In walking he shuffled rather than stepped. Dorothy Wordsworth remarked that he had bad teeth, and De Quincey says he had in his later years a lateral curvature of the spine—

both indications of a scrofulous constitution. 'After death,' wrote his daughter Sara, 'his body was opened, according to his own earnest request. The causes of death were sufficiently manifest from the state of the vital parts, but that internal pain from which he suffered more or less during his whole life was not to be explained, or only by that which medical men call nervous sympathy.' It is a pity no record has been kept of the condition of the brain, where, possibly, the secret lay.

There is, however, another record open to us in the fate of Coleridge's offspring, where the morbid characteristics of genius are so clearly written, that he who runs may read. Coleridge married Sara Fricker, sister of Mrs. Southey. As Mrs. Southey became insane, and as another Fricker died of paralysis, it is obvious that the marriage was a most undesirable one in a physiological sense. Whether the Coleridge or the Fricker heredity was the more to be dreaded it is impossible to say; but the blend of the two proved singularly disastrous to Hartley Coleridge, the first-fruit of this ill-starred union, who with great gifts combined great vices, and under the load of both sank into an early grave. Hartley Coleridge was a poet with more than a dash of insanity in his composition. He was never quite responsible for his actions. As a child he was even more precocious than his father. At five years of age he was a deep thinker, and was already in an agony of doubt as to the reality of existence; while seated on somebody's knee he would pour forth the strangest metaphysical speculations and poetic inventions. Between fact and fiction he was apparently unable to discriminate. He imagined a cataract bursting forth in a field near his home and forming an island, in which a community grew up; and this region gradually attained in his mind the dimensions of a new continent, with a people and a system of government of its own. He called it Ejuxria. Derwent Coleridge, in his memoir of Hartley, says: 'The history and geography of Ejuxria were at one time as familiar to me, to say the least of it, as any other portion, I was about to say, of the habitable globe.' From Hartley's vivid description Derwent knew the generals and statesmen of Ejuxria by name; he witnessed the jar of faction, traced the course of sedition, saw changes of government and the growth of public opinion. In a word, Hartley's hallucinations had all the features of a living reality, and he was able to convey a similar impression of it to others. He grew 'angry and mortified' if the literal truth of his words was doubted. 'His usual mode of introducing the subject,' says his biographer, 'was, "Derwent," calling me by name (for these disclosures in later years were made to me alone), "I have had letters and papers from Ejuxria." Then came his budget of news with appropriate reflections, his words flowing on in an exhaustless stream, his countenance bearing witness to the inspiration—shall I call it?— by which he was agitated. Nothing could exceed the seriousness of his manner and, doubtless, of his feelings. He was, I am persuaded, entirely unconscious of invention.'[1] It would be difficult to find a more striking example of an insane hallucination than this conception, which possessed the mind of Hartley Coleridge for so many years. Nor was this the only figment of his brain. As a boy he was accustomed to spin to his companions endless romances embodying a great variety of personages, his language on such occasions being as vivid as it was flowing. 'His sensibility was intense, and he had not the wherewithal to control it. He was liable to paroxysms of rage, self-accusation, and other painful emotions, during which he bit his arm or finger violently.' In his fits of depression he had hallucinations of hearing. To his friend, Chauncey Hare Townshend, he said, with reference to his hypochondriacal tendencies, 'I have even heard a voice—not a creation of the fancy, but an audible and sensuous voice, foreboding evil to me.' Along with these manifestations of insanity Hartley Coleridge displayed intellectual and poetic powers of a high order, and he also had the physical energy required to turn them to account. His misfortune was that, in a still greater degree than his father, he was destitute of the power of self-control. He took to drinking, and led an irregular and spasmodic existence till his death, which occurred from an attack of bronchitis at fifty-two.

[1] Derwent Coleridge: *Memoir of Hartley Coleridge.*

The genius which cannot regulate itself is not very distinguishable from insanity. Hartley Coleridge's brain was always teeming with ideas. These appear to have found but incomplete expression in the poems which he threw off almost without effort. In repose 'his countenance was stern and thoughtful in the extreme, indicative of deep and passionate meditation, so much so as to be at times almost startling.' 'Judging from his note-books and miscellaneous papers, the quantity, variety, and quality of the thoughts which passed through his brain in his latter years,' says his brother, ' would surely have ranked him among the most copious and instructive, as well as delightful, writers of his age had he exerted his resolution or possessed the faculty of combining his materials on any considerable scale or on any given plan.' The vice of Hartley Coleridge's organisation betrayed itself in his stunted stature, which barely exceeded five feet, and in his prematurely aged gait and appearance; his hair was latterly quite white.

Sara, the only daughter of Samuel Taylor Coleridge, inherited a feeble constitution, and with it, not only some of her father's poetic genius, but also his fondness for metaphysical inquiry. There is a close analogy between her case and that of her brother Hartley. 'Nervous sensitiveness and morbid imaginativeness,' she remarks, 'set in with me early.' She fell into a 'wasting illness' and died at forty-nine. During the last ten years of her life she was 'unchangeably depressed.' She married her cousin Hartley Nelson Coleridge, another sufferer from the evil heritage of the Coleridge blood, whose death from spinal paralysis has already been noted. The son who was born of this fatal marriage, Herbert Coleridge, was afflicted with stammering, and died of consumption at thirty-one. Derwent Coleridge, Hartley's younger brother, inherited the longevity of his paternal grandmother, dying at eighty-three. In his case the neuropathic tendency of the family assumed the form of ' constant attacks of acute neuralgia.'

Very similar to that of Charles and Mary Lamb was the association of Wordsworth and his sister Dorothy, except that throughout his long life—he died at eighty-four—Wordsworth's intellect was never deranged. Evidence of the neuro-

pathic element in his composition is afforded by the history of
his family, and chiefly by the insanity of Dorothy Wordsworth,
WORDSWORTH who, like Mary Lamb, was poetical and in the
closest sympathy with her brother's pursuits.
Wordsworth's father was a man of 'great force of character'
—a phrase which occurs with remarkable frequency in the
family history of the insane. What it means precisely in the
present instance cannot be gathered from biographical records, but if no neurotic characteristics existed in the poet's
father, who died suddenly at forty-two, of what is said to have
been 'inflammation of the lungs,' there is an unmistakable unsoundness to be traced to his mother, who died at thirty-one
of consumption. Wordsworth attributed his mother's decline
to her having caught cold from being put to sleep in a friend's
'best bed-room;' but, as the consumptive taint subsequently
appeared in his own children, it probably existed in the family
before the incident of the bed-room occurred. De Quincey's
description of Dorothy Wordsworth testifies to the strain of
insanity in the Wordsworth blood: 'Her eyes were not soft,
nor were they fierce or bold; but they were wild and startling, and hurried in their motion. Her manner was warm
and even ardent; her sensibility seemed constitutionally
deep, and some subtle fire of impassioned intellect apparently
burned within her, which, being alternately pushed forward
into a conspicuous expression by the irresponsible instincts of
her temperament, and then immediately checked in obedience
to the decorum of her sex and age and her maidenly condition, gave to her whole demeanour and to her conversation
an air of embarrassment, and even of self-conflict, that was
almost distressing to witness. Even her very utterance and
enunciation often suffered in point of clearness and steadiness
from the agitation of her excessive organic sensibility. At
times the self counter-action and self-baffling of her feelings
caused her even to stammer, and so determinedly to stammer
that a stranger who should have seen her and quitted her in
that state of feeling would certainly have set her down for
one plagued with that infirmity of speech as distressingly as
Charles Lamb himself.' The same writer further remarks:
'Miss Wordsworth was too ardent and fiery to maintain the

reserve essential to dignity'—in short, she was 'the creature of impulse' with 'a self-consuming fire of thought.'

Dorothy Wordsworth's poetic nature found expression in many passages of her diary, and she also wrote verses of a high order of merit. Physically her energy was prodigious; she was accustomed to walk twenty or thirty miles a day. In her fiftieth year her intelligence began to give way, a severe illness so prostrating her in body and mind that, according to Principal Shairp, she 'never recovered from it.' Three years afterwards an attack of brain fever supervened, leaving ' her intellect painfully impaired and her bright nature permanently overclouded.' It was not, however, until she was fifty-six that, in Wordsworth's euphemistic phrase, his sister became ' a confirmed invalid.' Loss of memory was the earliest characteristic of her disease, and she gradually fell into imbecility, which continued till her death at eighty-six. In her benighted condition she was accustomed to repeat the favourite small poems of her brother, as well as a few of her own. What is still more remarkable, her faculty for poetic composition remained, several pieces composed during her state of mental darkness finding a place in her biography.[1] At least one other member of the Wordsworth family showed signs of the poetic temperament. Concerning the seafaring brother who went down with his ship off the Bill of Portland in 1804, Coleridge wrote on one occasion to Miss Wordsworth : ' Your brother John is one of you—a man who hath solitary usings of his own intellect, deep in feeling, with a subtle tact and swift instinct of true beauty.' Wordsworth himself says that his brother John became a ' silent poet,' and was known among those of his own craft as ' the philosopher.' In Wordsworth's offspring the neuropathic taint unmistakably appears. One of his children, Kate, had a stroke of paralysis at the age of four, her left side being disabled. Some months afterwards she was discovered in a speechless condition in bed and suffering from convulsions, in which she died. Wordsworth's favourite daughter Dora grew to womanhood, with a character which Sara Coleridge described as 'most peculiar— a compound of vehemence of feeling and gentleness, sharpness

[1] Edmund Lee: *Dorothy Wordsworth, the Story of a Sister's Love.*

and lovingness, which is not often seen;' and at forty-three she died of consumption.

　　Robert Burns believed that poets had a 'stronger imagination, more delicate sensibility, and a more ungovernable

BURNS set of passions' than other men. He spoke from experience; in the words above quoted he faithfully describes his own characteristics. But while he had something more, he had also something less than other men. His ballads notwithstanding, he had no aptitude for music. Both the poet and his brother Gilbert took lessons in music, but, says their teacher, ' Robert's ear in particular was remarkably dull; it was long before I could get them to distinguish one tune from another.'[1] Burns's mother lived to old age without any notable ailment. His father, however, died of consumption, and was distinguished in life, says the poet in one of his letters, ' for a headlong, ungovernable irascibility.' Here we have explanation enough of the nerve-disorder of the son. The poet, in a letter, says : ' My constitution and frame were *ab origine* blasted with a deep incurable taint of melancholia which poisons my existence.' As a young man, according to his brother Gilbert, he not only suffered from depression of spirits but ' was almost constantly afflicted in the evenings with a dull headache, which at an after period of his life was exchanged for a palpitation of the heart, and a threatening of fainting and suffocation in his bed in the night-time.' With reference to these ailments Lockhart observes : ' I have heard from an old acquaintance of the bard who often shared his bed with him at Mossgiel, that even at that early period, when intemperance had surely nothing to do with the matter, those ominous symptoms of radical disorder in the digestive system—the palpitation and suffocation of which Gilbert speaks—were so regularly his nocturnal visitants that it was his custom to have a great tub of cold water by his bedside into which he usually plunged more than once in the course of the night, thereby procuring instant, though short-lived relief.'[2] Like Edgar Allan Poe, Burns fell a victim to drunkenness, and although his death at thirty-seven was immediately due to cold—the result of a drinking bout—we may

[1] Currie's Memoir.　　　　　　　　[2] Lockhart : *Life of Burns.*

conclude with Lockhart that the 'irritable and nervous bodily constitution,' inherited from his father, together with the 'exhausting excitement of an intensely poetical temperament,' was incompatible with length of days. Burns's sensibility was extreme. Once in Edinburgh, in the presence of Walter Scott, then a boy, Burns was shown a print representing a soldier lying dead in the snow, with his dog sitting in misery beside him; and the simple picture so affected him that he shed tears. Scott, who relates the incident, further remembers that Burns's eye was large and dark, and that it glowed— 'literally glowed'—when its owner spoke with feeling or interest. There was one thing that Burns loved as passionately as poetry—woman. 'In love,' says his brother Gilbert, and the passion began with him at fifteen, 'the agitations of his mind and body exceeded anything of the kind I ever knew.' Gilbert lived to the age of sixty-seven, but a younger brother died early, and although the poet had four sons I am not aware that there are any descendants of his at the present day.

The family of Walter Scott, whose pathological history stands out clearly in his own autobiographical notes and in Lockhart's admirable life of him, was permeated by nerve disorder. Scott's paternal grandfather, a farmer ＳＣＯＴＴ and dealer, was 'extremely active, quick, keen, and fiery in his temper,' and he married a woman whose character is vaguely indicated by the fact that she had a brother described by Scott as a 'weak, silly man.' Of the children born to this couple, the one with whom we have more particularly to do, Scott's father, also named Walter, died in his seventieth year 'after a succession of paralytic attacks, under which mind as well as body had by degrees been laid quite prostrate.' Unlike his father, this Walter Scott, although a lawyer, was a man of much simplicity of character, and devout. He married Anne Rutherford, daughter of an eminent physician. This lady, the novelist's mother, died also of paralysis at an advanced age, losing suddenly the use of speech and of one side; her brother, Dr. Rutherford, died of gout in the stomach after showing a partial failure of memory; while her sister, from some unknown cause, 'expired suddenly without a groan and without suffering.' That a robust family could be born

to such a couple was, of course, an impossibility. They had
twelve children, of whom six perished in infancy, and, writing
fifty years later, Lockhart sorrowfully observed that of the
remaining six four had left no descendants.

Sir Walter had four brothers and one sister, concerning
whom he has left on record some interesting facts. The eldest
brother, Robert, was in the army. 'His temper,' says the
novelist, 'was bold and haughty, and to me was often
chequered with what I felt to be capricious tyranny. In other
respects I loved him much, for he had a strong turn for
literature, read poetry with taste and judgment, and composed verses himself which had gained him great applause
among his mess-mates. . . . In bad humour he kicked and
cuffed without mercy.' This brother died of paralysis. The
second, John Scott, was also in the army, and died a young man.
Anne Scott, the novelist's only sister, was of a delicate constitution and died at twenty-nine. 'Her temper,' he observes,
'like that of my brother, was peculiar, and in her, perhaps, it
showed more odd from the habits of indulgence which her
nervous illnesses had formed. But, at least, she was an affectionate girl, neither devoid of talent nor of feeling, though
living in an ideal world which she had formed to herself by
force of imagination.' Thomas, the third brother, emigrated
to Canada, where he had a son and two daughters, who do
not appear to have left descendants. In Sir Walter's youngest
brother, Daniel, the inevitable ne'er-do-well of the family,
who treads upon the heels of genius, crops up. With a
marked 'aversion to labour,' or, rather, 'indolence,' 'he had
neither the vivacity of intellect,' says Sir Walter, 'which
supplies the want of diligence, nor the pride which renders
the most detested labour better than dependence or contempt.
His career was as unfortunate as might be augured from this
unhappy combination, and after various unsuccessful attempts
to establish himself in life he died on his return from the
West Indies.' Concerning Daniel, Lockhart supplies some
further particulars. 'The story is, shortly,' says the biographer, 'that the adventurer's habits of dissipation proved
incurable, but he finally left Jamaica under a stigma, which
Sir Walter regarded with utter severity. Being employed

against a refractory or insurgent body of negroes, he had exhibited a lamentable deficiency of spirit and conduct. He returned to Scotland a dishonoured man, and though he found shelter and compassion from his mother, his brother would never see him again. Nay, when soon after, his health, shattered by absolute indulgence, gave way and he died as yet a young man, the poet refused either to attend his funeral or to wear mourning for him like the rest of the family.' Twenty years afterwards, however, Scott spoke to Lockhart in terms of great and painful contrition for the austerity with which he had conducted himself on that occasion. Like others of his class, the unfortunate young man was a victim to the law of heredity; science, recognising that his faults were those of an inherited organisation, does him the justice that his own family denied him.

The paralytic ailment of his parents declared itself in Scott's case in infancy. At the age of eighteen months he felt a sudden loss of power in his right leg, and for the remainder of his life he was lame. During youth and manhood his nerves appear to have been dormant, but both paralysis and apoplexy were the afflictions of his later years. At the age of fifty, the novelist, writing to a friend with reference to the work on which he was then engaged, says, ' Peveril will, I fear, smell of the apoplexy.' This letter, adds Lockhart, ' contains the first allusions to the species of malady that ultimately proved fatal to Sir Walter Scott. He, as far as I know, never mentioned to any one of his family the symptoms he here speaks of. But long before any serious apoplectic seizure occurred, it had been suspected by myself, and by others of his friends, that he had sustained slight attacks of that nature and concealed them.' Three years later, in his journal, Scott speaks of feeling ' a tremor of the head, the pulsations of which become painfully sensible, a disposition to causeless alarm, much lassitude, and decay of vigour and activity of intellect.' An odd optical delusion also occurred to him. ' I have of late,' he writes, ' been accustomed for the first time to the use of spectacles. Now, when I have laid them aside to step into a room dimly lighted out of the strong light which I use for writing, I have seen, or seemed to see, the rim of the same spectacles which I have left behind me. At first the impression was so lively that I put my hands to my eyes, believing that I had the actual spectacles on at the moment; but what I saw was only the *eidolon* or image of the said useful servants.' More alarming was the hallucination of sight which occurred to Scott on hearing of Byron's death. He thought, for a moment, that he saw the image of his deceased friend, but on examination it proved to be nothing but the folds of some drapery. It was while Scott was writing the 'Tales of a Grandfather,' at fifty-eight, that his first alarming stroke of paralysis occurred. It rendered him speechless for ten minutes, and thenceforward his letters continued to drop hints as to the imminence of a recurrence of that ailment or apoplexy. His gloomy anticipations were soon realised. Repeated shocks of paralysis weakened him to such an extent, that he sank into a state of mental torpor, and, apoplexy supervening, caused his death at sixty-one.

The curse that overhangs the family of the man of genius fell with its wonted severity upon the offspring of Scott. He had two sons and two daughters. The former died as young men, childless. The elder daughter, Anne, laboured, for years, under a ' miserably shattered ' constitution, looking and speaking like one ' taking the measure of an unmade grave,' and finally succumbed to brain fever. Sophia, the younger, who became Mrs. Lockhart, died, like her sister, in what ought to have been the prime of womanhood, after a long ' illness '—most probably consumption—' which she bore with meekness and fortitude.' Mrs. Lockhart left two children, Walter and Charlotte; the former died young, without issue, and Charlotte, who became Mrs. Hope, succeeded to Sir Walter's estate at Abbotsford, but of her three children only one, a daughter, survived the period of childhood. ' The poet's ambition to found a family,' says Lockhart, ' sleeps with him.'

No poet was ever born in more prosaic surroundings KEATS than Keats. His father was a stableman, his mother a livery-stable keeper's daughter. The elder Keats was killed by falling from a horse at the age of thirty-six, and nothing is known of his parentage; but there is evidence enough that the poet derived his constitution mainly from his mother. Prodigal in her tastes, passionately fond of amusement, and, at the same time, 'saturnine in disposition,' Mrs. Keats suffered from rheumatism, and died of consumption—a neuropathic subject to the tips of her fingers. As a child Keats was 'violent and ungovernable,' and manifested emotional extremes, being one moment convulsed with laughter and the next bathed in tears. He was dwarfish in figure, barely five feet high, but his passions were so strong that he had to calm his nerves with laudanum. Lord Houghton saw him once in a state of physical excitement so intense, that it 'might have appeared to those who did not know him to be one of fierce intoxication.' He had a 'swooning admiration' for Fanny Brawne, to whom he wrote passionate love letters. When out of this vein he was plunged in despondency. On one occasion he wrote: 'The world is too brutal to me; I am glad there is such a place as the grave—I am sure I shall never have any rest till I get there.' The prophecy was too true. During his short life Keats was 'almost delirious' at times with his mental and bodily sufferings, and his agitation under the attacks of the critics is said by Shelley to have resembled insanity. No organisation could have been more responsive than his to outward influences. 'The humming of a bee, the sight of a flower, the glitter of the sun,' it is said, 'made his nature tremble; then his eye flashed, his cheek glowed, and his mouth quivered.' He died at twenty-five, of consumption. The same disease carried off his brother Thomas in early manhood, but his sister Fanny attained the age of eighty-six. Both these members of the family were as undistinguished as their ancestry, among whom no biographer has discovered the smallest trace of eminence.

Moore lost his memory some years before his death, which occurred at seventy-two. All his family, daughters and sons, predeceased him—Anne at five (as the result of a Moore fall, though, had she lived, said the doctors, it could only have been as an 'invalid from the bad state of her inward parts'), Anastasia Mary at seventeen, Olivia in infancy,

John at nineteen ('his constitution,' according to Lord John
Russell, 'being too delicate to carry him on to manhood'),
and Thomas at twenty-seven. The last named, who was the
eldest son, belonged to the ne'er-do-well class. Lord John
Russell says he ' was not physically strong, and had little
restraint over himself; ' his wild and dissipated life terminated
in consumption.

'All biographies begin with genealogy,' says Bulwer
Lytton, 'and with reason, for many of the influences that
BULWER   sway the destiny that ends not with the grave, are
LYTTON   already formed before the mortal utters his first
wail in the cradle.'[1] There never was a truer word spoken,
though it may be doubted whether Bulwer Lytton, who was
proud of his ancestry, grasped its full import as regards himself. His maternal grandfather, Richard Warburton Lytton,
was eccentric. The unbalanced condition of his mind
revealed itself in an extraordinary capacity for acquiring
languages ancient and modern. He wrote a drama in
Hebrew, intending it for the stage. This work he afterwards
burned in despair because, as he told a friend, he could not
find Jews sufficiently versed in Hebrew to act it. The friend
pertinently observed, ' And if you did, where on earth would
you find an audience sufficiently versed in Hebrew to understand it ? ' The old scholar was extremely short-sighted,
mismanaged his affairs, quarrelled with and lived apart from
his wife, and died of an apoplectic seizure. His daughter,
the novelist's mother, had a shy, sensitive temper, great self-
will, and a passionate fondness for poetry. There was something morbid in the long estrangement she set between
herself and her distinguished son on account of his marriage.
On the paternal side of Bulwer Lytton's family there was
also a strong neuropathic strain. His father, Colonel Bulwer,
suffered from gout, of which he died suddenly. Two uncles
were ' eccentric.' Colonel Bulwer, with his ' powerful self-
willed nature,' appears to have merited the same description.
The marriage of which the novelist was born was an extremely ill-assorted one. ' At first,' says Bulwer Lytton,
' though my father's temper was of the roughest, yet he was

[1] *Life and Romains of Edward Bulwer, Lord Lytton.* By his Son.

very much in love, and love has a good-humour of its own. But gradually the temper rose superior to the love, and gout, to which from early youth my father had been occasionally subjected, now fixed upon premature and almost habitual residence. He bore pain with the fierce impatience common to the strong when they suffer, and it exasperated all the passions which, even in health and happiness, that powerful and fiery organisation could but imperfectly control.' The mother's constitution, always delicate, also began to give way; her nerves were shattered, and 'to the dejected mind was added the enfeebled frame.' It was in her darkest hour that Bulwer Lytton was born. As a child he was weakly and delicate, and for some reason—no doubt a morbid caprice—his father always regarded him with a special aversion. At school the future author had a reputation for precocity and cleverness, and composed verses. He was only nine years of age when his master wrote to Mrs. Bulwer: ' Your son has exhausted all I can teach him. His energy is extraordinary. He has a vital power which demands a large field. He has it in him to become a very remarkable man.'

Exuberant natures with a morbid tinge are subject to strong reactions. In early manhood Bulwer Lytton's disposition took ' a morbid and even a dangerous inclination.' He had frequent ' fits of great melancholy and dejection,' and these moods were followed by impatient cravings for excitement. From the restlessness due to his great physical activity he sought relief in smoking, and all his works from the age of twenty-two were composed under the soothing influence of tobacco. At the same time his irritability was sometimes such as to render him 'absolutely unapproachable.' Although never robust, he had a devouring energy for work, and even in his early married days so incessantly was he occupied, that his wife seldom saw him for five minutes till two or three in the morning. A nervous pain in the ear caused him great suffering, and long before he was thirty his sensitiveness had become so morbidly acute that, to a visitor, he ' seemed like a man who had been flayed and was sore all over.' Ordinary worries were, to his exasperated brain, like friction to highly inflamed flesh. Hence the miseries and scandal of his married life.　The brutality of his father as a husband appears to have been far surpassed by his own. His outbursts of temper were such, that on one occasion he kicked his wife while she was near her confinement, and on another, ' springing upon her like a tiger, made his teeth meet in her left cheek.'[1]　Concerning the ear-ache above referred to, Lord Lytton writes of his father : ' To frequent and severe recurrence of that pain he was subject till middle age, and his public and social life was greatly affected by the deafness it induced.　When he was about forty, an abscess revealed itself in the ear from which he had thus suffered ever since the age of sixteen. He was then told by the aurists that any attempt to stop the discharge from the abscess might prove fatal.　In his seventieth year, after an exceedingly painful and prolonged attack of ear-ache, the discharge stopped of its own accord, and a few days after, he was dead.'

The characteristics of Macaulay were great physical activity, which expended itself in walking exercise, a mental

Macaulay vehemence and self-confidence to match, and a prodigious memory.　An uncle, Colin Macaulay, was a remarkable linguist, and Zachary Macaulay, father of the historian, devoted his life to the suppression of the slave trade with a zeal little short of fanaticism, a mental quality which, as I have elsewhere shown, is closely associated with nerve disorder.　Macaulay was a wonder-child, remembering without effort all that he read.　This faculty never deserted him.　He knew ' Paradise Lost ' and the ' Pilgrim's Progress ' by heart.　Poems read through once he could recall forty years afterwards without the omission of a single word ; the contents of a single page he could take in at a glance.　' To the last,' says his biographer,[2] ' he could read books more quickly than other people skimmed them, and skimmed them as fast as anyone else could turn the leaves.'　From the age of fifty he suffered from confirmed asthma, and at fifty-nine he died from stoppage of the heart's action.

The Brontë sisters were consumptive, deriving their unsound constitution from a father who was dangerously

<hr>

[1] *Life of Lady Rosina Lytton : a Vindication.*
[2] G. O. Trevelyan : *Life of Macaulay.*

'eccentric.' Himself a writer and versifier, the Rev. Patrick Brontë was tyrannical to his children, and was accustomed to carry about with him a loaded pistol, which he fired off in moments of temper. Another mania of his was always to dine alone; and his habits were otherwise solitary and peculiar. As in the case of George III., his insanity entailed early blindness. All the children born to this unamiable cleric were short-lived but strangely gifted. A daughter, who died at eleven, was, before her death, able to discuss the political questions of the day. The three sisters Charlotte, Emily, and Anne Brontë, who have rendered the family famous, were much alike in constitution, and all showed poetical and imaginative talent of a high order. Charlotte suffered from nerves and depression, her biographer, Mrs. Gaskell, noting the similarity of her brooding tendencies to Cowper's. On one occasion she had an hallucination of hearing, a voice seeming to recite to her some unknown lines of poetry. She was extremely weak-sighted, and suffered severely from neuralgia and sleeplessness. She died at thirty-nine, of consumption. A few years before her death she married, but left no children. Emily and Anne, consumptive also, died at thirty and twenty-nine, the latter suffering from asthma as well. In their brother, Bramwell Brontë, we have another example of the ne'er-do-well who dogs the footsteps of genius. Bramwell had a talent both for poetry and painting, but he was deeply tainted with vicious habits, took opium, drank to excess, and had repeated attacks of *delirium tremens*. The sisters were deeply distressed at his 'frantic folly,' and regarded him as 'hopeless.' This, indeed, he proved to be, losing all his situations through vice or culpable negligence. He died at thirty-one of consumption. All the members of the family were as undersized as they were precocious and clever. The same remark applies to Maria Edgeworth, who, like Charlotte Brontë, suffered from weak eyes and was the daughter of an eccentric father.

Charles Dickens was a 'puny, sickly boy, subject to attacks of violent spasm, which disabled him for any active exertion.' He outgrew his feebleness, however, and as a young man showed extraordinary vivacity

and force of character. In early manhood he had nothing to
complain of physically beyond 'a little weakness now and
then and a slight nervousness.' As he advanced in years he
became restless and irritable. His married life was 'a dismal
failure.' Neuralgic pains interfered with his work, and he
suffered from sleeplessness. Ultimately both gout and in-
cipient paralysis attacked him. In his fifty-sixth year he wrote
to a friend : 'My weakness and deadness are all on the left
side, and if I don't look at anything I try to touch with the
left hand I don't know where it is. Last Sunday I found
myself extremely giddy, and extremely uncertain of my sense
of touch both in the left leg and the left hand and arm.'
In the following year Sir Thomas Watson reported upon
Dickens's condition in the following terms : 'After unusual
irritability he found himself giddy with a tendency to go
backward and to turn round. Afterwards, desiring to put
something on a small table, he pushed it and the table forward
undesignedly. He had some odd feeling of insecurity about
the left leg, as if there was something unnatural about his
heel, but he could lift and he did not drag his leg. Also he
spoke of some strangeness of the left hand and arm ; he
missed the spot on which he wished to lay that hand unless
he carefully looked at it, and he felt an unreadiness to lift
his hands towards his head, especially the left hand, when,
for instance, he was brushing his hair. . . The state thus
described showed plainly that Charles Dickens had been on
the brink of an attack of paralysis of his left side, and possibly
of apoplexy.' Dickens also mentioned to his medical adviser
that he sometimes lost or misused a word, and that he forgot
names and numbers. Meanwhile he suffered from repeated
attacks of gout. At fifty-eight he died from effusion of
blood upon the brain. Forster, from whom these particulars
are derived,[1] is strangely reticent about the novelist's parentage
and connections, but the elder Dickens appears to have been
a thriftless man, and the existence of the ne'er-do-well member
of the family is admitted, though the details of the case are,
as usual. hushed up. The ne'er-do-well was Dickens's brother
Frederick, to whom, on his death, the novelist thus alluded :

[1] Forster : *Life of Charles Dickens.*

'It was a wasted life, but God forbid that we should be hard upon it, or upon anything else in this world that is not deliberately and coldly wrong.'

Both of George Eliot's parents appear to have contributed to her peculiar organisation, her father being a 'man of extraordinary determination of character,' and her mother 'a woman with an unusual amount of natural force,' but of an ailing habit. In childhood the novelist suffered from a 'low general state of health and great susceptibility to terror at night;' and, according to her biographer,[1] the liability to have 'all her soul become a quivering fear' remained with her through life. At school she showed great aptitude for English composition and music, and as an example of her sensitiveness it is related that after playing she would go and throw herself down in a flood of tears. Fits of depression beset her in womanhood, and from her thirtieth year she was a martyr to headaches. In her diaries and correspondence occur such jottings as the following: 1849 (at the age of thirty), 'terrible headaches;' 1850, 'lost whole weeks from headache, system shattered;' 1852, 'pity me! I have had headache for four days incessantly;' 1853, 'a crop of very large headaches, rheumatism in the right arm;' 1854, 'I have got into a labyrinth of headaches and palpitations.' In her latter years some disorder of the kidneys manifested itself, but the immediate cause of her death was a cold. A sister of George Eliot's married a surgeon and lived a homely life; and a brother was content to be, like his father, a land agent.

Sydney Smith's father was eccentric to the point of insanity. 'He was a man of considerable ability, endowed with great force of character and a keen sense of humour, but his disposition was selfish and his temper capricious; he was impulsive in his movements and arrogant in manner. He seems to have had a mania for doing rash and unaccountable things.'[2] One of these unaccountable things was to leave his newly-wedded wife at the church door and rush off to America, returning to her

---

[1] J. W. Cross: *Life of George Eliot.*
[2] Stuart J. Reid: *Life of Sydney Smith.*

only after he had spent some years in random excursions up and down the world. He lived to be eighty-eight. Sydney Smith's three brothers were, like himself, remarkably precocious, though, unlike him, they died comparatively early. One became an Indian judge and an ' Oriental scholar,' having a great facility for acquiring languages. Sydney Smith had gout and heart disease. His eldest son at twenty-four succumbed to a ' long and painful illness.'

Another great humorist, Thomas Hood, belonged to a consumptive family. An elder brother, James, was thought

HOOD to be the more promising youth. James was artistic, fond of literature, and a good linguist. He died, however, at an early age, a victim to consumption, which also carried off his mother and two sisters. Thomas Hood's life was one of much physical suffering ; he had rheumatism, breast spasms, heart disease, a disordered liver, and other complications, of which he died at forty-six.

De Quincey's father had a long period of ill-health, and died at thirty-nine. His mother's religious prepossessions

DE led her to a ' gloomy narrowness and austerity.' QUINCEY The famous opium-eater was himself of stunted growth, being barely 5 feet 3 inches high, was shortsighted, and took to opium as a relief from neuralgia and general nervous irritability. He had great aptitude for languages, being able to talk Greek fluently at fifteen, was fond of music, slovenly in his dress, and cared nothing for money, which he was all his life incapable of handling. In his later years he was subject to great vicissitudes of temperament and spirits, being frequently depressed and physically torpid, which condition, however, was not incompatible with a ' frightful recurrence of long ago imagery and veriest trifles of the past.' A brother, William, who died at sixteen, was a boy of ' remarkable character and energy, incessantly writing and inventing.' Consumption appeared among the members of De Quincey's family.

Thackeray died suddenly at fifty-two. He looked well

THACKERAY and strong enough to have lived twenty years longer, but for the last fourteen years of his life he was continually ailing and was subject to certain painful spasms, which were probably the immediate cause of his death.[1] His father, an Indian Civil Servant, also died suddenly.

All his life Wilkie Collins was a sufferer from his nerves, to calm which he was accustomed to take laudanum in immense doses. His head was mis-shapen. On the WILKIE right side there was a congenital swelling, and he COLLINS was accustomed to say that Nature, in his case, had been a bad artist, having depicted his forehead 'all out of drawing.' He had gout and was otherwise in bad health for many years. The beginning of his last illness, which came when he was sixty-five, was a stroke of paralysis. Wilkie Collins's paternal grandmother died in a fit after prolonged suffering from 'infirmities of body and mind.' His father was William Collins, the Royal Academician, who died of heart disease, and there was also a faculty for painting in his mother's family.

Although he attained the age of seventy-seven, Robert Browning had a curiously weak heart. Robert Buchanan writes of him : 'More than once at a time when he was in his prime, it was impossible to find at BROWNING his wrist any pulsation whatever, or a pulsation so slow and apparently feeble as to be scarcely noticeable.' In his latter years the poet also suffered from asthma. There is some obscurity about Browning's descent, but his father, although engaged in commerce, possessed the significant gift of verse-writing. In boyhood, Browning showed some disposition to be a painter. Elizabeth Barrett Browning, his wife and a poetess, was always weak and ailing, and died of a 'decline.' By Sarah Coleridge she was described as a 'little hard-featured woman, with long dark ringlets, a pale face, and a plaintive voice.'

In Balzac there was a converging heredity of nerve disorder. His maternal grandfather died of apoplexy, and his mother is described as a woman of 'great BALZAC vivacity of mind, untiring activity, and extra-ordinary firmness'—phrases which, in the circumstances, are of some significance to the pathologist. On the father's

[1] Anthony Trollope : *Life of Thackeray.*

side there was a pronounced strain of insanity. The elder Balzac was an *avocat* at Tours, 'where,' says his daughter, who has published the novelist's correspondence, 'his originality was proverbial, and manifested itself both in word and deed.' Although perfectly well in body, he took it into his head one day to lie in bed, and this he did continuously for twenty years thereafter, receiving his friends meanwhile, and even taking a part in public affairs. To everybody's surprise he got up one morning at half-past four, dressed himself—for he had always had his clothes kept in readiness—and went about his business as if nothing had happened. Among other peculiarities the elder Balzac had an extraordinary memory. This faculty the novelist inherited along with a feeble constitution. At school Balzac had an epileptic seizure, which so alarmed his teachers that they urged his parents to take him home. The illness was to them inexplicable, because he could not be accused of over-studying, being, in fact, a 'dull scholar.' Balzac does not seem to have had a return of this malady, which his sister, in her biography, curiously attributes to a 'sort of congestion of ideas;' for, although he cut a poor figure in the class at school, he was, it appears, an omnivorous reader. The weakness of his constitution finally assumed the form of hypertrophy of the heart—a disease which predisposes to congestion of the brain. Of this affection of the heart he died at fifty-one, leaving no offspring.

Balzac's literary energy was enormous. He owned to 'two immense desires—to be celebrated and to be loved'—and both of these he realised by dint of brain force alone; for physically he was the most insignificant of men, being barely five feet high. He was absorbed in his characters, and for weeks and sometimes months at a time he would not only disappear entirely from view, but all trace of him would be lost. At such times it was his whim to live in some garret under an assumed name—a proceeding not always necessitated by his pecuniary means. On one occasion he presented a play to the manager of the Odéon—for he dabbled for a time in dramatic authorship, though for the most part unsuccessfully. 'Where shall I apprize you of the rehearsals? What is your address?' inquired the manager. Balzac, being then in one of his eccentric moods, flatly refused the information. Ultimately it was agreed that a messenger should be sent every morning to a spot in the Champs Élysées where, 'underneath the twentieth tree from the Arc de l'Etoile on the left,' he would see a man pretending to look for a bird. To this man he would proffer a certain password, and on receiving the due reply he would hand him the message from the theatre. Passwords were a favourite device with Balzac; it was his custom to exact them even from the most intimate friends who called to see him when his abode happened to be known. Letters he received under such whimsical names as the Widow Durand. The same species of eccentricity he imported into his methods of work. His usual hours of sleep were from six in the evening until midnight. Then he would bathe, don the white robe of a Dominican friar, pose a black skull cap on his head, and, under the influence of coffee and by the light of a dozen candles, would work incessantly till he could work no more—from twelve to twenty hours at a stretch. His work was done mainly on proof sheets, the original ' copy ' of even his longest novels being at the most an outline, dashed off in a few nights of feverish anxiety. To no other member of Balzac's family was the gift of a creative imagination vouchsafed. One sister, who outlived him, published nothing but a meagre and colourless sketch of his life ; another died young ; and his only brother Henri was a ne'er-do-well, who sought his fortune abroad and failed to find it.

The father of Alfred de Musset died of gout. He was a man of ' stern and decided character.' A cousin of the poet on the same side committed suicide. His mother's family appears also to have been characterised by some nervous instability, his maternal grandfather having a prodigious memory, which enabled him at an advanced age to recite whole comedies by heart. With these credentials of a vicious heredity, Alfred de Musset started early upon a career of dissipation. He had the three weaknesses proverbially associated in all languages—women, wine, and play.

The first he developed almost in boyhood, conceiving a passionate attachment for a young cousin; at eighteen he regularly drank more than was good for him, and was a confirmed gambler. 'At the same time,' says his brother, who has written his life, 'he had an incredible activity of mind. Often he would write as many as fifty verses on leaving some late supper.' His gaiety alternated with fits of depression, in which it was his whim to don an old and ragged suit of clothes. In Italy, where he suffered one of his keenest *chagrins d'amour*, he had an attack of brain fever, and the disorder of his nerves for some time after was such that he could not speak of his troubles without falling into syncope. On one occasion a disposition to commit suicide appears to have been checked by the chance circumstance of his receiving an invitation from Rachel, the actress, to spend some days with her alone.

While recovering from an illness induced by his excesses he had some strangely vivid hallucinations, testifying to the morbid sensibility of his brain. Four little genii, with wings, seemed to him to be rearranging the articles on his work-table : bottles and other objects marched to and fro of their own accord. After the genii had put matters, as they seemed to think, in the state in which he had left them, the poet exclaimed, 'That is not right; there was some dust here and there.' Instantly there appeared a little man about three inches high carrying on his back a vessel of some sort with a tap, which he turned, and from which flowed a jet of fine dust as he walked, speedily bringing about the desired condition of things on the table. This vision was so forcible to De Musset, at the moment, that he had to question his brother who was present in order to distinguish real from imaginary objects, and while it was in progress he analysed his sensations precisely as if he had had a genuine spectacle before him. Symptoms of heart disease manifested themselves in De Musset soon after his thirtieth year. He also suffered terribly from sleeplessness, and had frequent attacks of syncope. Under these combined evils he died at forty-seven. George Sand, in her volume 'Elle et Lui,' describes a strange scene with Alfred de Musset in the

Forest of Fontainebleau, where the poet's visions, cries of despair, ecstatic joy, and nervous terror betrayed a nervous sensibility bordering upon absolute delirium. Some time before his death he was so worn with passion and debauchery that, according to Maxime du Camp, a lady who had come to admire the man of genius was moved to exclaim as he passed out of the room—the wreck of his former self—'Pauvre garçon!'

From about his twenty-third year Gustave Flaubert was an epileptic, and his nervous attacks rendered him morose and unsociable during the remainder of his life. Previous to his paroxysms he was accustomed to say that he had 'a flame' first in one eye then in the other, and that everything appeared to him under a yellow hue. This he called his golden vision. For months at a time, in dread of an attack, he would not go out of doors. A year or two before the malady set in, Flaubert's intelligence and intellectual power were observed to develop enormously, and Maxime du Camp believes that it was during this exceptional period that the future chief of the realistic school of novelists laid in his stock of observation.[1] Afterwards Flaubert's memory became fitful; he lapsed into a dreamy, indolent state which could not be shaken off without an effort, and he was at times so petulant and irritable that a trifle upset him. 'I have seen him,' says his friend and biographer, 'run about the room uttering cries because his penknife did not happen to be in its ordinary place.' Maxime du Camp naïvely observes that, but for his nervous malady, the author of 'Madame Bovary' would have taken a higher place in literature than he did. Readers of these pages will hardly be of this opinion. Without his malady and its clarifying effect upon the brain, Flaubert would probably have been an *avocat* at Rouen—the position to which he was destined by his father. It was in one of his convulsive attacks that he died at the age of fifty-nine. In his youth he had an admirable physique, being tall, broad-shouldered, ruddy, and blond. As a law student in Paris he was full of energy and enthusiasm

---

[1] Maxime du Camp: *Souvenirs Littéraires.*

for literature; but he had no passion for the fair sex, to whom, indeed, throughout his life he appears to have cherished an absolute repugnance. Like most neuropathic subjects, Flaubert was accustomed to pass rapidly from a state of exaltation to one of dejection without apparent cause. He was a most laborious writer, the question of style and literary form pre-occupying his mind incessantly to a degree that was positively painful to himself. The novelist's father was a medical man of 'remarkable energy and force of character;' a sister died from an attack of puerperal mania.

The exuberant imagination of Alexandre Dumas the elder is generally thought to have been derived from the negro blood in his veins. There is no physiological ground for such a supposition. Mulattos and quadroons—it was to the latter class that Dumas belonged—are not uncommon, but they are by no means distinguished for imaginative power. The germ of the great romancer's genius is to be traced rather to the eccentricity of his grandfather, a French noble, who at fifty suddenly sold his ancestral estates and exiled himself to the West Indies, where almost immediately he married a full-blooded negress of San Domingo. The existence of a legal contract in this case has been questioned; but there can be no doubt that the same ancestor, on returning to France twenty years later, after the death of his black consort, committed at the age of seventy-four a similar *mésalliance* in marrying his housekeeper. The San Domingo negress had an only son, who was subsequently known as General Dumas. This dashing soldier, the novelist's father, was celebrated for his courage and his enormous physical strength. It was said that he could crush a horse to death between his legs. He had a vehement temper and a want of restraint which ultimately brought him into disgrace with Napoleon. About this time he was also physically disabled for service by an apoplectic seizure, which destroyed or impaired his hearing. In retirement his constitution was further weakened by a troublesome disease, which would appear to have been gout, and of this he died at forty-four.

Shortly before his death General Dumas had married

a young woman, by whom he left in his turn an only
son, the author of ' Monte Cristo.' The alliance was
physiologically unsound, for Madame Dumas, the novelist's
mother, was subject to epileptic fits—she had one which
attracted public attention at the performance of her son's
first play at the Théâtre Français—and she died of apoplexy.
In the aggressive, vainglorious, extravagant, and even ridiculous life of Alexandre Dumas there is evidence of a want
of mental balance apart from his great creative faculty. In
his latter years he became imbecile, and, unfortunately, he did
not lay down his pen until he had partly ruined his great
reputation. In his sixty-eighth year, whilst being removed
from Paris on the eve of the siege, he was ' quite helpless
and almost unconscious of what was going on about him,'
and in the same state of darkness a few months later his
brilliant and romantic care r came to a close. Alexandre
Dumas' one son and namesake, the author of ' La Dame aux
Camélias,' presents the rare example of genius passing in a
direct form from parent to child.

Goethe's mother died of apoplexy, and the nervous unsoundness of her constitution revealed itself in the great
mortality of her offspring. Three of the poet's GOETHE
brothers and one sister died in childhood. Another
sister Cornélie lived to be twenty-seven, when she suddenly
expired from no known cause. Goethe's mother, writing of
the event, says, ' the flash and the stroke were one.' Cornélie
is described by Goethe in his autobiography as an ' incomprehensible being, with wonderfully brilliant eyes, while the
lineaments of her face, neither striking nor beautiful, indicated a character which was not and could not be at union
with itself.' Goethe had on one occasion a visual hallucination of a remarkable kind. He saw a spectral figure of
himself on horseback.[1] At all times he possessed a curious
faculty of visualisation, which is intimately associated with
hallucinations of sight. ' When I closed my eyes and depressed my head,' he observes, ' I could cause the image of
a flower to appear in the middle of the field of vision ; this

---

[1] Goethe : *Aus meinem Leben*, etc.

flower did not for a moment retain its first form, but unfolded itself, and developed from its interior new flowers, formed and coloured, or sometimes green leaves. These were not natural flowers, but of fantastic form, although symmetrical as the rosettes of sculpture. I was unable to fix any one form, but the development of new flowers continued as long as I desired it without any variation in the rapidity of the changes. The same thing occurred when I figured to myself a variegated disc. The coloured figures upon it underwent constant changes, which extended progressively from the centre towards the periphery, exactly like the changes in the kaleidoscope.'

Positive insanity is to be found in the family of Victor Hugo. This affliction befel the poet's elder brother Eugène, who died at thirty-seven in a lunatic asylum, where he was confined for many years. As a child Eugène Hugo was described by his mother as being *vif comme la poudre*; he had poetical tastes, and achieved some distinction at school for his effusions in verse. The first outbreak of his insanity occurred at Victor Hugo's marriage, the eccentricity which had for some time been growing upon him suddenly changing into an abiding incoherency of speech and action. Apparently the malady was inherited from the paternal side. Judging from his memoirs, General Hugo, the poet's father, possessed obstinacy and other angularities of character amounting to eccentricity. He fell into disgrace with his military superiors, separated from his wife, and passed his declining years in profuse scribbling—biography, fiction, and drama pouring forth from his restless pen. Victor Hugo's mother, for her part, had also some peculiarities, being, in particular, energetic and sensitive, with a pronounced taste for Voltaire's tragedies, of which, as a girl, she learnt long tirades by heart. As a woman she had indifferent health, and her death was sudden. If she did not contribute to, she probably did not correct, the eccentricity transmitted by the poet's father.

Victor Hugo's own angularities of character were sufficiently pronounced, although, unlike those of his brother Eugène, they appear to have kept within the bounds of reason. Concerning Eugène, there is a significant passage in one of the biographies of Victor Hugo. 'The two brothers, so intimately associated, appeared to have been destined for the same existence ; they had the same amusements, the same masters, the same poetical aspirations, the same restless activity ; they had never left each other a moment until the death of their mother. Suddenly Fate separated them, and threw the one into the dazzling light and turmoil of fame, the other into gloom and isolation.'[1] Of Victor Hugo's children, Charles, the eldest, and the translator of Shakespeare, died suddenly and mysteriously in the house of his mistress ; François fell a victim to consumption ; Adèle is confined in a lunatic asylum. The condition of the last-named is deplorable, and presents so eloquent a testimony to the evils that genius carries in its train that I cannot refrain from quoting the description given of her malady by a friend to whom I have applied for information on the subject :—' Adèle has passed her life in asylums, and since the death of Victor Hugo has been confined in a private institution at Suresnes. There she will probably remain till her death. She is not violent, but idiotic, putting sand and pebbles in her mouth instead of food. Victor Hugo was in the habit of seeing her at regular intervals, but the spectacle became too painful to him, and for some years before his death he had ceased his visits.' A grandson of Victor Hugo, George Hugo, has recently been placed in ' perpetual tutelage ' as being unfit to manage his affairs. A grand-daughter is described as ' flighty ' (*étourdie*).

Homer is reputed to have been blind. Sophocles was accused by his sons of being unable to manage his affairs. Molière was epileptic, and left a daughter who was childless. Voltaire had apoplectic attacks. Montesquieu became blind, and Lesage deaf. Bossuet suffered from fits, in which he lost the power of speech and hearing. Madame de Staël was eccentric and addicted to opium, and at her death was found to have a peculiar conformation of the skull. Dante, whose reputed skull exhibits an abnormal development of

---

[1] *Victor Hugo ; Raconté par un Témoin de sa Vie.*

the left side and two swellings of the frontal bone,[1] died suddenly, and his family became extinct in the second or third generation. Petrarch's constitution at sixty-four was 'entirely worn out;' he had several paralytic seizures and died of apoplexy. La Bruyère at fifty became suddenly deaf, and soon afterwards died of apoplexy. There was a marked strain of literary ability in Corneille's family, his brother Thomas and his nephew Fontenelle both achieving distinction. Racine's father died at twenty-eight, and his mother at twenty-nine. He was of an irritable and sensitive temperament, and, after a somewhat dissipated youth, became excessively pious. Ben Jonson had hallucinations, and died of paralysis. Dryden was gouty and deaf. Pope was deformed, deriving his rickety constitution apparently from his father, who expired 'without a groan.' The mother of the poet Savage was insane. Rogers's memory decayed to such an extent that he was accustomed to ask his servants whether he knew persons whose names he heard. Richardson died of apoplexy after suffering during the latter part of his life from 'nervous attacks.' Fielding's constitution was shattered by gout at forty, and he had a son paralysed. Henry Kirke White—like Chatterton a marvellous boy—was epileptic and died of consumption. Porson, the 'Greek scholar,' had a stupendous memory and great physical activity, combined with an irresistible craving for stimulants. Niebuhr, who lost both parents when a child, was constitutionally feeble. Gibbon was deformed. De Foe had an attack of apoplexy about his fiftieth year, suffered from gout and stone, and died at seventy 'in a lethargy.' Heine became paralysed at forty-seven. Schiller's father died of gout. The poet himself had a delicate frame, suffered from weak eyes, and passed through a melancholic period during which he was suspected of insanity.[2] He died at forty-seven, and a post-mortem examination showed that his lungs and most of the important organs of his body were seriously impaired. Hallam, the son of an over-anxious mother, belonged to a family in which there was great mortality, his own children dying

---

[1] Lombroso.   [2] Palleske.

in the prime of life. Gérard de Nerval, long intermittently insane, hanged himself to a lamp-post. Théophile Gautier died of paralysis. Prévost Paradol shot himself, following the example of his father, who committed suicide in the same manner.

CHAPTER VI

NEUROPATHIC ASPECTS OF SHAKESPEARE'S LIFE—EXTRAORDINARY MOR-
TALITY OF HIS BROTHERS AND SISTERS—CHARACTER OF HIS FATHER
AND MOTHER—CONJECTURES RESPECTING GILBERT, RICHARD, AND
EDMUND SHAKESPEARE—THE CIRCUMSTANCES OF SHAKESPEARE'S
RETIREMENT—NEW INTERPRETATION OF THE KNOWN FACTS OF HIS
DEATH—THE SIGNATURES TO HIS WILL AS EVIDENCE OF A PARA-
LYTIC ATTACK—UNFITNESS OF HIS OFFSPRING—PROOF OF PARALYSIS
IN HIS GRAND-DAUGHTER

IN any attempt to explain the conditions of genius it is impossible to avoid a reference to Shakespeare. A theory of
genius which did not accord with the ascertained facts in the
life of the greatest poet that the world has seen would
assuredly be unworthy of confidence. I purpose, therefore,
dealing with Shakespeare from the pathological point of view,
a task which, despite the immensely painstaking and far-
reaching character of modern research, is now undertaken
for the first time. Formidable, indeed, are the difficulties in
the way, the known events of Shakespeare's career and of his
family history being meagre in the extreme. Towards the
close of last century Steevens gave the substance of a
biography of Shakespeare in the following words:—'All
that is known with any degree of certainty concerning
Shakespeare is that he was born at Stratford-on-Avon,
married, and had children there, went to London, where he
became an actor, wrote poems and plays, returned to Stratford, made his will, died, and was buried.' If to this sum-
mary are added a few dates and a little contemporary history,
the whole authentic record of Shakespeare's life stands revealed. The only phrase in his actual handwriting that has
come down to us consists of the words ' by me,' prefacing one
of the three signatures to his will, and the one passage from
his pen in which he speaks *in propriâ personâ*, that is to say,

neither as a dramatist nor as a poet, but as a man, is the
fulsome dedication of ‘ Venus and Adonis’ to the Earl of
Southampton.   No biographer can piece together the scattered
fragments of the poet’s life without the aid of conjectures
and hypothetical interpretations for which there is little or
no warrant, and no exception can be made in this respect of
the works of Halliwell-Phillipps and Karl Elze,[1] in which the
latest results of Shakespearean research are embodied.

Still, there are facts in the poet’s life, which although
long known, acquire in the light of the present investigation
a new significance, and these I will briefly set before the
reader.   The first circumstances calling for attention are the
extraordinary mortality of Shakespeare’s brothers and sisters,
and his own comparatively early death.   The poet was one
of a family of eight, of whom only his sister Joan attained old
age.   Here is the testimony of the official register :—

Joan	baptized	1558	} died in infancy.		
Margaret	„	1562			
William	„	1564	died 1616	aged	52.
Gilbert	„	1566	„ 1611–12	„	46.
Joan	„	1569	„ 1616	„	77.
Anne	„	1571	„ 1579	„	8.
Richard	„	1573–4	„ 1612–13	„	39.
Edmund	„	1580	„ 1607	„	27.

Clearly this is not a healthy stock, the average life of
its members, with all the advantage of the second Joan’s
patriarchal age, being less than thirty-two years.   What
then becomes of the sententious remark of Halliwell-Phillipps,
that it is ‘ not very likely that a woman unendowed with an
exceptionally healthy and vigorous frame could have been
the parent of a Shakespeare ?’[2] This is quite in the customary
vein of biography, in which it is assumed, often in flagrant
contradiction to the facts, that the man of genius is necessarily
a fine animal.

The general unfitness of Shakespeare’s family for the
battle of life would, in all probability, be explained by the

---

[1] Halliwell-Phillipps : *Outlines of the Life of Shakespeare.* Sixth edition,
1886.   Karl Elze : *William Shakespeare : A Literary Biography.* London,
1888.

[2] *Outlines*, p. 28.

physical condition of their parents and ancestors, could a record of this be found; but unfortunately on this subject a Cimmerian darkness prevails. Nothing is known of John Shakespeare and Mary Arden, the poet's immediate progenitors, except that the former died in 1601 after a reverse of fortune, and the latter in 1608. These dates indicate for both parents a tolerably good age, but, judging by the mortality of their offspring, neither can have been normally sound. Joan's extremely long life as a member of a generally short-lived family is precisely what might be expected from such neuropathic conditions as determined the early death of Keats and his brothers, whilst enabling their sister Fanny to exceed the age of four score. As has been shown in a preceding chapter, an established inequality in the nervous system may signify either a depression or an exaltation of the vital forces, with a short or a long life accordingly. Through Joan alone, by her marriage with William Hart, the hatter, was the Shakespeare blood transmitted beyond the third generation.

No trustworthy indication can be found of John Shakespeare's character. With his wife he obtained a considerable amount of property, and as a successful tradesman of some sort he became one of the magnates of the Stratford Corporation. About five and twenty years before his death, however, the prosperity of the family began to decline, and in the year 1586 John Shakespeare's affairs were desperate. From this position he appears to have been latterly rescued by his distinguished son. The probability is that his health broke about fifty, and that from that period he led a rather shiftless existence. Of Mary Arden all that can be gathered is that she was her father's favourite daughter; at all events, he seems to have so regarded her in his will, made when he was 'sick in body.' The expression 'sick in body' rather implies that Robert Arden's illness was a lingering one, and his special provision for Mary, his youngest daughter, may have been a token of gratitude for her nursing. Although Robert Arden was a well-to-do farmer, it is gratuitous to assume, as Halliwell-Phillipps does, that because one of her sons was Shakespeare, Mary Arden possessed a 'romantic tempera-

ment' and the 'highest form of subjective refinement.' Such
assumptions the principles of heredity do not justify. It is
the besetting sin of the biographer in this, as in so many
cases, to recognise the law of heredity only to misapply it.
Farm life in Mary Arden's day was rude in the extreme. She
probably worked in the fields, ate her food with her fingers,
washed herself once a week in a pail, and slept at night on
the floor on sacks or straw. Among Robert Arden's effects,
as disposed of by will, there was only one bed.

Shakespeare's three brothers, Gilbert, Richard, and
Edmund, can have possessed none of their brother's ability.
They were probably weak and ailing men. They are not
known to have married; if they did marry they can have left
no descendants, seeing that while the poet, in his will, makes
bequests to the children of his sister Joan, there is no mention
of other nephews or nieces. There is evidence that Gilbert
was a haberdasher by trade; he is so described in a bail bond
where he became surety to a clockmaker of Stratford for the
sum of 19*l.*, but he does not appear to have been in business
for himself. His signature is extant, and is that of a neat
though not a fluent penman. According to the rules of
graphology it denotes a man of a methodical and parsimonious
turn, melancholic, destitute of vanity, and rather feeble in
resolution. The signature of Thomas Quiney, the poet's son-
in-law, on the other hand, would be interpreted as that of a
person who thought a great deal of himself, and who was at
once very attentive to his dress and appearance and fond of
display in other ways. I give this evidence for what it may
be worth.

Graphology contains no doubt a substratum of truth,
though it may not yield results as definite as those its votaries
claim for it. It is well known that insanity betrays itself
occasionally in the handling of the pen, and scientifically I
should expect that any depression or exaltation of the motor
centres for the wrist and the fingers, or of the associated
visual or auditory centres of the brain, would affect the character of the handwriting in respect of its neatness or sloven-
liness, its simplicity or its exuberance. No one accepting
the rules of graphology could say that Gilbert's handwriting

was that of a man of a lively or sanguine disposition. Its
'finals' are stunted, it is bare of all 'flourish,' the cross-stroke
of the 't' is very small; over or through the last syllable of
the surname there is a curious line which, beginning thick,
tapers to a point, and the signature shows a general tendency
to droop.

Of Richard Shakespeare, nothing is known beyond the
dates of his baptism and funeral at Stratford. The youngest
brother Edmund died in London, where he was a 'player.'
His age, twenty-seven, is a fatal one for those who have inherited the seeds of decline or consumption; and if I may
add my guess to the many others that have been made
concerning Shakespeare's family, consumption was the disease he probably died of. On the other hand, the greater
ages of Gilbert and Richard point to a more lingering
form of nerve-disorder. In 1693 Dowdall was told by the
parish clerk of Stratford that 'Shakespeare was the best of
his family'—a phrase implying that the poet's brothers were
not much respected in their native town. Can Richard have
been the ne'er-do-well who so often figures in the family of
men of genius? There is no evidence that he ever left
Stratford. Gilbert, who was enterprising enough to go to
London, appears to have been the more responsible and
trustworthy of the two brothers, inasmuch as he was entrusted
by William with the carrying out of an important legal
transaction on his behalf in 1602.

It has been doubted whether the Gilbert Shakespeare,
whose funeral is recorded as taking place at Stratford on
February 3, 1611–12, was the poet's brother. The precise
description is 'Gilbertus Shakespeare, adolescens.' The
'adolescens' is a curious word to apply to a man of forty-
six. Can it be the parish clerk's Latin for bachelor? Or
does it signify that a son of Gilbert's was then buried?
Shakespeare mentions no brothers in his will, and the natural
inference is that they were then all dead. On the other
hand, there is a tradition favouring the supposition that
Gilbert did not die in 1611–12. 'One of Shakespeare's
younger brothers,' says Oldys, who wrote about a hundred
years later, 'would, in his younger days, come to London to

visit his brother Will, as he called him, and be a spectator of him as an actor in some of his own plays. This custom, as his brother's fame enlarged and his dramatic entertainments grew the greatest support of our principal if not of all our theatres, he continued, it seems, so long after his brother's death as even to the latter end of his own life. The curiosity at this time of the most noted actors to learn something from him of his brother was great. They justly held him in the highest veneration, and it may well be believed, as there was besides a kinsman and descendant of the family who was then a celebrated actor among them, this opportunity made them greedily inquisitive into every little circumstance, more especially in his dramatic character, which his brother could relate of him. But he, it seems, was so stricken in years, and possibly his memory so weakened with infirmities which might make him pass the easier for a man of weak intellect, that he could give them but little light into their inquiries, and all that could be collected from him of his brother Will in that station was the faint, general, and almost lost ideas he had of having once seen him act a part in one of his own comedies, wherein being to personate a decrepit old man he wore a long beard, and appeared so weak and drooping and unable to walk that he was forced to be supported and carried by another person to a table at which he was seated among some company who were eating, and one of whom sang a song.'[1] If Gilbert Shakespeare did not die at the time specified, apparently he became of weak intellect.

The cause of Shakespeare's death—a matter of some importance to the present inquiry—has been the subject of much ingenious speculation. There is, however, a point of view from which it has never yet been considered. I refer to the peculiar character of the signatures the poet affixed to his will on his death bed. Examined in the light of medical experience, and taken in conjunction with the manifest unsoundness of the Shakespeare family, and notably with a remarkable failure of memory on the poet's part in the drawing up of his will, these signatures appear to me to be

[1] *Outlines*, etc. The part referred to is that of Adam in 'As You Like It.'

very significant, and to establish almost beyond a doubt the nature of Shakespeare's last illness. Concerning this illness, the only substantial report we possess is an entry in the diary of the Rev. John Ward of Stratford, made in the year 1663 in the following terms:—'Shakespeare, Drayton, and Ben Jonson had a merry meeting, and itt seems drank too hard, for Shakespeare died of a feavour there contracted.'

As there is no fever properly so-called which can be contracted by drinking, the reverend diarist's charitable assumption is clearly of no medical value. So much has been generally recognised. It is surprising, however, that while such a conscientious authority as Halliwell-Phillipps seeks to palliate or condone the drinking, he should un-hesitatingly accept the hypothesis of the fever, which stands upon a much less valid basis, and that he should furthermore strain and distort the indubitable circumstances of the case in order to make out that the particular kind of fever of which Shakespeare died was that arising from insanitary conditions, namely typhus or typhoid. This theory being the one now generally accepted both in England and Germany (where Elze has followed the English biographer's lead), it may be worth while to show in a few words why it is not scientifically acceptable. On January 25, 1616, a draft of Shakespeare's will was prepared under the direction of a lawyer named Collins, and was left in the rough, apparently for some emendation, the testator being then in legal phrase in 'perfect health and memory.' Halliwell-Phillipps thinks these words ought to be accepted literally, and not as a legal formula, but there is a curious proof in the body of the document that whatever Shakespeare's bodily health at the time may have been, his memory was by no means perfect; for, in ordering bequests to be made to his nephews, the children of Joan, he was unable to recollect the name of the second boy, Thomas. The provision runs thus: —'Item, I give and bequeath unto her (Joan's) three sons, William Hart, —— Hart, and Michael Hart five pounds apiece,' etc.

That is to say, the testator's memory failed him when he

wished to name his nephew Thomas, whom he was doubtless
in the habit of seeing every day, and the lawyer accordingly
left a blank in his draft. This is a striking circumstance,
and one that may help to explain various other omissions
and irregularities in the will so freely commented upon by
the biographers. However, Shakespeare was clearly in no
anxiety about his health at this time, for the draft of the
will was left untouched for two whole months, during which
time the marriage of the poet's daughter Judith with Thomas
Quiney took place.

Suddenly, in the latter part of the month of March, the
household at New Place was plunged into a state of alarm.
Shakespeare was thought to be dying. The draft of the
will was brought to his bedside, and there it was signed in
its rough state with a few verbal alterations made on the
spur of the moment. The word January was struck out of
the date, and the word March written in, while the day of
the month, the 25th, was allowed to stand. It is clear,
therefore, that on or immediately before March 25, 1616,
Shakespeare had an attack of something which was thought
to be eminently dangerous—so much so that no time was
lost in getting the will signed in its draft form, although
the preparation of a clean copy would only have been the
matter of an hour or two. But Shakespeare did not die the
day the will was signed. He lived for four weeks and a
day, his death occurring on April 23 ! This is not the
course of typhus fever, the third or fourth week of which
from the beginning is usually the fatal period. Nor are the
early symptoms of that disease of the alarming character
which would have induced a methodical lawyer to have a
draft will signed *talis qualis*. The business was so hurriedly
carried through that the blank space left for Thomas Hart's
Christian name was not filled up, but may still be inspected
by the curious at Somerset House.

In order to support the theory of fever as the result of
the insanitary condition of Stratford, Halliwell-Phillipps
assumes that in the will ' the alteration of the day of the
month was overlooked,' as, otherwise, ' there would be at
least a singular and improbable coincidence.' Why should

the coincidence be so singular and improbable? The 25th of March was a Monday, and the 25th of January a Friday. That because the draft of a will is made on a Friday the testator should not fall ill on a subsequent Monday, which happens also to be the 25th day of a month, is surely a strong, not to say unwarrantable assumption. Coincidence must extend to greater lengths than that before it can be rejected on its own demerits. 'It is probable,' adds the biographer, 'that the melancholy gathering at New Place happened somewhat later than the 25th of March, the fourth week being generally the most fatal period of typhus fever. We may, at all events, safely assume that if death resulted from such a cause on April the 23rd the seizure could not have occurred much before the end of the preceding month.' Thus, because the Rev. John Ward enters in his diary a bit of foolish, and possibly malicious gossip, concerning Shakespeare's death forty years after the event, and uses the word 'fever,' which was then applied to almost every complaint of an unknown character, a theory of the poet's last illness is constructed requiring for its acceptance the falsification of serious and authentic documentary evidence!

If this is the most plausible theory of Shakespeare's death that finds currency at the present day, it cannot be wrong to suggest another more in harmony with the facts. First, let us glance at the pathological circumstances of the case, as illustrated by the law of heredity, which no biographer of the poet has yet invoked. We have seen that Shakespeare's brothers and sisters, with one exception, exhibit the conditions of a strongly neuropathic family, unfit to live a life of the normal span, or to engender healthy descendants. Three sisters die in childhood, one brother in early manhood, and two others in what ought to be the prime of life, or, assuming Oldys's narrative to be well founded, one of these brothers passes into a state of imbecility. They none of them leave descendants. Joan, alone, by virtue of an exceptional organisation, has children approaching the ordinary standard of fitness, and even in her case, as the pedigree of the Hart family shows,[1] the Shakespeare blood has a hard

[1] French: *Shakespearana Genealogica.*

struggle to survive. Of the Harts in the first generation there are three sons and a daughter, namely, William, an actor, and probably the kinsman of the poet referred to by Oldys, dying at thirty-nine, Thomas at fifty-six, Mary at four, and Michael at ten. Thomas alone has children by his marriage with a woman of whom nothing is known except that her name was Margaret, and that she died twenty-one years after her husband, namely in 1682. Almost immediately the advantages of this infusion of presumably healthy blood into the Shakespeare stock begin to be seen. George, a grandson of Joan, attains the age of sixty-six, and has the good fortune to select in his turn a long-lived and presumably healthy wife, by whom he has a numerous and healthy family, descending lineally to the present generation. The last known survivor was a George Hart of Birmingham, who emigrated to Australia in 1864. In the third generation of Harts the death of one of its members, Shakespeare Hart, a plumber, is recorded at the advanced age of eighty-one. Judging from the prolific character of the Harts—for old age alone is no criterion of soundness—healthy conditions appear by this time to be restored to the family, but as health comes in at the door genius flies out by the window. Throughout their nine recorded generations the Harts are a family of utter mediocrities, plying the humblest callings, and for the most part miserably poor. Of the female descendants of Joan Shakespeare nothing is known; they intermarried with men of common names and common position, and are hopelessly lost in the seething ocean of humanity.

The few personal references to Shakespeare that have come down to us from Ben Jonson and others throw little light upon his physical condition. He appears to have been genial and well liked, and he was familiarly called 'Will' by his associates. Hypochondria, therefore, was clearly not one of his characteristics, at all events in his early days, as it probably was of his brother Gilbert. Further than this contemporary evidence does not go. That Shakespeare's health broke down, however, at forty-eight, or thereabouts —about the same period as his father's—may be inferred

from the curious fact that although in March 1612–13 he
purchases a dwelling-house in Blackfriars, he, about the
close of the same year, makes up his mind to retire definitely
to Stratford, where his apparently gloomy forebodings are
so far fulfilled that in little more than three years he is dead.
There is no evidence, moreover, that after his forty-eighth
year he wrote a single line of play or poem.   Now, without
ill-health is it likely that Shakespeare in the height of his
reputation, and in the flower of his age, would withdraw
from the literary pleasures of London and break with his
congenial associates in order to bury himself in a dull, unattractive town like Stratford ?   It is variously surmised
that his withdrawal to Stratford did not necessarily cut off
his connection with London society, and that he wished to
live the life of a country gentleman.   In view of the difficulties and hardships of travelling in those days the first
supposition can hardly hold good ; the second gains some
plausibility from the terms of his will, which betrays his
ambition to found a family upon the principle of entail, but,
without some overpowering physical cause the *cacoethes scri-
bendi* of the born poet is not in the ordinary course of things
to be suppressed at forty-eight.

The ' merry meeting ' with Drayton and Ben Jonson
probably took place about February 10, when Shakespeare's
daughter, Judith, was married to Thomas Quiney.   It is
extremely unlikely on any medical hypothesis that it could
be the cause of the poet's death, two months and a half later.
What the facts really point to is this—that shortly after the
merry meeting Shakespeare had an illness of some sort,
attributed by the gossips to his drinking bout, but not of a
sufficiently serious character to raise any question of the will,
and that on March 25 the attack was suddenly renewed in
such a grave form that his death was thought to be imminent.   On the face of it, this illness looks like successive
shocks of nerve disorder—the first slight, the second serious
and so shattering that death ensued in a month, the interval
being in all probability marked by further attacks and
periods of unconsciousness.   On this assumption the partial

loss of memory alluded to in connection with the drawing up
of the will becomes remarkably significant, such an infirmity being the almost invariable precursor of paralysis or
apoplexy.

There remains the evidence of Shakespeare's death-bed
signatures, which, so far as I know, have not hitherto been
critically examined from the medical point of view. The
will is written on three sheets of paper, on each of which the
testator's signature appears. On the first sheet the name is
almost illegible; it is written at the left-hand bottom corner,
where the paper is partially worn away, and it cannot now
be reproduced without a considerable amount of touching up.
Malone and Steevens have doubted whether it is Shakespeare's
handwriting at all. On this point I offer no opinion. Two
clear and undoubted signatures remain, and they are sufficient for my purpose. Here they are in fac-simile, reproduced from the original document in the archives of Somerset
House :—

Shakespeare's condition when he penned these signatures
must have been one of extreme nervous agitation. Brought
to death's door from fever, he might from physical exhaustion
have written in this fashion. But he was not at death's
door; he had four weeks longer to live, and the conclusion
is forced upon us that his ailment was a prostration of the
nervous system. What was the nature of this prostration ?
' In the precursory stage of disease of the brain,' says Forbes
Winslow, ' a tremulous state of the muscular fibre is occasionally observed. In one remarkable case, for nearly a fort-

night previously to any acute head symptoms, the patient was observed to have a tremulous state of the hand. He appeared at the time otherwise in good health. This condition of the muscles was succeeded by violent paroxysmal attacks of headache, causing the patient to scream from the intensity of the pain. He subsequently died paralytic. A post-mortem examination revealed a malignant tumour in the substance of the brain.' In another case the muscular tremor which attacked the patient's mouth and tongue was followed by a violent epileptic convulsion. He had a succession of epileptic fits at varying intervals for a period of twelve months, when his mind became deranged, and in this state he died two years after the first epileptic seizure. Forbes Winslow has observed this state of tremulousness in several cases of acute and chronic softening of the brain, as well as in general paralysis.

The circumstances of Shakespeare's death would accord with a paralytic or epileptic seizure of the kind here referred to. There is also something to be said in favour of *paralysis agitans*, or 'shaking palsy.' Parkinson thus describes this ailment, upon which he is the chief authority: 'The first symptoms perceived are a slight sense of weakness, with proneness to trembling in some particular part, sometimes in the head, but most commonly in one of the hands and arms.' The evil gradually extends until the patient 'seldom experiences any suspension of the agitation of his limbs,' but temporary relief is obtained in any particular limb 'by suddenly changing the posture.' After this the disease may become more vehement, until a fatal result ensues. The progress of 'shaking palsy' seems rather too slow to account for such an attack as that which brought the lawyer with the draft copy of the will to Shakespeare's bedside. On the other hand, while we know on the authority of the players that the poet in his prime wrote with such ease, that they 'scarce received from him a blot'—that is, scarcely a correction—'in his papers,' there is evidence of a considerable unsteadiness in his hand three years before the fatal seizure. In 1612–13—and in the very month of March—he signed documents relating to the purchase of the property in Black-

friars. Appended is a fac-simile of his signature on that
occasion :—

William Shakespeare (signature facsimile)

This is not a firm hand ; it has the cramped air which might
result from the writer's attempt to suppress a palsied tremor.
Thomas Carlyle had 'shaking palsy,' and the following signature of his, traced while he was suffering from that ailment, may be compared with Shakespeare's :—

Thomas Carlyle (Chelsea, 1865) (signature facsimile)

On the whole, it appears tolerably certain that in his latter
days Shakespeare was a victim to nerve disorder.

That the poet shared to some extent the physical disability of his brothers is the natural inference to be drawn
from the fate of his direct descendants. His only son
Hamnet died in his twelfth year. His daughter Judith had
three sons, who, however, all died early—(1), Shakespeare
Quiney at one year; (2), Richard at twenty-one ; and (3),
Thomas at eighteen. Susannah had one daughter, Elizabeth,
who was twice married, but by both husbands was childless.
Thus vanished the poet's dream of founding a family ; the
careful provisions of his will, which he imagined would affect
generations to come, became null and void in less than a lifetime. There may, of course, have been some taint in the
family of Anne Hathaway, the mother of Shakespeare's
children, also in the Quiney and Hall blood. The supposition is not borne out, however, by such facts as are known.
The Hathaways appear to have been a prolific family ; and
although they are strangely overlooked in Shakespeare's will
(with the exception of Anne, who received his 'second best
bedstead'), they are remembered many years afterwards in
the will of his granddaughter. Thomas Quiney, again, is

known to have been alive about the age of sixty-seven, and, what is more important, to have had numerous nephews and nieces. Finally, Dr. Hall died at sixty, not of a lingering illness apparently, but of some infectious disease, for he was hastily buried the day after. It is true that, according to his 'Select Observations,' he was afflicted a few years before with a slight delirium; but as this affection appears to have been cured by 'a pigeon cut open alive' and applied to his feet to 'draw down the vapours,' it can hardly have been serious.

There is hardly sufficient ground for the conjecture put forth in some quarters that Shakespeare was lame. The principal evidence in favour of it occurs in Sonnet XXXVII., where the poet thus speaks of himself:—

> As a decrepit father takes delight
> To see his active child do deeds of youth,
> So I, *made lame* by fortune's dearest spite,
> Take all my comfort of thy worth and truth.

Is this metaphorical, or is it put forward as a statement of fact? Scott has adopted the latter supposition in 'Kenilworth,' where Shakespeare is playfully alluded to as a 'halting fellow.' Elze thinks it would be an 'exceedingly strange coincidence' if Shakespeare had to be classed with Scott and Byron as a 'third lame poet.' On that score, however, no reader of the present volume is likely to share his opinion. At the same time, no contemporary allusion to Shakespeare's lameness has been discovered, while by Aubrey and others he is spoken of as a man of good parts and 'good shape.' Yet this is not conclusive, for Byron, despite his lameness, was accounted a handsome man, at all events, by the Countess Guiccioli. It has also to be considered that Shakespeare, as an actor, had curious limitations, suggestive of some physical infirmity. He appears to have been employed on the stage chiefly to represent old men, such as Knowell in 'Every Man in his Humour,' when he was still young, and Adam in 'As You Like It.' He is further believed to have played the ghost in 'Hamlet,' for the embodiment of which, of course, in the dim light of the scene a little lameness would not disqualify him. The testimony as to Shakespeare's physical infirmity, however, is altogether more curious than convincing. I give it merely for the sake of completeness; it is in no sense required to sustain the theory of genius as a form of nerve disorder.

Quite in accordance with this theory is the fact that Shakespeare's surviving daughters, the eldest of whom lived to be sixty-six, and the younger seventy-seven, appear to have been very ordinary, not to say poor, specimens of womankind. Both were virtually illiterate. Judith, who made her mark on the register of her marriage, must have been either very plain, or of an unamiable disposition. At the time of her marriage she was thirty-two, and her husband, Thomas Quiney, a vintner, was not only her junior by four years, but was not of good family, or particularly well-to-do. This would imply either that Judith was capricious in her rejection of previous offers of marriage, or that, despite her father being a man of means, no acceptable offers were made to her. Moreover, according to Halliwell-Phillipps, 'there was some reason for accelerating the nuptials' between the parties, for they were married without a licence, an irregularity for which a few weeks afterwards they were fined and threatened with excommunication by the ecclesiastical court at Worcester. Susannah made a better match. Dr. Hall, whom she married in her twenty-fifth year, was a man of good social standing; and, unlike her sister, Mrs. Hall was able to append her name to the marriage register. She also obtained a favourable epitaph, in which it was recorded in the conventional language of tombstone flattery that she was 'witty above her sex.' Unfortunately, this is all that can be told to her credit. Dr. Hall at his death left some interesting manuscripts for the press. So far from his widow setting any store upon these, however, she sold them in a heap to one James Cooke, from whose account of the transaction it appears that she did not even recognise her husband's handwriting, or trouble to make herself acquainted with what he had written. It is small wonder that such daughters should have preserved none of their father's books or papers.

To the fortuitous circumstance of Cooke's purchase in
1642 we owe an invaluable piece of information, tending to
establish the neuropathic condition of Shakespeare's family.
The manuscript notes of Dr. Hall, published in 1657, consist
of reports of cases of illness attended by the writer from the
year 1617 downwards. Had they begun but a year earlier,
they must have told us something of Shakespeare's illness
and death. As it is, they record that the poet's daughter,
Susannah, had attacks of ' scurvy,' also ' miserable pain in
her joints, so that she could not lie in her bed, insomuch as
when any one helped she cried out miserably '—the disease
being evidently rheumatism or gout. Furthermore, Elizabeth Hall, the poet's grandchild and last descendant, is
shown to have suffered from paralysis. ' At the close of the
year 1624 Elizabeth, my daughter,' says Dr. Hall, ' was
vexed with *tortura oris*, or convulsion of the mouth. At the
same time she suffered from inflammation of the eyes. She
was cured by January 5, 1624–5, but in the beginning of
April she went to London, and returning homewards the
22nd of the said month, she took cold, and fell into the said
distemper on the contrary side of the face ; before it was on
the left side, now on the right, and although she was grievously afflicted with it, yet by the blessing of God she was
cured in sixteen days. In the same year, May 24,' adds Dr.
Hall, ' she was afflicted with an erratic fever ; sometimes she
was hot by the sweating, again cold, all in the space of half
an hour, and thus she was vex't oft in a day.'[1] It is a
remarkable proof of the indifference which has hitherto been
shown to the pathological aspect of genius that Halliwell-
Phillipps, who in his ' Outlines ' collected, as he imagined,
every available scrap of information bearing upon Shakespeare, should have neglected the all-important evidence of
Dr. Hall's Medical Case Book.

<hr>

[1] *Select Observations on English Bodies : or Cures both Emperical and
Historicall performed upon very eminent Persons in Desperate Diseases.
First written in Latine by Mr. John Hall, Physician, living at Stratford-
upon-Avon, in Warwickshire, where he was very famous, as also in the
Counties adjacent. . . . Now put in English for common benefit by James
Cooke, Practitioner in Physick and Chirurgery. London, 1657.*

CHAPTER VII

THE MUSICAL AND ARTISTIC FACULTIES ALLIED TO INSANITY—EX-
AMPLES IN BACH, HANDEL, MOZART, BEETHOVEN, AND MENDELS-
SOHN—ABSOLUTE INSANITY OF DONIZETTI AND SCHUMANN—NERVE
DISORDER AMONG THE OLD MASTERS—MICHAEL ANGELO ECCENTRIC
—REYNOLDS'S BLINDNESS AND DEAFNESS—FLAXMAN DEFORMED—
THE INSANITY OF ROMNEY, COSWAY, HAYDON, AND LANDSEER—
TURNER'S CONDITION IDIOTIC—NEUROPATHIC CHARACTER OF THE
ACTOR'S GENIUS—EXAMPLES IN EDMUND KEAN, JUNIUS BRUTUS
BOOTH AND RACHEL

PATHOLOGICALLY speaking, music is as fatal a gift to its
possessor as the faculty for poetry or letters; the biographies
of all the greatest musicians being a miserable chronicle
of the ravages of nerve-disorder, extending, like the Mosaic
curse, to the third and fourth generation. The genealogy
of the Bach family has been traced for a period
of over 200 years. The founder of the family was
a baker named Veit Bach, who, in the sixteenth century,
settled in Saxe-Gotha. He played the guitar, and taught
music to his two sons. From these sprang numerous descendants, who not only cultivated music, but made it their
means of livelihood, filling a number of official posts as
organists or town musicians in Germany. Many of them,
of course, were mediocrities, but one or two Bachs in every
generation gained at least some local distinction. At first
sight the growth of this highly musical family, which
numbered at one time about 200 members, might be taken
to prove the feasibility of producing by means of heredity a
specially gifted race of men. If they did not marry in and
in, the male Bachs, in many cases, chose musical wives, and
music seemed with them to run in the blood. On a closer
examination of the family history, however, the prospects of

a successful breeding of musical geniuses on the system adopted with Derby winners and prize oxen, not only diminish, but become reduced to the vanishing point. Of the great majority of the Bachs little or nothing is known beyond the dates of their births and deaths. Yet the meagreness of the record does not disguise the growing ravages of nerve-disorder in their midst, the evil culminating at the point where the musical genius of the family is at its greatest, namely in the person of Sebastian Bach.

One of the grandsons of old Veit Bach was blind, as well as eccentric enough to be the subject of many strange stories; other Bachs appear to have been addicted to drunkenness, and Spitta, the historian of the family, makes a regretful allusion to the sickness and general misery with which the several generations of Bachs had to contend.[1] Christopher Bach, grandfather of Sebastian, died at forty-eight; he was a court musician, and his wife, herself the daughter of a musician, died the same year. Of his three sons, two were twins, John Ambrosius and John Christopher, born evidently of the same ovum, seeing that they had exactly the same temperament, suffered from the same disorders, and were so remarkably alike that even their wives could not distinguish them except by their clothes. Moreover, they died within two years of each other, and about the same early age as their father, whose feeble constitution they no doubt inherited. A sister of theirs, the aunt consequently of Sebastian, was an idiot.[2] John Christopher had a sickly family, some of whom suffered from weakness of the eyes. It was John Ambrosius, however, who became the father of the most illustrious member of the family in whom, observes Spitta, 'the genius

[1] Spitta: *Life of John Sebastian Bach.*

[2] At the burial of this hapless girl, whose life may be said to have been sacrificed on the altar of genius, the officiating clergyman preached from the text, 'For unto whomsoever much is given of him shall much be required,' and pointed out the strange distribution of human wealth and talents, saying:—'Our sister, who now rests in the Lord, was a simple creature, not knowing her right hand from her left; she was like a child. If, on the contrary, we look at her brothers, we find them gifted with a good understanding, and with an art and skill which make them respected and listened to in the schools and in all the township, so that through them the Master's work is praised.'

of the Bachs, after having diffused itself more or less widely through whole generations, culminated and exhausted itself.'

In Sebastian Bach the fatal inheritance of nerve-disorder first betrayed itself by short-sightedness in his youth. At sixty-five he became totally blind; a year later he was stricken with apoplexy, from which he died. Strange to say, ten days before his death, his sight was suddenly restored, from which it may be concluded that his blindness arose, not from a defect of the retina or a decay of the optic nerves, but from some disturbance of the visual centre of the brain, which the apoplexy temporarily corrected. Sebastian Bach was twice married, and had no fewer than twenty children. One of these was an idiot boy, who was thought for a time to have 'great genius.' Four other sons were musically gifted. With the whole family nerve-disorder played havoc. The eldest and most gifted son, Wilhelm Friedemann, was a man of obstinate and sombre disposition—more than half insane. He was said to be 'unable to adapt his style to circumstances.' During many years he depended for existence on the bounty of his friends, and died in extreme misery. Only a few of Bach's twenty children survived him, most of them indeed dying in childhood. One alone left issue, and with the death of Sebastian's solitary grandson, Wilhelm, court musician at Berlin, in 1846, the family of the great composer became extinct—a melancholy example of the unfitness of genius to perpetuate itself, or even to hold its own in the battle of life.

That a direct inheritance of musical gifts is essential to the constitution of musical genius is disproved by the case of Handel, whose family was of the respectable burgher stamp, and wholly unconnected with art. Handel's *HANDEL* musical bent in childhood was indeed sternly repressed by his parents. Yet he contrived to overcome all the obstacles in his path, and by the age of eight or nine was a composer. The mental constitution which carried with it the gift of music, he appears to have derived from his mother, who was subject to paralytic seizures, in one of which she lost her sight. About the age of fifty Handel was himself struck down with paralysis, which so seriously unhinged his mind

that for over a year he had to live in retirement.[1] The
effects of the malady are still to be seen in his changed
handwriting; in dating one of his compositions, moreover,
he makes the mistake of a whole year. It was a few years
after this period that the ' Messiah ' was given to the world.
Handel was always impetuous and choleric, and his nerves
were too irritable to endure the sound of tuning, so that the
musicians who performed in his orchestra were careful to
tune their instruments before his arrival. Like his mother,
he lost his eyesight, and during the last few years of his long
life—he died at seventy-five—was totally blind. Although
well grown and distinguished in appearance, he never married, and it is noteworthy that, despite his musical ear, he
never acquired a command of English, but spoke a jargon
compounded of German, English, French, and Italian.
Handel's mother had three other children, of whom only one,
a daughter, left issue, and of the five members of the second
generation it was again one daughter alone who transmitted
the Handel blood, which had thus a hard struggle to survive.
None of these members of the family gave any proof of the
possession of artistic gifts, so that among his relatives Handel,
as a musician, stands alone.

Like Bach, Mozart was the son of a musician, and may
be said to have imbibed music with his mother's milk. For
MOZART   the acquirement of the art he showed astonishing
aptitude, and at the age of four or five was able
to compose. Mozart's father died of gout; his mother also
succumbed to some nerve-disease apparently of an epileptic
character, attended by convulsions, delirium, and prolonged
insensibility. The offspring of such a couple could not be
physically strong. Both Mozart and his only sister Marianne,
who also displayed considerable ability as a musician, although destitute of the inventive faculty, suffered much from
ill-health. Soon after the age of thirty the composer broke
down mentally and physically. During the composition of
the ' Requiem ' he laboured under the delusion that he was
being poisoned, frequently swooned away, and became partially paralysed. Afterwards he fell into a delirious state,

[1] Rockstro: *Life of Handel.*

in which he still occupied himself with the 'Requiem,' blowing out his cheeks to imitate the trumpets and drums. In his thirty-sixth year he died of inflammation of the brain. The nerve disorder of the sister does not appear to have attacked any vital part of her system. She lived to an advanced age, but ten years before her death she became blind. Mozart's head was too large for his body, which was of stunted growth. Towards the close of his life he indulged in 'convivial excesses,' frequenting the society of 'low and unprincipled persons.' He left two sons, both of whom practised music, but with little success.

The eccentricities of Beethoven bordered upon insanity. He was constantly changing his lodgings, and, although miserably poor, had sometimes three or four places of abode to pay for at one time. He was always absent-minded and unpractical. Litigious and troublesome in disposition, he alienated both relatives and friends. He was in constant ill-health, and had some constitutional weakness of the eyes. From the age of thirty he gradually lost his hearing, and in his later years was completely deaf. Despite these afflictions he continued to play and compose, though sometimes ' he would unconsciously lay his left hand flat upon the key-board of the piano, and thus drown in discordant noise the music to which his right hand was feelingly giving expression.' The music he wrote during the latter half of his life was never heard by him in the ordinary sense of the word; it was conceived and perfected solely in his imagination. This is a feat which to a mind of ordinary calibre would be utterly impossible. Beethoven was most ungainly in his manners and habits. He was only five feet four inches in height, his head was unusually large, his hair bushy, and always in a state of wild disorder. He died at fifty-six, it is said of dropsy, which, however, is rather a symptom of some fatal malady than a malady in itself. More probably the vital functions were impaired through a deterioration of the brain. A post-mortem examination was made by one Joseph Wagner, who reported in the following terms:—'The auditory nerves were shrivelled and marrowless, the arteries running along them being stretched as if

over a crow-quill. The fourth ventricle of the brain was
filled with blood, and the brain substance was in this part of
a much firmer consistence than the rest. Generally the brain
was soft and watery, but its convolutions appeared twice as
deep as usual, and much more numerous. The skull was
throughout very compact and about half an inch thick.'
Beethoven never married. His ailments he appears to
have derived from his father, a tenor singer, who became a
drunkard.

No family could present more distressing conditions of
nerve-disorder than that of Mendelssohn, where deformities,
MENDELS- blindness, apoplexy, paralysis, and epilepsy are
SOHN found in unbroken sequence.[1] Moses Mendelssohn,
grandfather of the composer Felix Mendelssohn, was a
hunchback ; he stammered, and also suffered constantly from
violent headaches which nothing could relieve. At fifty-seven
he died of apoplexy. He wrote verses in his youth, and
afterwards achieved celebrity by his philosophical works.
To this feeble, ailing, and insignificant specimen of humanity
three sons and three daughters were born, most of whom
appear to have inherited some species of nervous affection.
The eldest son Joseph became a successful banker. As a
boy, according to a letter of his father's, he showed 'great
stubbornness and want of gentleness,' and was 'always of
that temperament which would ten times rather break than
bend.' At about his father's age he died 'painlessly and
suddenly.' He had two children, of whom one died young,
and the other left no issue. Abraham, the second son of
Moses and the father of the composer, was also an active and
energetic man of business, and of a hard and severe nature.
He became blind, and, like his elder brother, died suddenly,
no one supposing him to have more than a slight cold. His
age at death was fifty-nine. Nathan, the youngest, outliving
his brothers by a good many years, also died ' painlessly and
suddenly,' leaving a family who had pronounced musical
tastes. Although the cause of death in these cases is not
specified, the recorded symptoms point to apoplexy or to
some nervous affection of the heart. Not less afflicted in

---

[1] Rockstro : *Life of Mendelssohn.* Henschel : *Die Familie Mendelssohn.*

their way were the daughters of Moses Mendelssohn. Henrietta was deformed and never married, while Dorothea and Recha were somewhat disordered as to their passions, the former deserting her first husband to elope with a lover, and the latter being divorced. It is noteworthy that Dorothea had 'literary and poetic abilities,' and that Recha was also 'intellectually clever' but 'a very sickly woman.'

In Felix Mendelssohn there was, as has been observed in the case of Walter Scott and other great men, a converging heredity of nerve-disorder, Abraham Mendelssohn having married a woman 'of an excitable nervous organisation and prone to heart disease.' Leah Solomon, mother of the composer, excelled alike as a linguist, a musician, and an artist, and was also 'very lively and witty.' She died suddenly of 'spasm of the lungs.' By her marriage with Abraham Mendelssohn she had four children—Fanny, Felix, Rebecca, and Paul. Both Fanny and Felix had a decided predilection for music in childhood; the others were not so gifted. All were of feeble constitution. Fanny was of stunted growth, slightly deformed (having one shoulder higher than the other), and was weak-sighted. She was subject to alarming fits of bleeding at the nose, one of which lasted thirty-six hours. At forty-two she was seized with paralysis while seated at the piano, and died a few hours afterwards 'from a rush of blood to the head.' She was very 'lively, sensitive, and fond of the beautiful in all things.'

Felix, the composer, who in his short life—for he died at thirty-seven—made the name of Mendelssohn illustrious, was wayward as a boy. Writing to him at this period, his father observed:—'You have never been able to divest yourself of a tendency to austerity and irascibility, suddenly grasping an object and as suddenly relinquishing it, and thus creating for yourself many obstacles from the practical point of view.' Like Handel and Mozart, Mendelssohn was extremely susceptible to discordant sounds. The national melodies of Wales, as performed by itinerant musicians during his visit to the Principality in 1829, threw him into a frenzy. 'No national melodies for me,' he wrote. 'Ten thousand devils take all nationalities.' The airs of the country were to his ear 'infamous, vulgar, out-of-time trash,' and, he added, ' I am getting mad, and I must leave off writing till by-and-by.' By the age of thirty-five his health was ' hopelessly impaired.' This was soon after the composition of ' Elijah.' Rockstro remarks that Mendelssohn then appeared to be working himself to death. During the rehearsals of ' Elijah ' he had a ' worn look ' which it was distressing to witness. He next fell into a state of physical and nervous exhaustion, and was ' irritable to the last degree.' From this condition he never recovered. On hearing of his sister Fanny's death he fell down in a faint. Putting his hand to his head some time afterwards, he said mournfully, ' What is the good of planning anything? I shall not live.' The prediction was all too true. There is little doubt but that at this period Mendelssohn's mind was unhinged. His ' habits changed,' and he ' dreaded all contact with the public.' Epileptic symptoms appeared. He had shivering fits and headaches followed by periods of unconsciousness, and these attacks increased in violence until death supervened. Like his sister Fanny, Mendelssohn was undergrown. He was quick-tempered, lithe, and mercurial; his features were animated and expressive. Some of his vital forces, however, were deficient, for before his death, in what ought to have been the flower of his manhood, he began to be grey and bald. Rebecca suffered terribly from neuralgia, the pain being such that during her attacks she had to be held down in bed. At forty-nine she died of apoplexy. Paul escaped the family heritage of an early and sudden death; the unspecified malady that carried him off involved ' long and severe suffering,' which is no doubt referable to a deeply-impaired constitution.

In Donizetti and Schumann nerve-disorder attained the proportions of insanity. Both these composers also became DONIZETTI paralysed. Donizetti, who composed his numerous works with marvellous ease and rapidity, was during his latter years confined in a lunatic asylum. He died at fifty, leaving a son, like himself, insane. Schumann's insanity manifested itself in his youth, when fits of melancholia beset him, accompanied by suicidal impulses. Afterwards he had hallucinations, hearing spirit voices, melodies,

and harmonies, and having perturbations of smell and taste.[1]
For years he dreaded being shut up in a lunatic asylum, and
this was eventually his fate. He died at forty-six. The heritage
of nerve-disorder in Schumann's case appears to have been
exceptionally strong. There were no musical aptitudes in
the family; but his father, although engaged in trade, had
strong literary and poetic aspirations, and 'died in the prime
of life of a disease of long standing;' while the composer's
mother 'fell into an exaggerated state of romance and sen-
timentalism, combined with sudden and violent passions and
an inclination to singularity.' Three brothers all died in
early manhood, while a sister fell into an 'incurable SCHUMANN
melancholy' followed by dementia, and died in her
twentieth year. Physically Schumann was of middle stature,
inclining to stoutness. He was calm and dignified, but not
particularly intellectual in appearance, although his head was
square and firm, broadening in a marked manner at the
temples. A post-mortem examination was made with the
following results :—

The traverse folds marking the fourth cavity of the
brain were numerous and finely fashioned, and various
abnormal characteristics in the cerebral substance were
revealed, namely—

I. Distended blood-vessels, especially at the base of the
brain.

II. Ossification of the base of the brain and abnormal
development of the normal projections in the shape of a new
formation of irregular masses of bone, which partially pierced
the external hard covering of the brain with their sharp
points.

III. Concretion and degeneration of the soft coverings of
the brain and unnatural growth of the vascular covering and
the rear portion of the cerebrum.

IV. A considerable atrophy of the whole brain, which
weighed about seven ounces (Prussian Troy weight), less
than is usual in a man of Schumann's age.[2]

Wagner's origin is obscure. He has told us, however,
that his father, who occupied a humble position, died very

---

[1] Wasilewski: *Life of Robert Schumann.*   [2] *Ibid.*

early the year in which the composer was born. 'I hardly know,' says Wagner, 'for what I was originally intended.

WAGNER I only know that I heard one evening a symphony of Beethoven's, that I thereupon fell ill of a fever, and that when I recovered I was—a musician.' His tastes in the first instance were literary and dramatic, but he was a wild and disorderly boy, and infected with the wildest mysticism. At the beginning of his musical period he had 'while half dozing a day vision, in which fundamental thirds and fifths appeared to him incarnate.' Curiously enough, with all his genius for music, he was never able to acquire executive skill on the piano. For many years he suffered from hypertrophy of the heart, which was also Balzac's complaint. It was of this disease that he died. 'The most striking thing in Wagner,' says one of his biographers,[1] 'was the extraordinary energy that animated his frail (*chétif*) body, with its disproportionately large head and brow. This disproportion made him look smaller than he was in reality. He had a violent temperament; both in gaiety and anger he was tempestuous, and his wife was constantly on the watch to prevent or to repair the results of his uncontrollable actions.' 'Impatient, nervous, irritable, he seemed to take pleasure in rending in pieces men and things,' is another description given of him. He had a strange mania for silks and satins—a mania which increased with age. It was in these fabrics that he arrayed himself when about to compose, and in travelling he always carried about with him sufficient material of this kind to decorate his apartments, the room in which he died being upholstered in pink and pale blue satin.

Glück, avaricious and addicted to drink, died of apoplexy. Paganini, an inveterate gambler, was epileptic and consumptive. Weber lapsed into melancholia, and died of consumption at forty-two. The same malady carried off Hérold at the same age. Rossini had a cousin an idiot, and at times laboured under the hallucination that he was miserably poor.[2] Schubert's constitution was worn out at thirty-one. Bellini succumbed at thirty-three to an 'internal disease.'

<hr>

[1] Jullien.　　　　　　　　　[2] Lombroso.

Balfe died of asthma. Chopin was consumptive. The father of Berlioz was 'weakly in body and melancholic,' while his mother was 'fervently pious.' Gounod describes his brother-musician in the following terms :—'With Berlioz every impression and every feeling was carried to extremities; he only knew joy and sorrow at the pitch of delirium : as he said of himself, he was a volcano.' In the latter portion of his life Berlioz suffered excruciatingly from -'neuralgia in the intestines,' and his death was preceded by epileptiform fits.[1]

What has been said of music applies equally to the sister arts. Many of the greatest painters, sculptors, and engravers are but names to us; they live in their works, and MICHEL have otherwise no personal history. All the avail- ANGELO able evidence, however, points clearly to the existence of nerve-disorder as a fundamental element of genius in relation to colour and form. The publication in 1856 of the letters contained in the Buonarroti archives threw some light upon the previously obscure personality of Michel Angelo,[2] who, in consequence, is better known to us than any of the artists of his period. And it would be difficult to choose a more representative name, for the great sculptor also excelled as a painter, and was given to the writing of poetry as well. Like so many great men, unfortunately, he dwindles on acquaintance. The family correspondence does not show him to advantage. His suspiciousness, his irritability, and his want of calm judgment were the causes of infinite trouble to himself and his friends. These characteristics of the 'insane temperament' he appears to have inherited from his father—a 'man of narrow intellect and hasty temper, unreasonable, and unjust.' Some of the artist's greatest works were achieved while he was afflicted with severe nervous ailments. About the age of fifty-six he is described as suffering from sleeplessness, weak sight, pains in the head, and giddiness. Having been injured in a fall, he shut himself up in his room and refused all assistance, the surgeon being compelled to force his way to his bedside. If this was

---

[1] *Life and Letters of Berlioz.*
[2] C. Heath Wilson : *Life of Michel Angelo.*

the act of a sane man nothing but a morbid condition of mind could explain the artist's petulant and violent letters and his frequent explosions of temper. One of his letters, undated, but addressed to a friend to whom he was much indebted and, indeed, warmly attached, is so incoherent that he could not have been in his senses when he wrote it. It is such a letter as might emanate from Bedlam.

'Messer Luigi,' says the writer, 'you suppose that I shall reply to you as you wish, but it may well be to the contrary. You give me what I never requested. Truly you do not sin in ignorance, sending it to me by Hercules, being ashamed to give it to me yourself. He who has snatched me from the grave may censure me, but I don't know which weighs most on me, censure or death. In short, I pray and conjure you by the true friendship existing between us that you destroy that print and burn the other impression, and that if you make a profit out of me you will not make others do likewise. If you make of me a thousand pieces I will do as much not of you but of your affairs.'

The signature to this communication is not the least curious part of it. It runs thus :—

'MICHEL ANGELO BUONARROTI,
  Not painter, sculptor, or architect,
  But what you will. But not a drunkard
  As I told you at home.'

On the death of a lady to whom he was much attached Michel Angelo is said to have 'lost all control over himself.' He had an innate turn for art, which he adhered to notwithstanding that his father and uncles had recourse to blows to divert him from it as a boy. With the insane temperament he inherited from his father longevity, both dying at the age of ninety. The artist left no offspring, and, although many children were born to his brothers, few lived. 'It is not our fate,' wrote Michel Angelo, 'to multiply in Florence.' None of these brothers displayed any artistic gifts ; they were, indeed, men of very little capacity, and 'frequently played an unsatisfactory part in the family history.' Leonardo was infirm and of a pious disposition ; Giovanni Simone was the ne'er-do-well of the family. Only one brother, Buonarroti, had surviving issue.

From the biographical sketches of other old masters some significant facts may be culled. Giorgione, remarkable for his big body and big head, lived an extravagant life, and was notorious for his love adventures; Tintoretto died of an 'incurable disease of the stomach;' Paul Veronese left a gifted son, who died at twenty-six; Botticelli at sixty-four was completely broken down in health, and 'hobbled about on crutches;' Leonardo da Vinci's right arm became paralysed; Rubens died of gout, which attacked him at fifty; Raphael, addicted to sexual excesses, died at thirty-seven; Albert Dürer was consumptive; Claude Lorraine succumbed to gout; Salvator Rosa sank into imbecility; Benvenuto Cellini had hallucinations of sight in the form of ecstatic visions; Vandyck was melancholic, and died at forty-one of 'disappointment;' Watteau was also melancholic, his early death being attributed to 'deception in love.'[1]

Coming to English artists of the first rank, we meet with nerve-disorder in all its forms, not excepting mental derangement, and in one distinguished case—that of Turner—idiocy, or a condition nearly approaching it. Between the parentage of Samuel Taylor Coleridge and that of Sir Joshua Reynolds there is a curious similarity. The painter's father, like the poet's, was a clergyman and schoolmaster; he was also 'an absent man' and 'remarkable for his taciturnity.'[2] It is no surprise in these circumstances to learn that at the height of his fame Sir Joshua had a stroke of paralysis, and that some time afterwards, while engaged upon a portrait, he felt a sudden decay of sight in his left eye. Under the latter affliction he laid down the pencil, never to take it up again. His sight gradually darkened, and in a few weeks his left eye was totally blind. From similar causes, no doubt, the painter long suffered from deafness. Paralysis was not, however, the malady which was destined to end his days. He had an enlargement of the liver—a disease which perplexed the best physicians of

---

[1] Dohme: *Kunst und Künstler des Mittel-alters und der Neuzeit.*
[2] Northcote: *Life of Sir Joshua Reynolds.*

the time, but which is now known to be in relation with the medulla oblongata. From this we may conclude that the disturbance of function which had occasioned paralysis, deafness, and blindness of the left eye invaded yet another portion of the cerebro-spinal system before proving fatal. Sir Joshua, despite his social success, never married, and he otherwise appears to have indulged in what in any sanely constituted man of his position would have been an unaccountable eccentricity, namely, meanness in small money matters. 'In his household,' says Allan Cunningham, 'he was close and saving; while he poured out his wines and spread out his tables to the titled or the learned, he stinted his domestics to the commonest fare and rewarded their faithfulness by very moderate wages.' He was 'prudent in the matter of pins, a saver of bits of thread, a man hard and parsimonious.' Public opinion pictured him close, cold, cautious, and sordid; and an exhibition of his 'old masters,' which he set up in the Haymarket ostensibly for the benefit of a servant, excited a suspicion, because of his well-known love of gain, that he was a partaker in the profits.—Hogarth died of a sudden nervous spasm—probably *angina pectoris*.

The parentage of John Flaxman is obscure, his father having been a maker and seller of plaster casts in a humble FLAXMAN way, and nothing being known of his mother except that her name was Lee—a common gipsy patronymic. What the father of English sculpture inherited in a physical sense was a rickety, misshapen body which, in his early years, needed the support of crutches. As a child Flaxman was not expected to live; but an alert and tenacious spirit animated the puny frame, and after the perils of boyhood were past, he proved himself capable of sustaining the fatigue of incessant industry. Always drawing, the sickly youth became a precocious exhibitor and prize-winner. His health improved so much that he was able to lay aside his crutches, but he remained high-shouldered to deformity, his head always looked somewhat too large for his body, and he had an awkward sidelong gait. In religion he held stubborn and eccentric views. He was a believer in the Swedenborgian mysticism, and his opinions on this, as, indeed, on most subjects, were inflexibly rigid. In art, of course, he was an enthusiast. His genius was exclusively for form. With no model before him he had, even as a lad, instinctively grasped the true principles of Greek design, and he may be said to have recovered the art of combining ideal grace of form and the rhythmical composition of lines with spontaneousness and truth of pose and gesture. Flaxman married, but left no offspring. The immediate cause of his death at seventy-one was a cold. An elder brother, William, of whom nothing is known except that he also was a modeller, died at forty-two.

Other forms of artistic nerve-disorder—for it is only possible to give a selection of cases—are illustrated by Morland, Fuseli, Lawrence, Liverseege, Wilkie, Maclise, Doré, and Meissonier. Unlike Reynolds, Lawrence, MORLAND and many distinguished painters, George Morland came of an artistic family. His grandfather was a painter, his father also. The latter was what is known as a failure in life—a fact to which we may trace the germ of Morland's genius. This manifested itself early. At five or six years Morland drew wonderfully. He received no regular instruction. From the age of sixteen he was a drunkard, a spendthrift, a loafer about town, with the vulgarest tastes. Destitute of ambition, he worked only to supply the necessities of the hour. He painted with remarkable rapidity and often under the influence of intoxication, yet his pictures, observes Allan Cunningham, want nothing that art can bestow. His habits of debauchery obtaining the upper hand, he sank into the lowest state of destitution, while his personal character became an object of general contempt. At thirty-nine he was struck by paralysis. He recovered partially, but would often fall back senseless in his chair, and sometimes sank into sleep with his palette and brush in his hand. In his fortieth year he died, from the effects of swallowing an unusual quantity of spirits, in utter wretchedness and penury.

Fuseli was of 'diminutive stature and crabbed disposition,' and was all his life an eccentric, filled FUSELI with fiery impatience and untamable enthusiasm, which, before he took to the easel, found vent through literary and poetic channels. His style both in writing and painting was exaggerated and distorted, but always vigorous and animated. A consuming energy was his characteristic. To his friends and pupils his oddities, his jests, and his biting sarcasm were a constant source of amusement. He was subject to fits of despondency, and 'from these it was difficult and even dangerous to arouse him,' a violent explosion of temper being the usual result. In dispute he was eager, fierce, and unsparing, and he was too often morose and unamiable even with his best friends. The beautiful he saw chiefly with his mind's eye, for he was very near-sighted, and was obliged to study the effects of his pictures and to touch and retouch them with the help of an opera glass. For this reason, probably, his colouring has a kind of supernatural hue, well suited to beings of the spiritual world though not to those of flesh and blood. He died suddenly, but at an advanced age.

Sir Thomas Lawrence rivalled and, indeed, surpassed Sir Joshua Reynolds in tact, suavity, and courtliness of manner, although in pecuniary matters so unlike his distinguished predecessor in the chair of the Royal Academy that, despite his vast earnings and the fact that he remained unmarried, he was always in want of money. It is remarkable that Sir Thomas was one of sixteen children, nearly all of whom died in infancy, inheriting their instability of constitution from a ne'er-do-well father, who became successively attorney, poetaster, spouter of odes, actor, revenue officer, farmer, and publican, and prospered in none of these callings. The early history of the painter is painfully mingled with the fortunes of his father. He was exhibited as an infant prodigy, and at five years of age spouted poetry and took portraits for the delectation of the rustics in his father's bar-parlour. At twelve he was an established portrait painter at Bath, at three and twenty a London celebrity. Everything and everybody conspired to make him a coxcomb, for personally he was very handsome, and he was especially a 'ladies' man,' but his native good sense never deserted him except where money was concerned. Towards his sixtieth year his health became uncertain ; he had frequent headaches, and was liable to be overtaken by drowsiness in company—a symptom of brain disorder—and soon afterwards he died of heart disease.

The son of a harsh and cruel father who held a subordinate situation in a Manchester cotton factory, Liverseege was born weak and deformed. Afflicted with asthma from his cradle, he was of peevish disposition, but he was also thought to be quick in comprehension and eager for knowledge. He taught himself to draw and soon made. a livelihood by his portraits, which he afterwards quitted for more poetic subjects. During his brief and troubled existence, for he died at twenty-nine, he had alternate fits of melancholy and exaltation, and was always more or less ailing. A sudden nervous seizure of some kind cut short, in his case, a career of singular promise.

David Wilkie, 'the raw, queer Scotchman' of Jackson's description, was all his life, and despite his great success, a modest, diffident man, with little cultivation of manners, and wholly insensible to the charms and blandishments of the fair sex. Nervous ill-health weighed upon him from early manhood; and from before his fortieth year he was a confirmed invalid, going from place to place consulting one physician after another, and trying endless remedies all to no purpose. One symptom of his condition was a loss of the power of attention. This he recovered to some extent, though his later works are all inferior to his earlier ones. Haydon found him at forty looking 'thinner and more nervous than ever'—his 'keen and bushy brow, irritable, eager, and full of genius.' Returning by steamer in the Mediterranean from an Oriental tour, Wilkie had a nervous seizure 'which rendered his speech incoherent,' and to which he rapidly succumbed at the age of fifty-six.

Daniel Maclise was born of very humble parents, of whom nothing is known. Even the precise date of his birth is a mystery. He had two brothers, one of whom died with an 'undermined constitution,' the other attained some eminence as a singer. One sister married; another 'loved her brother Daniel so intensely that nothing would induce her to separate from him'—a circumstance recalling the devotion to their brothers of the demented Mary Lamb and Dorothy Wordsworth.   For some years this sister was an invalid.   Maclise's health was also unsatisfactory. About the age of thirty, when beginning to be famous, he wrote to a friend:—' I am really and truly unwell; it may be hypochondria, a return of my old ailment, but I was prohibited dining out.   I fell down at the door of my painting-room, and have had the most unquiet nights from palpitating fevers.'   Latterly Maclise's habits became very solitary and sedentary, and about the age of sixty he died of consumption, unmarried.

David Roberts, the Royal Academician, who began life as a house-painter, and who won his way to fame without any systematic instruction, had a marvellously retentive memory and a rapid execution.   These gifts he paid for in his sudden death from apoplexy.—To this complaint Gustave Doré succumbed.—Another wonderfully rapid worker was John Phillips, who was also originally a house-painter and who died from paralysis.—Meissonier, who suffered much from gout, was physically very active, for ever on the move, but hardly more than five feet high, with a large leonine head and great beard, set on a small body and supported by diminutive legs.

The degeneration of artistic genius into true insanity is exemplified by Romney, Cosway, Haydon, and Landseer. ROMNEY   Romney's father was a carpenter, and although successful in business was recognised to be ' something of a dreamer in curious projects and expensive plans'—a description which prepares us for the discovery of an unbalanced condition of mind in the son.   The artistic genius of Romney had its usual concomitants of extreme nervous sensibility and waywardness.   Hypochondria marked him for its own.   According to his friend Hayley, the painter laboured under a frequent dread that his talent would utterly desert him, and in the height of his fame his depression was such that he thought of relinquishing his art altogether. Romney in his letters speaks of his own ' distempered mind and body,' and in view of his friend's inexplicable fits of depression Hayley remarks :—' What can be more truly pitiable than to see great talents rendered frequently inactive by those wonderful variations in the nervous system that throw a shadowy darkness over the mind and fill it with phantoms of apprehension!' About the age of sixty Romney had a paralytic stroke which affected both his eye and his hand, and from this time impairment of his faculties proceeded rapidly. He built a whimsical dwelling at Hampstead, acting as his own architect; but this indulgence of an eccentric fancy brought him neither rest nor satisfaction. His dejection increased, and although he still busied himself with his paints and brushes, it was noticed that his skill had departed. By-and-by he ceased to recognise his friends or relatives, and thenceforward until his death at sixty-eight remained, as Hayley puts it, 'in that state of existence which is infinitely more afflicting to the friends who behold than to the mortal who endures it.' An elder brother of Romney's 'gave such proofs of genius in art as made his early death regretted.' By a wife whose existence he never acknowledged in London, and whom he neglected for nearly forty years, Romney left a son, who lived long enough to become a clergyman. In his youth the painter displayed a taste both for music and mechanics. For art he had an inborn aptitude; he was put to his father's trade, that of a carpenter, but began painting without having any models before him or receiving any artistic instruction whatever.

Very similar, in an artistic sense, was the origin of Cosway, whose taste for drawing, which made him the foremost miniature painter of his day, asserted itself in boyhood and in the face of the gravest difficulties. As a suite to certain 'infirmities' from which his father suffered, Cosway had a paralytic stroke which deprived him of the use of his right hand. Upon this hallucinations followed. These happily were of a pleasing order. Sometimes he would startle his friends by stating with a serious air that he had just had an interview with Praxiteles and Apelles, and that to the English Academy the former recommended a closer study of the human figure, the latter a less gaudy style of colour. Once as he sat at the dinner of the Royal Academy he turned to one of his fellow Academicians and said, ' Pitt while he

lived discouraged genius; he has seen his error now. He
paid me a visit this morning and said, " Cosway, the chief
fault I committed on earth was in not encouraging your
ta'ent." ' 'I have heard Cosway,' says another friend, ' relate
conversations which he held with King Charles I. (then dead
for 150 years) so seriously that I firmly believe he considered
everything he uttered to be strictly true.' According to
Hazlitt, Cosway professed to have held conversations with
more than one person of the Trinity, and to be able to talk
with his lady at Mantua through some fine ventricle of the
senses, as we speak to a servant downstairs through an ear-
pipe. The afflicted painter died at an advanced age, childless.

The 'clamorous, frenzied life' of Haydon is one of the
saddest in the annals of art. Inheriting a double strain of
HAYDON　　insanity, first from an eccentric father, who in re-
　　　　cording his birth in a diary, added that the wind
at the time was W.S.W., and secondly from a mother who
suffered from mental derangement, and who died of *angina
pectoris*, Haydon, besides his artistic genius, had two characteristics enormously in excess, a burning enthusiasm for art
and a prodigious vanity. Folly, extravagance, and lawsuits
had well-nigh ruined the family, and it is noted that Haydon's
paternal grandmother was a woman ' of great energy and
violent prejudices.' The painter suffered from suppressed
gout. In his youth he was threatened with blindness, but
this danger passed off, leaving him a prey chiefly to his own
inordinate ambition and self-will. He was apprenticed to
the bookselling business of his father, but his tastes were all
for drawing. ' I hated day-books, ledgers, and cash-books,'
he says in his autobiography; 'I hated standing behind the
counter, and insulted the customers. I hated the town
(Plymouth) and the people in it. I rose early and wandered
by the sea; sat up late and pondered on my ambition, and
my whole frame convulsed when I thought of being a great
painter.' In this passage we have the key to Haydon's
nature. Sent to London with 20*l.* in his pocket to make his
way, he imagined that he was destined to revive all the
ancient glories of painting, and worked with such energy
that his gums were ' sore from the clenched tightness of his

teeth.' His fiery zeal at first only brought him disappointment, his pictures being received with an indifference which to the impetuous young painter was 'agonising.' Success came by-and-by, though it profited him little. Out of the exhibition of some of his huge canvases he made large sums of money, but he was, nevertheless, constantly struggling with debt and addressing passionate prayers to the Almighty for protection. The vulgar necessities of daily life appear to have had a maddening effect upon Haydon's fervid soul. Repose he never found. ' My brain seems to require constant pressure to be easy, and my body incessant activity.' Three years later, disappointed with the result of an exhibition of his pictures, and suffering from a mental excitement which is vividly reflected in the following entry in his diary :— ' Slept horribly—prayed in sorrow and got up in agitation ' —he took a pistol and tried to shoot himself, failing in which attempt he cut his throat. A post-mortem examination revealed a long-standing irritation of the brain. There were innumerable bloody points throughout the cerebral substance, and the enveloping membrane was thickened and adherent.

Throughout the Landseer family the artistic faculty predominated. John Landseer, the father, was an engraver whose angularities of character enabled him to wage a prolonged quarrel with the Royal Academy. In LANDSEER consequence of the comparative failure of his efforts to raise the professional status of engravers, ' disappointment,' it is said, ' preyed upon his mind so deeply ' that he turned his attention from the practice of his profession to the study of archæology. He was also an attractive lecturer. Crabb Robinson described him as ' animated in his style,' adding that his ' animation was produced by indulgence in sarcasm and in emphatic diction.' In the absence of medical details, John Landseer's character may be said to be significantly indicated in these accounts of him. Two of his sons, Thomas and Charles, attained distinction as artists; two daughters also possessed artistic tastes. The third son, Sir Edwin Landseer, sketched from childhood. At six or seven he drew a cow from life, and constantly busied himself with his sketchbook in the fields thereafter. Like most great men, he was

thus a precocious genius. One of his first drawings of a dog
was done at the age of thirteen. As an example of the extraordinary manual dexterity he acquired, it is related of him
that at an evening party he with a pencil in each hand drew
simultaneously and without hesitation the head of a stag and
that of a horse, both full of his characteristic energy and
spirit. About his fifty-eighth year symptoms of the insanity
which darkened the close of Sir Edwin Landseer's life attracted
attention. The eccentricity of a picture entitled ' A Kind
Star ' alarmed his friends. This was exhibited in 1859, and
showed a Spirit with a star in its hair bending over a dying
stag. In the following year his ' Flood in the Highlands '
seemed to promise a restoration of his powers, but the promise
was not fulfilled. Always a man of ' extreme nervous susceptibility,' the painter ' had hints,' says his biographer,[1]
' that the human mind and the body which surrounds it are
mortal. He was constitutionally subject to nervous depression, but these attacks accumulated force as years went on,
and threatened the end which came with all its painfulness.'
Landseer died at sixty-nine, leaving no one to inherit his
name, the last bearer of which was a surviving maiden sister.

Turner stands alone as an example of a surpassing faculty
for colour, combined with the lowest intellectual powers.
Hogarth, according to Walpole, was a man of a
TURNER   ' gross and uninformed mind.' Nollekens never
had any notion of spelling or grammar. Reynolds himself
is said to have been deficient in scholastic attainments. But
Turner, as regards the general cast of his mind, was little
above the level of the idiot. His mother, always a woman of
fierce and ungovernable temper, became insane and had to
be placed in confinement ; his father was a loquacious barber,
mean and dwarfish-looking, and without much stability of
character. To this most unlikely couple there appears to
have been no other child born than the most renowned
landscape painter of England. Turner as a boy was impenetrably dull ; there was only one thing he was found to do
well, and that was, during the period of his apprenticeship
in an architect's office, the washing in of blue skies and

[1] F. G. Stephens.

orange gravel walks in architectural drawings. Here his
innate faculty for colour first showed itself. This, by degrees,
led to his becoming a student at the Academy, but he does
not seem to have profited much by the teaching he there
received. His genius, indeed, was remarkably slow in de-
veloping. Probably it would never have been recognised at
all had there not arisen an eminent critic who could see
visions of beauty in canvases which to the uneducated eye
looked like inchoate masses of colour. It is, indeed, acknowledged that some of Turner's works are ' fitful dreams, night-
mares of beauty rather than distinct images ; ' but this is said
to be the ' vision of the poet which, although perhaps less
definite, yet often catches further glimpses of truth and beauty
than ordinary sight can attain.' There is no doubt that
Turner's reproductions from Nature are at least untruthful
in outline. As pictures of real places—Kilchurn Castle and
Ben Cruachan, for example—they are absolutely misleading.
The colour sense was Turner's forte. With this he possessed
an extraordinary executive skill. His small hand was so
delicate that he could draw with a degree of refinement
astonishing even to opticians ; his arm was so steady that he
painted on upright canvases without the support of a maul-
stick, while his constitutional strength was such that he
could work fifteen hours at a stretch without fatigue, and eat
anything regardless of digestion. The only moral characteristic that he appears to have had in excess was avarice ; he
was saving even in the matter of half-pence, and haggled
with dealers like a Jew pedlar. For the rest, he fell infinitely below mediocrity. The mastery of English grammar
was beyond him, he could never write or speak like a person
of education, while his manners were slovenly, awkward, un-
conciliatory—boorish in the extreme. When he attempted
to explain himself on the subject of art his words were mere
gibberish. Here is an example of his philosophical observations, which the reader is invited to make sense of if he
can :—

They wrong virtue enduring difficulties, or worth in the bare
imitation of nature, all offers received in the same brain ; but
where these attempts rise above mediocrity it would surely not

be a little sacrifice to those who perceive the value of the success to foster it by terms as cordial that cannot look so easy a way as those spoken of convey doubts to the expecting individual. For as the line that unites the beautiful to grace and these offerings forming a new style not that soul can guess as ethics. Teach them of both but many serve as the body and the soul, and but presume more as the beacon to the head-land which would be a warning to the danger of mannerism and the disgustful.[1]

Yet, in this strangely muddled brain there appears to have been some occasional stirring of the poetic sense. His bad spelling and defective grammar notwithstanding, Turner appealed to the muses. 'Lead me along,' he sighs in one passage, 'with thy armonuous verse.' The result was always ludicrous. Much of his poetry, in fact, is sheer nonsense, like the following verse which may stand as an example :—

> If then my ardent love of thee is said with truth
> Agents the demolition of thy house forsooth,
> Broke through the trammels doubts and you my rhyme
> Roll into being since that fatal time.[2]

By way of explaining Turner's habitual sullenness, moroseness, and unsociability, it has been said that in his youth he was crossed in love. Remembering the strain of insanity in his composition, we may dismiss as groundless a story in support of which no biographer has been able to bring forward a particle of evidence. The mental constitution of the great colourist was, plainly speaking, that of the congenital idiot in whom, as we have already seen, there is often a special development of faculty. Ruskin places Turner among the seven supreme colourists of the world, the other six being in his estimation Giorgione, Titian, Veronese, Tintoretto, Correggio, and Reynolds. It certainly needs an abnormally constituted eye to appreciate Turner's colour, particularly his scarlet shadows in combination with white lights. That such shadows exist in nature, although they remained to be discovered by Turner, Ruskin asserts;[3] but the ordinarily constituted mind will be content to regard

---

[1] P. G. Hamerton : *Life of Turner.*   [2] *Ibid.*
[3] Ruskin : *Modern Painters*, Part IX. Chap. XI.

them either as a technical device of the painter's for obtaining a false brilliance or as an aberration of the visual sense. The latter years of his long life Turner passed in misanthropic seclusion in a house in Queen Anne Street, which he allowed to fall into the last stage of dilapidation. When friends called here they would sometimes find him 'quite dizzy with work;' it is believed that to other sordid vices he added drinking. His eccentricities were quite of the insane order. When Maclise called to tell him of Haydon's suicide, Turner scarcely stopped painting, but merely growled out between his teeth, 'He stabbed his mother, he stabbed his mother.' 'Good heavens,' said Maclise, so excited that he was prepared for any new horror, 'you don't mean to say, Turner, that Haydon ever committed a crime so terrible!' Still Turner made no reply, but slowly chanted 'He stabbed his mother, he stabbed his mother.' Nothing but this could his startled friend wring from him. The biographers suppose Turner to have meant that Haydon had injured the Royal Academy, but it is more reasonable to conclude that the words were an insane 'tic' such as is often to be found in the speech of lunatics.

The actor's art is not perhaps accorded as high a place in popular estimation as music, painting, and the literary faculty. Nevertheless, its pathological aspect, as EDMUND illustrated by the lives of the greatest actors, esta- KEAN blishes its identity of origin with the other forms of genius we have been considering. From both parents Edmund Kean inherited a strain of insanity. His maternal great-grandfather, Henry Carey, a composer of songs and a humourist of some repute, led a ne'er-do-well life, became blind, and hanged himself. Henry Carey's son, George, was a man of the same unsettled habits. Actor, musician, and itinerant lecturer by turns, he lived a life of continued hardship and struggle, his greatest talent being for the unprofitable business of mimicry. Nance Carey, George's daughter, and mother of the tragedian, proved in turn a worthy bearer of the family name. At fifteen she joined a company of strolling players, and the connection she formed soon after with Edmund Kean, the tragedian's father, was of the same fortuitous and unstable character as the family fortunes. She had no motherly affection, for she deserted her child three months after his birth, and only claimed him some years later, when there seemed a prospect of making a paltry profit out of his appearances on the stage.

Turning now to the paternal descent of the great actor, we find, if possible, a blacker record. Edmund Kean the elder was one of three brothers. Aaron was a drunkard; Moses was a tailor by trade, but earned his bread chiefly as a mimic, and had a wooden leg which probably had a neuro-pathic history if we but knew it, amputation being sometimes resorted to in severe rheumatic affections. With or without these collateral indications of nerve-disorder, there can be no doubt as to the constitutional infirmities of the third brother Edmund, father of the tragedian, with whom we are more immediately concerned. Early in life he was known as a fluent speaker at debating societies, although his calling was that of a clerk; and, after his acquaintance with Nance Carey, he drank heavily, lost whatever social position he had had, and finally sank into hopeless insanity, in which state he met his death by falling or throwing himself from the roof of a house into the street. In the tragedian's daily life as well as in his genius his mother's thriftlessness and his father's insanity were faithfully reflected. Kean not only drank heavily but committed strange acts, such as getting up at three o'clock in the morning, sending for a hackney coach, placing inside it a dog, a pair of pistols, a bottle of brandy, and two lighted candles, and gravely telling the coachman to drive 'to hell.'[1] He was constantly disgracing himself with the public by failing in his engagements through drunkenness or inattention. Visiting an American lunatic asylum, he walked out with some friends upon the roof, and after admiring the prospect, rushed suddenly to the edge, exclaiming, 'I'll make a leap; it is the best end I can put to my life.' With difficulty he was restrained from giving effect to his words. By the age of thirty-seven the tragedian's health, mental and bodily, was shattered, his memory began

---

[1] Molloy: *Life and Adventures of Edmund Kean.*

to play him false, even the extreme sensibility which was so long his unfailing characteristic occasionally deserted him, so that he walked through his parts 'with moveless muscle and glazed eye' like a man in the last stage of exhaustion. He lingered, however, a few years longer, acting to the last. In the midst of a performance of 'Othello' at Covent Garden he fell down insensible and was carried off the stage. From this attack he never recovered. It was found that his mind was unhinged, and in this condition death overtook him at the age of forty-six.

The great tragic genius of Junius Brutus Booth was as nearly allied to insanity as Kean's. Similar eccentricities marked his public and private life, though he does not appear to have been addicted to drinking. BOOTH When not in the humour to act he would disappear without a word of warning, leaving the managers who had engaged him in serious difficulties. In playing 'Richelieu' on one occasion he suddenly halted, tripped over to one of the characters, the priest *Father Joseph*, and, seizing him in his arms, waltzed with him round the stage, to the amazement of the house and the horror of the manager, who had the curtain dropped on this mad prank. Booth then disappeared and was not seen by his friends for some days. At thirty-five his eccentricities culminated in true insanity, the first outbreak of which occurred in the midst of a performance. In playing a tragic part at Boston, U.S.A., he suddenly dropped into a colloquial tone, and *à propos* of nothing said, 'Upon my word I don't know.' To the murmurs of the house he responded with a ringing laugh. The manager then rushed from behind the scenes and led him off, whilst he shouted 'I can't read—I am a charity boy—I can't read—take me to the lunatic asylum.' For some time after this incident Booth was an undoubted maniac. His mental aberration was, however, marked by lucid intervals in which he continued to act. While at sea off Charleston he jumped overboard, saying he had a message for an actor who had drowned himself near the spot some years before. He was rescued with difficulty and afterwards carefully watched. In a more or less demented condition he lived till the age of

fifty-six, dying then of a cold. His insanity he transmitted
to his son, Wilkes Booth, who assassinated President Lincoln.

The Kemble family exhibit a considerable variety of
nerve-disorder, whence inherited there is nothing
to show, save that the mother of Mrs. Siddons and
of John Philip Kemble was a woman of 'severe character.'
Old Roger Kemble and his wife Sarah, strolling actors, had
a large family, of whom Mrs. Siddons was the most gifted.
This great actress was a woman of extreme sensibility. She
had occasional fainting fits, and suffered from sciatica and
nervous depression. She was popularly said to be ' mad '—
a rumour which she took occasion pointedly to contradict.
Unquestionably she had a somewhat unbalanced mind, being
accustomed, artist-like, to attribute every adverse opinion and
every slight to deep-seated and malignant animosity. Before
the age of fifty physical weakness unfitted Mrs. Siddons for
acting, but she lived to an advanced age, and died of erysipelas. In her family consumption appeared, two of her
children dying of that complaint. John Philip Kemble, the
tragedian, and the most famous brother of Mrs. Siddons, was
a man of strange moods, who took opium and drank wine, it
is said, ' in pailfuls.' He had asthma, but a graver nerve
disorder seized him ultimately, in the shape of paralysis, of
which he died. Charles Kemble, inferior to his brother, but
still an actor of repute, became deaf before he attained the
age of forty. Another brother, Stephen Kemble, was noted
for his excessive stoutness—a defect which also characterised
Mrs. Siddons in her later years. Fanny Kemble attained
some distinction as an actress, but other members of the
family showed little or no aptitude for the boards.

In the case of Mrs. Curtis, youngest sister of Mrs. Siddons,
nerve disorder assumed what is commonly thought to be a
discreditable form ; she was lame, eccentric, incorrigibly im-
moral, and generally a ' disgrace ' to the family. At the same
time she had poetic and literary ability. While Mrs. Siddons
was at the height of her fame, the poor ne'er-do-well issued
a volume of miscellaneous poems, some of which she had
written at the age of fourteen, and others ' under a com-
plication of difficulties.' She also wrote romances. On one

occasion she added to her notoriety by attempting to poison herself in Westminster Abbey. But for her lameness it was thought she would have cut a respectable figure on the stage. Although known as the 'notorious Mrs. Curtis,' she was acknowledged to possess 'uncommon intellect.' She lived till the age of seventy-four, making the family uneasy all their lives, though latterly she was pensioned by Mrs. Siddons.

Rachel, the greatest tragic actress of the French, or indeed of any stage, was born of Jewish pedlars named Félix, and sang or recited in the streets as a child. She was abnormally thin and pigeon-breasted, but, as RACHEL an actress, her coal-black eyes glowed with passion and she had a something in her manner which made her silence even more expressive than words. The family were of a singularly mean and sordid disposition, and exploited Rachel in a shameless manner throughout her short but brilliant career. The great *tragédienne* was a 'bundle of nerves.' On the stage she was once seized with a fit of hysterics so violent and so prolonged that her reason was thought to be in danger. Her sister Rebecca died of consumption, and to this disease Rachel herself, after frequently failing in her engagements owing to 'ill-health,' succumbed at the age of thirty-seven. She was subject to fits of an epileptic character, and some time before her death was haunted by the vision of a giant's hand crushing in her chest. This was sometimes accompanied by an auditory hallucination, a voice saying to her, 'You shall die here, under my hand.' Rachel possessed no ear for music, being unable to distinguish time or tune; but she had a great passion for gambling. On the point of heredity it is to be noted that Rachel's father was subject to 'ungovernable fits of anger,' and that her mother was of a 'sharp, grasping, covetous nature'—defects which are acknowledged in the friendly sketch of the actress's life written by Madame de B——.

In not a few cases the genius of eminent actors has been coupled with neuropathic symptoms. Peg Woffington died of paralysis.—Monrose, the best *Figaro* of his day, developed insanity on the stage while playing his favourite character.—Mdlle. Mars, an inveterate gambler, died in a prolonged state of delirium which was attributed ignorantly to her use of hair dye.—Talma possessed the power of vividly picturing his audience to himself as unclothed skeletons.[1]—The beautiful and fascinating Rose Chéri belonged to a mad family.—Augustine Brohan was threatened with blindness.—Frédérick Lemaître drank heavily.—Aimée Desclée developed a strong religious vocation.—Robson, a pigmy in stature, drank himself to death. And Charles Kean inherited the nerve-disorder of his father in the form of gout.

[1] This curious faculty of Talma's was possessed by a medical man of Wigan's acquaintance who died of brain disease. In any large assembly his imagination gradually and slowly went on removing one article of clothing after another from all the persons present, then their integuments, then layer after layer of muscles, then the viscera, and at last left them all bare skeletons dancing before his eyes.

CHAPTER VIII

COMMANDERS AND STATESMEN AS NEUROPATHIC SUBJECTS—ALEXANDER
THE GREAT—JULIUS CÆSAR—MARLBOROUGH—CLIVE—NAPOLEON—
AND WELLINGTON—THEIR PARALYTIC AND EPILEPTIC TENDENCIES
—THE PROPHETICAL MISSIONS OF MAHOMMED AND JOAN OF ARC—
CHARACTERISTICS OF CHARLES V. AND FREDERICK THE GREAT—
UNSOUNDNESS OF THE CROMWELL BLOOD—THE PITTS, FATHER AND
SON—INSANE TENDENCIES OF THE FORMER—WARREN HASTINGS'S
PARALYSIS—BROUGHAM'S EXTRAVAGANCE AND IRRESPONSIBILITY—
THE NEUROPATHIC STRAIN IN BEACONSFIELD

A COMMON impression prevails that, be the weaknesses of
genius what they may, they are manifested exclusively in men
possessing literary and artistic faculty; but an examination
of the facts shows such a belief to be erroneous. Great
distinction is achieved in war and statesmanship under the
same conditions as in literature and art; there is a morbid
development of certain portions of the brain entailing a
hyper-sensitiveness or an impoverishment of other portions
with results that are disastrous either to the individual himself, or, by the operation of heredity, to his offspring and
connections. In all the military commanders of the world
of absolutely the first rank, a class so limited in number that
they may almost be reckoned upon the fingers of one hand,
the existence of such conditions is clearly proved upon the
evidence of history.

The parentage of Alexander the Great was of a most
unpromising character. His father Philip was violent in
temper, and given over to drunkenness and ALEXANDER
debauchery; his mother Olympias was a disso- THE GREAT
lute, ungovernable woman, who is said, previous to his birth,
to have had a remarkable vision of her son's greatness.
Alexander was himself addicted to orgies, in one of which he
died in his thirty-second year, but the neuropathic nature of
his genius was shown more particularly by an affection of the

muscles of the neck, which from birth compelled him to incline his head to one side, and by the circumstance that a brother of his, put to death by order of Olympias, was an idiot.

On the authority of Suetonius we learn that Julius Cæsar towards the close of his life became subject to JULIUS epileptic fits. This is confirmed by Plutarch, who CÆSAR states that while the battle of Thapsus was being fought Cæsar fell into convulsions. Two years after the close of his African campaign, and at the age of fifty-six, Cæsar was murdered. As repeated attacks of epilepsy impair the mental powers, it is possible that the daggers of Brutus and Cassius saved the dictator from a worse fate, that of lapsing into insanity.

From boyhood Marlborough was subject to headaches, giddiness, and what was called 'fever'—complaints which MARL- affected him greatly before and after the battle of BOROUGH Blenheim, his correspondence at the period containing frequent reference to his bodily sufferings. After his return to England in 1716 at the age of sixty-six, paralysis deprived him for a time of speech; and a series of epileptic attacks subsequently reduced him to a state of great bodily and mental debility. He was never himself again, he spoke with difficulty, and both his memory and understanding were impaired. At seventy-six his nervous attacks increased in violence and carried him off.[1] The hereditary influences which conduced to Marlborough's disorders are indicated in the fact that his father was a man of letters, and that his sister Arabella was a woman of dissolute character. In his own offspring neuropathic conditions were very marked, the evil tendencies of the Churchill blood having been aggravated, probably, by Marlborough's marriage with a woman of vehement temper. Marlborough's only son died in boyhood, a daughter Elizabeth died at twenty-six, and another daughter, Anne Countess of Sunderland, at twenty-nine, after having been 'long afflicted with a tedious disorder.' On Marlborough's death his title and honours descended to his daughter Henrietta, whose son became the Marquis of Blandford. This young man, though married, died childless at thirty-

[1] Coxe: *Life of Marlborough.*

two, and on the death of Henrietta the title and honours passed to the Sunderland line, in which they have since remained.

The hereditary influences that determined the career of Clive are obscure, though his own individual life shows them to have been of the usual neuropathic character.[1] His father, a country attorney, appears to have been CLIVE a thriftless person, consistently unsuccessful in life, and the future conqueror of India, by dint of that metamorphosis of heredity which has been so frequently illustrated in these pages, came into the world accordingly with a disposition of great impetuosity and waywardness. At school Clive was inordinately addicted to fighting, and was described by an uncle in a letter as flying into a temper upon every trifling occasion. He was also full of daring and adventure. Sent out to a writership in the East India Company's service, he proved irritable and impatient of control, and had fits of low spirits in which, as a lad, he twice attempted to kill himself, his life being saved only through his pistol missing fire. In a duel with a comrade he displayed an extraordinary degree of nerve ; he had called an officer a cheat, and when, having missed his aim, he stood at his adversary's mercy, he shouted ' Shoot and be damned, I said you cheated and I say so still.' The officer declaring the young man to be mad, threw away his weapon and there the matter ended. Clive's temperament called for strong and constant excitement, and this he eventually found in war. Of moral scruples he had none ; it is known that he stooped to forgery in order to circumvent a native opponent. At forty years of age Clive had conquered India and acquired a world-wide reputation. Yet in the height of his success he suffered from great depression of spirits, and his letters betoken a morbid, restless mind. He had a painful gouty rheumatic affection, to relieve which he took opium in large doses. With the untold wealth he had acquired in India, Clive indulged in extravagances that covered him with ridicule, ordering, for example, the costliest clothes, among other things a court suit, ' lined with parchment so that it might not wrinkle.' With everything at his

[1] Gleig : *Life of Clive.*

command apparently to make life worth living, riches and reputation without stint, he committed suicide at the age of forty-nine. Clive's book learning, according to his friendly biographer Gleig, was a mere blank. He had a harsh and heavy countenance, and his general manner in society was sullen and reserved. Lady Clive survived her husband a great many years, and her son, the first Earl of Powis, died at eighty-five.

There is nothing discoverable in the ancestry of Napoleon that foreshadowed his greatness except an excessive mortality, and the fact that his mother, Lætitia Ramolini, was a woman of 'strong character,' although illiterate, evincing firmness in certain matters, but in others, says the Duchesse d'Abrantès, 'an extravagant obstinacy.' Both the Emperor's parents were left orphans at an early age. Charles Bonaparte, his father, was a Corsican functionary of humble position, who died at thirty-nine of a cancerous affection of the stomach inherited from his father, who died about the same age. This also was the disease to which Napoleon himself succumbed, at little more than fifty. From boyhood Napoleon was irritable, obstinate, morose, splenetic and domineering, always more feared than loved. The sketches given of him by Bourrienne [1] and other observers reveal a disposition alternately sullen and impulsive, and lacking in all consideration for the feelings of others. 'His anger,' says the Duchesse d'Abrantès, 'was frightful, and though I am no coward I could never look at him in his fits of rage without a shudder.[2] His smile, it appears, was correspondingly winning. At school the only NAPOLEON branch of study for which Napoleon showed any special aptitude was mathematics, though he had some taste also for history and geography. To the last he was unable to spell correctly, while his handwriting was an unreadable scrawl, bearing in every slur and dash the traces of an impetuous temperament. Constant, his valet, who has written his memoirs, says that owing to his natural impatience and hastiness of manner Napoleon never attempted to shave without severely cutting himself.

[1] Bourrienne : *Mémoires sur Napoléon.*
[2] D'Abrantès : *Souvenirs historiques sur Napoléon.*

In an interesting study of Napoleon's handwriting,[1] the Abbé Michon, a graphologist, maintains that the Emperor's passionate vehemence and impenetrable dissimulation both stand revealed in the manner in which he wielded his pen. The furious illegibility of the Emperor's manuscript, the apparently unconscious leaps and bounds of the Imperial pen, convince Michon that Napoleon possessed the insane temperament. This conclusion he draws more especially from the strange abnormal form and excessive development of the letter p in Napoleon's handwriting. The Abbé states—and in this he is supported by medical authority—that the writing of the partially deranged usually exhibits some similar sign which he calls *la petite bête*, this sign generally consisting of a nervous, disordered, unusual stroke which falls fatally and spontaneously from the pen. Pascal, whose imagination, as already stated, was so far out of gear that he always saw an abyss yawning at his side, and whose writing in his later years Napoleon's most resembles, used an extravagant and accusing g. No doubt 'insane handwriting' is due to a morbid excitability of the motor centres, particularly those of the wrist and hand.

What, we may now inquire, is the direct evidence of a neuropathic condition in Napoleon himself? Brierre de Boismont[2] relates the following, which he heard from a friend to whom it was told by General Rapp:—'In 1806 General Rapp on his return from the siege of Dantzig, having occasion to speak to the Emperor, entered his study without being announced. He found him so absorbed that his entry was unperceived. The general seeing the Emperor continue motionless, thought he might be ill, and purposely made a noise. Napoleon immediately roused himself, and without any preamble seizing Rapp by the arm, said to him, pointing to the sky, " Look there, up there ! " The general remained silent, but on being asked a second time, he answered that he perceived nothing. " What," replied the Emperor, " you do not see it ? It is my star, it is before you, brilliant." Then, becoming animated, he cried out: " It has never

---

[1] Michon: *Napoléon I. d'après son écriture.*
[2] Brierre de Boismont: *Des Hallucinations.*

abandoned me, I see it on all great occasions, it commands me to go forward, and it is a constant sign of my good fortune."' Another authority, the historian of the Russian campaign, General Ségur, mentions Napoleon's star. Cardinal Fesch was begging him in 1811 to desist from his futile warfare, when the Emperor took him by the hand, led him to the window, opened it, and said, ' Do you see that star?' ' No, Sire,' replied the Cardinal. 'Look again,' insisted the Emperor. ' Sire, there is no star visible,' was the answer, to which Napoleon rejoined, ' I see it ' Whereupon the astonished Cardinal lapsed into silence, imagining that Napoleon intended to convey that his ambition extended even to the heavens.[1] This independent testimony in Rapp's favour is all the more convincing from its motiveless character, neither the Cardinal nor the historian having a theory of hallucinations to propound.

These stories of a guiding star of Napoleon's are rather unconvincing as they stand. There are unquestionable facts, however, that support them. Bourrienne says Napoleon ' frequently gave an involuntary shrug of his right shoulder which was accompanied by a movement of his mouth from left to right.' Meneval, who succeeded Bourrienne as the Emperor's private secretary, refers to the same peculiarity. While dictating, Napoleon, according to Meneval, ' experienced a sort of " tic," consisting in a movement of his right arm, which he twisted while pulling with his hand the lining of the cuff of his coat.'[2] This testifies to an abnormal excitability of the nerve cells in the motor area of the brain. A similar excitability in the visual or auditory area would tend to produce hallucinations of sight or hearing, and would account for the visions above described. It was persistently reported during Napoleon's lifetime that he was subject to attacks of epilepsy, though Bourrienne declares that during the eleven years he was with him he never observed any symptom of that malady. While it is significant that such reports should have been circulated at a time when no suspicion could be entertained of the relations existing between

<hr>

[1] Ségur: *Histoire de Napoléon et de la Grande Armée.*
[2] Meneval: *Napoléon et Marie Louise.*

Napoleon's genius and the epileptic habit, evidence of grave nerve-disorder on the Emperor's part is not wanting. Corvisart, his physician, told Madame de Rémusat that Napoleon's awakening from sleep was generally melancholy, and appeared painful, and that not unfrequently he had convulsive spasms in the stomach which made him vomit.[1] As bearing upon the question of epilepsy, it may be remarked, that during the Russian campaign, according to Ségur, Napoleon's memory became temporarily affected, particularly as to names and dates. For a time he was constantly confusing one person with another, and making odd mistakes as to the period of events. His strange fits of apathy, it is said, also attracted the attention of his generals. This, it is important to observe, was long after Bourrienne had ceased to be on confidential terms with the Emperor.

Nerve-disorder revealed itself unmistakably in Napoleon's brothers and sisters. Joseph Bonaparte had paralysis; Lucien was extremely short-sighted; Louis during the greater part of his life was an invalid, his infirmities, says the Duchesse d'Abrantès, giving him the appearance of an old man before his time; Caroline, like the Emperor, had cancer in the stomach; Pauline died of consumption. Alone among the family, Jerome lived to old age. The cause of death in all cases has not been recorded. But the curious dissimilarity in the character of the various members of the Bonaparte family is not without significance from the neurotic point of view. In extreme contrast to the Emperor, Joseph and Lucien were fond of literature; Louis was a mild, easy, good-natured man; Jerome was a spendthrift; Pauline was vain, capricious, unchaste, and generally foolish. Anomalies of physical growth are also to be noted in the family. While the Emperor was short and thick-set, Lucien was tall and thin, with legs, says the Duchesse d'Abrantès, like a field spider; the one brother had an excessively large head, the other a small one. Pauline was extremely graceful; Caroline, on the other hand, was ill-made, walked badly, and was undignified in her manners. Almost all the Emperor's nephews and nieces were very hasty-tempered. This is the testimony

---

[1] Rémusat: *Mémoires.*

of the Duchesse d'Abrantès, who adds: 'I have known Achille Murat (son of Caroline) so violently overcome by strong passion as to be thrown into convulsions.' The last piece of evidence I can offer as to Napoleon's nerve-disorder, is the early death of his only legitimate son, the offspring of Marie Louise. This poor young man, in whom the Emperor had centred his hopes of founding a dynasty, died at twenty, of what is described as a 'premature decay.' As a child, he was, like his cousins, self-willed and liable to strong fits of passion. Metternich visited him on his deathbed. 'It was a heartrending sight,' says the old diplomatist.[1] 'I have never seen a more mournful picture of decay.'

Wellington was epileptic. His father, the Earl of Mornington, was distinguished for his musical tastes, and an WELLINGTON elder brother had some poetic faculty. During Wellington's career as a statesman, after the battle of Waterloo, his fainting fits were repeatedly a subject of alarm to the nation;[2] and it was an attack of epilepsy that caused his death. In reference to the Duke's condition 'The Times' remarked: 'Of late years increasing infirmities —manifest though energetically resisted—the treacherous ear, the struggling utterance and the tottering step, all told their tale, and suggested even a fear that the greatest man of his age might live to illustrate the decay from which no greatness is secure.'[3] Longevity, a characteristic of Wellington's mother, who died at ninety, persisted in the family, but it is noteworthy that Wellington's elder brother left no issue by either of two wives, and that his eldest son and direct heir was childless.

Turenne, the greatest of French generals before Napoleon, had a weak constitution in boyhood, was a dull scholar, impatient of restraint, and showed dogged perseverance. He stuttered, and was subject to a convulsive movement of the shoulders.—Prince Eugène, who commanded the Imperial army of Austria at twenty-five, was deformed.—Gustavus Adolphus, shot in battle at thirty-eight, left a daughter, Christine, Queen of Sweden, who was of masculine habits

---

[1] Metternich: *Mémoires.*   [2] Greville: *Memoirs.*
[3] *The Times*, September 16, 1852.

and eccentric, and his great-aunt Cecilie led a dissolute and rambling life.—Charles XII., the son of an obstinate, harsh, and despotic father, began his wars at eighteen, and during the stormy life which he ended on the battle-field at thirty-seven displayed extraordinary courage, self-will, and cruelty.—Runjeet Singh, the founder of the Sikh Empire, whose father died at thirty, began his military career at seventeen, acquired large dominion, and at fifty could not stand without support, his health being said to be broken by excesses and low indulgence.

The prophetical missions of Mahommed and Joan of Arc, although belonging to a different order of mental phenomena from the foregoing, are equally traceable to physical causes. It need hardly be said that the ideas expressed to insane people by visionary characters are really their own. Blake conversed with his spirits not in words, but, as he expressed it, by 'intuition and magnetism.' Having summoned up the figure of Richard III., he was requested to ask the tyrant whether he could justify the numerous murders committed by him in the course of his life. The reply was immediate. ' Your question,' said Blake to his interlocutor, ' has already reached him. We have no need of words; this is the answer a little fuller than he has given it me, as you do not understand the language of spirits. He says, that what you call murder and carnage is nothing, that in butchering fifteen or twenty thousand people no harm is done, because the immortal part of them is not only preserved, but passes into a better world. A murdered man who reproached his murderer with killing him would be guilty of ingratitude, seeing that the latter procures him a more comfortable abode, and a more perfect existence.' Many epileptics are able to call up their hallucinations at will. They think of an object and it straightway appears before their eyes, or their unuttered thoughts are translated into audible speech.

A hundred millions of men now living upon the earth believe that Mahommed was sent by God, and that his visions were a revelation of the divine truth. Yet nothing can be more certain, scientifically speaking, than that the founder of Islam possessed no other source of inspiration than the morbid workings of his brain. We need not on that account deny Mahommed the credit of sincerity. There is no doubt that he was, in a great measure, sincere, and as much may MAHOMMED be said of all great religious teachers and prophets, both before his time and since. Traditions relating to Mahommed were industriously collected and recorded during the first three centuries of his era, and we have consequently a tolerably complete view of the prophet as a man. His parentage was not sound. His father, Abdullah, died at twenty-five, and his mother appears to have been a woman of nervous temperament. Frequently in a half-waking condition she fancied she was visited by spirits, and she died when Mahommed, her only child, was six years of age. In boyhood Mahommed had several epileptic seizures, the first occurring when he was four years of age, and causing great alarm to his nurse, who thought he was possessed by an evil spirit. These fits were afterwards regarded by the prophet and his disciples as of supernatural origin in accordance with a prevalent belief in the East. As a young man Mahommed showed great inactivity, and inaptitude for the ordinary duties of life. Until the age of twenty-five, when the widow Kadyjah chose him for a husband, he lived upon the charity of his relatives, and was reduced to the necessity of pasturing sheep, a humble occupation among the Arabs. After marriage he devoted himself to ascetic exercises and religious speculations, based upon the notions of Christianity which had penetrated into Arabia. His temperament was nervous and melancholic. He was generally low-spirited, pensive, and restless. About the age of forty he began to have visions and to hear spiritual voices. More than once he attempted suicide, and his friends were alarmed at the state of his mind. He himself thought he was possessed by a jinn or spirit. 'I hear a sound; I see a light,' he said to his wife. 'I fear there is a jinn in me.' Kadyjah went to consult a wise man. On returning she was told by Mahommed that the Angel Gabriel had appeared to him and told him that he was not possessed by a jinn. Subsequently it was a vision of Gabriel that determined Mahommed to declare his prophetical mission.

Walking on the hill near Mecca one day, he heard a voice

from heaven, and looking upwards he beheld Gabriel sitting with crossed legs upon a throne between heaven and earth. The angel cried out to him, ' Oh Mahommed, thou art in truth the messenger of God and I am Gabriel.' After this, came to him at short or long intervals the revelations set forth in the Koran. Tradition speaks of his being at such times either in a swooning or prostrate condition. ' Inspiration descendeth upon me,' he explained in two ways. ' Sometimes the revelation is communicated to me by Gabriel as by one man unto another, and this is easy ; at other times it affecteth me like the ringing of a bell, penetrating my very heart, and rending me as it were in pieces, and this it is which grievously afflicteth me.' Ayesha, his favourite wife after the death of Kadyjah, saw beads of perspiration on his brow as he received an inspiration on a very cold day. Othman, according to another tradition, related the following : ' When speaking to Mahommed one day he remarked that the prophet's eyes turned towards heaven and then to the right. His head moved as if he were speaking. After some time he turned to Othman and his face was then covered with sweat. Othman asked what was the matter, whereupon he repeated a verse of the Koran which had just been revealed to him.' Habitually the paroxysms may have been slight, but some of them were undoubtedly severe, as when the prophet ' fell heavily to the ground and snorted like a camel.' Besides the devout spirit, Mahommed displayed many of the qualities of a military commander, managing his affairs with tact and skill, and undergoing privation and danger with unflagging courage. It may be supposed that the cerebral disorder which produced Mahommed's visions tended in the latter half of his life to develop his erotic sensibility, and to give his religious system the sensual cast which distinguished it. Until his forty-ninth year the prophet contented himself with one wife ; afterwards he had a dozen, and received inspirations justifying 'the successive additions to his harem.

Hallucinations were at the bottom of the achievements of Joan of Arc. This heroine lived in credulous times ; her countrymen were longing to throw off the English yoke, and believed that she had a mission to lead them to victory, and her manifest sincerity inspired them with an invincible courage. How did she come by her mission? Supernatural voices and visions began to manifest themselves to her about the age of thirteen, a critical period in girlhood, when mental and physical disorders are not infrequent. She seldom heard voices without seeing a light, and when visited by the angels Gabriel, St. Catherine, and Michael, she was *kissed* by these celestials, and felt that they had a good *odour*. Thus she had hallucinations of hearing, sight, touch, and smell. At her trial Joan maintained the reality of her apparitions. ' I saw them,' she said to her judges, ' as plainly as I see you, and when they retired from me I wept, and much I wished that they would take me with them.' No one, whether friend or foe, seems to have thought Joan insane, and it is, of course, a well-established fact that hallucinations of all the senses may exist without intellectual derangement. The judges who condemned her to be burnt evidently believed that she was being deceived by evil spirits, who took the form of angels and saints. Had she lived in these days, poor Joan would have had a different fate; she would have been treated by doctors of medicine, not doctors of divinity; but happily the brain-disorder which brought her to the stake gave her also the fortitude to endure her martyrdom unflinchingly.

Statesmen and administrators of genius present the same characteristics as great commanders. The Romanoff dynasty became neuropathic soon after its accession to the Russian throne in 1613. Alexis, son of Michael, who died at sixteen, had by a first wife Feodor, Ivan, Sophia, and several other daughters. By a second wife he had Peter and Natalie. Feodor, who kept the throne for five years, was weak-minded, and Ivan positively imbecile, the latter being almost blind, unsteady in his gait, given to stammering, and subject to convulsions. On the death of Feodor his sister Sophia tried to make Ivan the Czar, in order to rule in his name. She was a woman of superior talents, a good writer, and a poet. She was also inordinately ambitious, but had to give way to the irresistible force of will of

her younger brother Peter, afterwards surnamed the Great
Thus, of the children of Alexis two were weak-minded, and
two had genius.   Peter was afflicted from infancy with nervous attacks which degenerated into epilepsy.   Excitement
often brought on these seizures, one of which is said to have
lasted three days.   Peter had six sons, five of whom died in
childhood.   The survivor, Prince Alexis, was a drunkard,
and so much given to insubordination and excesses of every
kind, that his father had him put to death.   Peter the Great
was succeeded by his wife Catherine, who was followed by
Peter II., son of the unfortunate Prince Alexis.   With this
youth, who died young, the male line of the Romanoffs
became extinct.

Charles V., in his day the most powerful ruler of Europe,
was a son of the insane Juana, sister of Catherine of Arragon.
Insanity had long been in the family, Juana's grandmother,
Isabella, having been demented, and her father, Ferdinand,
melancholic.   Juana was kept in confinement for many years,
being under the delusion that she was possessed by evil spirits.
She was also deformed.   In this poor lunatic's son administrative genius reached its highest expression.   Charles V.
had indeed a double heritage of insanity, as there are traces
of that disorder also in the family of his father, the Archduke
Philip.   In his youth Charles V. was epileptic.   CHARLES V.
His fits appear to have ceased about the time of his
marriage, but he remained subject to violent headaches, and
had gout from the age of thirty.   He was subject to melancholy, he stammered, was bald early, his lower jaw was longer
than the upper, and he had bad teeth, the sign of a scrofulous taint.   With these defects he combined great physical
strength and activity, extraordinary mental power and versa-
tility of intellect.   At fifty-six bad health compelled him to
retire, and two years later he died.   By a Flemish lady
Charles V. had an illegitimate daughter, who became regent
of the Low Countries.   She inherited the Emperor's gouty
diathesis, and was a woman of masculine character.   By
Octavio Farnèse she became the mother of Alexander of
Parma, a man of eccentric genius, and undoubtedly the
greatest general of his time.   The legitimate descendants of

Charles V. did not inherit their father's abilities. The eldest son, Philip II., was weakly, gloomy, severe, obstinate, and superstitious. By a marriage with his niece, Philip II. had Philip III., a man of feeble and indolent character. Another grandson of Charles V., Don Carlos, exhibited weak or unequal intelligence, and a fitful and turbulent character. He was five years old before he could speak, and afterwards he articulated badly ; he had the long protruding chin of his grandfather, the great Emperor, he was unintelligent, his beard was slight, and he was deficient in virility. In Philip IV., who composed a tragedy, the nerve-disorder of the family manifested itself in a taste for literature and the fine arts. The eldest son of this monarch had convulsions, and died early. His younger son became Charles II., a poor rickety, epileptic creature, deficient in intelligence, so malformed in his lower jaw that he could not masticate his food, twice married, but childless. Such was the last descendant in the male line of the ruler of Germany and Spain, the greatest European potentate of the sixteenth century.[1]

The father of Frederick the Great was eccentric to the point of insanity. Macaulay's description of him makes this sufficiently clear. 'The nature of Frederick William was hard and bad, and the habit of exercising arbitrary power had made him frightfully savage. His rage constantly vented itself to right and left in curses and blows. When his Majesty took a walk every human being fled before him, as if a tiger had broken loose from a menagerie. . . . But it was in his own house that he was most unreasonable and ferocious. His palace was a hell and he was the most execrable of fiends, a cross between Moloch and Puck. His son Frederick and his daughter Wilhelmina were in an especial manner objects of his aversion. His own mind was uncultivated. He despised literature. The business of life according to him was to drill and be drilled.' Again, 'his parsimony degenerated into sordid avarice ; his taste for military pomp and order became a mania. While the envoys of the Court of Berlin were in a state of such squalid poverty

Frederick the Great

---

[1] The neurosis of the Royal Family of Spain has been carefully tabulated by W. W. Ireland in his work *The Blot upon the Brain*.

as moved the laughter of foreign capitals, while the food
placed before the princes and princesses of the blood royal
was too scanty to appease hunger, and so bad that even
hunger loathed it, no price was thought too extravagant for
tall recruits.'[1] In view of the metamorphoses of heredity it
is no surprise to learn that the great Frederick, son of this
monster, was born with 'an exquisite ear for music, and
performed skilfully on the flute,' and that he wrote prose and
verse abundantly. It was by the merest chance, the cast of
Nature's die, so to speak, that Frederick did not become a
man of letters or a musician. As it happened, the qualities
predominated in his brain that made him, as soon as the
opportunity presented itself, 'a tyrant of extraordinary
military and political talents, of industry more extraordinary
still, without fear, without faith, and without mercy.' While
there was a wide difference between father and son as respected extent and vigour of intellect, 'the groundwork of
the character,' adds Macaulay, 'was the same in both. To
both were common the love of order, the love of business, the
military taste, the parsimony, the imperious spirit, the temper
irritable even to ferocity, the pleasure in the pain and humi-
liation of others. But these propensities had in Frederick
William partaken of the general unsoundness of his mind,
and wore a very different aspect when found in company with
the strong and cultivated understanding of his successor.'
To the last, amid all the cares of State, Frederick retained
his passion for music, for reading, for writing, and for literary
society. His conversation was lively, his manners to those
whom he desired to please were even caressing. But he had
a bad heart which betrayed itself in a taste for severe
practical jokes, 'a nature,' as Macaulay observes, 'to which
the sight of human suffering and human degradation is an
agreeable excitement.'

Oliver Cromwell did not come of a sound stock, nor was
his own offspring long-lived or prolific. His father, Robert
Cromwell, died prematurely, while an uncle, Oliver,   CROMWELL
was a gay spendthrift who dissipated a considerable
amount of property. It is stated that the Protector's father

---

[1] Macaulay: Essay, *Frederick the Great.*

was 'a sickly man judging by the languor of his countenance'[1] as shown in a contemporary portrait. By Robert Cromwell's marriage with Elizabeth Seward, he had, besides Oliver, two sons who died early, a daughter Elizabeth, who never married, another daughter Anna, who died at forty-two, and yet another daughter whom a 'lingering illness' carried off at fifty-one. Elizabeth Seward, the Protector's mother, was one of a family of seven, of whom only herself and a brother, Thomas Seward, survived. Thomas appears to have been weak-minded; at all events, Oliver Cromwell petitioned for a commission in lunacy against this maternal uncle, whom he believed to be incapable of managing his property. The Protector is said to have led in his youth a low boisterous dissolute life, and his letters seem to prove it. Apart from Royalist prejudices, such a career is what might well result from the neuropathic tendencies of his constitution. More importance may certainly be attached to this as evidence of the constituent elements of his genius than to the vision he is said to have had as a boy, namely, that of a gigantic figure pulling aside the curtains of his bed and telling him he would live to be the greatest personage in England. According to a document in Thurloe's State Papers, Oliver Cromwell's temper was 'exceedingly fiery.' Sir Philip Warwick says he was of good stature, but his countenance was 'swollen and reddish, and his voice harsh and untunable.' Among the Protector's distempers gout is mentioned. Thurloe speaks of his being dangerously sick in consequence of 'the retirement of the gout out of his foot into his body.'[2] The cause of his death at fifty-nine was ague, a malady the exciting causes of which are still unknown, but which is obviously of a nervous character. For some days before his death, his fits were so frequent as to be almost continuous.

By his wife, Elizabeth Bourchier, who appears to have been a woman of sound constitution, Cromwell had a large family, in whom, however, the evil influence of the Cromwell blood is apparent. Richard, who succeeded his father in the

---

[1] Noble : *Memoirs of the Protectoral House of Cromwell.*

[2] *Memoirs of the Protector and of his Son.* By Oliver Cromwell, a descendant of the family.

Protectorate, was a weak creature; Henry, the second son, who became Lord Deputy of Ireland, stated in a letter to his father that he seldom enjoyed good health for twenty-four hours together. He died at forty-seven of stone, a complaint associated with gouty and rheumatic tendencies.[1] Four of Cromwell's children predeceased him, including a grown-up daughter, Elizabeth, otherwise Mrs. Claypole, who appears to have died in a state of religious hypochondria, if not downright insanity. Mrs. Claypole had some internal complaint which none of her doctors understood. General Fleetwood, in a letter to Henry Cromwell, says it gave rise to 'great pains in the bowels and vapours in the head.' Mrs. Claypole on her death-bed reviled her father bitterly, and the scene, which occurred not long before his own death, is said to have impressed him greatly. Dr. Bates says: ' In her hysterical fits she much disquieted him by upbraiding him sometimes with one of his crimes, sometimes with another according to the furious distractions of her disease.' This daughter died at twenty-seven ; she had several children, none of whom, however, left issue.

The general ' unfitness ' of Cromwell's offspring is not a little remarkable, and may be taken to prove the existence, among them, of an acute degree of nerve disorder. Of the many children born to the Protector's sons and daughters, all but one either died young or were barren. Richard's eldest son, Oliver, was very weakly, and died at forty-nine, unmarried. At the age of twenty-one he made a will, showing that he was not then in good health. Three of Richard's daughters died in infancy, and one at the age of twenty. Another daughter remained unmarried, probably from ill-health or deformity ; and another, though married, was childless. Henry, the Protector's second son, had seven sons and daughters, all with one exception childless. This exception was Henry, among whose ten children only one, again, left issue. The survivor in this case was Richard. He had seven sons and daughters, of whom again but one, Thomas, had offspring—a phenomenon occurring for the third time in three successive generations. A daughter of Thomas's marrying an apothecary had a large and prolific

<hr>

[1] Dejerine.

P

family; and to this obscure but worthy couple is due whatever of the Cromwell blood may survive in England at the present day. On the female side of the House of Cromwell matters were still worse. We have seen that the Protector's daughter Elizabeth had a barren family; another, Bridget, who became Lady Fleetwood, was in similar case; and yet another daughter Mary, Lady Fauconberg, who 'greatly resembled her father in person,' and who in the decline of life is said to have been ' pale and sickly,' was herself childless. Such a record of sterility and physical worthlessness as the Cromwell blood presents is only to be found in connection with insanity or genius.

In statesmanship no greater names are to be found than those of the Pitts, father and son. Of the parentage of the CHATHAM elder Pitt, better known as the Earl of Chatham, the biographers have little to say, but contemporary records enable us to class him among the most afflicted of great men. From boyhood he was cruelly tormented with gout, and in his later life the fluctuations of this disease became a matter of state importance. Gout appears to have alternated in his case with true mental aberration. While he was in one of his strange moods, Lady Chatham wrote that ' no improvement could be expected in his lordship's health until he could have a fit of the gout.' On one occasion, according to Lord Mahon, Chatham suffered ' a dismal and complete eclipse of his powers for upwards of a year.' There was ' no morbid illusion of the fancy, but an utter prostration of the intellect.'[1] Junius, in one of his early letters, refers to Chatham as a lunatic brandishing a crutch. For a time Chatham's political opponents thought his malady was feigned, but Horace Walpole afterwards admitted that his great adversary's nerves were in a shattered condition. ' Added to the frenzy of his conduct,' writes Walpole,[2] ' a new circumstance raised again suspicion of there being more of madness in his case than mere caprice and impracticable haughtiness; he had himself put into the hands of Dr. Addington, a regular physician it is true, but originally

[1] Mahon: *History of England*.
[2] Walpole: *Memoirs of the Reign of George III.*

a mad doctor, who was selected as proper to the disease. . . .
So long did Lord Chatham remain without a fit of the gout, and
so childish and agitated was his whole frame, that if a word
of business was mentioned to him tears and trembling immediately succeeded.' At this time the great minister not
only did not see his subordinates, but did not even receive
letters. Walpole was persuaded of the reality of his madness by his eccentric proceedings on the estate left him by
Pynsent, trees being planted by torchlight 'because his
peremptory and impatient temper could brook no delay.'
Chatham's sickly and uncertain appetite was never regular.
'Hence a succession of chickens was boiling and roasting at
every hour, to be ready whenever he should call.' Even in
active Parliamentary life the disordered state of his intellect occasionally betrayed itself. In arranging to have
the subject of the East India Company brought before the
House of Commons, he passed over all his ministers, with
whom he assumed a sullen and mysterious attitude, and fixed
his choice upon a noisy, purse-proud, illiterate demagogue
named Beckford, who was a general laughing-stock. The
whole political world was thrown into a ferment by this
proceeding. In the midst of the confusion Chatham pro-
claimed himself gouty and retired to the country. On
returning after some time he shut himself up in the Castle
Inn at Marlborough, and remained there some weeks.
'Everybody who travelled that road,' says Macaulay, 'was
amazed by the number of his attendants. Footmen and
grooms dressed in his family livery filled the whole inn, and
swarmed in the streets of the little town. The truth was,
that the invalid had insisted that during his stay all the
waiters and stable-boys of the Castle should wear his livery.'
Walpole records that after executing a letter of attorney
giving full power to his wife, Chatham 'began singing.'
Again, having sold an estate to Thomas Walpole, he wanted
it back, and his discourse, it is said, 'grew very ferocious'
on the subject. Many other incidents in Chatham's career
suggestive of a disordered intellect could be quoted. His
fatal nervous attack came as he was attempting to address
the House of Lords. 'He fell down in a fit of apoplexy,

says Walpole, 'with strong convulsions and slobbering at the mouth,' and never recovered.

With his father's gout William Pitt inherited his father's genius for administration and debate, excelling his elder brother at all points.   Probably there was a double

PITT

heredity of nerve disorder in this case, inasmuch as Lady Chatham suffered in her later years from a 'painful disorder.'   Pitt was active and studious, and his abilities displayed themselves early.   At fourteen he wrote a tragedy. In this there was no love : the whole plot was political, one of the principal personages being a faithful servant of the Crown, the other an unprincipled conspirator.   Already his health was very weak.   His progress in learning, however, was extraordinarily rapid ; he had so peculiar a discrimination in seizing the meaning of an author that, as his tutor observed, he never seemed to learn, but only to recollect.   At the age of twenty-five Pitt had not only made a great name in Parliament but was Prime Minister.   'He was then,' says Macaulay, ' the greatest subject that England had seen during many generations.   His father had never been so powerful, nor Walpole, nor Marlborough.'   Youth as he was, he had brought into order the finances of the country, and he had decided and settled for seventy years the most anxious and perplexing of all questions—the principle of English government in India. Yet he was not dazzled by his success, but continued to be a great worker.   In the prime of manhood his health caused anxiety ; he had severe headaches and drank a great deal of port wine.   Ultimately his malady took the form of 'flying gout,' of which he died at forty-seven, unmarried.   Nerve-disorder betrayed itself in other members of Lord Chatham's family.   Pitt's elder brother married, but left no issue, the title becoming extinct on his death.   A sister, Lady Mahon, died at twenty-five, leaving three daughters, of whom one was the notorious Lady Hester Stanhope ; another, though married, died childless, and the third left a family.   Another sister of Pitt's died in childbed of puerperal fever, a malady of a nervous character.

Lady Hester Stanhope, grand-daughter of the great Lord Chatham, was eccentric, but is said to have had an 'inborn quickness of discernment, as well as a satirical tongue.' At the age of thirty-four she left England for the East, and established herself among the semi-savage tribes on Mount Lebanon. She adopted the garb of a Mahommedan chieftain, and by force of character obtained a great ascendency over the rude races around her, by whom she was revered as a prophetess. Among these people she died, with no European near her.

The greatest of Indian administrators, Warren Hastings, was of delicate constitution and stunted growth.[1] His father, Pynaston Hastings, the son of a clergyman, WARREN was a ne'er-do-well, very improvident and volatile. HASTINGS This unpromising youth married a butcher's daughter named Warren, whom he reduced to the greatest destitution. She, herself, was probably not too soundly constituted, for soon after giving birth to her eminent son she died. On the subject of his parentage Warren Hastings was always reticent, there being nothing in it, as he thought, to be proud of. No life, indeed, could have begun more inauspiciously than that of the first Governor-General of Bengal. Warren Hastings was sent to a charity school, where he first displayed the great industry, and the vivid and active imagination, which carried him to the pinnacle of fame. All his life he was subject to frequent attacks of illness. Despite his ailments he lived to a great age, but in his latter years, paralysis declared itself in his right side; he had also staggering fits, and hallucinations of hearing, his ears, as he records in his diary, being filled sometimes with slow music, sometimes with 'confused sounds of a distant multitude.' In the end his mental powers failed him to some extent, and at his death the organs of deglutition were paralysed. Twice married, he left only two children, both by his first wife; one died in childhood, the other in early youth. In his paralytic period Warren Hastings developed a taste for the composition of poetry which Macaulay ignorantly ridicules.

In Lord Brougham great accomplishments were combined with eccentricities that bordered upon insanity.[2] He

[1] Gleig: *Memoirs of the Life of Warren Hastings.*

[2] 'An Apology for Lord Brougham on Physical Grounds.' By D. D Tuke, M. D. *Journal of Mental Science,* 1869.

was irritable, restless, and insatiably vain. These characteristics he probably derived from both parents, for while
his father was noted for his 'originality,' his
BROUGHAM mother was a woman of 'remarkable intellect.'
As a young barrister of twenty-two, Brougham's conduct was
thought to show a tendency to madness, and his friends
were uneasy about him. Afterwards, his career, until he
became Lord Chancellor, was brilliant indeed, though marked
by many fantastical acts, explicable only on the ground of
mental derangement. The 'Edinburgh Review' complained
of 'the outrages he was in the habit of perpetrating, not
only on dignity but decency; his wearisome self-laudation,
his grotesque extravagances, his capriciously malevolent and
eccentric selection of the objects of his antipathies. . . .
From the end of the session, 1834,' said this organ, 'through
his wild visit to Scotland, and for many months afterwards,
his mind was clearly off its balance; his temper became for
a time uncontrollable, his perception of facts and of reasoning gradually disordered.' 'The Times' charged him with
drunkenness, and another newspaper ascribed his eccentricities to opium-eating. Lord Campbell considers that
Brougham's mind was 'very seriously affected.' During the
latter half of his long life, 'this impetuous and formidable
adventurer,' as 'The Times' called him, was not entrusted
with office. Before his death his mind gave way altogether.
He had a gaunt, ungainly figure, and the basis of his manifold
attainments seemed to be a strong memory, and an extraordinary power of application.

Washington exhibited an extreme development of the
osseous system, and lost his teeth early—signs of a rickety
constitution. He left no issue.—Richelieu had a sister insane, and a brother who was extremely pious.—Edmund
Burke had 'an imperious and uncontrollable temper;' he
fell into general debility accompanied by loss of muscular
energy and weakness of sight, and his one son died of consumption.—Széchenyi, the Hungarian patriot, founder of the
Magyar Academy, leader of the Revolution of 1848, promoter
of the navigation of the Danube, and of other public works
of great utility, died in a lunatic asylum.—The great Condé

family were dwarfish, and ravaged by nerve-disorder in various forms.—Charles James Fox, a lad of extraordinary promise, became a man of mark in the House of Commons at twenty-five, and was notorious for his drinking bouts, his gambling, and his amours. He was poetic, and had a violent temper. By his wife he had no issue, but he left an illegitimate son who was an idiot, deaf and dumb, and who died at fifteen. —Horace Walpole, son of Sir Robert Walpole, suffered from gout.—Sir S. Romilly, eminent as a law reformer, committed suicide.—The Canning family were distinguished for their sensitive and irritable temperaments.—Palmerston died child-less, as did also his brother, the title becoming extinct.— Cavour, after a series of apoplectic seizures producing an unwonted irritability of manner, died of congestion of the brain.—Beaconsfield's paternal grandmother lived to be eighty 'without indulging in a tender expression.' As the result of her 'insane temperament,' her son Isaac d'Israeli, besides being 'dreamy, eccentric, and poetic,' suffered from weakness of sight. The same strain manifested itself in Isaac d'Israeli's son Benjamin, afterwards Lord Beaconsfield. In early manhood he had fits of giddiness, which he described as like a consciousness of the earth's rotation. Once he fell into a trance, from which he did not recover for a week.[1] Gout was his chief ailment.

[1] Froude: *Life of Lord Beaconsfield.*
If we may trust the autobiographical details given in his novel, *Contarini Fleming*, Beaconsfield was well acquainted with the insanity of genius. 'I have sometimes,' he writes, 'half believed, although the sus-picion is mortifying, that there is only a step between his state who deeply indulges in imaginative meditation and insanity; for I well remember when I indulged in meditation to an extreme degree, that my senses ap-peared sometimes to be wandering. I cannot describe the peculiar feeling I then experienced, for I have failed in so doing to eminent surgeons and men of science with whom I have conversed respecting it, and who were curious to become acquainted with its nature. But I think it was that I was not always assured of my identity or even existence, for I have found it necessary to shout aloud to be sure that I lived ; and I was in the habit very often at night of taking down a volume, and looking into it for my name, to be convinced that I had not been dreaming of myself. At these times there was an incredible acuteness, an intenseness in my sensations. Every object seemed animate, and, as it were, acting upon me. The only way that I can devise to express my general feeling is, that I seemed to be conscious of the rapid whirl of the globe.'

CHAPTER IX

PHILOSOPHICAL AND SCIENTIFIC GENIUS—THE ECCENTRICITIES OF
SOCRATES—INSANITY OF BACON'S MOTHER—HIS BROTHER ANTHONY
DEFORMED—INSANITY OF SWEDENBORG AND AUGUSTE COMTE—
CARLYLE AND HIS ANCESTRY—NERVE DISORDER OF COPERNICUS,
GALILEO, AND KEPLER—ISAAC NEWTON'S INSANITY—THE HER-
SCHELLS—JAMES WATT—HUMPHRY DAVY—FARADAY—THEIR CHA-
RACTERISTICS AND AILMENTS—MISCELLANEOUS EXAMPLES OF NERVE
DISORDER AMONG MEN OF SCIENCE—THE ARITHMETICAL AND CHESS-
PLAYING FACULTIES—THE DARWIN FAMILY—ERASMUS DARWIN'S
ECCENTRICITIES—INSANITY OF ONE OF HIS SONS—THE WEDGWOODS
—CHARLES DARWIN'S DESCENT—THE PHYSICAL BASIS OF COMMER-
CIAL GENIUS, PHILANTHROPY, PIETY, AND CRIMINALITY—NEUROPA-
THIC ASPECTS OF PIETY IN LUTHER, BUNYAN, GEORGE FOX, AND
CARDINAL NEWMAN—NE'ER-DO-WELLISM AND GENIUS

THERE remains to be considered the important class of men
of genius whose labours are philosophical and scientific.

SOCRATES Some fifty years ago the French physiologist Lélut
wrote a treatise to prove that on the showing of his
disciples Socrates suffered, if not from insanity, at all events
from sensorial hallucinations;[1] and an examination of the facts
of the case in the light of modern science goes to establish
the truth of Lélut's contention. Socrates believed himself to
be attended by a familiar spirit whose voice he heard. There
is hardly in Plato a single dialogue where the 'demon' is not
spoken of. By literary students this has been accepted as
a figurative expression, but the philosopher's habits of life,
as recorded, are in perfect harmony with the hallucination
theory. Among the singularities of Socrates, Lélut enumerates his wearing the same mantle in all seasons, walking
barefooted on ice, and dancing and jumping alone without
apparent reason, leading in the eyes of the vulgar the oddest
kind of life, having no occupation but that of perorating
in public places, pursuing everybody with his irony, and

---

[1] Lélut : *Du Démon de Socrate.*

accepting nothing from his disciples or friends, but asking without hesitation for a coat when he needed one. Socrates had long reveries or ecstatic fits; and it often happened to him to stop suddenly in the midst of a walk or a conversation, saying that he heard the voice of his familiar. Clearly the father of philosophy was an eccentric, though his insanity may have been for the most part of a purely sensorial character.

The mother of Lord Bacon is believed for some years before her death to have been insane.[1] When Bacon was about thirty-eight, her health was said to be 'worn.' No letters of hers appear to have been written after this date, and only an occasional reference to her existence in Bacon's correspondence shows her to be alive. Spedding says: 'The supposition which seems to me most probable is that she lost the command of her faculties some years before her death, and that the management of her affairs was taken out of her hands.' In Bishop Goodman's ' Court of King James,' it is stated that Bacon's mother became ' frantic in her age.' In connection with this rumoured insanity it is important to find that Bacon's elder brother Anthony was lame throughout life, that at fourteen his eyesight was in danger, that he was always in a ' sickly state of body,' and that he died at forty-three.[2] Other collateral evidence as to Bacon's neuropathic condition exists. His mother's sister marrying William Cecil gave birth to Robert Cecil, first Earl of Salisbury, who was of weakly constitution, cold-hearted, selfish and deformed, but the ablest minister of his time. The philosopher's only brother Anthony was a man of some distinction, and it may be noted that of six children whom Bacon's father had by a first and presumably sound wife none attained eminence. The maternal heritage of nerve-disorder manifested itself unmistakably in Bacon's life. His health was always troublesome. He was so frequently absent from the Council in the Star Chamber that people began to doubt whether he would prove equal to his work. A contemporary writer says of him :—' His infirmity is given out to be gout. . . . But

BACON

---

[1] Spedding: *Life of Francis Bacon.*
[2] *Dictionary of National Biography.*

in truth the general opinion is that he hath so tender a constitution both of body and mind that he will hardly be able to undergo the burden of so much as his place requires.'[1] Gout may very well have been the complaint from which Bacon suffered, and which he so often alludes to as his 'sickness.' He died of an accidental chill, and left no off-spring.

The character of Swedenborg is a specially interesting study from the neurotic point of view. Swedenborg was not only an epileptic but at times an irresponsible maniac SWEDEN-BORG who, nevertheless, in his writings exhibits much subtle philosophical insight. Emerson calls him one of the mastodons of literature. Swedenborg's father was a 'bustling, energetic turbulently self-conscious man,' pious but keen in money matters, and possessing 'great energy of character.' That such qualities betray the presence of nerve-disorder we have frequently seen. Whether the evil influence was contributed to by the sage's mother there is no saying. Women of her class were accustomed to wear a top-knot, and it is related of her that a calf being born with something like a top-knot on its head, she 'took her own and her girl's hoods and threw them into the fire.' This was not, perhaps, a very sane proceeding, but she appears to have been for the most part a gentle and unassuming woman. As a boy Swedenborg was able to suspend his breathing, and his disciples supposed this to imply a power of entering the spirit world while still in the flesh. Until his forty-sixth year he studied and speculated largely about astronomy, anatomy, magnetism, and kindred subjects. The manner of his becoming a prophet was this: One night in London after he had dined heartily, a kind of mist spread before his eyes, and the floor of the room seemed to become covered with toads and other hideous reptiles. 'I was astonished,' he relates, 'having all my wits about me, and being perfectly conscious. The darkness gradually passed away. I now saw a man sitting in a corner of the chamber. As I had thought myself alone I was greatly frightened, when he said to me "Eat not so much." My sight again became dim, and when I recovered I found

[1] Spedding.

myself alone in the room.' The following night the same thing occurred, except that the man said to him, 'I am God the Lord, the Creator and redeemer of the world, and I have chosen thee to unfold to men the spiritual sense of the Holy Scriptures. I will myself dictate to thee what thou shalt write.'

Thenceforward Swedenborg abandoned all worldly learning, and laboured only in spiritual things. Previous to this, as shown by his diary, he had wonderful ecstatic dreams, distressing visions of temptations, persecutions, and sufferings. Some of these dreams were of a sensual character, and sensuality appears to have been his strongest passion. A break in Swedenborg's diary occurs when he had an attack of acute mania. This occurred while he was lodging in Fetter Lane, London, about his fifty-sixth year. Brockner, his landlord, found him foaming at the mouth and declaring that he was the Messiah in person. In the street he pulled off his clothes and rolled in the gutter. The outbreak occurred in connection with an epileptic seizure, and from this period onward Swedenborg's delusions were all of an insane character. He believed that the second coming of the Messiah had taken place in his own person, and that his existence was largely passed in the spiritual world. With a profound belief in himself he, nevertheless, showed considerable artfulness in evading attempts on the part of believers to put his miraculous powers to the test, alleging that the requests made to him were not sufficiently important to justify him in troubling the Almighty. His death was due to paralysis and apoplexy.

One of the most vigorous thinkers of modern times, Auguste Comte, founder of Positivism, fell into a state of insanity, and for nearly a year was confined in Auguste Esquirol's asylum. This occurred in 1826. Two Comte years later Comte published his ' Cours de Philosophie Positive,' the ' fruit of fourteen years' labour.'

Kant in his declining years became imbecile.—Descartes had hallucinations of hearing, thinking himself followed about by an invisible person, who entreated him to continue his researches.—Hegel's sister was insane.—Leibnitz was gouty, and subject to fits of giddiness.—Schopenhauer's father committed suicide in a fit of melancholia; an uncle was demented, and the philosopher himself was subject to strange manias and impulses.—James Mill was consumptive.—John Stuart Mill, a prodigy of learning in his youth, died childless, although his wife had issue by her first husband.

As to Thomas Carlyle's parentage we have copious information in his 'Reminiscences.'[1] The astonishing force and originality of his character had a distinctly neuropathic origin. On the paternal side, his ancestry and connections were marked by the insane temperament, and also suffered from some of the allied forms of nerve-disorder. The grandfather was a 'fiery, irascible, indomitable man, full of irregularities and unreason.' With his brother he maintained a bitter feud for many years—a very characteristic outcome of insane tendencies. Carlyle's father was a man of the same stamp, possessing 'great vehemence of insight, and a piercing emphasis of wisdom.' He was uneducated, had no appreciation of poetry, but was a man of action. 'We had all to complain,' says Carlyle, 'that we durst not freely love him. His heart seemed as if walled in. My mother has owned to me that she could never understand him.' That sturdy, angular figure of whom Carlyle writes with a curious awe-struck, wondering reverence, is however to be understood by the physiologist through the medium of his brothers and sisters. John the eldest brother had asthma, and was a 'sickly pallid man,' who died at forty-seven, leaving two sons and a daughter, 'none of whom came to anything but insignificance.' Francis, whom Carlyle remembered as having a tremulous palsied voice, was of cheerful demeanour, a quaint sociable man, and left two sons who prospered. Tom, the youngest brother, was 'fiery, passionate, and self-secluded,' dying at forty. All these uncles of the sage of Chelsea, small farmers or artisans, were evidently men of a peculiar endowment. Carlyle's aunt Fanny was likewise a woman of 'singular vehemence, inflexibility and energy—all uncultivated and ill-directed;' while another aunt, Margaret, died of consumption at twenty-seven. From

[1] Carlyle: *Reminiscences.*

boyhood, Carlyle himself was a martyr to dyspepsia and general ill-health. His irritability appears to have been excessive, and he suffered terribly from sleeplessness. In his diary he speaks of himself thus: 'Nerves all inflamed and torn up, body and mind in a hag-ridden condition.' He possessed, however, that great basis of knowledge a most retentive memory. For many years before his death, his right hand was palsied.[1] Carlyle's marriage was a barren one, and its painful discords may have been due to the fact that his wife was, equally with himself, a sufferer from nerve-disorder, which took the form of a keen and sarcastic wit, a turn for poetry and great self-will, as well as paralysis and sudden death.

In science, the lives of the greatest men, from Copernicus to Darwin, yield strong evidence of the existence of nerve disorder as an element of genius. The astronomers have been signal sufferers. Copernicus died of apoplexy, and before his death was 'paralysed both in body and mind.' He never married. Tycho Brahe in his latter days—he died at fifty-four—became weak-minded. He was of a sanguine temperament, but irritable and obstinate. He was one of a family of ten, none of whom became eminent, but his youngest sister, Sophia, is said to have been an accomplished mathematician. Galileo, the son of a musician and philosopher, had, from his youth, a 'chronic disorder accompanied with acute pains in his body, and loss of sleep and appetite.' As this attacked him at intervals during his life, it was probably gout. He fell into a state of melancholia, during which he felt 'as if he were being incessantly called by his daughter.' This daughter died suddenly. Galileo himself finally became blind, and also completely deaf. Kepler was the son of a man of good family, who ruined himself by his own misconduct, 'and died of apoplexy, while his mother had peculiarities of temper.' The astronomer was sickly as a child, and died at sixty of a 'violent fever accompanied by a brain disease, which baffled the skill of his physicians, but which was thought to have been produced by over-study.' By a first wife, Kepler left a son and a

EARLY ASTRONO-MERS

---

[1] Tyndall: *Fortnightly Review* for January 1890.

daughter whose fate is unknown; by a second wife he had three sons and two daughters who all died young.[1]

Isaac Newton, an only child, was so diminutive at birth that it is said 'he might have been put into a quart mug.'

NEWTON Very little is known of his parents. His father, a farmer, died at thirty-seven, from some unknown cause; his mother afterwards married a clergyman named Barrett, and had several children, none of whom became eminent. From this circumstance, and his father's early death, it may be concluded that the neuropathic influence in Newton's case was on the paternal side. No reasonable doubt can be entertained that Newton's mind gave way, and that temporarily at least he had some of the delusions of insanity. Sir David Brewster, his biographer,[2] is very angry at the suggestion, but the facts are too strong for him. In the MSS. left by Huygens there occurs the following note:—

'On May 29, 1694, Mr. Colin, a Scotchman, informed me that eighteen months ago, the illustrious geometrician Isaac Newton had become insane, either in consequence of his intense application to his studies, or from excessive grief at having lost by fire his chemical laboratory, and several manuscripts. When he came from the Archbishop of Cambridge, he made some observation which indicated an alienation of mind. He was immediately taken care of by his friends, who confined him to his house and applied remedies by means of which he has now so far recovered his health, as to begin to understand his "Principia."'

Huygens also mentioned the matter in a letter to Leibnitz under date June 8, 1694, in the following terms: 'I do not know if you are acquainted with the accident which has happened to Mr. Newton, namely that he has had an attack of phrenitis, which lasted eighteen months, and of which they say that his friends have cured him by means of remedies, and keeping him shut up.'

As the burning of Newton's laboratory and papers happened before 1684, it could have had no immediate connection with his illness, and in any case would be a very far-

---

[1] Brewster: *The Martyrs of Science.*
[2] Brewster: *Life of Sir Isaac Newton.*

f tched explanation of his state of mind. Concerning this,
we have direct evidence in Newton's own correspondence.
On September 13, 1693, when fifty-one years of age, he
wrote the following strange letter to Pepys :—

'Some time after Mr. Millington had delivered your
message, he pressed me to see you the next time I went to
London. I was averse, but he was pressing, and I consented
before I considered what I did. For I am extremely troubled
at the embroilment I am in, and have neither ate nor slept
well this twelvemonth, nor have I my former consistency of
mind. I never designed to get anything by your interest
nor by King James's favour, but I am now sensible that I
must withdraw from your acquaintance, and see neither you
nor any of my friends any more, if I may but leave them
quietly. I beg your pardon for saying I would see you again,
and rest

'Your most humble and most obedient servant,
'Is. NEWTON.'

This letter threw Pepys into consternation. He wrote
to Millington, to ask what it meant, saying : 'The letter
has put me into great disorder, lest it should arise from that
which of all mankind I should least dread from him, and
most lament for—I mean a discomposure in head or mind, or
both.' To Pepys, Millington replied in the following terms :—

'I was, I must confess, very much surprised at the inquiry you were pleased to make about the message that Mr.
Newton made the ground of his letter to you. For I was
very sure I never received from you, or delivered to him, any
such.'

Millington saw Newton on the subject. 'Upon his own
accord, and before I had time to ask him any question,'
continues Millington in his letter to Pepys, 'he told me
that he had written to you a very odd letter at which he
"was much concerned," and that he had done it under the
influence of a "distemper that seized his head, and kept him
awake for five nights together." Further, he desired that
I would reply to you on the subject, and beg your pardon,
he being very much ashamed he should be so rude to a

person for whom he hath so great an honour. He is now very well,' says Millington in conclusion, 'though I fear he is under some small degree of melancholy.'

While under his ' distemper,' Newton, on September 16, 1693, also wrote the following to Locke :—

'Sir,—Being of opinion that you endeavoured to embroil me with women and by other means, I was so much affected with it as that when one told me you were sickly and would not live, I answered, " 'Twere better if you were dead." I desire you to forgive me this uncharitableness, for I am now satisfied that what you have done is just, and I beg your pardon for having had hard thoughts of you for it, and for replying that you struck at the root of morality in the principles you expounded in your book, and designed to pursue in another book, and that I took you for a Hobbist. I beg your pardon also for saying that there was a design to sell me an office or to embroil me.—I am your most obedient and unfortunate servant,

'Is. Newton.'

Locke wrote Newton a magnanimous reply which called forth the following :—

' Sir,—The last winter by sleeping too often by my fire I got an ill habit of sleeping, and the distemper, which this summer has been epidemical, put me further out of order. So that when I wrote to you I had not slept an hour a night for a fortnight together, and for five days together not a wink. I remember I wrote to you, but what I said of your book I remember not. If you please, send me a transcription of that passage. I will give you an account of it if I can.—I am your most humble servant,

'Is. Newton.'

That these letters should never have been suspected by such a man as Sir David Brewster to contain indications of mental aberration on the part of the writer, shows how deeply rooted is the prejudice that genius is a strong and well-balanced condition of mind. After this period Newton was never himself again. His letters to Flamsteed on the lunar theory, written two years subsequently, exhibit a strange incoherence, and Professor de Morgan thinks that from the time of Newton's settling in London (he was appointed

Master of the Mint in 1696) 'his judgment underwent a gradual deterioration.'[1] While his distemper was incubating, that is to say about his forty-ninth year, he began to concern himself with the prophecies of Daniel and other theological questions, and to these he latterly gave himself up altogether. The part which piety plays in cases of mental aberration has elsewhere been dealt with. Newton lived to extreme old age, and died of stone—a disease belonging to the gouty diathesis. He never married, and was popularly believed to have a positive aversion to female society. As further evidence of neuropathic conditions on his father's side, one may point to the lamentable unfitness of the offspring of Newton's paternal uncle Robert. Sir Isaac's full cousin John was a carpenter, afterwards a gamekeeper, and this man's son, who became Sir Isaac's heir, was a youth of the most dissolute habits. One day while drunk, this scion of the house of Newton fell down with a tobacco pipe in his mouth, and the stem of the pipe sticking in his throat caused his death at the age of thirty. Ten years before this event a clergyman named Mason alluded to Newton's heir as a ' poor representative of a great man; ' adding very wisely, ' but this is a case that often happens.' Of course we know nothing of the influence which female heredity may have exercised in this case.

The native aptitude of the elder Herschell for astronomical research appears to have been a variation upon the musical tastes of his family—a species of metamorphosis THE familiar enough to the student of heredity, and HERSCHELLS having its basis in some inequality of nerve or brain function. The father of William Herschell was a musician, and everyone of the family, except the eldest daughter, possessed marked musical ability. Of the astronomer's brothers, three were professional musicians; he himself in boyhood was an excellent performer on the oboe and the violin. The father had a paralytic seizure, and also developed an asthmatical affection. Caroline Herschell shared her brother William's scientific tastes, and assisted him in his astronomical pursuits. From her diary[2] we gather some in-

---

[1] De Morgan: *Newton, his Friend and his Niece.*
[2] *Memoirs of Caroline Herschell.* By Mrs. John Herschell.

teresting facts in the family history. The sister who was unmusical was of a peculiar disposition. She married a man named Griesbach, but afterwards returned to her father's house. 'My sister,' says Caroline, 'was not of a very patient temper, and could not be reconciled to have children about her.' Dietrich, one of the musical brothers, appears to have caused his family some anxiety by his ne'er-do-well habits. About the age of fifty he was broken both in health and fortune, and his family appear to have been a sore disappointment to Caroline, who in her later years took up her abode with them in Germany. Caroline describes Dietrich as suffering from peevishness and weak nerves. Some painful details as to the Griesbach family, which might have been instructive from the heredity point of view, appear to have been suppressed in Caroline's published correspondence—a dis-service of a kind which the biographer of a great man too frequently renders to his readers. Caroline was at one time in danger of losing her sight, and she and her brother William, during their long residence in England, suffered from frequent illnesses. The nature of these is not always specified, but in her diary Caroline, nearly forty years before her death—she lived to be ninety-two—says she feels as if she would be an invalid for life, and speaks of her brother as suffering from constant fits of giddiness and low spirits. William's death occurred at eighty-two, 'after twenty years of nervous suffering.' The exact cause is not recorded, but Caroline's end was due to 'cramps and rheumatic complaints.' William Herschell married a woman who suffered from gout.

This alliance, unfortunate from the physical point of view, resulted in the birth of one son, a genius also. Herschell the younger continued his father's astronomical studies, in which he achieved similar distinction. He was also a highly accomplished chemist, and to his other gifts he added a deep poetic feeling. Curious sensorial hallucinations accompanied the younger Herschell's genius, as we gather from a lecture on ocular spectra delivered by him on one occasion before a scientific institute.[1] He often saw faces in the dark, some-

---

[1] Sir John Herschell: *Familiar Lectures on Scientific Subjects.*

times ten or a dozen appearing in succession, for the most part unpleasing though not hideous, and always h ving son e general resemblance to each other. Landscape also presented themselves to his inner vision, much more rarely than the faces, but much more distinctly. 'I was sitting one morning very quietly at my breakfast table,' he says, 'doing nothing and thinking of nothing, when I was startled by a singularly shadowy appearance at the outside corner of the field of vision of the left eye. It gradually advanced into the field of view, and then appeared to be a pattern in straight angular forms, very much in general aspect like the drawing of a fortification, with some suspicion of faint lines of colour between the dark lines. It appeared to advance slowly from out of the corner until it spread all over the visual area, and passed across to the right side, where it disappeared. I cannot say how long it lasted, but it must have been a minute or two.'

Several years afterwards the same geometrical spectrum presented itself to Sir John Herschell again. He adds: 'I have mentioned this experience to several persons, but have only met one to whom it has occurred. This was a lady of my acquaintance, who assured me that she had often experienced a similar affection, and that it was always followed by a violent headache, which was not the case with me.' Another waking vision of Sir John Herschell's was a 'round, deep purple, feebly luminous, spot, dying gradually away into darkness at the borders.' Various circular and geometrical forms often presented themselves to him. Once in the evening, while passing the site of a building that had been demolished, he was amazed to see the structure still standing projected against a dull sky. 'Being perfectly aware,' he adds, 'that it was a mere nerve impression, I walked on, keeping my eyes directed to it, and the perspective of the building appeared to change with the change in the point of view as it would have done if real.' Such impressions are to the visual centre of the brain what voices or other sounds would be to the auditory centre; they are, in fact, a true hallucination. Sir John Herschell was fortunate enough to marry a lady who gave him a numerous, and apparently healthy, family, in whom, however, his genius was not continued.

In the family of James Watt, genius was foreshadowed in the inventor's grandfather, Thomas Watt, who was a teacher of mathematics and 'an oddity,' and who had a weakly offspring. Three of Thomas Watt's children died in infancy, and a daughter at eighteen. Two sons survived, of these one died at fifty unmarried; the other, by his marriage with a woman named Agnes Muirhead, was the father of the inventor of the steam engine. In the absence of precise information as to the physical character of James Watt's parents, I can only note again the great mortality occurring in their offspring, three of the inventor's brothers and sisters dying in childhood, another brother at twenty-three, James Watt himself being the sole survivor in manhood of a family of five. The man who was destined to revolutionise the mechanical world was a born mathematician. Almost before he could read he was occupied with mechanical problems; he was of an abstracted and contemplative nature, and physically an invalid. In his youth the 'agony he suffered from continued and violent headaches,' says Mrs. Campbell, 'often affected his nervous system, and left him for days, even weeks, languid, depressed, and fanciful; at those times there was a roughness and asperity in his manner that softened with returning health. . . . He was alternately very active or apparently very indolent, and was subject to continual fits of absence.'[1] Again, as a young man he suffered from 'violent rheumatism and gnawing pain in his back, and weariness all over his body.' He had a good ear for music, and before occupying himself with the steam engine acquired some notoriety as a constructor of musical instruments. His health was always troublesome. In addition to his headaches he complained, about the age of thirty-four, of having fits of 'laziness, stupefaction, and confusion of ideas,' while his memory was accustomed to fail him in an alarming fashion. At forty-nine he wrote to a friend: 'My health is so bad that I do not think I can hold out much longer . . . I cannot help being dispirited, because I find my

[1] Muirhead: *Life of James Watt.*

head fail me so much.' Despite his ailments Watt lived to the age of eighty-three. He married a Miss Miller, by whom he had several children. Among these, nerve-disorder manifested itself strongly. A son and a daughter died in early life of consumption, another son James never married, but was a recluse and peculiar in his habits, and with his death at seventy-nine the Watt family perished.

Like the younger Herschell, Humphry Davy combined with his scientific genius a strong poetic feeling.[1] The neurotic condition is traceable in his family HUMPHRY through one or two generations. Grandmother DAVY Davy was a woman of 'fervid and poetical mind;' her son, the great chemist's father, died of a 'decline,' while his wife was carried off by some nervous illness. In his youth Humphry Davy, who thus appears to have had an evil heritage from both parents, was healthy and active enough. He learnt only by fits and starts, but was blessed with a most retentive memory. His imaginativeness developed itself early. In his youthful diaries he speaks of being 'pursued at night by horrible images.' 'After reading a few books,' he says, 'I was seized with a desire to narrate, and I gradually began to invent and to form stories of my own.' As he became eminent his health declined; it was then that the hereditary weakness of his constitution revealed itself. He suffered from his eyes; he had rheumatism in his right hand and arm, and generally a 'wretched condition of body.' Attacks of paralysis and apoplexy supervened, causing his death at fifty-one. He married the 'most amiable and intellectual woman he had ever known,' but left no offspring.

Faraday, after a brilliant career which he began as an errand boy, also died childless, and, like Humphry Davy, was much shattered by nerve-disorder, although he FARADAY lived to the age of seventy-five.[2] He was of the humblest parentage; his father was a blacksmith, and to the last his poor old mother, who was illiterate, never understood anything of her son's achievements in science. On the father's side an hereditary transmission of nerve-disorder is

[1] *Life of Sir Humphry Davy.* By his brother John Davy, M.D.
[2] Bence Jones: *Life of Michael Faraday.*

apparent. The elder Faraday died at forty-nine, and a few
years before his death he wrote:—'I am sorry to say I have
not had the pleasure of enjoying one day's health for a long
time. Although I am seldom off work for a whole day
together, yet I am under the necessity through pain of
being from work part of almost every day.' An uncle
of Faraday's died at twenty-four. Giddiness and loss of memory attacked Faraday before his fiftieth year. A course
of lectures which he delivered were afterwards so completely
obliterated from his memory that he delivered them again the
following year without a suspicion that they were not new.
Ultimately he became paralysed.

Joule, who discovered the mechanical equivalent of heat,
was deformed, and died of disease of the brain.—Ampère,
mathematician, electrician, and philologist, was eccentric. He
was self-taught, and had a most tenacious memory.—Volta's
skull was abnormal in shape, and he had a son insane.
—Linné, impetuous in character, was gouty and apoplectic,
and ultimately became weak-minded.—Cuvier died of a nervous affection, and his children of brain disease.—Augustin
de Candolle, a botanist of distinction, had water on the
brain in his youth and was poetic; while De Jussieu, the head
of an eminent botanical family, became blind.—Albert von
Haller, the father of modern physiology, was rickety and
gouty, and belonged to an hereditarily pious family.—Harvey,
who discovered the circulation of the blood, was gouty, hot-
tempered, and occasionally eccentric.—Swammerdam fell into
religious melancholy.—Zimmermann, the son of a nervous
mother and an ailing father, was hypochondriacal in his
youth, and became in his latter years completely demented;
his son was also insane, and a daughter died of consumption.—Lamarck became blind.—Cardan had delusions of
persecution, with hallucinations of hearing, smell, and taste.
His father had been insane, and Cardan in turn transmitted
insanity to his children.[1] This is indeed a remarkable case.
Cardan was one of the most distinguished men of the sixteenth century, revealing throughout his works 'an intellect of rare subtlety and force,' and occasionally letting fall

____
[1] Lombroso.

'hints of scientific principles so profound, looked at 'in the light of after years, that he himself cannot at all have even guessed at their significance.'[1] Voices told him to write his books. He is said to have been a stupid boy, and to have remained impotent till the age of thirty-four.—Of Charles Lyell, the eminent geologist, Charles Darwin wrote in 1875 : 'I cannot say that I felt his death much, for I fully expected it, and have looked for some little time at his career as finished. I dread nothing so much as his surviving with impaired mental powers.'—Sedgwick, to whom geology is also much indebted, was a sufferer from rheumatic gout and inflammation of the eyes.—In the family of Smeaton, civil engineer, brain disease was hereditary. He died of paralysis. —The same affection in the form of shaking palsy attacked George Stephenson, the railway engineer, whose mother was 'a delicat boddie an varry flighty.'—Telford, whose genius for engineering manifested itself along with a taste for writing verses, lost his hearing.

The marvellous arithmetical faculty of the American calculating boy Zerah Colburn, who was exhibited in Europe in the early part of the present century, may be ZERAH comprised in the scientific category. This prodigy COLBURN was the son of a carpenter, and began his arithmetical feats in childhood. The first manifestation of his power is thus described :—'When about one month under six years of age, his father being employed at his joiner's bench, Zerah was on the floor playing with the chips of wood. Suddenly he began to say to himself 5 times 7 is 35, 6 times 8 is 48, and so on. His father's attention becoming arrested by hearing this from a child who had only had six weeks' attendance at the district school, he left his work and began to examine him in the multiplication table. He thought it possible that Zerah had learnt his sums from other boys, but finding him perfect in the table his attention was more deeply fixed and he asked the product of 13 multiplied by 97, to which 1261 was instantly given in answer.[2] For the manipulation of numbers the boy, in short, was found to have

---

[1] *Chambers' Encyclopædia,* Ed. 1888.
[2] *Zerah Colburn : Memoir.*

innate gifts of a most exceptional kind. The matter became
noised abroad, and he was exhibited on tour. At the age
of six, when asked the number of seconds in eleven years,
he answered in four seconds 364,896,000. Being asked
how many hours there were in 38 years two months and
seven days, he answered in six seconds 334,488. At eight
years of age he was brought to London, and tested by
mathematicians who were surprised and disconcerted by the
rapidity and correctness of the boy's solutions to the most
difficult problems. He had the power of at once answering
questions to which no known rules applied, and he discovered
properties in numbers till then unsuspected.

Being questioned as to the principle upon which he proceeded, the boy declared that he did not know how the
answers came into his mind. Strangely enough, his power,
instead of improving with practice, gradually faded away,
and before he was old enough to explain himself it had completely left him. Its neurotic character is indicated by the
fact that the elder Colburn became insane, and died of consumption. There was also deformity in the family, the boy
and some of his near relatives being six-fingered. After the
disappearance of his arithmetical faculty, Zerah Colburn found
great difficulty in earning a livelihood. He subsequently
became a pious itinerant Methodist preacher, and died at the
age of thirty-six of a ' decline.'

Paul Morphy, the most brilliant of chess-players, who invented combinations on the chess-board previously unknown,
PAUL   began his chess career in boyhood and attained the
MORPHY height of his fame as a very young man. About
the age of thirty he became insane.

The genealogy of Charles Darwin, author of the ' Origin
of Species,' illustrates many of the neuropathic aspects of
ERASMUS genius, from insanity downwards. It will bear re-
DARWIN lating in some detail, for, unlike many men of genius
whose lives are obscure and imperfectly recorded, Darwin is
intimately known to us through his own memoirs and the
full biographical accounts which have been published of his
family for three generations.[1] To take first the paternal side

[1] *Life of Erasmus Darwin*, by E. Krause, with a notice by Charles Darwin.

of Darwin's ancestry. Erasmus Darwin, grandfather of Charles, and himself a man of genius, philosopher, poet, and physician, was noted for the great size of his frame, his physical energy, and the vividness of his imagination. Of all his characteristics, says Charles Darwin, ' the incessant activity of his mind was perhaps the most remarkable.' He had a special taste for poetry and mechanics. According to his son Robert, he was apt to be ' violent in anger.' Miss Seward adds that he ' stammered greatly' in his speech. He was clumsy in his movements, and is also said to have suffered from lameness, but, as this is ascribed to a carriage accident, it need not be insisted upon, notwithstanding the well-known fondness of the biographer for explaining everything according to his lights.

Miss Seward tells us of a freak once indulged in by Erasmus Darwin, which savours a little of insanity. At a picnic party, after luncheon, he surprised his companions by suddenly stepping from the boat into the middle of the river Trent; he then swam ashore in his clothes, and walked coolly over the meadows towards the town of Nottingham, where he was afterwards discovered in the market-place, ' mounted upon a tub in his wet clothes haranguing the mob in an extremely sensible manner on sanitary arrangements, and without his usual stammer.' Charles Darwin is persuaded that this narrative is ' largely the work of Miss Seward's imagination,' and that probably his grandfather, who was a great advocate of teetotalism, drank at the lunch ' something as weak which was really strong,' and so become ' half tipsy.' This hypothesis is a difficult one to maintain in face of the fact that Erasmus Darwin was a medical man, who would not readily be deceived as to what he drank. Besides, Miss Seward does not write in a vindictive spirit, and there is nothing inherently improbable in her narrative. Quite the contrary, when we remember that another philosophical physician of Erasmus Darwin's own time, and one equally eminent with himself, namely, Zimmermann, lapsed into a state of complete insanity.

Memoirs of the Life of Erasmus Darwin, by Anna Seward. *Life and Letters of Charles Darwin*, by his son, F. Darwin. *Life of Josiah Wedgwood*, by E. Meteyard. *A Group of Englishmen*, by E. Meteyard, etc.

Charles Darwin admits, in fact, that the owner of the boat, having been appealed to on the subject, said 'something similar' to Miss Seward's account did happen.

In his latter years, according to Miss Seward, Erasmus Darwin displayed ' the irritability, the disingenuous arts, and the jealousy of other reputations,' so often found in great minds. This charge the Darwin family indignantly deny, but surely there is nothing to be surprised at if an ancestor, to whom they concede the qualities of genius, should be shown to have some of the defects of that condition. Erasmus Darwin died suddenly in his arm-chair, after a shivering fit, at seventy. The doctors differed as to the cause of his death, but his son Robert, a medical man, believed it to be an affection of the heart. Erasmus Darwin was twice married; it is from his first wife, a Miss Howard, that the author of the 'Origin of Species' was descended. This poor lady, for many years an invalid, died at the early age of thirty. She told Miss Seward: ' The maladies of my frame were peculiar; the pains in my head and stomach, which no medicine could eradicate, were spasmodic and violent, and required stronger measures to render them supportable while they lasted than my constitution could sustain without injury.'

Of such a union it was hardly possible that a soundly constituted family could be born. There were three sons. Erasmus the younger committed suicide at forty in a state of insanity; Charles, who stammered like his father, and who also had a strong taste for poetry and mechanics, died at twenty of accidental blood poisoning; the remaining son Robert, who lived to a great age, became a successful medical man, and by his marriage with Miss Wedgwood was the father of Charles Darwin. As to the insanity of Charles Darwin's uncle Erasmus the younger, who was a solicitor, there appears to be no doubt. He drowned himself in a stream at the bottom of the garden. ' It is known,' says Charles Darwin in commenting upon the event, ' that a change of disposition generally precedes insanity, and Erasmus, from being an excellent man of business, had become dilatory to an abnormal degree. He was evidently conscious himself of some mental change, for he purchased, six weeks before his death, the small estate of the Priory near Derby, where he intended, though only forty years old, to retire from business, or, as his father expressed it, to sleep away the remainder of his life.' Miss Seward asserts that when the body was found, the father said in a low voice, ' Poor insane coward.' Charles Darwin doubted the truth of this, but the remark was surely not an unnatural one.

Robert Darwin was of enormous size, standing six feet two inches, and weighing twenty-four stone. This was not the only, though it was the most conspicuous, evidence in his case of an abnormality of the nervous system, by which, as we have seen, the nutrition or growth of the body is regulated. He suffered from gout. He was a good man of business, and contrived to amass a fortune in his medical practice. He also had ' curious intuitions,' which he could not explain, and an extraordinary memory. In marrying Miss Wedgwood, daughter of Josiah Wedgwood, he, like his father, formed an alliance which must have fostered rather than corrected the neuropathic tendencies of the Darwin blood. On its own account the genealogy of the mother of Charles Darwin merits attention. It has the additional advantage, however, of making us acquainted with a man whose achievements entitle him to an independent place in this book, namely, Josiah Wedgwood, the creator of British pottery as an art.

During the seventeenth and eighteenth centuries, the births, marriages, and deaths of the Wedgwoods fill half the parish registers of Burslem. The family was JOSIAH prolific, and apparently prosperous through WEDGWOOD several generations, but its history begins with Josiah. In this, the fourth generation of the Staffordshire potters, by a coincidence for which the reader will be prepared, genius and nerve disorder unmistakably manifested themselves side by side. The evil appears to have been slowly preparing. Already in the third generation there were neurotic symptoms in the family. Thomas Wedgwood, father of Josiah, made a deathbed will, in which, while providing for a younger daughter, he sternly prohibited his eldest daughter Ann from sharing in his estate. Unforgiveness on a death-bed, like those prolonged and bitter family feuds originating in a trifle, of which the world occasionally hears, is a frequent sign of the insane temperament. Nor does the wife of Thomas appear to have been particularly sound. She is described as a 'small and delicately organised woman of unusual quickness and sensibility.' Of the children born to this couple Josiah was the youngest. They exhibited forms of nerve-disorder, ranging from genius to idiocy. Thomas, brother of Josiah, left his affairs in a 'sadly unsettled state.' Miss Meteyard says he was an 'incompetent, careless man,' and one of his sons was weak-minded. Writing of this nephew of his, Josiah (who, like the typical biographer, is ready with a reason for the thing he describes) says: 'The shock he received from his father's death, and the foolish education and behaviour of his mother, made him for some time quite an idiot. . . . He will never be qualified to do any business, and what we shall do with him I do not know.' A second son, brother of the idiot, was 'as unwilling as he was incapable of being taught or managed to any good purpose.' Richard Wedgwood, another brother of Josiah's, died of 'a long course of drinking and irregular living.' A son of Richard's, as the result of a worn-out constitution, died early.

Two ne'er-do-well brothers, and three ne'er-do-well nephews in the family of a man of genius, is a large allowance. It is true that the genius of Josiah Wedgwood was of no common order. It was many-sided. Pottery, when he took it up, was a rude and barbarous manufacture; he raised it to the dignity of an art. He was a man of much general culture. He also accumulated a vast fortune, promoted public works, and exercised a princely liberality. For these achievements a heavy price of bodily suffering had to be paid. Josiah Wedgwood became lame in boyhood; some years afterwards his leg, being increasingly troublesome, had to be amputated. Before his fortieth year he began to have spectra in the eyes; he also suffered from constant headaches and sleeplessness. It is well known that pain can be felt in an amputated limb, the explanation being that the severed nerves continue to convey sensation to the brain, which has no knowledge, so to speak, of its habitual communications from the limb in question being interrupted. It is as if the wire of the door-bell were cut midway, and the short end pulled as usual. For twenty years after the amputation Josiah Wedgwood felt severe pain in what he called his 'no-leg.' He died of mortification of the jaw at sixty-five.

Given a man of such feeble physique as Josiah Wedgwood, it is evidently important in the interests of the unborn generation, that if he marries at all, he should choose as his wife a woman normally constituted, or at least nervously sound. This Josiah Wedgwood did not do. He married a Miss Sarah Wedgwood, a distant cousin of his own, who appears to have had a share of the family disorder; and seeing that she became afflicted with a 'severe rheumatic affection,' together with what were called 'fever fits' and ague, the offspring of this union were necessarily born to a heritage of suffering. A daughter, Mary Ann, became paralysed and blind, but died in childhood. Less fortunate was a son Thomas Wedgwood, whose manhood, through disease, was rendered an indescribably weary burden to him. It was not until his thirty-fourth year that he was relieved from his pain. His mental powers were of a very high order; indeed, Thomas Wedgwood is himself entitled to rank as a man of genius, although his ill-health and his early death cut short the promising scientific researches in which he was engaged. Before his twentieth year he was prying into the secrets of nature, particularly in relation to the problems of light and heat, and he was the virtual discoverer of photography. For ten or twelve years before his death, however, he could do little but suffer, bodily and mentally. His brief life shows what terrible evils genius may bring in its train. Who can read without being moved to pity of the vain yearnings after health and strength of this poor young man, to whom his immense fortune was only a mockery? He travelled, he was always buying new estates, he tried opium, he thought of bhang, nothing procured him relief. Dr. Robert Darwin, who attended him, anticipated that his life would close in frenzy or paralysis, and paralysis it was which carried him off in the prime of manhood. He was remembered by one of his nieces as a 'tall, pale, sickly gentleman, moving feebly with the aid of a stick,' for with his brain affection he combined an incurable disease of the stomach.

Another of Josiah Wedgwood's sons, John, had infirmity without the solace of genius. He was a hypochondriac, and a restless traveller. A daughter Catherine by her marriage with a Unitarian preacher, named Willett, became the grandmother of the eminent physician, Sir Henry Holland; it was the other daughter Sarah who married Dr. Robert Darwin. This lady died comparatively early 'after a long decline,' but not until she had given birth to Charles Darwin. Thus we see that the great biologist, whose discovery of the principle of Natural Selection has revolutionised modern thought, was sprung both on the paternal and the maternal side from an insane and paralytic stock, in whom the great neuroses alternated not only with genius but with the special maladies of the drunkard and the ne'er-do-well.

Charles Darwin, with his heavy heritage of nerve-disorder, lived an ailing life. 'For nearly forty years,' says his son, CHARLES 'he never knew one day of the health of ordinary DARWIN men. . . . His life was one long struggle against the weariness and strain of sickness.' He had his 'bad days,' when he suffered from 'swimming in the head.' He had a peculiar stammer on the first word of a sentence. 'I can only recall this,' says F. Darwin, 'with words beginning with W. Possibly he had a special difficulty with this letter, for I have heard him say that, as a boy, he could not pronounce W, and that if sixpence were offered him to pronounce "white wine" he would pronounce "rite rine."' 'Swimming in the head,' or giddiness, is most probably an affection of the cerebellum. 'The malady exhibits itself,' says Forbes Winslow, 'at all periods of the day, and in all possible positions of the body. . . . I have known clergymen attacked whilst preaching in the pulpit, merchants when engaged at the desk, or on the Stock Exchange, barristers whilst addressing Courts of Law.' Attacks of giddiness, as we have seen, were a premonitory symptom of Dean Swift's insanity. They may be experienced for years and 'frequently terminate,' says Clutterbuck, 'in apoplexy or palsy from the extension of the disease in the brain.' Difficulties of articulation are, also, of course, indications of brain disorder. Severe fainting fits attacked Charles Darwin in his latter years. The chief affliction of his life was dyspepsia; his death was due to *angina pectoris*. He married a cousin, Miss Emma Wedgwood, daughter of one of the sons of the great Josiah.

In Charles Darwin's brother, Erasmus Alvey Darwin, we have the *contre-coup* of genius. 'His health from boyhood,' says Charles, 'had been weak, and as a consequence he *failed in energy*. His spirits were not high, sometimes low, more especially during early and middle manhood.' Carlyle refers to this Erasmus as a 'most diverse kind of mortal,' with 'health so poor,' that it 'quite doomed him to silence and patient idleness.'[1] Miss Julia Wedgwood thought his mind had the same kind of playfulness, the same lightness of touch, the same tenderness, perhaps the 'same limitations' as that of Charles Lamb.[2] A sad but suggestive comparison!

Several minor descriptions of genius remain to be mentioned. Men who amass wealth or who initiate and successfully carry out great commercial schemes are not usually accounted geniuses, but there is no doubt that the qualities of mind which bring them to the front are in many cases identical in their origin and nature with the literary or artistic gifts. That is to say, they are the result of an exaltation or depression of certain brain-areas and are associated with the various ailments incident to an instability of the cerebro-spinal system. It is necessary, however, to discriminate as to the means by which wealth is acquired. A lucky speculation is not necessarily a proof of mental capacity on the part of the speculator; and large fortunes are made by persons who accidentally obtain a monopoly of some commodity for which there is a general demand. In such cases no genius need be presumed. Skill, foresight, and industry, however, are native qualities of mind, for the absence of which no training can compensate; they are important constituents of the business faculty. Avarice, again, which frequently goes to the amassing of wealth, is a distinctly neuropathic characteristic.

[1] *Reminiscences.*   [2] *Spectator*, September 3, 1881.

Side by side with legal, poetic, musical, and literary gifts, the parsimonious spirit crops up with curious frequency in the biographies of the famous North family, who, dating from the reign of Queen Elizabeth, were illustrious through several generations. Francis North, the Lord Keeper of James II., was one of a family of five brothers and one sister. The father of these brothers wrote poems; he was also 'economical.' In the sons the latter characteristic appears in various forms. The Lord Keeper was crafty and designing. Macaulay accuses him of selfishness, cowardice, and meanness. There is no doubt, however, but that his abilities were very varied, and of a high order. Besides studying the law, he 'pursued his inquiries into all ingenious arts, history, humanity, and languages, whereby he became not only a good lawyer but a good historian, politician, mathematician, natural philosopher and musician in perfection.' He is said to have been always fanciful about his health. Roger North, brother of the Lord Keeper, wrote excellent biographies of the family and was musical.

Dudley North, another brother, contrived to make a large fortune in the Levant and, retiring to England, became a noted financier. The financial career of the latter began at school when he trafficked with other boys; he afterwards cheated sadly, and even his brother Roger allows that 'as to all the mercantile arts and stratagems of trade which could be used to get money from those he dealt with he was no niggard.' He was very energetic and a great swimmer. Macaulay admits that Dudley North was 'one of the ablest men of his time.' In another brother, John North, Master of Trinity College, Cambridge, we discover the neuropathic taint which produced these excessive abilities. As a boy John North was of a 'nice and tender constitution,' and affected with a 'non-natural gravity' for his years. He became penurious and hoarding, but was a thinker of great earnestness and a remarkable Greek and Hebrew scholar. According to the jargon of the biographer who so persistently mistakes effects for causes, study ruined his health. 'His flesh became strangely flaccid and soft, he was weak and shuffling, often crossing his legs as if he were tipsy; his sleep was seldom or never easy, but interrupted with unquiet and painful dreams, his active spirit had rarely any settlement or rest.' Finally, he had a stroke of paralysis, of which he died at thirty-eight. The sister, Mary North, afterwards Lady Spring, had a prodigious memory. According to her brother Roger, she used to recite ' by heart prolix romances with the substance of speeches and letters as well as passages, and this with little or no hesitation, but in a continual series of discourses—the very memory of which is to me at this day very wonderful.'[1] The Lord Keeper's eldest son and successor in the family title was a nonentity, but his daughter, Dudleya North, inheriting her uncle John's characteristics, ' emaciated herself with study, whereby she had made familiar to her not only the Greek and Latin, but the Oriental languages.' She died not long after the birth of her first child, and the child speedily followed her to the grave.

Through the alliance of heiresses with noble families, some indirect evidence is furnished of the neuropathic character of the money-making faculty. The heiresses who win a title are generally the daughters of men who have made large fortunes in trade, and, as books of the peerage show, there is a well-marked tendency on their part to sterility, about one-fifth having no male children at all, a third one child, and three-fifths two children only. For various reasons, however, one of which is the possible unsoundness of the husbands of these heiresses, trustworthy statistics on the subject are not obtainable.

It is more important to note that the money-making faculty alternates, as we should naturally expect it to do, with prodigality, and the usual functional disorders in families where a neuropathic taint exists. Men of genius are not necessarily thriftless. Perhaps the majority are so, but Reynolds and Turner were avaricious, Shakespeare contrived to retire early with a competence, Josiah Wedgwood built up one of the largest fortunes in the world, and the Darwins were excellent men of business. On the other hand, Byron, Coleridge, and Scott, were incapable of handling money, while Corneille, according to his nephew De Fontenelle, had an

[1] Roger North : *Lives of the Norths.*

R

incapacity for business, which was only equalled by his aversion to it. Frequently a father laboriously amasses a fortune, which his son as recklessly squanders. The phenomenon, a common one in social life, is explained by the variations of heredity. As between father and son, there is a shifting, so to speak, of the nervous centre of gravity with a consequent modification of faculty, such as we see in the families of men of genius. But just as among the accidents of variation a man of genius may have a son who is gifted also, so the successful man of business may likewise have a son of his own calibre.

Harvey, the discoverer of the circulation of the blood, a gouty and eccentric subject, had brothers in trade who amassed large fortunes. The Mendelssohn and Meyerbeer families comprised bankers of great ability. Heine's father was an improvident person, always struggling with misfortune. His uncle Solomon, on the other hand, starting in life with 'only a pair of leather breeches and sixteen groschen in the pocket of them,' rose to the highest place in the financial world, and died a millionaire. Anatole Demidoff, who married into the Napoleon family, and who was notorious under the Second Empire for his extravagance and debaucheries, belonged to a trading family in St. Petersburg, from whom he inherited an enormous fortune, and with it paralysis. His brother, Paul Demidoff, also a celebrity in Parisian society, was accounted half mad. Amid his eccentricities and cruelties, however, Paul Demidoff was singularly impressionable to the sufferings occasioned by infirmity and poverty, and spent thousands of pounds yearly in philanthropic acts.

As with avarice, so with philanthropy. It is a constitutional characteristic, and its connection with an unstable condition of the cerebro-spinal system is readily shown. Howard, the prison reformer, was a sickly child. The son of a pious upholsterer, he was himself strongly imbued with the religious spirit, but this did not prevent him from being excessively self-willed and tyrannical in his own household.[1] In his youth he was thought to be con-

[1] Stoughton: *Howard the Philanthropist*

sumptive, and he had attacks of what the biographer calls 'nervous fever;' but his death was due to some contagious disease contracted in his wanderings. The philanthropist left a son who was an inveterate drunkard, and who finally became insane and had to be placed under restraint. This young man, of whose mother nothing is known, except that she died in childbed, ended his days in a lunatic asylum at thirty-four. In his own person Howard exhibited eccentricities unaccountable to his friends. It is related that in Venice, during a hard winter, he took it into his head to 'go about the streets without boots or gaiters, with no great coat, and sometimes even no cravat on,' to the amazement of the natives. The cruelty exercised by the philanthropist in his domestic relations has always been a subject of perplexity to his admirers. But they have succeeded in explaining it away to their own satisfaction. 'He had a theory of family discipline,' observes Stoughton, 'which, however conscientiously formed, will be approved by only a few in the present day. His idea of obedience was not the submission of love, but a subjugation of will through the influence of fear, or through the force of authority. But,' adds this reverent apologist, 'we see in his case not parental unkindness, not insensibility, not a hard, severe, ungenerous mind,—only a *misjudgment*, an *unwise* opinion.' Quite so! But insensibility and misjudgment belong to the same order of mental phenomena as insanity itself. There can be no doubt that Howard's domestic tyranny was as much the outcome of a disordered brain or nervous system as his philanthropy.

Nield, a prison reformer who followed in Howard's footsteps, is also said to have been 'somewhat eccentric.' Another notable worker in the same field, Sarah Martin, was, in her latter days, 'greatly afflicted.' Similarly George Moore, 'merchant and philanthropist,' one of the worthies whose life has been written by Smiles, suffered at times from 'intense pains in the head,' and felt his nervous system to be 'much shattered.'—John Ellis, a working shoemaker of Norwich, who had a passion for establishing reformatory schools, presented a strange, uncouth, unkempt figure, shambling in gait, and with a style of speech that could only be described as a half inaudible mumble. He worked at his philanthropic projects night and day. He had also a turn for mechanical invention. At eighty years of age, in a fit of religious melancholy, he committed suicide by thrusting his head into a leather-cutting machine.

William Wilberforce, the great enemy of the slave trade, was all his life a valetudinarian. 'His frame from infancy was feeble, his stature small, his eyes weak—a failing which, with his many rich mental endowments, he inherited from his mother.'[1] An unusual thoughtfulness for others is said to have marked his earliest childhood. Piety descended upon his mother in her later life. Wilberforce exhibited some religious leanings in boyhood, but these gave place at college and at the opening of his Parliamentary career to a degree of worldliness, upon which, in after years, 'he could not look back without unfeigned remorse.' He was then intellectually clever, ready-witted, an accomplished singer, and a good mimic. At the age of twenty-six he became suddenly alive to his state of sin and corruption, and thereafter was a changed man, so much so, that he made a 'frank avowal of his altered views' to those with whom he had hitherto lived in levity and thoughtlessness. During his life, Wilberforce's nervous condition expressed itself in occasional 'seizures' of so alarming a character that, for hours, he was 'utterly insensible.' Like many neuropathics, however, he lived to a great age, leaving two sons, whose inherited piety carried them into the church.

The relation of fervid piety to certain states of the cerebrospinal system has been referred to in a preceding chapter. Further examples of this are furnished by Luther, Bunyan, George Fox, and Cardinal Newman. Luther was a man of powerful imagination, subject to nerve-affections, which he put down to the devil. 'This toothache and earache (neuralgia) that I am always suffering from,' he writes, 'are worse than the plague. When I was in Coburg I was tormented with noise and buzzing in my ears, just as though some wind were tearing through my head. The devil had something to do with it.' He also complained of giddiness.

____
[1] *Life of Wilberforce.* By his son.

IIe sometimes saw the devil, but more frequently heard him. In fact, the devil and he were upon the most familiar terms. ' Once in our monastery at Wittenberg,' says the great reformer, ' the devil, interrupting my studies, came into my cell and thrice made a noise behind the stove, just as though he were dragging some wooden measure along the floor. As I found he was going to begin again, I gathered my books together, and got into bed.' On another occasion he says: ' I heard the devil above my cell walking in the cloister, but as I knew it was the devil, I paid no attention to him and went to sleep.'

John Bunyan was a violent, passionate boy. He says of himself that for lying and swearing he had no equal; and the disorder of his brain is attested by the ' fearful dreams and visions' to which, at this period, he was subject. He saw evil spirits in monstrous shapes, orgies of devils, archangels, and what not. Apparently these visitations kept his evil nature in check, or he thought they did. They suddenly ceased when he was about seventeen. God then left him to himself as he puts it, and gave him over to his own wicked inclinations; whereupon he fell into all kinds of vice and ungodliness without further restraint. Among the young tinker's acquaintances there was an ale-house-keeper who had a half-witted son. For the amusement of his guests, this ale-house-keeper used to torment the lad so as to make him curse his father, and wish the devil had him. ' The devil did, at last, have the ale-house-keeper, and rent and tore him till he died.' ' I,' says Bunyan, who relates this incident as a miracle, ' was an eye and ear-witness of what I here say. . . . I saw the father himself possessed, his flesh being gathered up in a heap about the bigness of half an egg, to the unutterable torture and affliction of the old man.' They attempted to smoke the devil out, but he would not come, and he afterwards carried the sufferer out of the world.

In Bunyan's conversion this miracle appears to have played an important part. Yet we can now see that it was a simple case of epilepsy; the father of the half-witted son having a convulsive seizure which proved fatal. About the age of twenty Bunyan's visions returned, but they assumed a beatific character. He heard spiritual voices and saw Christ Himself looking down upon him from the sky; and the exalted mental condition of which these hallucinations were the outcome, made him in due time not only a fervid preacher, but the author of the 'Pilgrim's Progress.' Of Bunyan's ailments nothing is known; but one of his children was blind.

It was in a vision that the founder of Quakerism, George Fox, like Francis d'Assisi, and other holy men, received the consecration of the Spirit. In the early days of his mission his visions were frequent; in these he nearly always *heard* the voice of the Lord, and on one occasion he records, 'the creation gave *another smell* to me than before beyond what words can utter.' Every crazy impulse that passed through his mind he regarded as an inspiration from on high.

In the family of John Henry Newman, the musical faculty and a strong strain of ne'er-do-wellism were associated with intense religious convictions. Newman's father was an enthusiastic musician, but thriftless and unsuccessful in business. The ne'er-do-wellism existed strongly in his youngest brother, Charles Newman, who was eccentric and apparently destitute of all moral principle. This person was accounted a disgrace to the family. While emerging from his teens he renounced all his relatives on the ground that they were too religious. He was sent to a German university, but left it without offering himself for examination, a step he explained by saying that the judges would not grant him a degree because of the offence he had given them by his treatment of faith and morals in an essay which they had styled *teterrima* ('most abominable'). Julius Hare, a clergyman, to whom he was known, used to make excuses for the religious and moral obliquities of this member of the Newman family on the ground of 'partial insanity.'[1]

NEWMAN

Religious conversion presents some instructive features to the psychologist. One of the most rapturous cases of conversion on record is that of a young woman in her twentieth year, a disciple of Wesley's, whom she calls her 'dear and most honoured father in Christ.' The change in her condition

[1] *Contemporary Review*, September 1890: 'Cardinal Newman and his Contemporaries.' By Wilfred Meynell.

began with a *violent agony* of about four hours' duration. 'Then,' says the patient, 'I began to feel the Spirit of God bearing witness with my spirit that I was born of God. Oh, mighty, powerful, happy change! The love of God was shed abroad in my heart, and a flame kindled there with *pains so violent, yet so very ravishing*, that my body was almost torn asunder. I sweated; I trembled; I fainted; I sang. Oh, I thought my head was a fountain of water. I was dissolved in love. *My beloved is mine and I am his.* He has all charms; he has ravished my heart; he is my comforter, my friend, my all. He is now in his garden feeding among the lilies. Oh, I am sick of love. He is altogether lovely, the chiefest among ten thousand. Oh, how Jesus fills; Jesus extends, Jesus overwhelms the soul in which He dwells.' [1]

Experiment has shown that exaltation of this kind can be produced by hachisch.[2] Moreau of Tours, who experimented upon himself with that drug, has left his sensations on record. 'It is really happiness,' says this writer, 'which is produced by hachisch, and by this I imply an enjoyment entirely moral and by no means sensual as we might be induced to suppose. This is surely a very curious circumstance, and some remarkable inferences may be drawn from it—this, for instance, among others, that every feeling of joy and gladness even, when the cause of it is exclusively moral, may be nothing else than sensations purely physical developed in the interior of the system. For the hachisch-eater is happy, not like the gourmand, the famished man, or the voluptuary who has satisfied his appetite, but like him who hears tidings of great joy, the miser counting his money, the gambler successful in play, or the ambitious man whose hopes are realised.' In cases of religious conversion there would seem to be a profound disturbance of the different sensory and motor centres of the brain; and it is more than probable that this occurs only in organisations which are naturally excitable, and at the same time deficient in memories of a corrective kind, and therefore peculiarly open to the contagion of

<hr>

[1] Southey: *Life of Wesley.*
[2] Moreau: *Du Hachisch et l'Aliénation Mentale.*

example. If so, the most vigorous proselytising is likely to be successful only in a certain proportion of cases, many persons being condemned by their organisations to remain insensible to the most rousing appeals from the pulpit or the platform.

The passages italicised in the statement of Wesley's convert, above quoted, testify to the existence of a purely physical process in the brain and nervous system, and it is curious to note how the sexual organisation is called into play without the sufferer's knowledge. The erotic influence is not so clear in this case, however, as in that of an ecstatic young woman observed by Moreau, who has left copious accounts of her experience where she evidently confounds her carnal appetites with the 'Divine Love.' One passage of Mdlle. X.'s confessions may be quoted: 'During my long hours of sleeplessness in the night,' she observes, 'my beloved Saviour began to make Himself manifest to me. Pondering over the meditations of St. François de Sales in the Song of Songs, I seemed to feel all my faculties suspended, and crossing my arms upon my chest, I awaited in a sort of dread what might be revealed to me. . . . I saw the Redeemer veritably in the flesh. . . . He extended Himself beside me, pressed me so closely that I could feel His crown of thorns and the nails in His feet and hands, while He pressed His lips over mine, giving me the most ravishing kiss of a divine Spouse, and sending a delicious thrill through my entire body.'[1]

A derangement of the sexual sense is common in insanity, especially in female patients. In the days of a belief in witchcraft many poor women, labouring under hallucinations, confessed to having commerce with the devil. Male converts are less subject than female to such erotic influences, though the excesses alleged to occur at the love feasts of certain sects may be assigned to this cause. All 'conversions,' however, appear to be essentially neurotic in their nature, exhibiting during their fervid period the same tendency to fluctuate as ordinary hallucinations.

John Wesley's younger brother Charles, a valetudinarian through the greater part of his long life, in consequence, it

---

[1] Moreau : *La Psychologie Morbide.*

was believed, of having 'injured his constitution by close application and excessive abstinence at Oxford,' had two sons who, by a familiar metamorphosis of heredity, were 'among the most distinguished musicians of their age.'[1] The musical performances of these young men were held by some of their pious friends to be 'dishonourable to God.' Their father was less bigoted. In a letter to his brother he said : 'I am clear without doubt that my son's concert is after the will and order of Providence.' When John Wesley printed this letter after his brother's death, he added in a note : 'I am clear of another mind.' It is almost pathetic to reflect that the piety which urged John Wesley to this uncharitable conclusion was, in a scientific sense, of the same genesis as the artistic accomplishment he censured. Among the early leaders of the Methodist revival movement nerve-disorder manifested itself strongly. John Oliver was seized with a spirit of fanaticism as a boy, and afterwards became a starring preacher. He was afflicted with a scrofulous disorder, inherited from a father who had 'a most violent temper.' Grimshaw in his unconverted state, according to Southey, ' was certainly insane.' Afterwards he was always more or less eccentric. His change of mind, which was not till he had been ten years in Holy Orders, was 'preceded by what he supposed to be a miraculous impression upon his senses,' probably a neuropathic affection, and 'the only son of this singular man became a drunkard, notwithstanding that he had been favoured with a religious education,' says his father's biographer, ' and had been prayed for by some of the holiest men in the land.' One of Wesley's pupils was a young man named Hall. He was, for a time, very pious, and married one of Wesley's sisters. By-and-by, Hall fell into strange moods and fancies. 'He publicly and privately recommended polygamy as conformable to nature, preached in its defence, and practised as he preached. Soon he laid aside all pretension to religion, professed himself an infidel, and led the life of an adventurer and a profligate at home and abroad, acting sometimes as a physician, sometimes as a priest, and assuming any character according to the humour or the convenience of

----

[1] Southey: *Life of Wesley.*

the day.' After some years, however, his piety returned, and he died in the odour of sanctity. There was much nerve-disorder in the ranks of the eminent Protestant Divines who flourished in Europe from the Reformation down to the close of the last century. Middleton's lives [1] abound in examples. Wickliffe died of paralysis, Melancthon's health required constant care, and Calvin was thin and consumptive. George Herbert, who was consumptive, and subject to frequent 'fevers' and other infirmities, appears to have grown more pious as he became more stricken; he was also a poet. Philip Henry, called the 'heavenly Henry,' was weakly as a child, and was subject to great excitement in the pulpit, where 'he sweated profusely as he prayed fervently;' he died of apoplexy. Harvey, who died at thirty, was such a weakly, puny object that his father did not like his becoming a minister, lest his stature should render him despicable. Hervey was weakly, and was terribly emaciated before his death. Guise became lame and blind. Toplady struggled constantly against ill-health, until he succumbed at thirty-eight.

A noteworthy circumstance from the physiological point of view is, that not a few of Middleton's worthies were, like Bunyan, irregular and wild to begin with, piety supervening upon prodigality in strict accordance with pathological principles. Some of them in their youth were given to drunkenness and profanity, others to licentiousness. Allowing for the exaggerated view which a religious biographer would naturally take of worldly proclivities, the 'conversion' of these good and gracious men is an instructive detail in mental science. Further evidence of the essentially pathological nature of religious enthusiasm is to be found in the fact that the children of extremely pious parents often turn out badly. Upon this, as upon so many other matters that seem to tell against his *protégé*, the biographer is curiously, one might almost say dishonestly reticent, but the fact is one of common observation, and is quite in accordance with the principle of the metamorphosis of heredity. The direct transmission of piety from father to son appears to be in pretty much the

[1] Middleton : *Biographia Evangelica.*

same ratio as that of epilepsy or any other special affection
of the nervous system. Matthew Henry, son of Philip above
mentioned, was devout from infancy, and precocious. At
three years of age he could read and even comment upon the
Bible. He was weakly when young, and is said to have
further injured his constitution by 'fervent preaching' and
overstudy. The mother of George Herbert was a woman of
'extraordinary piety.' Other examples might be quoted, but,
generally speaking, piety appears to be the result of indirect
transmission; the biographer with the best intentions in the
world being unable in the majority of cases to employ more
definite phrases with reference to the parentage of his subjects
than that the father was a worthy man, the mother an excellent
woman, and so forth. Of George Herbert's brothers one was
a sceptical writer, the second a renowned duellist, and the
third a dashing naval officer—the two latter showing that
courage, like so many forms of genius, depends upon a congenital want of mental balance. The jumpings, contortions,
and shoutings of the converted at revival meetings, are only
the physical outcome of violent cerebral action. Just as anger
makes a man walk sharply up and down a room and throw
his arms about, so strong religious emotion passing into the
motor area of the brain induces violent and aimless movements of the limbs, and the emission of senseless sounds.
Much the same effect is produced by the excitement of battle,
as savage war-dances and the excesses of civilised soldiery
testify.

It is startling enough to find that, not only the 'lunatic
and the poet,' but the successful merchant, the philanthropist,
and the fervidly pious person 'are of imagination all compact.'
What shall be said if, to the list, be added the criminal?
Yet, in sober truth, there is every reason to believe that the
habitual criminal owes his characteristics to the same set
of causes as the types above named. He, too, is a man of
genius in the sense that he is differently constituted from his
neighbours. That criminality is congenital is shown by an
overwhelming mass of evidence collected by Lombroso,
Dugdale, and other investigators of the present day. In a
large proportion of cases, criminals have abnormal skulls

and brains approaching the idiotic type; they are epileptic, alcoholic, and otherwise afflicted with nerve-disorder in a high degree; physical malformations and sensory defects are frequent among them. The progenitor of the infamous Jukes family in America, whose genealogical tree has been made out for seven generations, and who now number nearly six hundred individuals, all more or less stained with crime, was evidently of the neuropathic temperament. He is described as a 'hunter and fisher, a hard drinker, jolly and companionable, averse to steady toil, working hard by spurts and idling by turns, *becoming blind* in his old age and entailing his blindness upon his children and grandchildren.' In the Jukes family 'harlotry,' among other vicious proclivities, is shown to be largely due to heredity, there being among women of the Jukes blood over 20 per cent. more harlots than among other women of the same class intermarrying or cohabiting with the Jukes.

Like men of genius, criminals show a considerable inequality of faculty. They are often excessively vain and excessively addicted to venereal pleasures. While remarkably shrewd, too, in some respects, they are just as obtuse in others. 'Some young criminals,' says Barwick Baker, 'appear to have scarcely the power of determining between good and evil. Yet, strange to say, there are among them boys whom almost any schoolmaster would class as of remarkably high intelligence, their arithmetic, their knowledge of Scripture, their answers, not merely as to facts but as to reasoning, being very far above the average of boys of their age. . . . In the case of the passionate, the bad, or the idiot,' this writer adds, 'it does not seem as if punishment would have much effect.'[1] The truth is that punishment operates as a deterrent only in cases where there is no great departure from normal conditions; the criminal propensity may be so strong as to be ungovernable, in which case it may be classed as a true insanity.

Closely related to criminality is the ne'er-do-wellism which

---

[1] Lombroso: *L'Uomo delinquente*. Dugdale: *The Jukes; a Study in Crime, Pauperism, and Heredity*. Barwick Baker: *War with Crime*.

is so constantly found in the families of distinguished men.
This condition has been shown to occur in an aggravated form
in near relations of Newton, Southey, Campbell, Scott, the
Brontës, Mrs. Siddons, William Herschell, Warren Hastings,
Josiah Wedgwood, Balzac, and Dickens. It is the border-
land between crime and genius.

CHAPTER X

MEMORY AS AN ELEMENT OF GENIUS—AUTOMATIC ACTIVITY OF THE BRAIN—CREATIVE GENIUS AS DISTINGUISHED FROM TALENT—DREAMS OF EMINENT MEN—WAKING VISIONS—INSPIRATION—ITS PHYSICAL BASIS—THE IMPULSE TO PRODUCE—ACTIVE AND SLUGGISH GENIUSES—LITERARY STYLE—METRE AND CADENCE AS SENSORI-MOTOR EFFECTS—THE VISUAL ELEMENT IN LITERATURE—WIT AND PUNNING—THE ARTISTIC FACULTY AS AN ASSOCIATED SENSORY AND MOTOR ENDOWMENT—EXAMPLES IN MUSIC AND PAINTING—ACTING CONSIDERED AS A MOTOR SUSCEPTIBILITY—ITS INDEPENDENCE OF INTELLECT—MILITARY GENIUS AND EPILEPSY—BRAIN-MECHANISM OF THE ORATOR, THE STATESMAN, THE PHILOSOPHER, THE MAN OF SCIENCE, THE PHILANTHROPIST, THE RELIGIOUS ENTHUSIAST, THE MAN OF BUSINESS, THE NE'ER-DO-WELL, THE MISER, AND THE CRIMINAL

THE external manifestations of genius having been set forth in some detail, there remains to be considered its action in the individual, with special reference to the character of his work. This brings us back to the subject of brain-structure, where alone the solution of such problems as reason, judgment, imagination, and inspiration is to be sought. As we have seen, there are many grounds for believing that our sensations are represented by so many groupings of nerve-cells and fibres in the brain, that ideas consist of organic cohesions or associations among such groupings, and that the so-called exercise of reason, judgment, or will is an automatic struggle for predominance between revived and associated impressions, one set of which finally asserts itself, and is translated into action. If all brains were constituted alike, all men would think and feel alike. But this is not so. As there are diversities of brain-structure, so there are diversities of intelligence and intellect. Before a sight, a sound, or a touch can become an idea, it must be coupled with other sensations or movements to which it is in some way related; there must be a cohesion formed between the present sensation and a group more or less extensive of past sensations; and just in proportion as these associations are readily established and far-reaching, will the person's ideas be simple or complex. The individual, therefore, is clever or stupid, sharp or dull, according to the receptivity of his centres of sense and the facility with which in these, hosts of associated feelings can be summoned up. The centres of the sensations which accompany muscular action and which form in part the basis of our ideas of movement would appear to be distinct from the motor centres themselves and to be merely associated with these. The destruction of the motor centres in the gray matter paralyses the power of execution, but not the ideal conception of the movement itself. For a dog with its motor centres destroyed has a distinct notion of the movements desired when asked to give a paw, though it makes only ineffectual struggles to comply with the demand. Nevertheless, highly developed and susceptible motor centres necessarily re-act upon our sensations and thus assist in the production of thought.

If an ordinary man were to be suddenly equipped with the brain of a Shakespeare, he could not for many years be as witty or as wise as his prototype, because he would have no fund of past experience or observation to go upon. He would have to accumulate his knowledge before he could apply it. A good memory is an essential element of genius. Macaulay's memory is proverbial. Ben Jonson's must have been nearly as good, for until he was forty, as he tells us, he could repeat all that he had ever written and whole books that he had read. Niebuhr, the historian, restored from recollection a large book of accounts that had been accidentally destroyed in one of the public offices of Denmark. Gibbon, Pascal, Leibnitz, Burke, and many other eminent men, are noted for their memories. It is said that Themistocles could call by their names the 20,000 citizens of Athens, and that Cyrus knew the name of every soldier in his army.

The nerve-cells of the brain are not merely retentive,

they may also be spontaneously active, and without any external stimulus throw into all sorts of shapes and combinations the existing material of thought. This is the secret of the hallucinations of insanity, and there is no doubt that the same excitability of the nerve-cells of various regions of the brain is the cause of what is called creative genius. A choleric temperament like Walter Savage Landor's represents a rapid discharge of nervous energy. Many men of genius are of very active habits, and an excess of energy in the motor area of their brain is no doubt a necessary condition of their productiveness. If the sensory centres alone are active, the individual will pass his life amid visions and reveries which he will not exert himself to give to the world in the shape of poetry, fiction, or art. On the other hand, activity may be confined to the motor regions, in which case we have a fussy, bustling personage, whose energy expends itself to no purpose, having no basis of observation to work upon. In order that genius may incontestably assert itself, there must be a special excitability of both the sensory and motor areas of the brain. The energy so manifested may be rapid and temporary, or slow and persistent. In the former case we have men of brilliant achievements, like Shelley, Byron, and Brougham; in the latter, slow and laborious workers like Wordsworth and Flaubert. When the spontaneous activity of the nerve-cells is great the condition of the brain is a morbid one; whence the close relationship of genius to insanity.

The following notes by a medical man of the course of an insane patient's ravings, illustrate most aptly both the spontaneous generation of ideas in the brain and the mechanical process whereby one train of thought is associated with another :—' Bring the tea—tea comes from China—wall of China—wall *mur*, *muraille*, difference between them in French—French habits—habit a coat—long-tailed coats for soldiers—jackets—division of Spaniards into jacquitos and habitos—civil war—murder of Cabrera's mother—mother a widow—widows—suttee—cremation—Inquisition—Catholic faith—Pope of Rome—Capitol—Tarpeian Rock—mode of punishing criminals—Central Criminal Court—Court of Victoria—visit to the King of France—Queen Bess—female sovereigns

—lady who thought herself Mary Queen of Scots—Highland dress not ancient—introduced by an Englishman—Englishmen all over the globe—Colonies best resource of the poor—Poor Law—introduced by the Whigs—Whigs and Tories—origin of the names—surnames from trade—state of trade—Board of Trade—Board of Green Cloth—green—composition of light—polarisation—Poland—sympathy with Poland—nerves and muscles—poisoning from mussels—poisoning—new style of novel writing—printing has superseded writing—printing reports—cannon—attack on Afghanistan—Progress of British Empire—Emperor—Napoleon—snows of Russia—Russian leather—binding — Bodleian Library.'[1] And in the delirious rapidity of thought, peculiar to the insanity that arises from over-excitability of the nerve-cells, not only is the patient unable to control his ideas, but his mechanism of articulation is strained to the uttermost by the rapidity of its action.

Nicolai, whose hallucinations have already been referred to, found that the figures he saw before him came and went without his being able to control them. 'The phantasms,' he remarks, 'appeared to me involuntarily, as if they had been presented externally like the phenomenon of nature, though they certainly had their origin internally.' Similar observations were afterwards made by a medical man named Bostock, to whom, after a period of nervous prostration, figures like those of Nicolai appeared. What chiefly struck Bostock was that the figures which were best defined and longest visible were such as he had no recollection of having previously seen. 'For about twenty-four hours,' he says, 'I had constantly before me a human figure, the features and dress of which were as distinctly visible as those of my real existence, and of which, after many years, I still retain the most lively impression ; yet neither at the time nor since have I been able to discover any person previously known to me who resembled it.' It is proved by the experience of hypnotic patients that many impressions are made upon our senses of which we are unconscious, and no doubt Bostock at some time or other saw the figure he speaks of. He may have

[1] Wigan.

seen, indeed, only the component parts of it, for the spontaneous action of the nerve-cells is capable of blending several past impressions into one, as when an insane patient sees floating before him portions of human faces and bodies which suddenly combine to form a grotesque and impossible whole. All images and ideas that pass through the mind are necessarily either revivals in whole or in part of actual sensory impressions, or of their induced effects. An image may rise before us different from anything we have actually seen, but it will be found to have been suggested by something in our past experience through the faculty whereby we discriminate the like and the unlike.

Dreams, in all their variety, are the product of the automatic action of the brain. 'The degree of the soul's creativeness in sleep,' says Lamb, 'might furnish no whimsical criterion of the quantum of poetic faculty resident in the same soul waking.' The remark is absolutely just. A brain well stored with impressions will always furnish richer dreams than one which is less susceptible. It was only a Coleridge who could have dreamt the poem of Kubla Khan. Coleridge's account of the origin of this poem is as follows :—'In the summer of the year 1797, the author, then in ill-health, retired to a lonely farmhouse on the confines of Somerset and Devonshire. In consequence of a slight indisposition an anodyne had been prescribed, from the effect of which he fell asleep in his chair at the moment that he was reading the following sentence in Purchas's Pilgrimage :—" Here the Khan Kubla commanded a palace to be built, and a stately garden thereunto, and thus ten miles of fertile ground were enclosed with a wall." The author continued for about three hours in a profound sleep, at least of the external senses, during which time he has the most vivid confidence that he could not have composed less than from 200 to 300 lines, if that, indeed, can be called composition in which all the images rose up before him as things, with the parallel production of the correspondent impressions without any sense or consciousness of effort. On waking he appeared to himself to have a distinct recollection of the whole, and taking his pen, ink, and paper instantly and eagerly wrote down the lines that are here preserved.' Before he had transcribed much of his poem, Coleridge was called away, and on resuming his task some time afterwards he found to his mortification that, ' with the exception of some eight or ten scattered lines, all the rest had passed away like the images on the surface of a stream into which a stone is thrown.'

Southey's dreams are remarkable for their originality, and show what wild work may go on in a brain which is morbidly excitable. They are all such conceptions as might originate with a madman. For example : He dreamt that he met a human head which had been so born, without any body belonging to it. Afterwards he thought he was in a castle where there were several such heads, well born and enjoying respect and all the comforts that could be given them. They were sustained by odours, and had all the pleasures of taste, but swallowed nothing, and they had power enough of motion to turn themselves as they liked. Equally fantastic was the dream that he had been left a legacy of ten thousand pounds on condition that he should never wear breeches, pantaloons, trousers, or any description of that masculine garb, and that he was deliberating whether to adopt Moorish or Highland dress, though afraid the former would not be allowed. The following is pictorially vivid :

' I thought a fiend and a good spirit were shooting arrows at each other, many of which fell near me, and I gathered them, and endeavoured to shoot at the fiend also, who was very little, but never could get them to fit the bow. The good spirit at last heaped coals and peat upon the head of his enemy, so as to bury him completely till he, by the fieriness of his nature, kindled them and they blazed and burned, burning him who yet could not be consumed.'

And here are all the elements of a romance :—

' To my great surprise I discovered that my wife had a former husband living. He was either by birth or descent a Spaniard, but in the English army. He had been dotingly fond of her, and she of him, till in some action he received a musket ball in his leg, which, as long as it remained there, rendered him feeble, and he would not suffer it to be extracted because some old woman had told him it would be fatal.

Upon this he abandoned his wife. I now, however, understood that he was perfectly recovered. The way I learnt this was by seeing a Spanish grammar, so philosophically and ably arranged as to make me inquire for the anonymous author, who proved to be this person. Upon questioning Edith she said it was all true. . . . I asked her if I should write to him or find him out. She said no, because she still felt a regard for him which he did not deserve.'

Dr. Johnson says: 'I was often during sleep engaged in controversial discussions, and whilst recognising that my antagonist occasionally had the best of the conflict, I entirely forgot that my own arguments as well as those advanced by my opponent were supplied by myself.' Newton is alleged to have solved a subtle mathematical problem while sleeping, and Condorcet recognised in his dreams the final steps in a difficult calculation which had puzzled him through the day. Hartley Coleridge's dreams were intensely painful. 'There are figures always at me in my dreams,' he writes, 'hooting, pelting, spitting at me, stopping my way, setting all sorts of hideous, scornful faces at me, oppressing me with indescribable horrors, to which waking life has no parallel.' Shelley also had vivid and distressing dreams, which he has not left on record.

Apart from actual hallucinations there are waking experiences as vivid and as fantastic as any dreams. Examples of what Galton calls the visualising faculty prove how, by the automatic activity of the nerve-cells of the brain, conscious and unconscious memories are worked up into new and startling combinations. 'When passing a shop in Tottenham Court Road,' says a correspondent, 'I went in to order a Dutch cheese, and the proprietor, a bullet-headed man whom I had never seen before, rolled a cheese on the marble slab of his counter, asking me if that one would do. I answered yes, left the shop, and thought no more of the incident. The following evening on closing my eyes I saw a head detached from the body rolling about slightly on a white surface. I recognised the face, but could not remember where I had seen it, and it was only after thinking about it for some time that I identified it as that of the cheesemonger who had sold me the cheese on the preceding day. I may mention that I have often seen the man since, and that I found the vision I saw was exactly like him, although, if I had been asked to describe the man before I saw the vision, I should have been unable to do so.'

Still more remarkable is the recorded experience of a well-known clergyman. Whenever he shuts his eyes and waits he is sure in a short time to see before him the clear image of some object or other, but usually not quite natural in its shape. It then begins to change from one form to another, and continues to do so as long as he cares to watch it. One of these initial images seen by him was a cross-bow. This was immediately provided with an arrow remarkable for its pronounced barb and superabundance of feathering. Some person, but too indistinct to be recognised except in the hands, appeared to shoot the arrow from the bow. The single arrow was then accompanied by a flight of arrows from right to left, which completely occupied the field of vision. These changed into falling stars, then into flakes of a heavy snow-storm; the ground gradually appeared as a sheet of snow, where previously there had been vacant space. Then a well-known rectory, fish pond, walls, etc., all covered with snow, came into view most vividly and clearly defined. The rectory suggested a bed of tulips. These all vanished, except one, which gradually became denuded of its petals until only the stump was left. And so on. When this process is in full activity the writer says he feels as if he were a mere spectator at a diorama of a very eccentric kind, the succession of images refusing to be modified or interfered with by the will. The same writer gives another example. He thought of a gun. The stock immediately came into view, the metal plate and wood-work being very distinct. As he was scrutinising it, the stock oscillated up and down and crumpled up, turning into something like a tuning fork. He then proceeded to examine the lock and get it well into view, the rest of the gun disappearing. It turned out to be an old-fashioned flint-lock. It immediately began to nod backwards and forwards in a manner suggestive of the beak of a bird pecking. Consequently it became forthwith converted into the head of a bird with a long curved beak, the knob on the lock becoming the head of the bird. He then looked to the right, expecting to see the barrel, but the snout of a saw-fish, with the tip distinctly broken off, appeared instead. He had not thought either of a flint-lock or of a saw-fish, both came spontaneously.[1]

In all minds of a creative turn some process like that above described is constantly going on, though it may not always come within the scope of consciousness. The old material of thought is being constantly moulded afresh. Old material it is, inevitably. Nothing absolutely new ever is or can be evolved by the automatic action of the sensory centres, which, from their nature, can only be concerned with impressions already received in one form or another from the outer world. Hence the highest conceptions of genius must have some actual basis of observation to go upon, and the richer a person's stores of observation, the more retentive of their impressions his various sensory centres are, the better he is equipped for the creative operations of the intellect. In all De Quincey's visions[2] the reader can perceive how fragments of conscious memories in his brain are worked up into fantastic images, each with a power of seemingly endless growth and self-reproduction due to unconscious memories. The visions of the English opium-eater are those of a man who has read history and who has a literary knowledge of the East; they are revivals of images and conceptions that have passed through his brain in his waking hours. For the function of opium is to arouse not only known, but all sorts of unknown, that is to say, forgotten or unsuspected, nerve-groupings in the brain—memories which have never been vivid or consistent enough to make us conscious of them. These lie buried in the living tissue of the cerebral substance, but are ready to be revived, like invisible ink, in due season. The dreams of the opium-eater necessarily take shape from his own sensory impressions; they are portions of his past sensory impressions, conscious or unconscious, recalled into a state of activity. To have the visions of a De Quincey one

---

[1] Galton : *Inquiry into Human Faculty.*
[2] De Quincey : *Confessions of an English Opium-eater.*

must have the general reading and knowledge of a De Quincey. The reveries of the illiterate Malay sailor to whom De Quincey once gave a dose of his drug, would differ from those of the author of the 'Confessions' almost as widely as the dreams of the rabbit in his warren differ from those of the fox in his hole. There would be an entirely distinct order of cerebral memories aroused in each case.

The mysterious gift of inspiration, essential to all literary and artistic genius, is evidently nothing but the automatic activity of the nerve-cells of the brain—a phase of that morbid condition which finds its highest expression in insanity. For this reason inspiration can never carry us beyond the limits of experience. Milton's archangels are only disguised men. They are animated by purely human motives, and their warfare is based upon the strategy of human battles; while the poet's conception of the universe is in accordance with the Ptolemaic system, which was generally accepted in his day. If the most highly gifted writer of fiction attempted to describe the inhabitants of another planet, he would inevitably draw upon his experience of human or animal life. The Deity himself has a human shape assigned to him by the loftiest imaginations.[1] When Milton wrote 'Paradise Lost' he was blind, but the imagery he employed in it was that which he had stored up while he had the use of his eyesight; it is very largely visual. Had he been born blind, the poem would not have been written or must have taken a wholly different shape. Again, Dante wrote in an age when tortures were commonly practised by rulers; hence his conception of hell and purgatory, which he would inevitably have modified had he been writing at the present day.

The difference between genius and talent may be thus defined. In genius there is a spontaneous morbid activity of the nerve-cells and fibres of the brain whereby new combinations of sensory impressions and memories are constantly being formed. This condition is identical in kind with that

---

[1] In *Paradise Lost* Raphael tells Adam that God 'did wisely' not to divulge his secrets to be scanned by those who ought rather to admire, and that if they choose to conjecture, he has perhaps left the fabric of the universe to their disputes in order that they may 'move his laughter' by their quaint opinions.

which obtains in certain forms of insanity; but whereas in the latter case the nerve-connections or memories which enable the patient to keep in touch with his surroundings are weakened or destroyed, in genius such connections remain intact. Hence, while the lunatic's actions are uncontrolled by past or present experiences, owing to his having no sufficient basis of comparison to go upon as between the real and the ideal, the man of genius, with similar conceptions seething in his brain, is held in check by his actual perceptions, and is more or less amenable to ordinary human motives. Talent, on the other hand, implies a great extension of the basis of comparison owing to the multiplicity of the memories which may be aroused by a given stimulus; the nerve-connections existing between the various centres are very complete and active, but there is little spontaneous activity in the nerve-cells, and consequently little of the creative faculty. Originality of thought is a characteristic of talent as well as of genius, and is due to a wider faculty of discrimination between the like and the unlike; a more extensive nerve-connection than exists in average brains. In the superior forms of genius there would seem to be present all the conditions of talent with a spontaneous overflow of nerve-energy in addition. Owing to the complexity of the brain-functions, however, there is room for infinite shades or degrees of both genius and talent. Both states of mind, when in excess, are probably morbid. Genius is unquestionably so, entailing as it does the same instability of the nervous system and being attended by the same train of functional disorders as positive insanity.

It is a characteristic of the creative mind that its possessor is, in some sort, impelled to produce. He cannot help himself, he is the victim of his organisation. 'The author,' said Beaconsfield on one occasion, 'is a being with a predisposition which is irresistible, a bent which he cannot in any way avoid, whether it drags him to the abstruse researches of erudition or induces him to mount into the fervid and turbulent atmosphere of imagination.'[1] This is proved by the early ex-

[1] Beaconsfield · *Speech at the Anniversary of the Royal Literary Fund,* 1868.

periences of many men of genius, who have followed their bent despite unfavourable surroundings and often in the face of violent opposition from their parents. An instructive glimpse of the creative mind is given us by Bulwer Lytton, who, writing at the age of forty-two, says: ' For sixteen years I can conceive no life to have been more filled with occupation than mine. What time was not given to action was given to study, what time not given to study, to action—labour in both! To a constitution naturally far from strong I allowed no pause or respite. The wear and tear went on without intermission, the whirl of the wheel never ceased. Sometimes, indeed, thoroughly overpowered and exhausted, I sought for escape. The physicians said " Travel," and I travelled, " Go into the country," and I went. But at such an attempt at repose all my ailments gathered round me—made themselves far more palpable and felt. I had no resource but to fly from myself—to fly into the other world of books or thought or reverie, to live in some state of being less painful than my own. As long as I was always at work it seemed that I had no leisure to be ill. Quiet was my hell.' [1]

The foregoing extract illustrates curiously enough what has been said about the will. The writer thinks that his action was voluntary. 'To a constitution far from strong,' he remarks, 'I allowed no pause or respite.' In reality the automatic forces of his brain drove him to what he did. Among the private papers of Bulwer Lytton was found a criticism of his own character, written at the age of forty-three, in which a further illustration of this argument presents itself. 'Thought,' says the writer, ' is continually flowing through my mind. I scarcely know a moment in which I am awake and not thinking. Nor by thought do I mean mere reverie or castle building, but a sustained process of thinking. I have always in my mind some distinct train of ideas which I seek to develop, or some positive truth which I am trying to arrive at. If I lived for a million years I could not exhaust a millionth part of my thoughts.'

Defoe believed that the premonitions he sometimes felt as to coming events were spirit warnings, and a passage in

---

[1] Bulwer Lytton: *Confessions of a Water Patient.*

his works bearing upon this subject may be taken to illustrate the automatic character of his inspiration. 'I have never,' he writes, 'had any considerable mischief or disaster attending me, but, sleeping or waking, I have had notice of it beforehand; and had I listened to these notices I believe I might have shunned the evil. Let no man think this is a jest.' He further says, 'I know a man who made it a rule to obey these silent hints, and he often declared to me that when he obeyed them he never miscarried.' This man, ——, there is good reason to believe that Defoe means himself; at all events, he seems to write from his own experience. —— came under the ban of a Government prosecution, and was much perplexed as to what he should do. 'In this extremity,' writes Defoe, 'he felt one morning just as he had waked and as thoughts of his misfortune began to return upon him, I say he felt a strong impulse darting into his mind, thus: "Write a letter to them." It spoke so distinctly to him, and as it were forcibly, that, as he has often said since, he could scarcely persuade himself to believe but that he heard it; but he grants that he did not really hear it too. However, it repeated the words daily and hourly, till, at length, walking about in his chamber where he was hidden, very pensive and sad, it jogged him again, and he answered aloud to it as if it had been a voice: "Whom shall I write to?" It returned immediately, "Write to the judge." This pursued him again for several days, till at length he took his pen, ink, and paper.' He was puzzled what to say, but on beginning to write, 'the words flowed upon his pen in a manner that charmed even himself,' and the letter was instrumental in averting the prosecution.

Mrs. Gaskell says of Charlotte Brontë that it was not every day that she could write. Sometimes weeks, or even months, elapsed before she felt that she had anything to add to that portion of her story which was already written. Then some morning she would waken up, and 'the progress of her tale lay clear and bright before her, and she had only to sit down and write out the incidents and consequent thoughts, which were, in fact, more present to her mind at such times than her actual life itself.'

Whether the creative power is active or sluggish would seem to depend upon a greater or less degree of energy in the nerve-cells. Both conditions are met with among distinguished men of letters. Irritated by current reports that he was suffering from mental aberration, Byron said to Nathan, who set the 'Hebrew Melodies' to music, that he would try for once to write like a madman. Hastily seizing the pen, he stared for a moment into vacancy and then wrote down, as if by a flash of inspiration, and without erasing a single word, the beautiful verses beginning:—

> My soul is dark—oh! quickly string
> The harp I yet can brook to hear;
> And let thy gentle fingers fling
> Its melting murmurs o'er mine ear.

There was nothing laboured in Hartley Coleridge's inventions. 'Intense, glowing, ever-kindling genius,' says Townshend, 'breathed in every word he uttered. Originality was the life and soul of his most common converse.' And, as with Hartley Coleridge's conversation, so with his written compositions. ' His poems,' says his brother Derwent, ' including the best, were thrown off with the greatest facility and in the most casual manner. . . At any hour, in any place, or in any company if the fit took him, he would ask for a scrap of paper and produce a short piece of poetry, perhaps a sonnet, often of very perfect construction.' He had a great contempt for what he called ' baker's poetry,' poetry that had to be kneaded and pounded by its author. His own thoughts, according to his friend Thomas Blackburne, ' always came out finished cap-a-pie like a troop in quick march.'

Byron assured Leicester Stanhope that the gift of poetry had ' burst upon his mind unexpectedly,' and had excited his wonder, as he was not previously conscious of its possession. Goethe found himself impelled to turn into an image or a poem everything that delighted or troubled him, and Coleridge ' from childhood ' was accustomed to ' abstract, and as it were unrealize,' whatever of more than common interest his eyes dwelt upon, and then, ' by a sort of transfusion and transmission of his consciousness, to identify himself with the object.' Brougham wrote with extreme rapidity. There seemed to be no bounds to his energy or to the impetuosity of his spirit. His accomplishments were manifold and dazzling. It was said of him that if a new language were discovered in the morning, he would be able to talk it before night, and that if locked up in the Tower without a book he would be able to write an encyclopædia.

The foregoing examples represent a very high degree of morbid excitability. Wordsworth's brain, on the other hand, had little of the actual glow of insanity, though sensitive to rhythm and harmony. He had to slowly grind out his grandest poetry, and had few compensatory bursts of inspiration. He records as a remarkable feat of fancy his shaping out a single sonnet off hand. His sister's journals are full of lamentations over the sad hours he passed at his desk when out of the mood, hunting with a dismal sense of failure after thoughts and expressions that eluded him. Though a vigorous pedestrian and indifferent to weather, a trifle would interfere with his literary work, such as the pinch of a tight shoe.

In literary and poetic genius there would seem to be a considerable excitability of the visual centre, with more or less extensive cohesions in other centres. Describing in 'Facino Cane' his own early life, Balzac says: 'Observation had become to me intuitive. It penetrated the spirit without neglecting the body; or, rather, it seized external details so clearly, that it immediately went beyond them. It gave me the power of living the life of any individual upon whom it was exercised, and permitted me to substitute my personality for his. . . . While listening to the poor people around me, I espoused their life. I felt their rags on my back, my feet marched in their tattered shoes; their desires, their needs all passed into my spirit, and mine into theirs; it was the dream of a waking man. . . . To relinquish my identity, to become another through the intoxication of the moral faculties, and to play this game at will, such was my sole distraction. I have sometimes wondered if this gift were one of those whose abuse leads to madness, but its causes I have never sought. I know merely that I possess and make use of it.'

Balzac's characters were as realistically vivid to him as people of flesh and blood, and he spoke of them as friends and acquaintances. 'I am going to Alençon,' he would say; 'you know Mdlle. Cormon lives there,' or, 'I am off to Grenoble, the abode of M. Benassis.' 'Let us talk of realities,' he one day said to Jules Sandeau, 'let us talk of Eugénie Grandet;' and at another time, when his sister asked him for some information about Captain Jordy, Balzac replied very simply, 'I never knew the man before he came to Nemours, but if he interests you I will try to learn something of him.'

'Dickens once declared to me,' says George Henry Lewes,[1] 'that every word said by his characters was distinctly heard by him,' and the eminent critic accounts for the novelist's vividness of imagination, much to the disgust of Dickens's biographer, John Forster, by a theory of hallucination. 'When he (Dickens) imagined a street, a house, a room, a figure, he saw it not in the vague schemetic way of ordinary imagination, but in the sharp definition of actual perception, all the salient details obtruding themselves on his attention. He, seeing it thus vividly, made us also see it, and believing in its reality, however fantastic, he communicated something of his belief to us. So definite and consistent was the image, that even while knowing it was false, we could not help for a moment being affected, as it were, by his hallucination. . . . The imagination of the author laid hold of some well-marked physical trait, some peculiarity of aspect, speech, or manner which everyone recognised at once; and the force with which this was presented made it occupy the mind to the exclusion of all critical doubts; only reflection could detect the incongruity. . . . Dickens sees and feels, but the logic of feeling seems to be the only logic he can manage. I do not suppose a single thoughtful remark on life or character could be found throughout his twenty volumes. Keenly as he observes the objects before him, he never connects his observations into a general expression. Compared with that of Fielding or Thackeray his was merely an animal intelligence, *i.e.* restricted to perceptions.' The hallucination theory of Dickens's art is

____
[1] *Fortnightly Review*, February 1872.

supported by a letter of his to Forster. 'May I not be forgiven,' he writes, 'for thinking it is a wonderful testimony to my being made for art, that when in the midst of this trouble and pain I sit down to my book, some beneficent power shows it all to me and tempts me to be interested, and I don't invent it—really do not—but *see it* and write it down ?'

What seems to limit Dickens's genius is the fact that while his perceptions are vivid, their cohesions in the brain are not extensive, and, unlike those of Balzac, for example, embrace no profound experiences of human nature. Scott's genius is also largely pictorial. He draws his materials from history and legend, but the automatic activity of his brain blends so many impressions that his picturesque scenes deviate widely from the pattern of past realities ; and while he is not without a shrewd knowledge of the world he depicts rather the actions of men than their motives. Yet with all the spirit Scott had none of the executive faculty of the painter. 'The humble ambition which I long cherished of making sketches of those places which interested me was,' he writes, ' totally ineffectual. After long study and many efforts I was unable to apply the elements of perspective or of shade to the scene before me, and was obliged to relinquish in despair an art which I was most anxious to practise. But show me an old castle or a field of battle and I am at home at once, filling it with its combatants in their proper costume and overwhelming my hearers by the enthusiasm of my description. In crossing Magus Moor, near St. Andrews, the spirit moved me to give a picture of the assassination of the Archbishop of St. Andrews to some fellow travellers with whom I was accidentally associated, and one of them, though well acquainted with the story, protested that my narrative had frightened away his night's sleep.' Scott's defect evidently lay not in the visual centre of his brain, but in the nerve-connections between that and the motor apparatus for the hand.

Given morbid conditions of the brain a conceived idea may assume the force and vividness of a fact. It is a common delusion among the insane that they have taken part in great historical events. George IV. was convinced that he had fought at the Battle of Waterloo, and was accustomed to call upon the Duke of Wellington to corroborate him. Balzac described with enthusiasm to Madame Delphine Gay a superb white horse which he wished to present to Sandeau. A few days afterwards he believed that he had really given the horse, and meeting Sandeau asked him how the animal was doing.[1] Gustave Flaubert, like Dickens, had remarkably quick perceptions intimately associated with each other. While describing the death by poison of his famous character Emma Bovary, he felt the taste of arsenic so sharply in his mouth that he made himself ill and vomited his dinner.[2] His epileptic visitations were a dread to him, but the 'poetic vision' he frequently experienced with pleasure. 'Very often,' he observes, ' it comes slowly, bit by bit, like a scene set on the stage. At other times, however, it is sudden and fleeting. Something passes before your eyes and it must be seized quickly or it is lost.' Théophile Gautier, passing by the Vaudeville Theatre in Paris one day, noticed on the printed bill a commonplace phrase which stuck in his memory. He found himself repeating it mechanically. After a time it sounded in his ear as if uttered by a third person in a clear and distinct voice; and this continued intermittently for several weeks. From the repetition of a single phrase, such voices readily pass into a threatening key, make prolonged and more or less appropriate remarks, order the patient to do this or that, and finally assume all the characteristics of an insane hallucination.

Shakespeare's perceptions must have been extraordinarily keen and persistent. His mind must have photographed everything he saw. Natural scenery, natural objects, human character, society and its usages—all must have been vividly impressed upon his brain, and there associated with extensive and hardly less vivid memories. Probably had we known the man we should have discovered that he had limitations. All we can gather from his writings is that his surroundings must have impressed him with a force out of all proportion to the attention he could have given them, and that his

---

[1] Taine: *De l'Intelligence.*   [2] *Ibid.*

impressions being retained must have furnished him with an enormous amount of intellectual material and a basis of comparison infinitely greater than that possessed by ordinary men. He seems to have been untravelled, and to have had but a moderate knowledge of books; yet by dint of his acquisitions—mainly visual in their origin, but extensively cohering together and thus creating a great identifying or constructive faculty—he was able to people foreign scenes and the ancient world with appropriate characters, and to supply them with incidents to match. Such immense creative power as Shakespeare's can only be understood in connection with a morbid impressionability. Walter Scott and Charles Dickens, of all English authors, have probably drawn the largest number of distinct characters after Shakespeare, and their imaginative faculty, as we have seen, was associated with an extremely unsound condition of the nervous system. Thomas Kenny, although ignorant of this physical aspect of genius, makes some suggestive observations upon Shakespeare's character as a man. Accepting the sonnets in common with most English commentators as pure autobiographical material, Kenny finds that they exhibit throughout a 'teeming, unchecked, more or less disordered profusion of thought and imagery in the mind of the writer,' and from Shakespeare's unparalleled faculty of transporting himself into the state of mind of every species of human being, he concludes that the poet cannot have possessed a very resolute character of his own.[1]

From the absence of all mention of him by his contemporaries outside a small theatrical circle, it is indeed not unlikely that Shakespeare may have looked a comparatively insignificant person, gliding through life quietly and unpretentiously. Masson, after a close analysis of his works, comes to the conclusion that he was 'essentially a meditative, speculative, and, even in his solitary hours, an abject and melancholy man, rather than a man of active, firm, and worldly disposition.' Instead of being a calm, strong observer of life and nature, a 'bird singing on the bough,' as Carlyle puts it, he was, in Masson's view, 'a man of the gentlest and

[1] Thomas Kenny: *Life and Genius of Shakespeare.*

most troublesome affections; of sensibility abnormally keen and deep; full of metaphysical longings; liable above most men to self-distrust, despondency, and mental agitations from causes internal and external; and a prey to many secret and severe experiences which he did not discuss at the Mermaid Tavern.'[1] Physically and mentally this is precisely what a man of Shakespeare's surpassing genius might be expected to be.

Style, so important an element of literary genius, consists in the choice of words, images, metaphors, and illustrations appropriate to the subject in hand. It has its basis in our sensory and motor cohesions, and is therefore dependent upon the reciprocal action and retentiveness of the several centres of the brain. The great writer is one who has a profusion of words at his command, together with a great stock of observation, and who is able out of the plenitude of his resources to convey the exact shade of meaning he desires—to communicate to others the precise effect, pictorial or comparative, which has been produced by something upon his own mind. A necessary part of the faculty of choosing the right word is to be able to discriminate between the associations of one word as compared with those of another which may have pretty much the same meaning. Such associations may be extremely delicate, in many cases almost indefinable. 'Acute' and 'sharp' are obvious examples of a distinction without much fundamental difference. Most people know or feel which of the two in a given connection is the more suitable. It is less easy to say why 'plenitude' is sometimes a better word than 'fulness,' or 'stupendous' than 'vast,' though every skilful writer prefers one or the other according to circumstances.

Some remarks by George Henry Lewes[2] on the difficulties of making an adequate translation of poetry, illustrate the delicate effects of association and suggestion in the use of words, effects of which the poet's mind takes account. The line,

The river wanders at its own sweet will,

---

[1] David Masson: *Essays Biographical and Critical.*
[2] *Life of Goethe.*

T

is not adequately rendered by this other, although the meaning is the same :

The river runneth free from all restraint.

In the first case, a landscape is somehow brought before the mind, probably by the word 'wander' in conjunction with a river. The words of the parody, on the other hand, have only bad associations. 'Runneth,' 'free,' and 'restraint' are in no way associated with rural scenery, but rather with Bow Street or the Old Bailey. Walter Scott speaks of the verse of an old ballad which haunted his boyhood. It is this :

> The dews of night began to fall.
> The moon, sweet regent of the sky,
> Silvered the walls of Cumnor Hall
> And many an oak that stood thereby.

Lewes renders the verse as follows, and asks, as well he may, 'Where is the poetry of it ?' :

> The nightly dews commenced to fall.
> The moon, whose empire is the sky,
> Shone on the walls of Cumnor Hall
> And all the oaks that stood thereby.

The beauty and the force of the original lie mainly in the phrases 'sweet regent,' which gives the moon a personality, 'silvered,' which pictorially represents the effect of her light, and 'many an oak,' which conveys a sense of vagueness and romance incompatible with such a precise and matter-of-fact statement as 'all the oaks.'

In general, that style is clearest and best which enables the nerve-currents in the reader's brain to travel along easy and direct tracks. Long parentheses or suspensions of the interest are fatiguing from the greater expenditure of nerve-energy required to establish the necessary organic cohesions in the brain, and for the same reason, vague, abstract terms call for a greater effort on the reader's part than direct word-pictures. To 'send a man to prison' is a more forcible expression than to 'punish him in accordance with the regulations of the penal code.' 'Beware of the bottle' is better than 'be careful not to indulge excessively in intoxicating fluids.' A word learnt and used in childhood has more meaning to us as a rule than one acquired in after life, the reason being that it lies upon a well-established track of nervous impulse, and has easily aroused associations. The fancied superiority of Latin to Saxon English is only a question of early use. It so happens that an English child's vocabulary is almost wholly Saxon. Hence, 'sour' has always more forcible associations in the average Englishman's mind than 'acid,' though to a Frenchman who has learnt English the cases are reversed. The words of a foreign language seldom become as vivid to us as those of our mother tongue, but increasing familiarity with them brings increased rapidity and ease of comprehension.

A good style of writing is one that is constantly arousing pleasing and illustrative associations. To express everything overloads the reader's mind with detail. The skilful writer feels how much may be left to the average reader's imagination, and is careful not to say more than he need for the purpose in view. Much of the effect of style depends upon the sequence of the ideas presented, and there is also the music of language to be considered—the rhythmic effect of words and phrases upon the ear. All these niceties of writing are governed by the degree of the susceptibility of the writer's brain, the physical basis of language being the innumerable nerve fibres that run between the visual, auditory, and articulatory centres. The enjoyment of a good style by the reader necessarily depends, of course, upon the reader's own faculties. If he has no associations, his author cannot be expected to stir them into activity.

It may further be laid down that the extreme sensibility which raises the individual's faculties of perception and expression to the level of genius is a morbid condition, which, if it were not demonstrated by the pathological history of great men, could still be proved from the records of insanity. Gérard de Nerval, the friend of Théophile Gautier and Gustave Flaubert, in the lucid intervals of an insanity which afflicted him from his youth upwards, and which terminated in his suicide, was a prolific writer of fiction, and his colleague, Maxime du Camp, pointedly observes that he possessed 'a great *finesse* of style ' and a rare gift of ' subtle observation,' as, indeed, every reader of his works will acknowledge.

Nothing is more remarkable in Shakespeare than the easy flow of his language. ' Abundance, ease, redundance,' observes a literary critic, ' a plenitude of word, sound, and imagery which, were the intellect at work only a little less magnificent, would sometimes end in sheer braggardism and bombast, are the characteristics of Shakespeare's style ! On and on the poet flows : words, thoughts, and fancies crowding upon him as fast as he can write, all related to the matter on hand, and all poured forth together, to rise and fall on the waves of an established cadence. Such lightness and ease in the manner, and such prodigious wealth and depth in the matter, are combined in no other writer.' The little we know of Shakespeare the man attests his extraordinary fluency. Ben Jonson says : ' I remember the players have often mentioned it as an honour to Shakespeare that in his writing he never blotted out a line.' ' Shakespeare,' his brother poet adds, ' had an excellent phantasy, brave notions, and gentle expressions, *wherein he flowed with that facility that sometimes it was necessary he should be stopped !* His wit was in his own power. Would the rule of it had been so too ! Many times he fell into those things which could not escape laughter, as when in the person of Cæsar, one speaking to him, " Cæsar, thou dost me wrong," he replied, " Cæsar never did wrong but with just cause," and such like, which were ridiculous. But he redeemed his vices with his virtues. There was ever more in him to be praised than pardoned.' The editors of the First Folio, Hemynge and Condell, remark of Shakespeare : ' His mind and hand went together, and what he thought he uttered with that easiness that we have scarce received from him a blot on his papers.' Fluency of expression occurs in insanity, and may be temporarily increased by alcohol and other drugs. Evidently, therefore, it depends upon a morbid excitability of the nerve-cells and fibres of the brain.

The susceptibility of the mind to the minutiæ of style may, in extreme cases, seriously impede a writer's productiveness. Gustave Flaubert exhausted himself in corrections.

He would toil for hours at a single phrase. It is recorded that in one of his pages of manuscript the word 'mais' at the beginning of a sentence is struck out and written in eleven times before being allowed to stand. Latterly his life was a perpetual irritation, his work haunting him in his feverish sleep, and his days being consumed in frenzied attempts to push the art of composition beyond the limits even of perfection. Probably there is some affinity between such a condition and the somewhat rare form of insanity called by the French *la folie du doute*, and by the Germans *Grübelsucht*, or prying-mania, the essential feature of which is the obsession of the mind by a perpetual interrogation—a constant and urgent morbid impulse to inquire into and investigate everything of however trivial a nature, a tendency to spin an endless web of questionings, an inability to accept the ordinary facts of experience.[1] The assonance of words in a sentence produced as violent an effect upon Flaubert's nerves as a discord did upon those of Mozart.

Closely allied to the choice of the right word is that curious sense displayed by some famous writers of fiction of the appropriateness of names. Balzac was very scrupulous in the naming of his characters. He never invented names; he discovered them. They could no more be fabricated, he held, than granite or marble; they were all the work of time and revolutions. It is told of him that for a whole day he scrutinised the signboards of Paris in company with Léon Gozlan for a name for a personage in his 'Scènes de la Vie Politique,' and found it at last on a tailor's signboard. It was 'Marcas,' to which he took the liberty of prefixing the initial 'Z.' 'A certain harmony,' he afterwards wrote, of the character whom he called Marcas, 'existed between the man and the name. This Z with which Marcas was preceded presented to the imagination a something indescribably fatal. Marcas! Repeat to yourself the name! Does it not seem to have a sinister significance? Does it not seem as though its owner were born to be martyr'd? . . . I would not dare affirm that destiny is uninfluenced by a name, for between

---

[1] A curious example of this malady is reported in the *Journal of Mental Science* for October, 1888.

the deeds of men and their names there are inexplicable affinities and visible discords which at once astonish and surprise. But the subject will some day assuredly form part of the occult sciences. Does not the Z present a thwarted and contradicted appearance? Does it not represent the contingent and fantastic zig-zags of a tormented life? What ill wind can have blown upon this letter that in every language to which it is admitted it commands barely fifty words? . . . Examine the name again—Z. Marcas! The entire existence of the man is contained in this fantastic assemblage of seven letters. Seven!—the most significant of the cabalistic numbers! Marcas died at the age of thirty-five; his life, therefore, was composed of but seven lustres. Marcas! Does not the sound convey to you the idea of something precious broken in a noiseless fall!' Very few people, perhaps, will discover as much as Balzac in the conjunction of letters referred to, but the anecdote is instructive as pointing to the existence in certain minds of subtle appreciations of harmony and discord in words, akin to the musical sense.

Susceptibility to metrical cadence is a natural endowment. It is more or less developed in individuals, and when brain disease occurs it is liable to be depressed or elevated. To Swift, during one phase of his insanity, it was 'as hard to find a rhyme as a guinea.' On the other hand, patients in lunatic asylums sometimes rhyme with marvellous facility. I apprehend that the metrical faculty has its main seat in the area of the brain concerned with articulatory movements, and that it is largely dependent upon the efficiency of the nerve-fibres passing between that area and the auditory centre. Of the muscular element in rhyme we may assure ourselves by a simple illustration. In walking along the street, or, still better, in going down stairs, a rhythm is established in the movements of our limbs. The concussions of our steps recurring in a definite order, we automatically adjust the muscular resistance needful for each concussion; the body husbands its resources so as to meet the calls made upon it. Then, if our foot knocks against an unexpected obstacle, or if at the bottom of the stairs there is a step more or less than we counted upon, we receive a shock. Precisely the same thing happens in

rhyme if we come across a misplaced accent or a super-
numerary syllable. In both cases there is an erroneous pre-
adjustment of our muscular forces. A special susceptibility
of the motor as well as of the auditory centres and their connections would therefore seem to be essential to the writing
of verse.

But rhyme does not necessarily go with reason nor cadence
with poetry. Coleridge observes that the words—

> Behold yon row of pines that shorn and bowed
> Bend from the sea-blast, seen at twilight eve—

contain so little poetry that if re-arranged they would not be
out of place in a book of topography, or in a description of a
tour. The same image, however, rises into a semblance of
poetry if thus conveyed:

> Yon row of bleak and visionary pines
> By twilight glimpse discerned! Mark how they flee,
> From the fierce sea-blast, all their tresses wild,
> Streaming before them!

Whence comes the difference? Surely from the identity unexpectedly established between the row of trees and some form
of moving animal life. The visual and motor centres, with
their respective memories, contribute to the creation of the
image.

The part played by the visual sense in poetry is very
great, hearing, touch, taste, or smell furnishing comparatively
few metaphors or illustrations. Frequently a mere optical
effect is reproduced with great force and propriety. For
example:

> As when far off at sea a fleet descried
> *Hangs* in the clouds, by equinoxial winds
> Close sailing from Bengala, or the isles
> Of Ternate or Tidore, whence merchants bring
> Their spicy drugs; they on the trading flood,
> Through the wide Ethiopian to the Cape,
> Ply, stemming nightly toward the pole: so seem'd
> Far off the flying fiend.

Here the word 'hangs' governs the whole image, and the
optical effect is further heightened by representing the fleet, an

aggregate of many ships, as one mighty person whose track is upon the waters. Another example of the same kind is Milton's description of the Messiah:

> Attended by ten thousand thousand saints
> He onward came ; far off *His coming* shone.

What finer abstraction could there be than His coming, which merges into a single optical effect a multitude of individuals ? Shakespeare abounds in visual images. Here is a fine example:

> Night's candles are burnt out and jocund day
> *Stands tip-toe* on the misty mountain tops.

A similar picture presented itself to the poet while he was writing his sonnets, and was thus rendered:

> Full many a glorious morning have I seen
> *Flatter* the mountain tops with sovereign eye.

In both cases the optical virtue of the words italicised is very marked. Wordsworth delighted in the exercise of

> —that inward eye
> Which is the bliss of solitude.

The woods, the fields, the seasons, and aspects of simple rural life, alone moved the poetic spirit of Wordsworth to expression. The most exciting and dramatic public events scarcely interested him. He visited France during the great Revolution and saw the first French politician sent to the guillotine. To this subject he alludes casually in his letters ; but he notes nothing of it in his verse, though he could make sonnets on the sunsets on the banks of the Loire. Turner the painter had, of course, the pictorial eye required by the poet, but he was deficient in the rhythmic sense. His verse was very jolting, and his command of words ludicrously inadequate to the task of writing even passable poetry. Wordsworth's deficiency was evidently in the perception of the dramatic and social or historical element in events. It was the pictorial sense that he excelled in, and, unlike Turner, he had the necessary command of words and rhythm to give it poetic expression.

Graphic writing is due to the possession of a strong visual faculty. It is more telling to say that a ' field is *black* with

people,' than that 'thousands of people are in a field.'
Carlyle, ridiculing a doctor who failed to cure him of his
dyspepsia, says he might as well have poured his tale into
' the long, hairy ear of the first jackass' he met. In penning
this, Carlyle must have had the picture of the jackass, with
its long, hairy ear, in his mind.

The identifying faculty whereby unsuspected likenesses
and analogies are discovered, is strong in all forms of literary
genius; it is exceptionally strong in wit, and even in the
despised form of wit called punning. Sydney Smith's theory
that surprise is an essential ingredient of wit is probably the
true one. The best joke loses its effect on repetition, and
the reason would seem to be that the 'sudden joy,' the 'flash
of astonishment' with which it was first received is not re-
kindled in our minds. 'The greater the surprise,' says
Sydney Smith, 'the greater the pleasure.' Voltaire was
praising Haller to a Swiss gentleman. 'I am astonished,'
said the Swiss, 'you should speak so well of Haller, for he is
outrageous in his abuse of you.' 'Well, well,' replied Voltaire,
'I believe the truth is we have both formed very erroneous
notions of each other.' 'Here,' says Sydney Smith, who
quotes the anecdote, 'surprise is excited by the connection
discovered between the apparent candour and the real severity
of Voltaire. We expect from the first physiognomy of the
answer that he is going to say something kind and conciliatory of his enemy, when at the same time he overwhelms
him with the keenest satire.' When surprise is accompanied
by other feelings the sensation of wit is almost entirely lost.
This is aptly illustrated by Sydney Smith. 'In looking over
the various parts of a steam engine,' he remarks, ' the mind
is repeatedly affected by sensations resembling those of wit;
the mode in which the valves open and shut, etc. But, at the
same time, we begin to speculate upon the importance of the
discovery; to reason upon its utility, and the sensation of surprise no longer remains pure and unmixed. In the mind of
a child capable of understanding these mechanical discoveries,
the unexpected relation between the parts and movements
would excite nearly the same feeling as wit would do; he
would enjoy the pure surprise and speculate little, if at all, on

the matter.' Hobbes thought the pleasure of wit lay in the implied superiority of the person expressing it or hearing it, and it is undoubtedly true that wit is nearly always derogatory to somebody or something. On reflection it will be found, however, that surprise is a more constant ingredient of wit than detraction. When a joke is twice told the detraction remains, but in the absence of surprise its characteristic effect is lost.

Many of Sydney Smith's own recorded witticisms are as perfect in the element of surprise as the one he quotes from Voltaire. Such were his remarks : to a boy, who was trying to please a tortoise by stroking its shell, that he might as well stroke the dome of St. Paul's to please the Dean and Chapter, and his pithy reply to the medical men who advised him to 'take a walk on an empty stomach'—'On whose?' This, again, is a fairly good specimen of wit: 'The observances of the Church as to feasts and fasts are tolerably well kept upon the whole, since the rich keep the feasts and the poor the fasts.' Just as wit depends upon an identity of intellectual conceptions, so does punning consist in establishing an identity of word sounds. A good specimen of a pun is the following:

Customer (to Tailor) : Were you at Balaclava ?

Tailor : No! Why ?

Customer : Because you *charge* so magnificently.

Here the memorable charge of the Six Hundred is unexpectedly associated with such a trivial matter as a tradesman's bill, and, as in wit, surprise is evoked. Generally, however, punning is confined to identities of sound. It stirs a much more limited circle of associations in the brain than wit and is justly accounted inferior. Remarkable wits and punsters like Voltaire, Sydney Smith, and Thomas Hood, have invariably been of the morbid type as regards their nervous organisation, and it is probable that excellence, either in wit or in punning, is only attained at some cost to the other faculties. Wits and satirists, it has been observed, are themselves peculiarly sensitive to ridicule. This, one would expect from their keen sense of the ridiculous in others.

In the exercise of the fine arts, both a sensory aptitude and an associated muscular endowment are called into play.

The musician's discrimination of sound is acute, and there is a wealth of sound-memories accumulated in his auditory centre; but the perception of time is as obviously as much a question of muscular movement as the metrical sense. Again, the painter, like the poet, has an extensive perception of colour in nature together with a strong retentiveness for all kinds of pictorial display. With this, however, he also possesses a faculty for delicate movements of the hand and fingers. If he is good at drawing, his sense of touch and the muscular adjustments of his eye will be keen. Whence his perception of form—an endowment likewise of the sculptor. The mere colourist, on the other hand, will rely chiefly upon his optical sense and his mechanical aptitude.

As few musicians write poetry, or poets music, it may be concluded that time in music and metre and cadence in poetry are not identical. I have associated rhyme with the speech-centre. Considering how prone we are to beat a measure with hands and feet, and how greatly music conduces to dancing, it is probable that time in music is connected with movements of the limbs. Individuals differ widely in their perceptions of music, and although the ear may be improved by cultivation, the musical faculty is essentially a natural gift, that is to say, dependent upon the number and the susceptibility of the nerve-cells and fibres in the auditory and motor centres. Executive power, involving the use of the hands in conjunction with the visual reading of the musical notes, is a distinct faculty from that of musical creativeness or the mere taste for music. Wagner confessed to being a poor hand at the piano. Other musicians, such as Paganini, have been great executants with little creative power.

Like visual images, sounds are revived by association. They, too, form more or less extensive cohesions, and it is probable that the educated musician has many thousand such cohesions at his command. A memory for sounds is as important to the musician as is a visual memory to the man of letters. Revived combinations or sequences of notes, whether conscious or unconscious, are the raw material of musical composition, and creativeness in music is due to precisely the same cause as creativeness in literature, namely, the spontaneous action of the nerve-cells and fibres of the brain, the only difference being that the auditory and general motor areas are affected in place of the visual and the articulatory.

In Mozart the impulse to compose manifested itself in his fifth year, by which time he was already a good player. His ear was extremely delicate. 'Until he was about ten years old,' says his early friend Schachtner, 'he had an insurmountable horror of the horn when it was sounded alone without other instruments; merely holding a horn towards him terrified him as much as if he had been threatened with a loaded pistol.' Schachtner once blew the horn in the boy's presence notwithstanding. 'Mozart no sooner heard the clanging sound than he turned pale and would have fallen into convulsions had it continued.' To be creative it is necessary that the musician should have his mind well stored with musical memories. Mozart said of himself: 'It would not be easy to find a celebrated musician whose works I have not often and laboriously studied.'[1] Wherever he happened to be, Mozart was incessantly occupied with musical thoughts. 'I am,' he wrote, 'steeped in music so to speak; it is in my mind the whole day and I love to dream, study, and reflect upon it.' He was always strumming—on his hat, his watch-fob, the table, the chairs, as if he were at the piano, and even in conversation with his friends he seemed to be carrying on an under-train of musical thought. More remarkable still, when music was going on that did not interest him, he had the power of working upon his own musical ideas. At the opera, his friends could tell by the restless movements of his hands, by his look, and the motion of his lips as if he were singing or whistling, that he was entirely engrossed by his internal musical activity. It is further related of Mozart that, in walking or driving, he would be occupied in inventing, arranging, and elaborating melodies, often humming or singing aloud, and growing red in the face with excitement, and the briefest indications in black and white sufficed to preserve these studies in his memory.

It is often quoted as a proof of Mozart's wonderful

[1] Otto Jahn.

memory that, as a boy, he was able to recollect and write down Allegri's ' Miserere ' after hearing it once ; but this was by no means a solitary feat of the kind on his part. Concertos that he had not heard for a long time he could play by heart ; he wrote the trumpet and drum parts of the second finale in ' Don Giovanni ' without a score ; on one occasion he wrote only the violin part of a sonata for violin and piano, playing himself the piano part without having heard the piece, and he could write a composition at once in parts without having scored it. Compositions that he had once thought out he could recollect with perfect clearness in their minutest details. In composing he was not obliged to have recourse to the piano ; his mind pictured the whole work when he had once conceived it. According to his wife, ' he wrote music like letters and never tried a movement until it was finished.' He could, however, improvise marvellously. At such times, ' the bold flights of his imagination into the highest regions and down again to the very depths of the abyss caused the greatest masters of music who heard him to be lost in amazement and delight.' The impressions produced, says one of them, were like the gift of ' new senses of sight and hearing.'

Mozart, in the height of his activity, lived in a delirium of invention, often working so hard that, as he himself expressed it, he did not know whether his head was on or off. Concerning his method of work he wrote : ' It is when I am, as it were, entirely myself, alone and in good spirits, that my ideas flow best and most abundantly. Whence or how they come I know not, nor can I force them. Those that best please me I retain in my memory, and I am accustomed, as I have been told, to hum them to myself. If I continue in this way, it soon occurs to me how I may turn this or that *morceau* to account, agreeably to the rules of counterpoint and to the peculiarities of the various instruments. All this fires my soul, and, provided I am not disturbed, my subject enlarges itself, becomes methodized and defined, and the whole, though it be long, stands almost complete and finished in my mind, so that I can survey it, like a fine picture or a statue, at a glance. In my imagination I hear the various parts, not successively but all at once. What a delight this is I cannot tell. All this inventing and producing takes place in a pleasing, lively dream. Why my productions take from my hand that particular form and style that makes them "Mozartish" and different from the works of other composers is probably owing to the same cause that renders my nose Mozart's and different from the noses of other people. For I really do not study or aim at any originality; I should not, in fact, be quite able to describe in what mine consists. At least, I know that I have not constituted myself either one way or another.'[1]

Other great composers have similarly been controlled by the automatic forces of their brain. Handel was not only born of unmusical parents, but was sternly forbidden to practise music and, as a boy, received no instruction in the art whatever. Yet his earliest delight was a mimic orchestra of toy drums and trumpets, horns, flutes, and Jew's harps. He practised on an old clavichord in secret, and by dint of his unaided efforts made such progress in executive power and artistic expression as to astonish all who heard him the first time he was allowed to touch an organ. At eight or nine years of age he was consumed by the fire of inspiration. Of Beethoven, Schindler relates that he would not infrequently, in a fit of the most complete abstraction, go to his washhand basin and pour several jugs of water upon his hands, all the while 'humming and roaring, for sing he could not.' After splashing in the water till his clothes were wet through, he would pace up and down the room with a vacant expression of countenance and his eyes frightfully distended. These were his moments of profoundest meditation. Again, 'when one of his musical ideas took possession of his mind, he would look upwards, his eyes rolling and flashing brightly, or stare straight in front of him with his eye-balls fixed. These fits of inspiration frequently came to him when he was in company or even in the street. In public, at such moments, he naturally attracted attention and ridicule.' The fact that Beethoven went on composing after his hearing failed him, shows how his brain must have seethed with musical material. Mendelssohn's fits of inspiration were sudden. 'Sometimes

[1] Holmes: *Life of Mozart.*

I have a feeling like this,' he remarked to Rockstro, twisting his hands rapidly and nervously in front of him—'and when that comes I know that I must write.'

The key to this great creative activity in music is furnished by the insanity of Schumann. While in a beer saloon one evening Schumann threw down a newspaper he had in his hand, saying to a friend, 'I can read no more; I hear an incessant A.' Afterwards he imagined he heard a tone which pursued him incessantly, and from which harmonies, and even whole compositions, were gradually developed. Spirit voices whispered in his ear; now gently, now rudely and reproachfully. These hallucinations robbed him of sleep for the last two weeks of his wretched existence. One night he rose suddenly and called for a light, saying that Schubert and Mendelssohn had sent him a theme which he must write out at once, and this he did in spite of his wife's entreaties. During his illness he composed five piano variations upon this theme, which was his last work.[1] Taken in conjunction with Mozart's remarkably lucid statement of his methods, nothing could more conclusively establish the automatic character of musical inspiration than this experience of Schumann's.

That musical inspiration is subject to pretty much the same rules and exceptions as literary, is shown by the fact that Chopin, like Flaubert, had a mania for corrections. Chopin's creations were spontaneous; the idea came to him without his seeking it. It would come to him at the piano suddenly and completely, or it would spring up in his mind out of doors when he would hasten to fix it upon paper. 'Then began,' says Madame George Sand, 'a painful labour of correction. Chopin wrote, erased, added, diminished, transformed, and, finding his idea still inferior, would sink into the depth of despair. For whole days he would be shut up in his room, marching to and fro, weeping, tearing his hair, tearing up his written sheets, breaking his pens, changing a hundred times a measure, a harmony, a note. He would spend six weeks torturing a page only to restore it ultimately to its original form.' Such incessant correction would seem to arise from a persistent flow of fresh combinations upon a

[1] Wasilewski.

given theme, if it is not, as already suggested, a form of *la jolie du doute*. Music requires little or no basis of general observation in the individual; it has few cohesions outside the auditory area and the motor centre where it finds expression. As a class, consequently, musicians do not strike one as exceptionally intelligent or well-informed men.

Painters have a much keener perception of light and shade in a given object than the ordinary observer. They see their model as a patch of diversified colour apart from tactile and motor suggestions of a disturbing character. The eminent French painter Delacroix was exclusively a colourist, with little idea of form. He was bad at drawing, but in the manipulation of colour his genius was marvellous. 'I have seen him,' says Maxime du Camp, 'take coloured skeins of wool, mix and group them, and by that means produce extra-ordinary effects of colouration.' Delacroix once remarked that the finest picture he had ever seen was a Persian carpet. In his portraits he achieved but an indifferent likeness, but his pearl necklaces and jewels were startlingly real. Destitute of colour, his compositions tended to the grotesque.

'What do you see, sir?' said Fuseli one day to a student, who, with his pencil in hand and his drawing before him, was gazing into vacancy. 'Nothing, sir,' was the answer. 'Nothing! young man,' rejoined the eminent painter; 'then I tell you you ought to see something—you ought to see distinctly the true image of what you are trying to draw. I see the vision of all I paint, and I wish to Heaven I could paint up to what I see.' At the same time Fuseli was near-sighted, so much so that, while painting, he was obliged from time to time to retire from his easel to a distance and examine his picture by means of an opera glass, then return and retouch the defective places.[1] The faculty of seeing their subject in the mind's eye is not an uncommon one among painters of genius. Leonardo da Vinci organised a festive meeting of peasants, fed them, watched them closely, and afterwards painted them from memory. Hogarth writes: 'I had one material advantage over my competitors, namely, the early habit I acquired of retaining in my mind's eye, without coldly copying it on

<hr>

[1] Allan Cunningham.

the spot, whatever I intended to imitate.' Gustave Doré and David Roberts, the inspired house-painter who rose to be a Royal Academician, possessed the same gift. Of Roberts a biographer says: 'With a few touches he could produce an effect, rivalling in apparent elaboration the most careful productions, and far excelling them in breadth and power. He seemed to be able to photograph objects on his eye, for I have again and again been with him while he was sketching very elaborate structures, or very extensive views, and he took in a large mass at one glance, not requiring to look again at the portion until he had completed it in his sketch.'

How morbid is this faculty of optical retentiveness may be gathered from a remarkable case that came under Wigan's treatment. It was that of a painter of note, who executed portraits with remarkable facility. He required but one sitting, and his system he thus explained: 'When a sitter came, I looked at him attentively for half an hour, sketching from time to time on the canvas. I wanted no more. I put away my canvas and took another sitter. When I wished to resume my first portrait, I mentally took the man and set him in the chair, where I saw him as distinctly as if he had been before me in his proper person—I may almost say more vividly. I looked from time to time at the imaginary figure, then worked with my pencil, then referred to the countenance, and so on, just as I should have done had the sitter been there. When I looked at the chair I saw the man.' The artist possessing this strange susceptibility was very popular for a time and made a great deal of money. Gradually, however, he began to lose the distinction between the imaginary figure and the real person, and sometimes disputed with sitters as to whether they had been with him the day before. Madness supervened, and he remained for thirty years in an asylum. A short time before his death he resumed his pencil and painted nearly as well as formerly.

Another celebrated artist of Wigan's day (probably Haydon), whose fertility of imagination was a general subject of wonder and admiration, is said to have remarked that the preposterous faces and figures he put forth always seemed to him to exist already on the paper, and that his hand did nothing more than trace the outlines and fix them with the pencil. Here we have an example of that spontaneous activity of the nerve-cells of the visual centre which is at the bottom of creative art. Another illustration is furnished by the case of an 'eminent artist' known to Forbes Winslow. This person died of apoplexy, and, before his death, he exhibited a curious derangement of the visual centre. The cerebral symptoms showed themselves several years before the fatal attack, in the form of flashes of light before the eyes, to which were afterwards added pains in the head and diminished distinctness of sight. This last symptom gradually increased, till the patient's sight was totally destroyed. From that time he suffered from a series of the most dazzling images, playing apparently upon the optical apparatus by day and night. Their brightness was unspeakably distressing. Sometimes they would assume the form of angels with flaming swords, every motion of which seemed like an electric flash to blind the eye and sear the brain by the intensity of its light. With the exception of some irritability of temper, there was not the slightest affection of the intellectual powers. The memory, imagination, and judgment were unimpaired, and there was no change in the coats or humours of the eye.

The actor's genius consists mainly in a special command of voice, facial expression, gesture, and action. Actors do not feel more acutely than other people, but they are able to express their feelings more vividly, and this faculty may be ascribed to a special susceptibility of the area for the articulatory apparatus and for the movements of the body and limbs, more particularly the face, arms, and hands. Of all the arts, acting probably requires the least assistance from the sensory centres. It does not seem to be necessary that the actor should closely observe or have a specially retentive memory for life and character. Working by analogy, he can successfully enact a murder though he may never have assisted at one, and he constantly depicts feelings, such as those of a king or a criminal, which he has never actually experienced. Some of the greatest actors are callous to the emotions they portray; they seem to feel but in reality they do not. Sarah

Bernhardt's pulse does not quicken in her violent scenes of passion. Robson could electrify his audience by his emotional changes ; yet Palgrave Simpson described him as one of the stupidest actors at rehearsal he had ever met, and apparently without an idea in his head. Actors who have played with him, relate that in his most pathetic scenes, while he was thrilling the house to tears, Robson could try to make his stage companion laugh by some *sotto voce* remark upon a trivial subject, showing himself to be completely unmoved.

Probably there is little in the greatest acting that goes beyond the mechanical aptitudes described. The intellectual *finesse*, so much admired in certain impersonations, is one of the many illusions of the stage. No actor ever possessed it in a higher degree than the elder Farren, who, nevertheless, in private life, according to George Henry Lewes, was ' rather stupid than otherwise.' An actor may, of course, be an acute thinker, but at the same time he is not bound to be intellectual, exceptional powers of observation not being essential to his art as they are to that of the man of letters or the painter, though he must, of course, have intelligence enough to make-up in character, and to adapt himself to the *optique* of the stage. Children with no knowledge of the world act remarkably well, whereas we never hear of infant prodigies in literature or of Royal Academicians of tender years. I am speaking, be it remembered, of the actor's natural endowment, the gift of imitation, which constitutes his speciality. With this a very ordinary degree of intelligence will make a great display, and without it the highest intellectual attainments will avail nothing. Shakespeare was a mediocrity on the boards—at all events, nothing has been recorded in praise of him as an actor, and it is a matter of common observation in theatrical life that the author, who necessarily feels the pathos of what he writes, is usually unable to give it effective expression personally. In the mounting of a play, much of the painter's faculty for colour and form may be displayed ; but this, properly speaking, lies outside the actor's province, as does also the business skill required for the successful management of a theatre.

The impulsive actor is one whose muscular mechanism is

highly responsive to the induced emotion of the scene. When Edmund Kean was at his best, ' the fury and whirlwind of the passions,' says a contemporary writer, ' seemed to endow him with supernatural strength. His eyes were glittering and bloodshot; his veins were swollen, and his whole figure restless and violent.' The very looks of a great tragedian are as terrible to his fellow actors as to the public. Murdoch, an actor who played with Junius Brutus Booth, thus describes a scene in which he took part with that tragedian : 'I turned, and there, with the pistol held to my head, stood Booth, glaring like an infuriated demon. Then for the first time I comprehended the reality of acting. The fury of the passion-flamed face, and the magnetism of the rigid clutch upon my arm paralysed my muscles, while the scintillating gleam of the terrible eyes, like the green and red flashes of an enraged serpent, fascinated and fixed me spell-bound to the spot.' And a moment's reflection will show how much the functions of the muscular system are indicated in the following description by Lewes of the genius of Rachel : ' In her early days nothing more exquisite could be heard than her elocution—it was musical and artistically graduated to the fluctuations of meaning. Her thrilling voice, flexible, penetrating, and grave, responded with the precision of a keyed instrument. Her thin, nervous frame vibrated with emotion. Her face, which would have been common had it not been aflame with genius, was capable of intense expression. Her gestures were so fluent and graceful that merely to see her would have been a rare delight. Very noticeable is it,' adds the eminent critic, ' that Rachel could not speak prose with even tolerable success ; deprived of the music of verse, and missing its *ictus*, she seemed quite incapable of managing the easy cadences of colloquial language. The subtle influences of rhythm seemed to penetrate her, and gave a movement and animation to her delivery which were altogether wanting in her declamation of prose.'[1]

I have already shown what ground exists for believing that our perception of rhythm is connected with the motor area of the brain. On the theory of dramatic expression as a

[1] George Henry Lewes : *Actors and the Art of Acting.*

muscular endowment one can understand how Macready was able to prepare himself for rendering the rage of Shylock by violently shaking a ladder and cursing in an undertone behind the scenes. Had Macready, however, been an actor of surpassing genius, that is to say, of surpassing susceptibility as regards his muscular system, the induced emotion of the scene would have lashed him into a rage, or the semblance of a rage, without the aid of the ladder.

That the actor or actress can shed tears on the stage is perfectly true; but this, again, is a purely mechanical effect. It is not the expression of a genuine grief. The same automatic action of the lachrymose glands in obedience to a stimulus is experienced by the spectator of a play, who weeps at, while he secretly enjoys, the harrowing scene enacted before him. There is in the brain a mechanism of grief and gladness—a cohesion of sensory and muscular nerve-groupings which is operated upon by direct or induced sensations. The stimulus may be real or false; of that the brain takes no account. A lever is pulled, and the fountains play whether the occasion be a great or a small one. In insanity, examples of automatic grief are frequently met with. For example, a young woman treated by Maudsley passed her time moaning and weeping abundantly. She was not really, however, as miserable as she looked, for in the midst of her sobbing, if a ludicrous remark were made, she would look up calmly, speak quietly, and even smile for a moment before relapsing into her habitual condition. The motor centres for the expression of grief were evidently subjected to some morbid excitement. All theatrical emotion, whether on the stage or in the auditorium, is of this automatic kind, the impressionability of the auditor, like that of the actor, depending upon his cerebral organisation. A special susceptibility of the articulatory apparatus would confer the faculty of learning long speeches by heart, and this the actor possesses in an unusual degree.

It is not a little remarkable that the greatest military commanders in the world have been epileptics. Cruelty or indifference to the feelings of others is a special feature of epilepsy, which seems to sap or destroy the links of association productive of sympathy. Epileptics are notoriously destructive; they break, maim, or kill without apparent motive, and this characteristic is developed even in children. Napoleon made war as an epileptic smashes the crockery in his room or murders his own child, namely, from a wanton desire to destroy something or somebody. Bourrienne often heard Napoleon say, 'Friendship is but a name; I love nobody.' When physically idle, Napoleon never knew what to do with himself. So great was his natural impatience and hastiness that he could not shave without gashing his cheek. Clive's indifference to consequences has already been noted in his duelling experience. In a military commander of genius there is, of course, much more than mere destructiveness. In addition to great energy and quickness, he must have a keen perception of the effects of strategic movements—a motor susceptibility in combination with quickness of vision, whereby he is enabled to be superior to his enemy at the point of contact; and he must have a spirit of reckless daring calculated to inflame the courage of his soldiers. Of literary or artistic culture he need have none. Clive, one of the greatest of generals, was almost illiterate; Napoleon's scholastic attainments were very moderate. The epileptic is indifferent, not only to the fate of others, but also to his own, as the great frequency of motiveless suicides among epileptic patients attests. In this respect he resembles the born general who, by his calmness, coolness, and courage in the hour of danger carries his men to victory.

The orator, whether in Parliament or in the pulpit, requires the actor's control of voice and gesture, together with a great fluency of speech and command of verbal imagery. Chatham seems to have had all the physical resources of Edmund Kean. 'In his look and gesture,' says a contemporary, ' dignity and grace were combined. . . The terrors of his look, the lightnings of his eye, were insufferable. His voice was both full and clear, his least whisper was distinctly heard, his middle tones were sweet, rich, and beautifully varied. When he lifted his voice to its highest pitch the house was completely filled with the volume of the sound. The effect was awful, except when he wished to cheer and animate; then he had spirit-stirring notes that were perfectly irresistible. But the terrible was his peculiar power. Then the whole house sank before him.'[1] The keen lighting of Chatham's eye is said to have 'blasted the courage of the most intrepid of his opponents.' Profusion of language implies a great retentiveness in the various cerebral centres concerned. From the testimony of his grand-daughter, Lady Hester Stanhope, we know that Chatham's visual memory was great. 'On passing a place where he had been ten years before,' she relates, 'he would observe that there used to be a tree, or a stone, or something that was gone, and on inquiry it always proved to be so. Yet he travelled always with four horses at a great rate.' Chatham was a wretched financier, and his administrative faculties generally were poor. For statesmanship in its highest form, not only a rich store of facts and figures, but also a far-reaching identifying faculty, is required. In this respect the philosopher and the statesman approximate, though the latter is more alive than the former to considerations of practical expediency. If the philosopher dabbles in statesmanship he is apt to become a doctrinaire.

Men of science, also, are distinguished for their discernment of likeness in diversity. It was this identifying faculty which enabled Newton to couple with a falling apple the moon's deflection to the earth, and James Watt to see the possibilities of the steam-engine in the boiling kettle. In the same way, from the facts laid down by Malthus showing that the increase of population was limited by the supply of food, Darwin deduced the principle of natural selection. In all these discoveries there was a great stretch of identifying genius—an enormous generalising power displayed. The identifying faculty was very great in Faraday. Bence Jones say he had 'a sort of divination or scientific second sight which led him to anticipate results that he or others afterwards proved to be true.' He laboured to establish the actual identity of all the forces of nature—a conception borne out in part by Joule's discovery of the mechanical equivalent of heat, and by the later developments of the molecular theory in physics.

Of the scope and power of Darwin's mind we have an

[1] Charles Butler: *Reminiscences.*

interesting record in his autobiography. 'For many years,' says the author of the 'Origin of Species,' 'I cannot endure to read a line of poetry; I have tried lately to read Skakespeare, and have found it so intolerably dull that it nauseated me. I have also almost lost my taste for pictures or music. . . . My mind,' he adds in his autobiography, written five or six years before his death, 'seems to have become a kind of machine for grinding general laws out of large collections of facts.' This bent declared itself in his early youth, when he always had 'the strongest desire to understand or explain whatever he observed,' and he had the patience to 'reflect or ponder for any number of years over any unexplained problem.'

In scientific genius the faculty of long-sustained attention is very marked. 'The difference,' says Sir William Hamilton truly enough, 'between an ordinary mind and the mind of Newton consists principally in this, that the one is capable of the application of a more continuous attention than the other; that a Newton is able, without fatigue, to connect inference with inference in one long series towards a determinate end, while the man of inferior capacity is soon obliged to break off or let fall the thread which he had begun to spin.' In the case of the poet, who likewise possesses it, the identifying faculty is affected by strong human sympathies. To these the man of science is commonly as much a stranger as he is to the perception of verbal rhythm. The arithmetical faculty of Zerah Colburn probably consisted in a tenacious recollection of forms, as visible in the ten numerals and their combinations. George Bidder, another famous calculator, relates that, having a great liking for figures, he gave himself up to the study of numbers, learning first the ordinary multiplication table by making lines and squares of peas, marbles, and shot, and then enlarging upon this, until at last he had a multiplication table of his own, rising to a million.

The faculty of fixing and sustaining attention is assigned by modern physiology to the frontal area of the brain, whence the movements of the head and eyes are controlled. What has been called the identifying faculty, must also, however, be concerned with some automatic process carried on between various cerebral centres, inasmuch as solutions of problems, glimpses of truth, so to speak, occur to the mind when one is not actively engaged in considering the subject in hand ; when, indeed, the attention is relaxed. Swedenborg's great inventive genius, based upon a morbid excitability, was clearly of the automatic order. The sub-marine torpedo-vessel, the balloon, and the steam-engine, he anticipated long before they became accomplished facts,[1] while the shrewdness of not a few of his observations is remarkable. 'Nature,' he said, 'is the same everywhere, in suns and planets, and in the smallest particles'—a view which spectroscopic analysis and chemical research at the present day tend to bear out. In physiology, again, his theory that the angels read a man's history in his brain and physical structure after death, is not one that any reader of this book will scoff at. And most of these pregnant thoughts appear to have come to him, not by dint of conscious reasoning, but spontaneously, or automatically, in visions.

The prudential faculty, so important in business, appears to consist in a lively memory for pains or inconveniences, and a consequent eagerness to avoid a recurrence of them. If the mind is untenacious of its worries it will not be prudent. The improvident man is one whose perception of the evils that threaten him is feeble ; he is a careless, happy-go-lucky person, who does not realise the force of the sage counsels tendered him from time to time, and who gathers nothing from his own past experience. Bain offers some shrewd remarks on the qualities which ensure success in life : 'As an artist feels at once the effect of every touch in the total of his picture, so some men,' he observes, 'discern in a moment whether they have given offence or caused delight, while to others no indication of either is apparent. The art of reading countenances and interpreting the full force of words, tones, and gestures, belongs to the politician, to the diplomatist, to the man that keeps free of quarrels, and

---

[1] These inventions took the form in Swedenborg's mind of (1) a sort of ship in which men might go below the surface of the sea and do great damage to an enemy ; (2) a flying chariot ; and (3) a machine driven by fire for pumping water.

to most of those that attain popularity and rise in the world. Some men may do many foolish things, but by being distinguished in this one branch of circumspection, they procure the reputation of prudence, caution, and foresight, which by sinister applications degenerates into cunning. We cannot doubt that in some corner of the human cerebrum there is a distinguishing development in the instances where this quality of the observation of men is strongly manifested. It may not be an ultimate fact in our constitution, but it is a genuine fact of character unequally displayed in individuals. It is a chief mode of being wide-awake, and an instrument in the hands of every one engaged in ruling, persuading, guiding, instructing, or moulding human beings.'[1] In the mental processes above described, one can perceive a quick responsive action between the chief centres, in conjunction with cohering trains of past experiences. A dull mind brought into contact with the same facts would be irresponsive and deficient in its memories.

In the ne'er-do-well there is not only improvidence, but a warp of the organisation conducing to drunkenness and even to crime. Avarice is a haunting prepossession like the 'fixed ideas' of insanity; for the miser has been known to starve himself to death in the midst of his possessions. Philanthropy, benevolence, and the kindred sentiments of compassion and friendship, again, are excited through the sensory centres. To experience these sentiments we must realise the pain or discomfort of those who stand in need of our services. Distresses that are incomprehensible to our minds, that is to say, of which we have no experience direct or indirect, awaken no benevolence within us. A tender-hearted man will kill a minute insect without compunction, though he may hesitate to injure an animal of larger growth more nearly resembling himself in organisation.

Simple piety or veneration seems to resolve itself into an absence of the identifying faculty, the generalising power which is so marked in scientific genius. It is not to be confounded with the theological spirit, which is often well versed in the methods of controversy. A typically pious

[1] Bain: *On the Study of Character.*

mind would have been incapable of discerning, as Franklin did, that electricity and lightning were identical. True religion is the antithesis of self-esteem. The mind imbued with it distrusts itself and is fond of relying upon authority or dogma. The identifying faculty, if not pushed to the extreme which produces the genius of a Newton, is a great safe-guard of mental stability. Hallucinations of sight or hearing do not affect the reason if there is a strong identifying faculty in the individual whereby he is enabled to keep in touch with his actual surroundings. By dint of extensive memories and cohering impressions in his brain he *knows* that the figures he sees or the voices he hears can have no objective reality. He can even calmly study the phenomena as the result of some disorder of the visual or the auditory area. If, on the other hand, he is without the identifying faculty, he is carried away by his errors of sense. A man like Nicolai knows that his phantoms have no reality, but an ignorant French peasant girl who sees the Virgin accepts her vision as a miracle. Swedenborg combined in a remarkable degree the most opposite qualities, reminding one a little of Coleridge, who was as much a philosopher as a poet. But the Swedish prophet was not an example of ordinary piety ; his sensory hallucinations were too strong for him and so warped his understanding. Religious inspiration, like the inspiration of the poet, never transcends the actual knowledge of its own day. No ancient prophet anticipated the Copernican theory of the universe. Mahommed's inspiration was coloured by his ideas of Judaism and Christianity. George Fox believed that the Lord had given him 'a spirit of discerning,' by which he could see the inward condition of people, and the use he put this to was to 'discern witches.' 'As I was going to a meeting,' he says, 'I saw some women in a field and I discerned them to be witches,' upon which he told them his mind. Swedenborg, in his ecstatic trances, conversed with the inhabitants of all the planets except Uranus and Neptune, which, unfortunately for his pretensions, had not then been discovered.

Of criminality there are many varieties, but a common feature underlies them all—an obtuseness with regard to the consequences of unlawful acts, whether as affecting the criminal himself or his victim. The criminal can hardly be expected to study the welfare of society when he is indifferent to his own. In civilised communities, crime most emphatically does not pay ; it is in the long run a losing game. Yet it is taken up by a regular percentage of individuals, generation after generation, who persist in their evil courses despite the cumulative punishments meted out to them. The investigations of Lombroso and others leave no room for doubt that crime is literally a moral insanity, depending in the main upon congenital causes. In extreme cases, the vicious proclivity manifests itself in childhood, and the individual, acute though he may be in many respects, betrays a total incapacity to appreciate the moral bearings of his offence. There are, of course, degrees of this insanity as of every other. Punishment may deter a large class who hover on the brink of crime, or normally constituted individuals who, through passion or stress of circumstances, are tempted to break the law ; but when the congenital bent is strong no repressive measures avail.

The great frequency among criminals of anomalies in the shape of the skull testifies to a special mental organisation ; and this is confirmed by an anatomical study of the convolutions. So complex is the mechanism of the brain as a whole, and so numerous the functions called into activity even in the commission of crime, that no constant set of anomalies in the brain-structure of criminals can be looked for. But so far as one can judge from the recorded confessions of malefactors of all descriptions, the working of the criminal mind revolves itself into a partial, instead of a general, activity of the different centres. The murderer strikes, the thief steals, in obedience to a first impulse. His associated impressions or memories are comparatively few ; his cohering trains of ideas are imperfect. The question then arises : Ought the criminal to be relieved of the penal consequences of his acts ? My answer is, No. The welfare of the community is the supreme consideration. If he is a danger to it he must be suppressed. The majority have the right to protect themselves against him as they would against a madman, a venomous reptile, or a wild beast.

CHAPTER XI

PHRENOLOGY AND ITS LIMITATIONS—EVIDENCE IN FAVOUR OF IT—
THE FOREHEAD AS AN INTELLECTUAL REGION — EFFECTS OF
INJURY OR DISEASE OF THE FRONTAL LOBES—THE CONCENTRATIVE
FACULTY—CRIMINAL HEADS—LOCALISATION OF WIT—SWIFT'S
SKULL—PARALLELISM BETWEEN THE OLD PHRENOLOGY AND THE
NEW—CORRECT AND INCORRECT LOCALISATIONS—SIZE AND WEIGHT
OF BRAINS—HEADS OF REMARKABLE MEN—SAVAGE AND CIVILISED
BRAINS—THE PHRENOLOGY OF THE FUTURE

AFTER suffering much neglect and obloquy from the scientific
world, phrenology begins to appear in a somewhat more
favourable light than heretofore. No doubt any method of
guessing at the functions of the brain from the shape of
the head must in a great measure be untrustworthy. The
volume of the brain is not the only point to be considered;
the quality of it is a matter of importance, and this it
seems to be impossible to gauge through the skull. But
such a condemnation as Bastian passes upon phrenology
is obviously too sweeping, namely, that it is 'fallacious in
almost every respect,' 'eminently unsatisfactory in its localisations, and altogether defective in its psychological analysis.'
Bain's conclusion is more just: 'There is much that is
noticeable in the coincidences between the shape of the head
and mental peculiarity, and of the entire number of such
included in the phrenological system, it is possible that some
may stand and others turn out mistaken.' The elements of
character are very numerous, and they are found united in
individuals in infinitely varying proportions. That particular
functions are carried on by the various centres of the brain is
proved beyond a doubt, and it follows inevitably that all
mental functions, however complex, have an equally material
basis. To concede this, as physiology must do, is to concede
the principle of phrenology. The only question that can arise

is as to the particular regions of the brain where the various
mental functions are exercised.

The phrenologists, it must be owned, have been singularly
rash. They have not only carried their pretensions to an
absurd pitch, but they have shown an almost incredible laxity
and credulity in their investigations. ' It is impossible,' says
Spurzheim, ' to unite a greater number of proofs in demon-
stration of any natural truth than may be presented to place
the seat of the amative propensity in the cerebellum.' What
these so-called proofs amount to is this : The effects of lesion
or disease in the cerebellum have been shown in repeated
instances to be accompanied by a disturbance of the amative
propensity, while unusual force of the feeling has been seen to
accompany a large cerebellum, and weakness of the propensity
a small one. There is nothing, however, in these cases to pre-
clude the possibility of mere coincidence ; and in point of fact
the only proved connection of the cerebellum with amativeness
is that the nerve-connections between the hemispheres and
the organs of generation pass near it, and are therefore liable
to be affected by disease in the cerebellar region, just as the
telegraphic communications between London and Edinburgh
might be disturbed by floods in the Midlands. Of Gall many
amusing anecdotes are related. He is said to have mistaken
the skull of an imbecile for that of his colleague Spurzheim.
On one occasion he went to the prison of Bicêtre for the purpose of examining the heads of some notorious convicts. In
anticipation of the visit, Pariset dressed up a dozen of the
worst criminals as warders and presented them to Gall, with
the result that the founder of phrenology found nothing remarkable in them. After Gall's death, three portions of
skulls were found in his museum representing the organs of
' music,' ' caution,' and ' amativeness.' They were labelled as
having belonged to a musician, a baroness who had committed
suicide in a fit of monomania, and a merchant who had lost
his reason through love. Leuret found that the three cranial
specimens were all parts of the same skull.

All allowance being made for coincidence, however, there
is still a certain amount of evidence in favour of the theory
that the shape of the head bears some relation to mental

capacity.   Phrenology need not be thrown over altogether.
It was originated at a time when knowledge of the functions of
the brain was extremely limited, but it roughly accords, not
only with general experience, but in some important respects
with the latest discoveries in physiology.   The forehead has
long been regarded as an important seat of the intellectual
faculties.   Now, the electric stimulus produces no effect upon
the frontal lobes of the brain ; but the fact of their being connected with the sensory and motor centres by great bands
of fibres shows that they play some important part in the
cerebral economy.   Of this there is also some negative evidence.   Animals whose frontal lobes are destroyed become
stupid.   They eat freely enough but cannot look for their
food.   If a bone is thrown to a dog so injured, it will run to it
with great alacrity, but it has not the sense to stop at the
right moment ; it overshoots the mark.   Then, instead of
turning round and looking for the bone in a methodical way,
it appears to forget what it was after and runs on heedlessly
until the object is again brought under its notice.   Meanwhile the animal is able to hear, see, smell, touch, and taste
perfectly, but it has a stupid expression of the eyes and
inability to fix the gaze.   The same results are observed in
monkeys.   When their frontal lobes have been removed,
' instead of as before,' says Ferrier, ' being actively interested
in their surroundings and curiously prying into all that comes
within the field of their observation, they remain apathetic, or
dull, or doze off to sleep, responding only to the sensations and
impressions of the moment, or varying their listlessness with
restless and purposeless wanderings to and fro.   While not
demented,, they have lost to all appearance the faculty of
attentive and intelligent observation.'
Evidence directly bearing upon the functions of the frontal
lobes in man is very scanty, disease being seldom entirely local
in its effects and special experiments with the electric stimulus
or the cautery being forbidden even in the case of the worst
criminals.   Several cases are recorded, however, in which disease
or accident to the frontal region has produced in man an
intellectual deficiency and an instability of character exactly
as in monkeys and dogs.   An American workman, for ex-

ample, had his frontal lobes injured by a crowbar and lived twelve years after the accident. Before sustaining the injury he was steady, shrewd, intelligent, persevering, and well-mannered; afterwards the balance of his intellectual faculties appeared to be destroyed, and he became nervous, irritable, impatient, obstinate, capricious, disrespectful, and profane in his language—a child in intellect, a man in his passions and instincts. Idiots in whom the frontal lobes are notably undeveloped have no power of concentration whatever, but turn from one object to another without gathering any informing impressions. Darwin's head, on the contrary, showed a striking development of the pre-frontal region. Immediately over the eyes it jutted forward so much as almost to be a disfigurement. This peculiarity is very marked in a photograph dating from 1854, when he was forty-five, and is still more so in the portraits of his latter years. The brain of Gauss, the mathematician, was very much convoluted in the frontal regions. Rudolph Wagner compared his frontal lobes with those of an artisan and found a marked difference between them. Bastian examined the brain of another mathematician, De Morgan, and although the convolutions were by no means so intricate as those of Gauss, the frontal development was still very large. In the lower races of mankind the frontal lobes are comparatively small.

The anatomical evidence by which Ferrier seeks to establish the solidarity of the post-frontal region, whence the movements of the eyes and head are governed, with the pre-frontal region, which are not electrically excitable, is plausible, and no better conclusion can at present be arrived at than that the whole frontal area of the brain is concerned with intellectual observation. It is here that the phrenologists locate the perception of facts, movement, and cause, together with the faculty of comparison. This last is the identifying faculty, already noted as so important an element of the higher intellectual operations. Its exercise one can almost feel to be muscular, prolonged concentration of thought producing fatigue like a severe physical effort. The connection of thought or attention with muscular action is not at first sight apparent, but it is none the less real. In hypnotism, suggestions may be conveyed through the muscular system as well as through the sensory centres. The operator places a limb in such a position as to suggest an act, and the subject spontaneously completes the act so suggested. This shows that, just as sensory impressions tend to call up movements, so the excitation of movements tends to call up by association the various sensory factors with which these particular movements cohere. Now, as movements of the head and eyes are intimately concerned with attention to an object actually placed before us, it follows that, if the portion of the brain governing these movements be well developed, there will be a special faculty for reviving these movements ideally and so reacting upon the associated sensory cohesions that constitute the fabric of thought. If, on the other hand, the portion of the brain referred to be poor as regards the number or the activity of the nerve-cells, there will be no persistence of the muscular effort with which the whole mechanism of thought coheres; our ideas will slip from our grasp, so to speak, and we shall find ourselves thinking of nothing. Men differ greatly in this power of concentrating their attention. It is unquestionably a natural endowment, and there is every reason to believe that its seat is in the frontal region of the brain. As the material of thought is supplied by the sensory and motor centres, well-developed frontal lobes do not, by themselves, imply acute mental powers; they may be like an excellent machine which has nothing passing through it, and which consequently produces nothing. Rudolph Wagner remarks, however, that ' the convolutions and fissures, as a rule, are better developed in all portions of the brain when the frontal convolutions are specially complex.'

Among criminals a low or narrow forehead is common. This bears out to some extent what Lombroso says of them morally. ' Taken as a whole, criminals show a great want of coherence and continuity in their mental operations, which, if occasionally powerful, are intermittent.' Some famous criminals no doubt have shown remarkable cunning in their enterprises, but they have generally failed through over-looking some source of danger which a mind of scientific

x

calibre would have perceived and guarded against. The scientific mind is, *ipso facto*, the least criminal of any. With the doubtful exception of Bacon, criminals of scientific attainments are virtually unknown.[1] On the other hand, men of poetic and artistic gifts are not indisposed to crime, especially crime arising from the passions. Notwithstanding the frequency of low and narrow foreheads among convicts, however, criminality is most assuredly not a question of the size of the frontal lobes or of the shape of the head alone. The brains of criminals are in many cases found to be defective in a manner which could not possibly be detected outside the skull. They exhibit a deterioration of the gray or white substance, the blood circulation is imperfect or the convolutions are abnormally fissured.[2]

Wit is located by the phrenologists in the frontal region, and in view of what has been said of this faculty as consisting in an identification of the like with the unlike, the presumption is in their favour. Swift's skull when disinterred proved, however, to be phrenologically disappointing. The forehead was extremely low, and the so-called organs of wit, causality, and comparison were scarcely developed at all. This relic of one of our greatest humorists was, in 1835, handed to an eminent phrenologist, who 'pronounced it to be a very common-place head indeed—nay, from the low frontal development, almost that of a fool.'[3] This reading the phrenologists afterwards sought to explain away on the ground that the skull must have collapsed during Swift's period of mental derangement. That a skull previously normal alters its form in insanity is not, however, a physiological fact, as Esquirol proved by a long series of observations upon the inmates of his asylum.

Examined in the light of the new phrenology, Swift's skull is pretty much what we should expect it to be. Its sensory and motor capacity is very great. A medical man who examined it at the time of its exhumation, after remark-

---

[1] The principal cases are those of Eugene Aram, Doctor Dodd, Mercadante, an able Italian chemist who put himself at the head of a gang of thieves and a number of medical men of no great professional eminence.
[2] Lombroso.   [3] Wilde.

ing upon the lowness of the forehead, goes on to say : 'The head rose gradually, and was high from benevolence backwards. The portion of the occipital bone assigned to " philoprogenitiveness " and " amativeness " appeared excessive. The side view showed great elevation above the level of a horizontal line drawn through the ears. The front view exhibited extreme width of the forehead. It was, however, when looking into the interior and examining the base that the wonderful capacity of the skull became apparent. The room for the anterior lobes of the cerebrum was very great ; the depressions also for the middle lobes were very deep. The cerebellum must have been very small, and the posterior lobes very large. . . . Although the skull, phrenologically speaking, might be thought deficient, yet its capacity was in reality very great. I took an ordinary skull, and making a section of it on the same level with Swift's, I compared their outlines, drawn on paper, and found that the latter exceeded the former in a remarkable manner, particularly in its transverse diameter.'

It has already been remarked that the smallness of the cerebellum would account for Swift's fits of giddiness, which made his gait so frequently that of a 'drunk man.' As for the hugeness of the posterior and middle lobes, representing the visual, auditory, and chief motor centres, this formation would clearly favour an accumulation of intellectual material. Ignorant as we are of the precise functions of the frontal lobes, it is impossible to say what other uses Swift might have made of this material had his forehead been of the three-storey order of architecture so much affected by artists since the rise of phrenology, but a mere lateral extension of the frontal area is evidently not incompatible with the exercise of a keen satirical humour. Probably, however, there was little reflection or sustained thought in Swift's writings. Swift's skull showed the blood supply of his brain to be unequally distributed. In the posterior lobes the marks of the bloodvessels were large and deep ; in the middle they were ordinary ; and in the frontal area small. One may certainly conclude from the general plan of the brain that the discriminating faculty called wit has its seat somewhere in the frontal lobes, but it is by no means proved that the possession of it is coincident, as the phrenologists contend, with a high and square forehead.

Although 'form,' 'size,' 'order,' and 'weight' depend somewhat upon ocular adjustments, there can hardly be any warrant for the phrenological localisation of those faculties round the eye. They are probably associated with sight and touch. Language, again, is auditory, visual, and motor in its genesis. To locate 'colour' in the frontal region is clearly a mistake. The optical sense pure and simple must be assigned to the visual area at the back of the head. Jeffrey, of the 'Edinburgh Review,' had a hollow where the bump of colour is supposed to be, but he had, nevertheless, a keen enjoyment of bright hues; and this difficulty Combe, the phrenologist, tried rather disingenuously to get over by detecting Jeffrey in the admission that his pleasure had to do, not with the intrinsic effects of the colours themselves, but with their associations, the red of flowers suggesting a lovely season, and so forth. Arithmetical calculation or 'number' is probably dependent in some degree upon a memory for naked forms or visual abstractions, and 'locality' would seem to resolve itself into a sense of forms and colours in combination with muscular movements. Both faculties are assigned by the phrenologists to the forehead. The primary seat of both must be in the sensory and motor areas, but it may be in the frontal region that the raw material of judgment in such matters is utilised. In dogs, 'locality' is essentially a memory for smells.

Over some portion of the motor area the phrenologists have come wonderfully near the truth. Thus, their bump for 'imitation,' the actor's art, is almost identical with Ferrier's centre ' for the extension forwards of the arm and hand '—in other words, for gesture, one of the main elements of the actor's genius. The seat of 'imitation,' however, must be more extensive than the phrenologists have supposed; it must cover at least another of Ferrier's centres in a downward direction, that, namely, for ' movements of the lips and tongue,' as in articulation. With the centres for movements of the hand and arm, again, the 'constructiveness' of the phrenologists has evidently a close affinity. 'Constructiveness' is a talent for the mechanical arts, as found in engineers, engravers, painters, operative surgeons, and mechanics of great skill. It consists in nice powers of muscular discrimination in the hand. With a pressure or sweep of the fingers or a turn of the wrist the operator produces a desired effect, and he retains for future use an exact memory of the degree of muscular force expended. Meissonier's fingers were so sensitive that he could, with his eyes shut, lay on the exact amount of colour that he wanted at a given spot, if somebody placed the point of the brush upon it. The phrenologists are probably right, therefore, in associating mechanical constructiveness with a bump on the side of the head, though it ought not to be exactly where they locate it, namely, between the eye and the ear on a higher level, but a little further back over the ear, where Ferrier places the centres for movements of the fingers and wrist.

The emotional constructiveness of the poet or the playwright is a totally different endowment. Unlike mechanical constructiveness, which is a pure nicety of touch, as the actor's diction is a nicety of articulation, emotional constructiveness is a co-ordination of sensory and motor impressions, which probably has its seat in the frontal region. 'Music,' as already shown, must be both a motor and an auditory endowment, and I should expect it to be denoted by a lateral bulge of the head covering the centres for movements of the limbs and trunk, and for hearing. Similarly, a poet ought to be well-developed in the articulatory centre, the probable seat of rhythm, which is a motor faculty. The phrenologists appear to place 'music' rather too far forward. Some of the perceptions involved in musical composition may belong to the frontal region, but the main constituents of time and tune must be motor and auditory. In the motor region, also, will lie the executive faculty of the painter. All the arts, indeed, on their executive or motor side, would seem to be indicated in phrenology by the vague term of 'ideality,' which is obviously not a special faculty at all, but a mass of widely different feelings or aptitudes.

All that can physiologically be said for phrenology is probably summed up in the foregoing pages. As regards. the frontal region and the fore portion of the side of the head, the system of Gall and Spurzheim contains elements of truth which no doubt serve to keep it alive. But all its localisations in the back and upper parts of the head are very contestable, even allowing for the fact that the physiologists talk a different language from the phrenologists, as when Ferrier says 'movements of the fingers and wrist,' and Gall 'constructiveness.' The visual centre in man covering the back part of the head, has, no doubt, manifold functions to perform. But one cannot satisfactorily connect 'love of home,' 'friendship,' 'cautiousness,' 'combativeness,' 'love of approbation,' or 'love of offspring,' with visual images. Equally incompatible are 'destructiveness,' 'acquisitiveness,' or 'secretiveness,' with effects of hearing, smell, or taste. The 'self-esteem' of phrenology is almost identical with Ferrier's centre for 'movements of the leg and foot such as are concerned in walking.' Here, again, there is no reasonable parallelism to be established. Nor is there between 'firmness,' 'conscientiousness,' 'veneration,' 'hope,' 'benevolence,' or 'wonder,' and the different motor centres for the legs, arms, etc., actually underlying them. Many of these phrenological faculties are not simple but compound. Such characteristics as vanity, veneration, and philanthropy cannot be the outcome of so many particular bumps, but must rather depend upon a combination of qualities or defects in the brain. Under analysis, vanity seems to resolve itself into an automatic persistence of the various images and effects, sensorial and motor, affecting the personality; the main feature of veneration, on the other hand, an absence of the identifying faculty—that main-stay of the scientific mind— probably arises from some weakness in the frontal lobes or their nerve-connections, while philanthropy is, in the main, sympathy—a ready emotion induced by the susceptibility of one or more of our sensory centres to the painful experience of others.

The size and weight of the brain are important, but not so much so in an absolute as in a relative sense. Usually the elliciency of a brain-centre bears some proportion to its development, and so far the system of phrenology is justified. But size is not always a trustworthy criterion. With a brain smaller than a pin's head, the ant is capable of acting in an organised community and exercising mental functions as complicated at least as those of a bullock. The muscular movements of an animal consume a great deal of nerve-energy, and a large brain may be expected to go, therefore, with a large body. It is mainly for this reason, no doubt, that the male human brain on the average weighs one-tenth more than the female. More important, however, than size is elliciency. One brain, without being greater in volume than another, may be better supplied with nerve-cells and fibres, and the same may be said of one area of the brain as compared with another. Acknowledged genius, again, is a very uncertain test of brain-elliciency. Of the many different kinds of genius, some may arise from the inordinate activity of one or two centres, while their possessor as regards the common concerns of life may be a very ordinary person indeed, or even a fool.

Among men of genius, accordingly, all sizes of heads are found. Napoleon's head always appeared to the Duchesse d'Abrantès to be 'too large for his body,' and his portraits show great lateral breadth in the motor region. Mozart's head was also disproportionately large. As Napoleon and Mozart were physically small men, it may be inferred that they had both a great deal of superfluous nerve-energy. Wordsworth had a good forehead. Landor, in a letter to a friend, describes it as 'broad though somewhat heavy,' adding: 'There are few indications in the forehead, however. I would not say *nulla fides*, but one of the emptiest heads I ever saw was a man's so exactly like Erskine's that you might look at both together and doubt which was which, and I once saw a postilion at La Cava as exactly like Napoleon.'

On the other hand, Keats, Byron, and Shelley had all small heads. Leigh Hunt, who had not himself an abnormal head, says he could not get their hats on. Hartley Coleridge and Charles Lamb, too, were small headed. The average circumference of the heads of Englishmen is from $22\frac{1}{4}$ to $22\frac{1}{2}$ inches. Nevertheless, Galton has found ' thirteen eminent scientific men with heads under 22 inches, and only eight with heads of 24 inches or upwards, and of the thirteen there were only two or three who had not " remarkable energy." ' As he omits to tell us, however, what size of body accompanied his small heads, his figures are rather inconclusive. A little man with the same size of head as a big man will, other things being equal, possess more energy. In weight of brain, again, considerable differences exist among men of acknowledged power. The average weight of the male brain in civilised races is about 49 ounces. Cuvier's brain weighed 64 ounces; Abercrombie's and Schiller's 63 ; De Morgan and Gauss, the mathematicians', $52\frac{3}{4}$ and 52 respectively. But Grote, the historian, had a brain only three-quarters of an ounce above the average, while the brains of Tiedemann, the anatomist, and Hausmann, the mineralogist, fell 5 and 6 ounces below it.

In congenital idiots the average weight of brain is low, as is also that of persons dying in lunatic asylums; and Gratiolet says that where it falls below $31\frac{3}{4}$ ounces ordinary human intelligence is impossible. But many idiots and lunatics have been found with brains far above the average in weight; Thurnam, for example, having met with an epileptic butcher, barely able to read, whose brain turned the scale at 62 ounces. Among men of the artisan class who were perfectly sane, but by no means superior in endowment, brains of this weight have occasionally been found. The heaviest known human brain belonged to a Sussex bricklayer, who died of consumption in University College Hospital in 1849. It exceeded 67 ounces, and was well proportioned; while in physical size its owner was not greatly above the average, being 5 ft. 9 in. in height and of robust frame. But the man could not read or write, though he was said to have a good memory and to be fond of politics. Age makes some difference in brain weight, but not enough to materially affect the foregoing figures.

At the same time the brains of civilised races are considerably heavier on the average than those of the uncivilised and also

more convoluted, showing a general correspondence between
size and function.   Thurnam's figures establish a difference
between Europeans and African negroes of about 5 ounces.
A Bushwoman's brain examined by Marshall was found to
be remarkably deficient in its convolutions, especially in the
occipital, the middle and lower frontal and the temporal regions
—a formation which would clearly conduce to poverty of ideas.
The human brain of the lowest type approximates in fact to
that of the monkey.   Le Bon estimates the cranial capacity
of the gorilla at 600 cubic centimetres, the poorest African
or Australian black's at 1,200, and the modern Parisian's at
from 1,800 to 1,900.   So that some human races would seem
to be mentally nearer to the gorilla than to the highest
civilised type.   Among Frenchmen, Le Bon has found head
measurements running in the following order : 1st, scientific
and literary men; 2nd, tradesmen; 3rd, nobles of old families;
4th, male domestic servants; and 5th, peasants; while both
he and Broca conclude from an examination, the one of
Egyptian mummies, the other of French skulls of the twelfth
century, that civilisation tends to increase the cranial capacity.[1]

Not only the frontal but all the lobes of the brain appear
to grow in bulk and complexity as the race advances in
intelligence.   Apart from the localisations actually proved,
there is a presumption amounting to certainty that every
variety of human character is represented by some variety of
detail in the cerebral system.   The phrenologists have had a
glimmering of the truth ; it is to physiology we must look
for the further light that may be thrown upon this interesting
subject.   So much of our mental action depends upon the relations of the different centres to each other, independently of
the shape of the skull, that phrenology can never be made an
exact science.   But clearly if the moral localisations of the
brain are to be attempted on anything like the scale adopted
by the phrenologists, the existing chart of so-called faculties

---

[1] Thurnam : 'On the Weight of the Human Brain,' *Journal of Mental
Science*, 1866 ; Marshall : *Proceedings of the Royal Society*, 1875 ; Gratiolet :
Anatomie Comparative du Système Nerveux; Le Bon : *Revue d'Anthro-
pologie*, 1879.

must be recast into certain main visual, auditory, tactile and motor effects with manifold combinations. Meanwhile, it may safely be asserted that an ample forehead, provided the brain be otherwise well proportioned, will commonly be found associated with powers of reflection and concentration of a high order, and that breadth of head is a good indication of that executive energy without which no kind of genius will be able to make itself felt.

CHAPTER XII

MEN OF GENIUS MORE SUBJECT TO NERVE-DISORDER THAN THE COM-
MUNITY AT LARGE—COMPARATIVE STATISTICS ON THE SUBJECT—
PHYSICAL CONDITIONS OF GENIUS RARE—EXAMPLES OF IMPERFECT
GENIUS—VARIETIES OF FACULTY AND TEMPERAMENT IN EMINENT
MEN—VANITY—THE SEXUAL PASSION—GENEROSITY AND MEAN-
NESS—POETRY AND SCIENCE—IMPORTANCE OF THE NATURAL BENT
—THE PERFECT MAN UNKNOWN—FAMILIES IN WHICH GENIUS
MAY BE LOOKED FOR—NEUROPATHIC UNIONS AND THEIR BEARING
UPON DARWINISM—INAPPLICABILITY OF NATURAL SELECTION TO
MAN—UNKNOWN AGENCIES AT WORK—ORIGIN OF THE FITTEST—
EVIDENCE OF A GROWTH-FORCE IN NATURE—GENIUS AS A LAW

It will be seen that the connection of genius with nerve-
disorder manifests itself in two ways, positively by the
neuropathic character of all the great men enumerated in the
foregoing chapters, and negatively by the difficulty, I may
say the impossibility, of finding a single celebrity of the first
rank who, the facts of his life being sufficiently well known,
does not either personally or by heredity fall into the morbid
group. Taken by themselves, of course, these considerations
are still not conclusive. If it could be shown that all men,
great and small, distinguished and undistinguished, were
equally subject to nerve-disorder, the theory of genius as a
neurosis would fall to the ground. It is important, therefore,
to see in what proportion nerve-disorder affects mankind at
large compared with that small section of mankind with
whom we are specially concerned.

Altogether I have dealt specifically with some 250 men
of genius. Selected upon no other ground than their eminence
in the first instance, the total number of these are found to be
neuropathic, suffering from, or dying of, some description of
nerve-disorder. Now the Registrar-General's returns for

England for 1888 exhibit the proportion of deaths from the chief constitutional or nerve-diseases to a million deaths—from all causes in round numbers as follows :—

Phthisis, 86,500; pneumonia, 60,000; convulsions, 40,600; inflammation of the brain, and brain paralysis, 34,000; apoplexy, 31,500 ; heart-disease, various forms, 17,000 ; hydrocephalus, 13,000 ; scrofula, 9,600 ; rheumatism, various forms, 7,000 ; softening of the brain, 6,000 ; epilepsy, 5,600 ; asthma, 4,600 ; diseases of the spinal cord, 3,700 ; syncope, 3,300 ; diabetes, 3,000; chronic alcoholism and delirium tremens, 2,800 ; rickets, 1,600 ; angina pectoris, 1,300 ; gout, 1,000 ; stone, 500 ; and paralysis agitans, 390.

Other constitutional diseases there are, though comparatively unimportant, but for the sake of contrasting the ordinary death-rate with that of genius I mention only those disorders which the biographer, as a rule, has been able or has thought fit to specify in the case of eminent men. The death-rate of the general population from the above-mentioned diseases would appear to be about one in $3\frac{1}{4}$. Among the men of genius enumerated it is at least three times greater.   Certain varieties of nerve-disorder, moreover, such as gout, paralysis, and epilepsy, occur in an enormously greater proportion among men of genius than among ordinary individuals.   So likewise with insanity.   Of this, however, owing to the fact of there being so many degrees of mental unsoundness unrecorded in statistical returns, no trustworthy percentages can be arrived at, though it is clear from the biographical portion of my record that the proportion of eccentricity or insanity observed in great men and their families is very much in excess of that prevailing in the community at large.

Very notable as a sign of nervous degeneration is the extreme mortality of the family stock to which the greatest men belong, and more especially among the immediate heirs of an illustrious name. Examples abound in the biographical chapters.   As a rule the families of great men die out in the course of a few generations; occasionally they recover themselves through an admixture of healthy and undistinguished blood, but in that event the period at which the man of

genius makes his advent will be found to coincide with the
lowest ebb of the family vitality. Had the human race consisted three hundred years ago of Shakespeares, Miltons, and
Cromwells, it would long since have disappeared from the
face of the earth. Napoleon divorcing Josephine with the
view of obtaining by another marriage a dynastic heir, is at
the best a sorry example of human vanity; it is doubly so
when we perceive, as we now do, that the very greatness which
the conqueror of Europe sought to perpetuate was itself fatal
to his hopes. Nature is rich in compensations. The undistinguished citizen, centuries after his death, is represented by
the vital principle which he has transmitted to his descendants;
the great man has often to be content to influence posterity
indirectly by his works.

Here, a plausible objection to the theory of genius as a
neurosis suggests itself and has to be met. There are many
insane persons, many paralytics, many epileptics, many gouty
subjects, many consumptives, in a given generation, while the
men of genius are few and far between. Why so? In answer
to this, it can only be said that the physical conditions from
which genius results are highly complex, and that the chances
of a member of a neuropathic family uniting in himself all
those conditions are exceedingly small. They may be compared to the chances of an unmusical person being able to strike
by accident on the key-board of a piano a succession of harmonies. Given the sensory endowment requisite for a painter
or a poet, there may be a lack of executive power or *vice versâ*,
and the disability may be of all degrees. The colour sense,
for example, without making a man a painter may dispose
him merely to a fondness for the concrete in life and a repugnance to abstractions; combined with the literary faculty
it may make him merely a writer upon art.

Side by side with undoubted geniuses, there ought, on
this showing, to be a multitude of imperfect or fractional
geniuses—men possessing some of the elements of greatness
but not all. This is, in fact, what we find. Many persons are
to be met with, extraordinarily gifted, but just falling short
in some particular of true genius—the genius which not only
conceives but executes, and which has persistence enough not

to grow weary in well-doing whatever obstacles may lie in its
path. The imperfect genius does not make his mark in the
world unless, like Blake or George Burges, he happens to err
on the side of insane whims or extravagance. Nevertheless
he is on record. To such a type belonged Bulwer Lytton's
grandfather, Richard Warburton Lytton, who had an extraordinary faculty for acquiring languages, and was a profound
student of science and metaphysics, but who imparted none
of his wisdom to the world. Bulwer Lytton says of this not
very distant ancestor :—

' He loved learning for learning's sake. He disentangled
himself from the world—from pleasure, from ambition, from
all the usual aspirations of a man who unites knowledge and
talent to wealth and station. The image of his life was like
a statue, cold in its complete repose, and shattered into fragments on his tomb. Nothing remains of it—nothing but a few
notes and comments, scattered here and there, through remote
regions and down recesses of that silent world in which he
lived unseen. . . . To me, amid the hum and buzz that
accompany the feeblest fame, the most fleeting celebrity,
there is something unspeakably impressive in the oblivion to
which this solitary scholar was carried, with all the spoils and
trophies of his vast research.'

Another example of the imperfect genius is that of the
gifted W. M. Praed, whose bright and varied talents obtained
him an enviable position at the University, but who died at
thirty-seven of consumption, without achieving anything of
note. He swept away prizes and scholarships, was the
readiest and most forcible debater in the Union, was match-
less in dancing, never missing a ball, though it were on the
eve of an examination. He excited at the University the
same kind of haunting personal interest that Byron was then
exciting in the world, and speculation was freely indulged
in as to his future—as to whether he would be most renowned
as poet or wit, essayist or orator. But he lived as long a
life as Byron, Mendelssohn, or Raphael, and left only a
collection of pretty but feeble poems, which the world has
made haste to forget.

Within the limits of true genius many varieties of faculty

and temperament are to be observed. Vanity is generally supposed to be the characteristic of little minds, and to be incompatible with true greatness, but this is not so. It is to be found on both sides of the account. There have been many great men who thought little of themselves. Shakespeare took no care of his writings, nor did Swift. Walter Scott had an extreme simplicity of manners. 'It was impossible,' says Robert Chambers, 'ever to detect in his conversation a symptom of his grounding the slightest title to consideration upon his literary fame, or of his being even conscious of it.' On the other hand, Milton had a curious vein of egotism and unbashful self-assertion. 'In his later years,' says Masson, 'he evidently believed himself to be, if not the greatest man in England, at least the greatest writer. All that he said and wrote was backed, in his own consciousness, by a sense of the independent importance of the fact that it was he, Milton, who said or wrote it.' Wordsworth, again, was excessively vain, as Carlyle shows in the following amusing passage of his ' Reminiscences : '—

'One evening I got him (Wordsworth) upon the subject of great poets, which I thought might be admirable equally to us both, but was rather mistaken as I gradually found. Pope's partial failure I was prepared for; less for the narrowish limits visible in Milton and others. I tried him with Burns, of whom he had a singularly tender recognition, but Burns also turned out to be a limited, inferior, creature ; even Shakespeare himself had his blind sides, his limitations. Gradually it became apparent to me that of transcendent and unlimited genius there was to this critic but one specimen known—Wordsworth himself. He by no means said so or hinted so in words, but his pride in himself was so quiet, so fixed, so unappealing—like a dun, old lichened crag on the wayside.' And not poets alone, but all men of eminence suffered the same depreciation at Wordsworth's hands. 'One saw the great Wilberforce and his existence visible in all their lineaments, but only as through a reversed telescope, and reduced to the size of a mouse and its nest, or a little more ! This was in all cases the result brought out—one's self and telescope of natural, or perhaps, preternatural size, but the object, so great to vulgar eyes, reduced amazingly with all its lineaments recognisable.'

Byron was similarly filled with an inordinate vanity. He was vain of his personal appearance, and it was for this reason he dreaded corpulency, and found his club foot such a source of vexation—vain also of his aristocratic birth, and a passion for celebrity seems to have been the motive of his actions through life. Shakespeare's fame excited his mortification and jealousy. He told Lady Blessington that Shakespeare owed half his popularity to his low origin, and the other half to the distance of time which separated him from the nineteenth century. Except Pope, and of course himself, he regarded the English poets as barbarians. Goethe's writings and recorded conversations betray a great deal of the self-consciousness which is not far removed from vanity ; and the existence of this element in his nature is further proved by the readiness with which he was able to break off detrimental attachments. Chatham was full of affectation. Walpole described him as a comedian even in his dress, and in fact the crutch upon which he hobbled about when in mourning for the King of France was covered with black velvet.

Equally marked are the differences exhibited in the sexual passions of great men. It is by no means true, as many suppose, that the poet is necessarily a flighty person. From his earliest youth a solemn and austere demeanour of mind was the characteristic of Milton. Wordsworth, Southey, and Scott were strait-laced in their domestic relations. Despite appearances, it may be doubted whether Goethe was a man of strong passions, seeing that at twenty-five he was able to give up a beautiful and innocent girl from the philosophical conviction that it was better to do so. Licentiousness, on the other hand, was the characteristic of Byron and Shelley, as it has been perhaps of the majority of poets and artists. Shakespeare does not seem to have been exempt from this weakness. There is evidence that while in the prime of his intellectual powers he was the abject slave of a dark-complexioned woman who was faithless to him and whom he cursed in his heart.

Apart from vanity and amativeness, which are perhaps the most strikingly varied characteristics of great men, many inequalities of character or faculty accompany genius. Milton and Wordsworth were wholly destitute of humour. Pitt and Fox, resembling each other in their wonderful powers of debate, were otherwise as opposite as the poles, the one being lanky, slender, cold and ascetic, except in the matter of port wine, the other corpulent, slovenly, and given to all manner of sensual indulgence. Byron was niggardly in small things, and lavish in great. His memory for scenes and events was extraordinarily retentive, but he could never acquire a competent knowledge of arithmetic. Both Wordsworth and Scott were wanting in the sense of smell. In the senses of taste and hearing, too, Scott was curiously deficient. Lockhart says he was unable to tell madeira from sherry, while the incurable defects of his ear rendered it impossible for him to acquire a knowledge of music. To the last, complicated harmonies seemed to the author of 'Waverley' a 'babble of confused though pleasing sounds,' and this although his father was musical and a performer on the violin.

The metamorphosis of faculty and character is necessarily as varied as that of nerve disorder. Where a general soundness of the brain and nervous system exists, there is perhaps a tolerably equable transmission of mental and moral endowments; but given in the parent those inequalities from which genius arises, we may expect in the offspring great uncertainty or capriciousness of function. In the reshuffling of the cards, so to speak, it is impossible to predict which member of the family, if any, will hold the trumps. The Darwin family exemplifies in a striking degree this inequality of faculty. Great in some directions, Charles Darwin's powers were in others curiously limited. His want of ear was such that he could not distinguish the commonest tunes. 'I have no great quickness of apprehension or wit,' he wrote in his latter years. 'I am therefore a poor critic; a paper or book when first read generally excites my admiration, and it is only after considerable reflection that I perceive its weak points. My power to follow a long and abstract train of thought is very limited, and therefore I could never have succeeded with metaphysics or mathematics. My memory is extensive, yet hazy; it suffices to make me cautious by telling me that I have heard or read something opposed to the conclusion which I am drawing, or on the other hand in favour of it, and after a time I can generally recollect where to search for my authority. So poor in one sense is my memory that I have never been able to remember for more than a few days a single date or a line of poetry.' A memory for dates was, however, the special gift of Charles Darwin's father, Robert. 'My father,' says the author of the 'Origin of Species,' 'knew the day of the birth, marriage, and death of a multitude of persons in Shropshire, and he once told me that this power annoyed him, for if he once heard a date he could not forget it, and thus the deaths of many friends were often recalled to his mind.' With this was combined an excessive sensibility. 'I once asked him,' says Charles Darwin, 'when he was old and could not walk, why he did not drive out for exercise, and he answered, " Every road out of Shrewsbury is associated in my mind with some painful event."' The uncle, Erasmus Darwin, the younger, who committed suicide, had for his part a peculiar taste for statistics. 'When a boy, he counted all the houses in the city of Lichfield and found out the number of inhabitants in as many as he could, and when a real census was first made his estimate was found to be nearly accurate.'

Although the only trace of the poetic faculty in the Darwin family was in the ill-fated Charles, who died in his youth, the gift of poetry is not incompatible with scientific genius. Humphry Davy was fond of poetry and romance. According to his brother and biographer, he was 'sanguine, with an excess of sensibility and irritability, and of vital action combined with corresponding activity of mind, and a certain warmth and impetuosity of temper.' He was a many-sided man. Besides poetry he dabbled in religious and metaphysical speculation, before engaging in the chemical studies which brought him fame. Yet he had not the wit to perceive, or the fairness to acknowledge, the equally brilliant genius of his assistant, Faraday, whose election to the Royal Society he opposed. The younger Herschell wrote poetry;

the sons of Arago, the mathematician and astronomer, displayed literary and artistic gifts, and the Bernoulli family, distinguished for mathematics and science, comprised an orator of exceptional powers. It has already been remarked that philosophy and the business faculty were combined with music in the family of Mendelssohn, and the business faculty with poetry in that of Heine. A great variety of faculty is presented by the Meyerbeer (or Beer) family. The father was a successful banker, the mother was noted for her philanthropy. One of the sons, William Beer, devoted himself successfully to scientific studies; another, Michael Beer, became a dramatist and poet of distinction, although he died at thirty-three; Jacob or Giacomo Meyerbeer, always remarkably sensitive and irritable, was from childhood a musician, and of the gifted members of his family he alone attained to old age.

A natural bent asserts itself in the face of all obstacles. The poet lisps in numbers. Burns was a local celebrity at sixteen, Campbell published his 'Pleasures of Hope' at twenty, and Schiller his 'Brigands' at twenty-three; Byron awoke and found himself famous at one and twenty; and Keats was dead at twenty-five, the age at which most men are only buckling on their armour for the battle of life. The poet, the painter, and the musician, employ their innate faculty as naturally as a cat uses its claws, or a bull its horns. There were no artists in Michel Angelo's family, and no musicians in Handel's, and the parents of both tried in vain to thrash them out of their predilections. Claude Lorraine began life as a poor uneducated boy apprenticed to a pastry-cook. Reynolds as a lad eagerly copied all prints that came in his way, and was a good artist as Handel was a good musician before he received a single lesson. Hogarth's school exercises were more remarkable for their ornament than for their matter; apprenticed afterwards to a silversmith, he was nobody's pupil in art, but painted life as he saw it. To some extent the statesman and the military commander may be creatures of circumstance. There may be a Clive or a Warren Hastings now languishing at his desk in the Indian Civil Service of to-day; there may be a Napoleon in the village bully. But as in letters and art, so in science and philosophy, genius insists upon making itself felt. Faraday was not lost because he began life as an errand boy, nor did Carlyle find the world unwilling to listen to a voice from Craigenputtock. The natural endowment for some one or other of the great spheres of human activity is the all-important point. With this, minor and non-essential details of character may be combined in infinite variety. Hogarth, for example, was gross and unpolished in his manners, Reynolds was suave and miserly, Lawrence was a dandy and a spendthrift; but all three were born artists. As regards education, it is vain to expect boys by means of a system of hothouse forcing to excel or even to attain proficiency in studies for which they have no natural aptitude.

If it is impossible to say exactly upon what plan the variations of heredity proceed, it may confidently be affirmed that genius implies some inequality of brain and nerve function tending to be morbid, if not actually so. Probably a dead level of capacity is impossible, for we have all our strong and our weak points. The soundest man is he who most nearly approaches the mean. He will assuredly not be a genius, but having the power to do many things well, though none superlatively, he may be—indeed, must be—a good citizen. Such a man, we may take it, exerting all his powers in a given direction, will achieve those respectable results in life commonly ascribed to talent. Benjamin West must have been a painter of this stamp. At all events it is curious and suggestive, that he who was accused of a lack of imagination and a want of fire and poetry,[1] should at the same time have been a most amiable and upright man, enjoying good health and a long life. Conceivably there might be soundness in a general levelling up of faculty to the highest point, but this is a phenomenon we are never likely to meet with, since the man who was gifted in that degree would be a Shakespeare in literature, a Reynolds in painting, a Mozart in music, a Kean in acting, a Chatham in oratory, a Pitt in politics, a Napoleon in war, and a Newton in science. The respectable, law-abiding, healthy, long-lived

[1] Allan Cunningham.

family is not that into which the man of great genius may be expected to be born. In his parentage there will be symptoms of the insane temperament, or of its allied functional disorders; he will stand side by side with the ne'er-do-well, the paralytic, and the consumptive, and his offspring, for the most part, will be puny, ailing, unintelligent, and generally ill-equipped in body and mind.

This being so, the stud-book theory of genius, which seems to possess most attraction for the public mind, must be definitively abandoned. It is to some extent true, as Galton says, that 'ability is not distributed at haphazard, but clings to certain families.' This does not imply, however, that genius is *per se* hereditary. What runs in the blood is nerve-disorder, of which genius is the occasional outcome. Genius is not to be compared with the physical perfections of the Derby winner; it is an accident of the cerebral and nervous organisation, and one which different races estimate differently. Among a hardy tribe of savages, the sensibility which we esteem in the musician or the painter would be a positive drawback; half our men of genius indeed, with their feeble frames and their indifferent health, would be merely so many despised camp-followers, unable to take a scalp or to capture a buffalo.

There is no evidence that sexual selection plays any considerable part in obviating such unions as are likely to prove disastrous from the physical point of view. Insanity or deformity renders its victims unattractive no doubt to the opposite sex, but neuropaths, who suffer from more disguised though equally serious forms of nerve-disorder, do not instinctively avoid each other. On the contrary, they seem to be drawn to each other's society. Southey and Coleridge made most unfortunate matches, seeing that there was insanity in the Fricker family into which they married, but the former at least was much attached to his wife, and his second marriage, with Miss Catherine Bowles, a poetess and a confirmed neuropath, was from the physical point of view no better. De Quincey says Coleridge assured him that his marriage was not his own deliberate act, but was 'in a manner forced upon his sense of honour by the scrupulous

Southey, who insisted that he had gone too far in his attentions to Miss Fricker for any honourable retreat.' De Quincey, however, adds: ' A neutral spectator of the parties protested to me, "that if ever in his life he had seen a man under deep fascination, and what he would have called desperately in love, Coleridge in relation to Miss F. was that man."' The neutral spectator's opinion is supported by the evidence of Coleridge's poems, from which it may be gathered that for the first two or three years at least his marriage was a happy one.

Among Byron's many ' loves,' again, none could have been less suited to him, as a partner, than Lady Caroline Lamb. More than half crazy, this woman had a touch of genius in her composition. ' There was a wild originality in her talk,' says Bulwer Lytton, ' combining great and sudden contrasts from deep bathos to infantine drollery; now sentimental, now shrewd, it sparkled with anecdotes of the great world, and of the eminent personages with whom she had been brought up or been familiarly intimate; and ten minutes after, it became gravely eloquent with religious enthusiasm, or shot off into metaphysical speculations—sometimes absurd, sometimes profound, generally suggestive and interesting. A creature of caprice, and impulse, and whim, her manner, her talk, and her character shifted their colours as rapidly as a chameleon.' At forty-three, Lady Caroline Lamb lapsed into a state of ' partial insanity,' and died of an epileptic attack. She was, therefore, as unsoundly constituted as Byron himself. Nevertheless, Byron and she fell in love with each other almost at first sight, and their attachment while it lasted was strong. The poet said Lady Caroline was the only woman who never bored him. Among other notable attachments in which there have been strong neuropathic tendencies on both sides, may be reckoned those of Sara Coleridge and her cousin, H. N. Coleridge, Flaxman and his wife, Scott and his wife, Campbell and his wife, and Charles Darwin and his cousin, Miss Wedgwood.

Elsewhere I have suggested that our growing knowledge of the danger of neuropathic unions may gradually create an instinctive dislike to them,[1] but this is necessarily a mere speculation with respect to the distant future. In the face of the examples quoted and the common experience of life, it is unsafe to assume that sexual selection necessarily tends to the immediate and physical improvement of the species ; and although errors of the sexual instinct may be supposed to be corrected by natural selection or the principle of the survival of the fittest, this in its turn has serious, nay, insuperable difficulties to encounter when it comes to be applied to man. Darwin was latterly constrained to enlarge the scope of natural selection so as to include the preservation of variations beneficial to the community, although not to the individual,[2] and under this head he reckoned the scientific and artistic faculties to which is mainly to be attributed the advance of the race from barbarism to civilisation. But now that the exact genesis of those faculties has been studied, such an argument is seen to be open to grave suspicion.

'If in each grade of society,' says the author of the 'Descent of Man,' 'the members were divided into two equal bodies, the one including the intellectually superior, and the other the inferior, there can be little doubt that the former would succeed best in all occupations and rear the greatest number of children.' Considering the excessive mortality and the general unfitness that attend upon genius, this does not by any means follow. 'At the present day,' continues Darwin, 'civilised nations are everywhere supplanting barbarous nations, and they succeed mainly, though not exclusively, through their arts, which are the product of the intellect. It is therefore highly probable that with mankind the intellectual faculties have been gradually perfected through natural selection. Again, this is an absolute *non sequitur*, as even Darwin seems to feel from the admission he is constrained to make in another passage, namely, that, allowing for natural selection, 'an unexplained residuum of change, perhaps a large one, must be left to the action of unknown agencies.'

Weismann, whose investigation of the germ-plasm has been so fruitful in suggestion, adopts the Darwinian view.

---

[1] *Op. cit.*   [2] Darwin : *The Descent of Man.*

'Human intelligence in general,' he observes, 'is the chief means, and the chief weapon which has served, and still serves, the human species in the struggle for existence. Even in the present state of civilisation, disturbed as it is by numerous artificial encroachments and unnatural conditions, the degree of intelligence possessed by the individual chiefly decides between destruction and life; and in a natural state, or still better in a state of low civilisation, this result is even more striking.' All this is undeniable. Intelligence, under which are included the inventive and the mechanical faculties, is the great means of advancement for the human race. The savage may have greater muscular strength and greater powers of endurance than the European, yet the superior mental capacity of the latter ensures him in every field an easy victory. 'Here again, therefore,' continues Weismann, 'we encounter the effects of natural selection.' Why 'therefore?' Weismann's easy acceptance of this conclusion prepares us for his next remark, which is that chance alone determines in what direction a man's faculties shall be developed, and incidentally he adds that 'at the present day there are many men of science, who, had they lived in the time of Bürger, Uhland, or Schelling, would probably have been poets and philosophers,' also that 'Raphael might have been as great a musician as he was a painter if, instead of living during the historical high-water mark of painting, he had lived under favourable personal conditions at a period of highly developed and widespread musical genius.'[1] When Weismann ventures upon such a speculation as this, it is plain that he has given no attention to the subject of mental faculty at all.

That human intellect is progressive there can be no question. The fact is shown by the greater development of the brain among civilised as compared with savage races. But the causes of this advance in intellectual capacity cannot yet be said to be determined. For many years past, natural selection has been a phrase to conjure with; it has been glibly used to explain everything. But its insufficiency as applied to man latterly began to dawn upon Darwin himself. 'In one of my latest conversations with Darwin,' says Alfred

[1] Weismann: *Biological Memoirs*, 1889.

Russel Wallace, 'he expressed himself very gloomily as to the future of humanity, on the ground that in our modern civilisation natural selection had no play and the fittest did not survive.'[1] As if the human race could abrogate or suspend any great law that truly underlay its existence! Wallace himself also circumscribes considerably the principle of which he was the co-discoverer, confessing himself wholly unable to explain by natural selection the growth of the mathematical and artistic faculties in man, and taking refuge in the hypothesis of 'an unseen universe—a world of spirit to which the world of matter is altogether subordinate.'[2] Other evolutionists, while accepting natural selection up to a certain point, hold that the intellectual gap between man and brute is too great to be bridged over by Darwinian principles alone.

The kernel of the question is clearly the origin of the so-called 'spontaneous variations' upon which the principle of natural selection is based, and concerning which Darwin has remarked: 'We know not what produces the numberless slight differences between the individuals of each species, for reversion only carries the problem a few steps backward, but each peculiarity must have its own efficient cause.'[3] It seems to be established by the study of morbid heredity in man that variations in structure including the brain, and consequently the intellectual capacity, have their origin in a molecular instability of the cerebro-spinal system which follows a law of alternation in heredity and is little affected by environment. These variations Darwin has never professed to explain, his system of natural selection starting from the point where they appear, and being essentially 'restrictive, directive, conservative, or destructive of something already created.' What an investigation of the physical basis of genius seems to disclose is that human progress through the practice of the arts and sciences is mainly due to the molecular instability of the nervous system above referred to, operating not only without aid from sexual selection or natural selection, but in direct opposition to those principles.

[1] Wallace: 'Human Selection,' *Fortnightly Review*, September, 1890.
[2] Wallace: *Darwinism*, 1889.   [3] Darwin: *Op. cit.*

By the use of clothes and fire man renders himself independent of climate; his weapons give him a power for offence and defence far transcending that of beak or claw; and the inventive faculty which thus extends his dominion in nature is not the attribute of a race, but only the apparently accidental endowment of a few individuals in each generation who, in the Darwinian sense, are to be classed with the 'unfit'—a category to which Darwin himself, with his forty years of persistent and disabling ill-health, might not improperly be assigned. Victorious generalship and skilful administration, again, both important factors in determining supremacy of race, are likewise the outcome of a cerebral organisation which is wholly personal to individuals and not necessarily transmissible by heredity or otherwise amenable to the Darwinian law.

These considerations appear to me to be of great importance, lending as they do an unexpected support to the view of the small but not uninfluential group of evolutionists above referred to, and favouring the still more heterodox speculations of the new American school of biologists, who, upon different grounds, believe in the existence of a special developmental force in nature which they term 'bathmism,' or growth-force, and which they conceive to act by means of 'retardation and acceleration' and 'without reference to fitness at all.'[1] Cope rightly observes that the theory of the survival of the fittest leaves the origin of the fittest entirely untouched. Growth-force, in his view, is the vital principle which supplies material for selection; its direction is determined in part by effort and use, but from its automatic action it may also tend to the production of useless characters.

The grounds upon which the American biologists seek to establish this theory of the origin of the fittest may not be conclusive, but in the molecular variations of heredity, as illustrated in genius, we certainly seem to come upon some such agency as the so-called growth-force—an agency no longer subject to natural selection, but eluding it and deter-

---

[1] Cope: *The Origin of the Fittest: Essays on Evolution.* New York, 1887.

mining human advancement by independent means. To growth-force may be attributed small racial differences like those which exist between Celt and Saxon and which are not explicable by the Darwinian law. It does not follow that man is to be regarded as a special creation—a type apart in the animal kingdom. His close anatomical resemblance to the higher apes—not merely in body, but in brain—forbids such a supposition; and if growth-force be accepted as a factor in human development, it must also be allowed for in the case of the lower animals, though possibly the shaping influence of natural selection may be all-powerful until the higher intellectual processes come into play. After all, growth-force is only another name for ' spontaneous variations,' and the true point at issue is how far it is governed by outside conditions favourable or unfavourable. In man it appears to be largely independent of such conditions.

To discuss the new aspect of evolution thus opened up would, however, carry me far beyond my present purpose. This I have fulfilled if, in availing myself of the latest acquisitions of knowledge in more than one field of research, I have succeeded in reducing to a law those higher manifestations of the intellect which have so long perplexed, while they have stirred the admiration of, mankind. Some prejudices may have been hurt in the process. It is the facts, however, which speak rather than I, who merely group them so that they may be mutually explanatory of each other; and as to the wisdom of Nature's courses it behoves us to be dumb.

INDEX